STEALTH POWER

VIKKI KESTELL

NANOSTEALTH | BOOK 2

Faith-Filled
Fiction™

STEALTH POWER

Nanostealth | Book 2
Vikki Kestell
Also Available in eBook Format

BOOKS BY VIKKI KESTELL

NANOSTEALTH

Book 1: *Stealthy Steps*
Book 2: *Stealth Power*
Book 3: *Stealth Retribution*

A PRAIRIE HERITAGE

Book 1: *A Rose Blooms Twice* (free eBook, most online retailers)
Book 2: *Wild Heart on the Prairie*
Book 3: *Joy on This Mountain*
Book 4: *The Captive Within*
Book 5: *Stolen*
Book 6: *Lost Are Found*
Book 7: *All God's Promises*
Book 8: *The Heart of Joy—A Short Story* (eBook only)

GIRLS FROM THE MOUNTAIN

Book 1: *Tabitha*
Book 2: *Tory*

The Christian and the Vampire: A Short Story
(free eBook, most online retailers)

STEALTH POWER

I must survive. For Dr. Bickel's sake, I must survive.

But how does a hunted woman—an *invisible woman* with no identity—outrun and outwit the enemies of a visible world?

Weakened by the nanomites' drain, Gemma flees from General Cushing's pursuit. She seeks refuge in Dr. Bickel's vacant safe house—and finds a temporary haven while her body recovers from the nanomites' damage.

While the mites search for Dr. Bickel (intent upon facilitating his rescue), Gemma appropriates a new identity and, piece by painstaking piece, secures a foothold in the real world, one that allows her to move about unnoticed.

Having forged a shaky ceasefire between the nanomites and herself, Gemma begins to rethink her attitude toward the unwanted pests and begins to doubt her decisions: Is she taking the wrong approach? Is her greatest resource right under her nose?

With reluctance, Gemma admits that she may be discounting her best defense.

"Nano, I wish we could find a means to function better. Together. More efficiently. I guess what I'm trying to say is that I'm interested in improved relations and faster and more effective communication. Enhanced communication could lead to, um, greater exchanges of information and understanding, maybe even, um, *consensus* (*gag*) and cooperation. An enriched relationship could result in, um, superior decisions—perhaps collaboration and mutual support—especially when we are in tight spots."

To Gemma's amazement and grave misgivings, the nanomites, who had previously withstood her every overture, show themselves to be her allies.

Or are they?

The struggle for control is on.

DEDICATION

In honor of the
139 police officers and **89 firefighters**
who fell in the line of duty during 2016
while I was writing *Stealth Power*.
Thank you
for your service and your sacrifice.
Lord, please bless and comfort
the families they left behind.

ACKNOWLEDGEMENTS

Many more thanks to my wonderful team,
Cheryl Adkins and **Greg McCann**.
You give more of yourself
with every book—even through
life's difficulties and pain.
I love and appreciate you.
Our *gestalt* is a continual blessing.

Special Thanks
to **James Rutske**
for his technical expertise.

Cover by
Vikki Kestell

PROLOGUE

As the boot completed, my laptop pinged a new email. I hadn't received many emails of late, but I didn't much care. Tonight, I was divesting myself of all that remained of Gemma Keyes. As soon as I was finished here, she would be gone.

I almost ignored the ping. Shrugging, I opened my email for the last time. My Inbox read one new email. I didn't recognize the sender but the subject line gripped me. Ice water poured over me in waves, scrambling my skin.

Sorry about the spam.

I couldn't move.

"No, no, no, no, no. Not possible! Not!" The mites stirred, uneasy at my dismay and the panic that held me in a constricting vise.

Frantic, I clicked into my spam folder and sorted through the junk mail. Nothing of note.

I started at the top and did it again. Nothing.

My hands were wet with perspiration but I was freezing. I scrubbed my hands on my jeans and then hugged myself. I stared again at the new email: *Sorry about the spam.*

It's how he contacted me the first time, I told myself. *Who else could have sent it?*

"But it's not how we communicated after that," I whispered. We'd used a message in my Draft folder with the subject line *Position Description* to communicate.

But I purged that file not long after I realized Cushing would, eventually, be looking at me, snooping in my life.

Hands shaking, I opened the draft folder. There, in a folder I had *emptied*, was a lone draft message with subject line *Position Description*.

The date stamp read *today.*

I clicked on the email and scanned the hasty, garbled message.

G,
Yes, alive. Top S. mil installation don't no where Purge draft folder after. 1 guard @night; 3 rotate nights. Taught all Samba.

I was dizzy, light-headed. "Why in the world? But . . ."

Guard lax. Left smart phone on card table; went to answer phone at desk. Enuf time 4me to get to anon email account.

7

He put more care into the next lines, signaling their importance.

Told you I uploaded research to secure place in cloud. No such place. "Cloud" still real server with actual hard drives. Vulnerable. Uploaded all—every part of life's work—to only place could never be hacked. You know. Safe

The message ended there.

He ran out of time to write more. My finger traced the words on the screen, rereading and reading between the lines. It had been enough.

. . . as I said, Gemma, five tribes. Alpha Tribe holds the nanocloud's collective memories and learning. Think of them as being the library—the historians—of the nanocloud.

I knew, then. I knew why the nanocloud clung to me and refused all my commands to leave. I understood *what I carried* and the great, the awesome responsibility thrust upon me.

I finished reading, purged the folder, and closed my email. I sat in front of my laptop, considering, for the second time, news of Dr. Bickel's return from death to life.

For a while I let my thoughts roam over happier days spent in the lab under the mountain, his pride in the nanomites, his struggle to hold his cards right, his shy pleasure when he brought out one of his fantastical desserts.

"Oh, Nano," I whispered. "We need to find him. We need to find Dr. Bickel and get him out. We need—"

I covered my eyes with my hands, overcome that my dear friend was still alive, overwhelmed by the futility of such a task.

The room behind my closed eyes brightened. I lowered my hands and stared at the laptop's screen. On a bright silver background, in bold, glowing blue words, it read,

WE CONCUR GEMMA KEYES
STAND BY
SEARCHING
MESSAGE ORIGINATION

⌘⌘⌘⌘

PART 1: SURVIVAL

CHAPTER 1
LATE OCTOBER

My overwhelmed brain fixed on the blue letters glowing in my dark living room, but I had trouble translating them, understanding what they implied.

WE CONCUR GEMMA KEYES
STAND BY
SEARCHING
MESSAGE ORIGINATION

Then, like a line of falling dominoes, bits and pieces of evidence and observation fell into place and began to gel, to make sense. What had Dr. Bickel said?

"Alpha Tribe holds the nanocloud's collective memories and learning," he'd bragged.

While I stared at the screen, the truth synced. It clicked into place.

I understood.

The *nanomites* carried Dr. Bickel's research! *They* were the "safe" place to which he'd uploaded his data!

My eyes returned to the nanomites' three lines of text. The statements were simple; the inferences were huge. Immense! My hands remained frozen on the keyboard as I fumbled my way through the significance of the nanomites' message: They were aware of what went on around them.

When I'd uttered the words, "We need to find Dr. Bickel and get him out," they had heard me. More than that, they agreed with me—and they were already tracing Dr. Bickel's email, attempting to pinpoint his location.

Dr. Bickel's email!

Oh, Dr. Bickel! You are alive? Where are you, my sweet old friend? Can the nanomites uncover your location? Is there any way—any hope— that the nanomites and I could find you and help you escape?

I shifted my eyes away from the screen as additional realizations disturbed and clogged my thinking: The nanomites were communicating with me? After these many weeks of frustration, after all my efforts and many attempts to reach them, to reason with them, to get them *off* me and *out* of me—*NOW* they were speaking?

And, apparently, they *did* know my name and actually "heard" and paid attention to what I said?

Grrr!

The bright message superimposed upon my laptop's screen began to fade, disclosing the body of Dr. Bickel's email behind it. I shook myself, set aside my anger—however justified—and copied the email text into a new file, deleted the email, then purged the folder and the trash.

The screen glowed silver again, interrupting my tasks. More blue words appeared.

INTRUSION DETECTED
NETWORK COMPROMISED
WIRELESS ACCESS
TERMINATED FROM
REMOTE TERMINAL

I sucked in a breath. *Cushing! She didn't leave—she's here and monitoring me in real time!* And I still needed to upload the file containing Dr. Bickel's email and the all-important file that documented my experiences with the nanomites.

As I groped for the flash drive, I reproached myself for my stupidity. *Why, oh, why did I write everything down? For what purpose? How could I have been so foolish? So stupid!*

I didn't need to answer my own censure. I had been a different person "back then," before the nanomites had invaded me. My trials since then had made me wiser.

New words flashed onto the screen.

GO NOW
GEMMA KEYES

Cold sweat prickled my skin, but I couldn't leave my journal for Cushing to find—Abe, Zander, and Emilio were named in it! And if I deleted the file but did not trash the hard drive, her IT people would recover the deleted file.

Again, the screen flashed.

GEMMA KEYES
GO NOW
NOW
NOW
NOW

The mites stung my hand to spur me into action. I was out of time—but was I out of options? No—because the nanomites could hear me.

Fine. Then let *them* do the work.

"Nano!" My voice was harsh. Ragged. "Upload files, 'Gemma's Log' and 'Email Text.' Then burn the hard disk!"

I resigned myself to whatever happened next: The mites would either listen and do what I commanded or they would ignore me—as they had for the most part so far.

If the mites refused to follow my directions, then I was done for. I was determined to deny Cushing my firsthand testimonial—that ill-conceived record of my experiences with Dr. Bickel's nanomites. With that file in her possession, Cushing would know my current predicament and all my vulnerabilities. More than that, she would know who my friends were—the people I loved—and she would not hesitate to use them as leverage to bend me to her will.

So, if the nanomites refused my instructions, I would stay and delete the files and try to trash the hard drive. Even if it meant capture.

I would let Cushing take me before I placed my friends in harm's way.

While those thoughts flashed through my mind, I jammed the flash drive into the USB port and opened a command prompt—but before I could begin to type, two blue streaks jetted from my fingertips. My hands jerked and pulled away, yet the two streaks of light converged on the screen, unfurled as a blue aura that overspread the flash drive and body of the laptop, retracted, returned to me, and vanished.

The laptop's screen dimmed and died. Wisps of smoke tried to follow the laser beams as they withdrew into my hands, but they could not.

The smell of fried electronics wafted up to my nostrils.

"Huh!"

The background thrum in my head rose in volume and urgency.

I raced for the back door, leaving my bug-out bags on the couch. I had my hand on the door handle when I heard the rush of booted feet upon the driveway.

Too late. Cushing and her thugs hadn't left after all. She'd used an age-old military ploy, *a feigned withdrawal*—and I'd fallen for it.

The back door crashed open—almost flattening me against the wall behind it. I dropped into a crouch as a stacked line of armed men clad in black tactical garb and gear poured into my tiny house. They shouted, "Federal agents!" and "Gemma Keyes! Show yourself!"

Not a chance.

I pushed my backside into the crack between the fridge and the wall where I stored the broom and mop.

As the first man charged by me—his head canted toward the dining room—I saw he was equipped with weird goggles that protruded forward, beyond his face.

Night vision goggles? Thermal imaging? If the man wearing the goggles looked my way, would he see my heat signature?

Or would the nanomites mask it?

I had no idea—and right then was no time to find out. I curled into a ball and made myself as small a target as I could manage. My crouch sank into a deep squat; my thighs screamed in protest.

The last man rushed by me and turned the corner into the dining room. From farther within the house I heard multiple shouts of "Clear!"

I wasn't going to wait around for them to come back. I bolted out the back door and swung left, heading around the garage. If more of Cushing's goggle-geared goons were about, I needed to put distance and as many physical barriers as possible between them and me. Although I could still hear shouted commands and responses coming from inside my house, I rounded the back of the garage without anyone raising an alarm at my escape.

In the rear corner of my lot, I shimmied up and over the rough cinder block wall into a neighbor's yard. I landed on the other side and did not pause to consider the scrapes and bruises I'd sustained. I raced through the yard, tripped over a sprinkler, got up, stumbled past the neighbor's confused dog and out their side gate. I hit the open street and headed toward the downtown area where, if Cushing's men followed me, I hoped barhopping foot traffic would confuse their thermal-imaging readings and make pursuit difficult.

Of course, I couldn't make it all the way downtown in one effort. I ran until I could run no farther, then slumped down between two parked cars. My lungs were on fire. The huge adrenaline boost my body had produced was wearing off, and I shook all over.

Out on the street, all was dark and quiet.

No pursuit so far.

After ten minutes, I made myself get up and get moving.

Good thing I had a place to hide.

Because I could never go back home.

⌘⌘⌘⌘

CHAPTER 2

I arrived at Dr. Bickel's safe house midmorning. I was beyond exhausted; I was teetering on the ragged edge of a breakdown, physically and emotionally.

After evading Cushing and her soldiers the night before, I had pushed on until I reached the downtown area and mingled with crowds of partiers and bar hoppers. I wandered down Central until I was beyond the nightclubs and foot traffic. Once I was the lone heat signature on the street and no longer felt safe, I ducked into a twenty-four-hour pancake place, found a corner to collapse into, and slept.

I awoke, stiff, bleary-eyed, and lightheaded. It was very early morning, and the breakfast rush was just starting. A kink throbbed in my neck.

The clock on the restaurant wall told me I'd slept a solid six hours, but the fatigue reaching its fingers deep into my bones persisted. Had it been only yesterday when the nanomites drained me in their attempt to keep me quiet about them? Had it been only yesterday when I defied them and told Zander and Abe everything? When I begged Abe to take Emilio in? When Cushing and her swat team stormed the cul-de-sac and my house? Not once but twice?

I struggled to my feet and slumped against the wall. After the dizziness passed, I helped myself to a large coffee in a to-go cup, left two crumpled dollar bills next to the cash register, and jostled by a couple of high school students as they came in.

No one saw me sitting outside against the restaurant's east-facing wall, sipping my coffee while warming myself and massaging the knot out of my neck. The coffee helped wake me up a little, but the caffeine did nothing for the black depression swimming around in my gut.

Here I sat, no better than a vagrant on the street. Pursued. Hunted like a criminal.

Alone.

I'd never felt so . . . forsaken.

My fingers picked at the chain around my neck, and I pulled the cross hanging from it into my hand. Its smooth, polished surface comforted me—and reminded me of Emilio and the hours he must have spent carving it, rubbing it until the wood glowed.

All while perched on the curb outside his uncle's house.

Just a child.

Alone and neglected.

Yeah, you have it so *rough, Gemma. Quit whining and get moving.*

The last of my coffee swirled at the bottom of the cup. I downed the dregs and crushed the paper. When I felt that I had some wits about myself, I trudged toward a transit stop. Two transfers later, I stepped off a bus a few blocks from my new digs.

So weary! Three blocks seemed three miles.

I stumbled down the alley, over the wall, to the back door, and performed a cursory check for recent footprints or other signs that Cushing had found my hiding place. Seeing nothing out of the ordinary, I let myself in. I closed and locked the door behind me.

Safe. Safe for the moment.

I glanced around the simple kitchen and sighed. After all my careful preparations, I had brought nothing with me, not one thing: no spare clothes, no personal items, no food. No treasured keepsakes. Just what I wore—Uncle Eduardo's baggy old shirt over worn jeans and t-shirt—and some wadded-up cash in my pocket.

I wonder what Cushing will make of my bug-out bags and the chunk of change I left in them?

I was grateful for the few dollars in my pocket; I was more grateful for the large stash of bundled bills I'd hidden in the wall behind the kitchen stove here in Dr. Bickel's house. Yeah, I'd lost my shopping bags and would have to jury-rig another set, but what were my handy-dandy bags in comparison to my freedom?

Still, I felt their loss. Those items would have lent familiarity and comfort to this foreign place where I'd gone to ground.

With growing pessimism dogging my steps, I wandered through the house and took stock: typical single-floor, one-bath, three-bedroom, ranch-style home, circa 1950-something—so archetypical of the "mid-century modern" look that was coming back into vogue. Thick, lined drapes covered every window, blocking all but the brightest of outside light—and, I figured, blacking out interior lights, too. Dr. Bickel had prepared this place to hide in, after all, had the circumstances dictated.

The shotgun kitchen was clean and functional but dated like the rest of the house. It included an old-school microwave featuring real numbers that flipped over when you turned the timer knob rather than a touchscreen digital readout. Bifold doors near the back door hid an aged washer and dryer. I say "aged," because they looked exactly like the washer and dryer Aunt Lucy owned when I was a kid—and that set had seemed ancient back then.

Dr. Bickel's appliances were at least twenty-five years old, but they still looked new. Like they'd been set in place decades ago and were still waiting to be used.

Yeah. Weirder and weirder.

The tiny bathroom echoed when I stepped inside. The room had no window and, like the kitchen, the enameled fittings were an outmoded pinky-flesh tone and the tub's tiles were plain white interspersed with a smattering of faded turquoise ones. Dr. Bickel had not stocked the bathroom—it contained not a single item: no hand soap, no towels, no bathmat, no shower curtain.

No wonder it echoed!

Oh. And no toilet paper.

Thanks a lot, Dr. Bickel. Were you planning on grabbing a roll or two before you ducked in here to hide? Or did you leave an old Sears catalogue handy?

The smallest bedroom was unfurnished; the largest had an empty dresser and a single bed. I stared with longing at the bare mattress. A pillow and folded sheets and blankets waited on the bed. I pounded the pillow, shook fine dust out of the sheets and blankets, and—*sneeze, cough*—made up the bed, after which I checked out the last room.

Dr. Bickel had, at one time, used the middle-sized bedroom as an office. The room contained an old desk, a chair, and some discarded office supplies. I could tell where a computer and printer had sat at one time—a power strip and some cords lay scattered under the desk; even spied a few five-and-a-quarter-inch floppy disks in the trash.

Wow. Way old school.

I picked up a cheap extension cord from the office floor. I went back to the bedroom, plugged the cord into a wall outlet, and collapsed into the bed with the cord's other end clutched in one hand. I stared at the ceiling in the dim light, declining the invitation to give in to despair—but only because I was too tired to indulge in full-blown depression. Besides, the hopelessness would be waiting for me when I woke up.

I will have plenty of time to wallow in self-pity.

The last thing I remembered before sliding off a cliff into oblivion was the tingling sensation of electrical current pulsing through my hand as the nanomites fed.

***

General Imogene Cushing walked the length of the table and considered the "take," the various objects her people had retrieved from the home of Gemma Keyes. The array of belongings spread out on the table seemed an odd, eclectic collection.

"What are these?" She pointed to two fabric grocery bags and addressed the three agents hovering nearby.

The two men slanted looks at each other and then at the third agent, a woman. Agent Janice Trujillo sneered at the men before answering Cushing. "We found these bags and the laptop in the dining room after the second team went in, ma'am."

"They weren't in the house during the first raid?"

"No, ma'am."

"Really, Miss Trujillo? How *interesting*." Cushing fingered one of the bags. "And what do you make of these, er, sacks?"

Trujillo swallowed. "They are ordinary, reusable shopping bags, ma'am, but the straps have been lengthened so that, we assume, Keyes could carry them over her shoulders."

"And all these items were in the two bags?" Cushing eyed the bags' contents, including a large amount of cash, laid out on the table in a neat line. "Even the money?"

"Yes, ma'am."

"What do you deduce?"

"The bare essentials, ma'am: clothing, toiletries, food, water, cash, cell phone. Everything she would need on the run."

"What of the phone?"

"Never used, ma'am. No incoming or outgoing calls. Ever."

"And yet she left all these things."

"I believe we surprised her with the second raid—as we'd intended."

Cushing held herself erect; her silvered hair sat at the nape of her neck in an elegant, knotted braid, not a strand out of place. She was polished and commanding, the epitome of a career military woman. However, she was not a tall woman; Cushing was, in fact, short and somewhat rounded.

Those moderating factors, nevertheless, did nothing to allay the anxiety in the room: Every agent under her authority knew that Cushing suffered no fools.

"Ah. We surprised her, did we? And yet she was, somehow, able to wipe and destroy the hard disk of her laptop in a matter of minutes? Or seconds?"

She spoke her question with mild curiosity, but the strain around her grew.

Agent Trujillo focused her sight on the wall over Cushing's shoulder rather than risk being snared in the net of Cushing's deep, beady eyes—much as a doomed deer is caught by the headlights of an oncoming truck.

"Yes, ma'am, she was, and the forensic team has not been able to ascertain the, uh, method by which she destroyed the hard disk."

"Oh?"

Tensions ratcheted up another notch.

"The disk was burned, um, *melted* while inside the laptop, and yet the laptop's case bears no evidence of a point of entry. The forensic team says they are, um, stumped as to how she burned the disk without leaving an entrance point."

"What could melt a hard disk in this manner, Miss Trujillo." General Cushing did not ask; she demanded.

"Our technicians suggest a tiny, focused laser would do similar damage, ma'am. Again, however, they are unable to ascertain how a laser could be brought to bear on the laptop without melting the plastic case surrounding it."

"And they could pull absolutely nothing from said disk?"

"Nothing, ma'am, not even fragments. One of our technicians suggests that the disk was degaussed prior to it being melted."

"Harrumph." Cushing's glare could have blistered Trujillo had the younger woman's eyes not been fixed on that invisible point somewhere over the general's shoulder.

Cushing turned on her heel and picked up the offending laptop. She turned it over in her hands. "A laser, you say."

"One possibility, ma'am."

"You have another possibility in mind, Miss Trujillo? Care to share?" Cushing barked.

"N-no, ma'am."

"But if a laser did this, then how did it leave no mark on the outside?"

Trujillo realized that Cushing was speaking to herself and, wisely, made no answer.

Cushing set the laptop down and placed a hand upon one of the grocery bags. She muttered under her breath, "She had these bags packed and ready to go, but she left them—and yet she took the time to burn the hard drive on her computer, to wipe it first and then melt it? How? And why? What was on the laptop that was of more importance than survival gear? Than this money?"

Cushing's focus shifted. "Where did the cash come from, Miss Trujillo?"

"The forensics team is working to track the serial numbers, ma'am, but none are sequential. The team did detect trace amounts of cocaine and methamphetamine on the plastic wrapping and on the bills themselves."

"Drug money?"

Trujillo nodded. "That would be my assumption, ma'am."

"Gemma Keyes and drug money? Absurd." But Cushing replayed her conversation with Gemma's twin sister from the night of the raid.

Gemma's sister had smirked and said, *"Whatever my sister's involvement in your 'serious national security incident' might be, I can guarantee that it is minimal—at best. She is not what you'd call the sharpest tool in the shed."*

And Cushing had replied, *"I believe Gemma likes to give that impression, Miss Keyes. However, I've become convinced that she is, ah, sharper than you credit her."*

Cushing's upper lip twitched. *Yes, Gemma Keyes, you are sharper than even I had believed. Where are you, dear Gemma? What are you up to? And how did you manage to escape my agents not once, but twice?*

Not for the first time did Cushing's puzzlement turn to the interviews of Gemma's neighbors from that same night. Of particular interest were the comments of Gemma's next-door neighbor, the ever-so-helpful Mrs. Calderón: *"Why, I haven't seen Gemma in weeks, even though I know she is in there. She ignores me and will not open the door when I knock and ring the bell . . . she picks the mail up after dark and she puts the garbage out during the night before collection day and puts the can back the night after . . . ."*

At Cushing's frustrated growl, the three agents stood straighter, but the general did not notice.

I am missing something. It is right here, in the evidence, in the melted hard drive, in the witness statements.

Her upper lip lifted in what might have been construed as a smile by those who were unacquainted with Imogene Cushing.

The three agents exchanged covert looks: They knew better.

It was not a smile; it was a predator's snarl.

Cushing's mouth curved more, and her eyes narrowed. *It is only a matter of time before I put the pieces together, Miss Keyes.*

⌘⌘⌘⌘

CHAPTER 3

I slept through the afternoon, evening, and night and awoke before dawn, groggy and disquieted. I had dreamed of Zander, Abe, and Emilio; of Mateo and Arnaldo Soto and his dead eyes; of General Cushing and my evil twin, Genie. My dreams had mashed all these people together into strange, implausible scenarios and anxiety-generating chases.

As I came awake, my heart was thumping; my mouth was dry.

No bueno.

While I downed two glasses of water, I forced myself to mentally pull apart my mashed-up dreams, sorting truth from lie, fact from fiction:

Zander, Abe, and Emilio—my friends and the good guys. *Check.*

Mateo and Soto—gangsters and very bad dudes. *Check.*

Genie and General Cushing—baddies and bosom buddies (not!) who registered at a whole other level on the Universal Scale of Evil. *Check.*

My friends—safe for now. No one chasing them. *Check.*

My enemies—unaware of my location or state of invisibility. *Check.*

I was safe.

My friends were safe.

The dreams were figments of my exhausted body and overstimulated imagination.

Check and check.

I rinsed my face and more cobwebs from my mind. I needed coffee in the worst way and my stomach rumbled its needs, too.

The lengthy sleep had done me good, but what the mites had done to deplete me—followed so closely by Cushing's assault on my home—had worn me down to a nub. It would take time to heal from the nanomites' drain, and I would not be able to do much until my body recovered its strength. To recuperate, I would need fuel.

I wandered into the kitchen and opened cupboards. The kitchen was furnished with most everything I'd ever need to prepare meals except for, you know, actual *food*.

"Great."

Yet I had to eat, and soon.

I snuck out the back door in the predawn light and walked four blocks to the nearest gas station/minimart. Those four blocks seemed like miles and took most everything I had left. Inside the little store, I grabbed a handful of little packs of cashews, some bags of trail mix, and two energy bars and stuffed them under my t-shirt, tucking the hem of the shirt into my jeans to hold the items. The cashier was busy with a line of customers gassing up on their way to work, so I grabbed a coffee, too.

The hot cup was too dangerous to carry around under my shirt, but the nanomites provided cover for it before I asked them to.

It was downright galling how the mites could be so accommodating one minute and utterly obstinate the next.

As the line to the register began to clear out, I left a grimy twenty-dollar bill on the counter and pushed through the door. The cashier looked up from habit when the buzzer on the door sounded, but I kept going.

What's he gonna do? I mean other than think he's lost his ever-loving marbles?

I didn't much care. I was famished. Weak. I plopped down on a patch of grass not far from the gas station and pulled my loot out from under my shirt. I selected an energy bar, but broke off and ate only half of it.

I don't know how long I'll need to make these last, I told myself. Besides, what my convalescing body wanted, the food I *really* craved and needed, was hot and filling—like the full-on breakfasts they were serving at the pancake house when I'd awakened early yesterday.

I sipped the coffee and ate the rest of the energy bar anyway. I was just too hungry. Then I walked home—not to the comforting familiarity of my little *casa*, but to Dr. Bickel's sterile safe house. My new digs.

Guess I should be thankful to have a place, any place, I admitted, even as my stomach demanded more fuel.

Inside Dr. Bickel's home, I penned "to do" and shopping lists and salivated at the images dancing in my head: platters of buttery scrambled eggs, syrupy waffles, and fat, juicy sausages.

Oh! And steaming hash browns, all golden and crispy on the outside. Gurgle. Growl. Drool.

I sighed and penned "car" at the top of my list.

I can't do much on foot. I need transportation.

Big problem.

I had cash, so money wasn't the hitch—human interaction was.

I'm so stinking tired. I must have food, real food to recover. Then I need a phone. A computer and Internet access. And—

The astonishing events of two nights past popped into my head: Apparently, the nanomites could do a whole lot more than I'd thought they could. I simply needed to figure out how to use them differently. Make them shoulder more of the load.

"Nano." I spoke aloud and felt that inner stillness as the nanomites came to attention. "Nano, we had better get on the same page, you and I. No more ignoring me—or, worse still, fighting me and my decisions. We are stuck with each other, but I drive this boat, not you."

The quiet in my head persisted; I closed my eyes to revel in it.

That peaceful, welcome solitude had been my underappreciated norm prior to the nanomite invasion. However, since that day, I'd endured a continual hum in the back of my head when the mites were at rest—an indefinable but incessant vibration some might describe as "white noise"—not to mention the chittering, buzzing, chipping, and droning of their activity when they were up to something.

At present, they were still—and the hush was bliss.

I'd figured out that absolute silence on the part of the nanomites meant one of two things: Either they were waiting for me to speak, or they were holding a confab. A confab, Dr. Bickel had told me, was a summit of the five nanotribes, a meeting where they presented data, reasoned with each other, and arrived at a consensus regarding a decision or a course of action.

Were they listening or confabbing?

"Nano! Do you hear me? We have got to work together to survive and find Dr. Bickel. You need to help me when I ask for it, like you did when you burned my laptop. Um, thank you for that, by the way."

I waited and the intermission lengthened. I guess I was waiting for an answer, but we hadn't hammered out a communication strategy, a means for them to respond to me—now that it was obvious that they could communicate if they chose to.

How could I prod them into regular communication? If—and a very big "if" at that—*if* the nanomites were willing to talk, how could I get them started? What would it look like?

I had already tried everything I could think of, to no avail: The mites had been determined to ignore my overtures. But now that we knew Dr. Bickel was alive, could the nanomites have changed their collective mind?

I thought back to Dr. Bickel's lab in the tunnels. He had spoken aloud to them and the swarm had propelled itself into the air and bunched up to form letters.

HELLO

That was how they had greeted me in Dr. Bickel's lab under the mountain—in blue letters hanging in the air within the glass cage Dr. Bickel had constructed, the letters formed by the shimmer of the mites' billions upon billions of coordinated mirrors reflecting light. The problem here and now was that the swarm was *in* me, not in front of me—and they had shown their obdurate, *pigheaded* election to never leave me.

Could I convince them to allow a cluster of the swarm to leave my body, to "exit the building," even temporarily, so we could communicate?

They had done just that only two nights ago: They had sent letters and words to the screen of my laptop, so I knew that what I was proposing was possible. The question was, would they?

I napped away the day, rationing my food, eating tiny meals whenever I awoke, recovering my strength in increments. As evening shadows lengthened, I found myself curled up in a chair in the living room, deep in thought, avoiding the specter of a bleak future by focusing on finding a route through the dilemma-fraught maze that lay before me. I opened no drapes and switched on only a small table lamp. I couldn't chance the neighbors noticing that the house was occupied.

"Nano."

I paused for them to fix their attention on me. "Nano, we need to talk to each other. Would you please leave my body and make words in the air?"

Their response was a fierce, tickling thrum that went on for five seconds.

"So, that's a 'no'? But you wrote messages on my laptop's screen, right? Some of you left me for a bit. A minute or so?"

More (but less vehement?) clicking answered me.

I looked around the room. The décor wasn't horrible, mind you, just minimal and impersonal. Not a single intimate touch. No magazines or knickknacks. One print of a Southwestern water color hung opposite the sofa. Other than that, entire walls were bare.

Entire walls.

Bare.

I jumped up and faced the off-white paint of one naked wall. "Nano! Can you project words on this wall?"

I waited.

Silence.

"Nano! We *must* begin to communicate. We must! I know Dr. Bickel told you to hide me, but can't you send one of the tribes or part of a tribe to paint a word on this wall like you did on my computer screen?"

More silence.

"You are *not* that freaking *stupid*!" I yelled. I slapped the wall with one hand and left it there. My frustration levels were not improved by the hunger lurching around in my stomach.

"Nano! Give me a sign that you are listening! That you hear me!"

Warmth shot down my arm, into my palm, out my splayed fingers. Blue letters leaked from my fingertips and formed on the wall.

WE HEAR

I sighed. Shuddered. My pent-up anxieties seemed to unravel and ooze away.

"All right then. We have work to do. What do you need to trace the origin of Dr. Bickel's email?"

All was silent—which told me that they were either ignoring me or discussing my question. A full minute later another set of letters sparkled on the otherwise blank wall.

TERMINAL

"Right. Like I'm gonna stroll into an electronics store and walk out with a new laptop. And what about an Internet connection? A computer is worthless without connectivity."

More deafening silence.

I paced the living room floor, sifting through schemes by which I might acquire a laptop. The easiest, most logical method to acquire what I needed sported a six-inch, all-cap, above-the-fold headline:

GEMMA KEYES EMBRACES LIFE OF CRIME

As I ranged back and forth across the room, growing more frustrated with each crossing, I scowled. *Moral scruples be hanged! As Invisa-Girl I can stroll into any store I want and take away whatever fits under my shirt—without the hassle of payment.*

I had a good excuse. It was, after all, a matter of survival.

And, well, wasn't "appropriating" whatever I needed the safest, most sane route to go?

"Pride goeth before destruction, Gemma," Aunt Lu's voice chipped in, *"and a haughty spirit before a fall."*

Riiiight. Cuz I hadn't heard that all my life.

I shrugged off the arguments on both sides. "Fine," I informed the nanomites. "I'll figure out a way to get a computer—but you'll have to figure out the connectivity thing. I'm not calling the cable company."

It dawned on me, as I proposed—and scrapped—various tactics over the next hours, that pirating a neighbor's network would be child's play for the mites if they chose to cooperate. So would spoofing an IP address or otherwise masking our computer.

I snorted. *"Our* computer?"

Strange alliances.

While I schemed and strategized, I also thought about Zander, Abe, and Emilio. I ached to find out how Abe and Emilio were getting along. I wanted to know if Abe had called CYFD yesterday and reported Emilio's uncle for neglect.

And I wondered if CYFD would leave Emilio with Abe, if they would approve Abe for custody of Emilio.

I itched to know the answers to these concerns—and a simple, five-minute conversation with Zander would put my fears to rest. *Except* (and here I swallowed down a fresh burst of anxiety) except I needed to proceed with extreme caution. Because of Cushing. Because of what she would do to my friends if I slipped up.

Even once.

Zander. How would I communicate with him on the "down low"? Maybe I could slip into some random store or business and use a land line to call Zander at his office—but what if the church secretary picked up instead? Or, more concerning, what if Cushing had already tapped DCC's phones?

And what means could we arrange for him to reach me in an emergency? What we needed was a new and covert means of communication. A secret means.

The phrase "burner phone" popped into my head. Dr. Bickel had given me what he called a burner phone. I'd left it in my bug-out bags, and it was likely in Cushing's possession now.

"What exactly is a burner phone?" I asked aloud. "And where can I get one?"

I noodled that around and realized I would need two phones. *Well, of course! One for me, one for Zander.*

By default, I was back to a Walmart Supercenter. I could think of no other store that was open 24/7 and that had, in one location, everything I needed—maybe not the best of what I needed, but usable. Shrugging, I also admitted that at Walmart I could avoid theft by checking out at the self-serve registers.

I started a list: *Laptop, two burner phones, food, and clothes. Personal items. Might require two trips into the store and out to the ca—*

"Oh, yeah. No car. So, how exactly do I get to Walmart and back? Walk three miles and tote all that stuff home? The mites can't hide everything I need to pick up—and I sure can't carry it all home in one trip."

While my strength was returning, I would not be strong enough to undertake anything so physically demanding. All my planning led straight back to the transportation quandary: I needed a car!

The tenuous grip by which I kept my emotions in check slipped another notch—until out of the downward spiral sprang the glimmer of an idea.

⌘ ⌘ ⌘ ⌘

CHAPTER 4

FBI Special Agent Ross Gamble studied the burned-out shell of an old building. He glanced around, taking in details, assessing the markers of the rundown southwest Albuquerque neighborhood: weeds growing up through cracked and buckled sidewalks; boarded-up shops and gang-tagged walls and fences; broken streetlights and the disreputable dumps the area residents called homes.

The ruin before him had been a respectable bodega at one time—back when every Albuquerque neighborhood boasted of its own little corner market. If one believed the news, the seedy storefront had most recently been used to cut, package, and distribute drugs—meth, coke, and heroin.

Gamble rehearsed what the Albuquerque news outlet had reported: *Sources in APD's gang unit believe that the building had housed a drug processing hub belonging to a local gang with ties to a Mexican cartel. A spokesperson for the gang unit, who asked not to be identified, suggested that the fire might have been started by a rival gang out of California seeking to horn in on the market and trafficking routes through Albuquerque. The unit has cautioned APD to be on the alert for gang-related reprisals.*

Gamble and the other agents of the FBI's Albuquerque field office didn't involve themselves in local gang activity unless a case had direct international ties and/or crossed over into terrorism—or unless APD requested assistance from DEA's Organized Crime Drug Enforcement Task Force, OCDETF. The FBI participated in the OCDETF, as did APD; however, most federal law agencies left the menial, small-town stuff to local law enforcement.

But today? Gamble was here today because of one tiny tidbit a confidential informant had slipped to him—a name: *Arnaldo Soto.*

Arnaldo Soto. The hair on the back of Gamble's neck bristled.

An unmarked car pulled up to the curb, and two men stepped out. Gamble spied his contact in the APD gang unit as he exited the passenger side. He raised his hand in greeting. The driver, who was unfamiliar to Gamble, nodded in his direction. The man scanned the area, lit a cigarette, and stood watch while his partner approached Gamble.

"Hey, man. Good to see you." Pete Diaz thrust his hand toward Gamble and they shook.

"You, too, Pete. Who's your friend?"

"Don Benally. Good man. Been with the gang unit five years."

That was the extent of the pleasantries. Gamble and Diaz had too much on their plates to waste time with chitchat.

Gamble jutted his chin at the gutted storefront. "So, what did RCFL come up with?" The Regional Computer Forensics Lab served all New Mexico law enforcement agencies, federal and otherwise.

"They confirmed that the fire was arson. It was set from the inside, and whoever did it intended to make a statement. If you look over there, you can make out the safe."

Gamble spied the blackened hulk, its door hanging open on twisted hinges, and nodded for Diaz to continue.

"When the fire started, the door was open just like you see it. We think whoever set the fire emptied the safe, piled everything that was in it on the floor, and lit the fire there. No accelerant, though."

"Huh. Any idea what was at the ignition point?"

"Sure. The forensics geeks found traces of drugs and cash, couple of handguns, and the scorched remains of ammo casings."

"The arsonists burned cash?"

"Apparently."

Gamble, hands on his hips and a scowl on his face, surveyed the heap of rubble. "I don't get it. I thought this was a rival gang hit."

"That's the word on the street—except no rival gang has taken credit for it. Besides, that theory doesn't make sense, does it? Ever hear of a gang burning money and drugs instead of taking them? Nope. Doesn't hold water."

"So, if not a rival gang, then who?"

Pete shrugged. "Not too many possibilities. For instance, couldn't have been a greedy employee, right? Greed and 'let's burn the drugs and cash' don't jibe. If it had been an inside job, they would have taken the money and left town in a hurry."

"Sounds right. So, who else?"

"Maybe a disaffected *ex*-employee? Someone with a grudge against the gang leadership? Possibly a vigilante?"

"Speaking of gang leadership . . ." Gamble let his question hang.

"Guess you've heard the same rumors. You're here because of Soto."

"Well, suppose I am?"

"Yeah, and if Soto is in Albuquerque and the fire proves to be a rival gang hit, the streets are gonna run with blood."

"What if it wasn't another gang?"

"Then Soto is going to thin his own organization, weed out any loose or suspicious members, and shake down anyone who might have an inkling of who burned him out. You know Soto's reputation for payback: If he even *thinks* he knows who did this, it ain't gonna be pretty. He will make an example of them."

"Yeah, I get that. He's feared by those who work for him and eyed with caution by those up the chain. If he weren't connected by blood at the top—" Gamble let that thought linger before he asked, "Any idea why he was sent to Albuquerque?"

"The gang's local leader, one Mateo Martinez, had a bit of a problem a few weeks back. Seems his girlfriend clobbered him over the head, hog-tied him while he was unconscious, stole the gang's take from the night before—and Martinez's prized muscle car—and burned rubber. Got clean away. Quite the loss of face for Martinez. His superiors sent Soto to temporarily take the reins, assess Martinez's standing, and shape up the organization."

Gamble looked unconvinced. "Over what? A domestic dispute and a small chunk of change?"

"That and the disturbing news that someone *other* than his girlfriend called the cops on Martinez—from his own phone, even. That means an unknown participant was inside his house, someone party to Martinez's girlfriend's theft. When the officers arrived, they found Martinez trussed up like a Thanksgiving turkey—and a brick of coke sitting on his table in plain view. The gang higher-ups want to know who ratted them out."

"Still seems like overkill, sending in Soto's kind of, er, management style."

"Yeah, well, I've heard rumors."

"Of?"

"Of Soto screwing up bad in Mexico, of him being sent here to 'think on his sins.'"

Gamble didn't comment; he returned to the curious details around Martinez. "Whoever messed up Martinez and called the cops also left the drugs on the table for the police to find?"

"Uh-huh. So . . . care to share your interest?"

Gamble didn't answer. He looked down at one polished shoe tip and, instead of answering, he pondered what Diaz had told him.

In both cases, neither drugs nor money seemed to have mattered. Could there be a connection between the burned-out drug house and Mateo's girlfriend? Between this fire and the call to APD from Mateo's house? A common thread?

Pete Diaz and the APD gang unit didn't mind partnering with the Albuquerque Division of the FBI, but they didn't like working in the dark—and Gamble had evaded Diaz's gentle probe.

Time to probe less gently.

"Give it up, Gamble. Why your interest in Soto?"

The FBI man shrugged. "Arnaldo Soto is a sociopath who needs to be taken out of play. Wherever he goes, law enforcement agencies have to restock their body bags. Isn't that interest enough?"

Pete shook his head. "Nope. I'd appreciate a little more detail."

Gamble's smile was thin. "You know the whole 'I'm not at liberty to discuss the specifics' spiel, but . . . I guess I can tell you that Soto is a suspect in the deaths of several Mexican undercover cops. Unfortunately, one of those undercover operatives was FBI, working with the Mexican authorities. Another was DEA."

"Okay, so it's agency interest. Not personal."

Gamble's eyes hardened. "I didn't say that."

"So, it *is* personal. To you."

"I didn't say that, either."

Pete's nod was almost imperceptible. "Got it."

"Thanks. You'll be calling me?"

"I'll keep you in the loop."

The two men shook hands again and strode to their respective vehicles.

***

I rested another entire day, parceling out the remainder of the snacks I'd bought at the minimart, taking naps, drinking copious amounts of water. All the sitting around wasn't good for my mental state, though: I had too much time on my hands to think without being able to act. I tried to ignore the nagging sense of despair, but it adhered to me like static cling.

When the food ran out, it forced me to get moving, to confront my logistical problems.

Remember my "glimmer of an idea"? After dark that evening, I made a careful circuit of my near neighbors' homes, taking note of the cars parked in driveways and along the curbs.

What if . . . what if I were to 'borrow' a car for a few hours in the middle of the night? I wouldn't keep the car; I'd just use it and put it right back.

The Ghost of Aunt Lucy Past rattled its chains at me, but I kept walking, looking for the "right" vehicle. Zander's disapproving face hovered at the edge of my vision, too, but I refused to look at it.

I returned home, fed the nanomites, and waited until after midnight. Then I turned off the living-room lamp, slipped out the back door, climbed over the wall, and headed down the alley. At the corner, I turned right and jogged two blocks.

I'd spotted a likely candidate on my earlier reconnaissance.

Three cars lined the driveway of a single-story stucco-and-brick house. A fourth car sat on the street.

Sheesh. How many cars do people need?

I waltzed up to the car at the curb and placed my hand on the driver's window near the locking mechanism. My next moves depended on the nanomites and their cooperation.

"Nano," I breathed. "Unlock this car."

Silence.

I waited. Fidgeted.

"Nano. Remember what you asked for? A laptop? I said, *unlock this car.*"

A few chitters and seconds later, a tiny blue light jumped from my fingers and through the window. I watched the light touch down on the manual door latch.

Saw the lock rise.

I blew out a pent-up breath. "Nano. Make sure the interior lights don't come on when I open the door."

I waited while the twinkling blue specks did their thing. When I lifted the handle, the door opened, but the car's inside lights remained off.

"All right . . ." I whispered. I slid into the driver's seat, eased the door closed, and sat there, watching the house. When nothing happened, I buckled up and studied the dash for a minute.

"Nano. Start the car."

While staring at the house I counted under my breath, "One, one thousand; two, one thousand; three, one thousand; four, one thousand; five—"

The engine turned over and caught. I didn't move; my eyes were glued to the house: No alarm; no lights. A full minute later, I slipped the gear shift into drive and let the engine's impetus roll the car down the street. I glanced back at the house. Still no lights. No shouts. No movement. I put my foot on the gas and, at a sedate speed, headed toward the nearest Walmart.

I spent the drive down Candelaria thinking through what had just happened.

The nanomites had obeyed my voice commands in two recent instances: They had uploaded my files and burned the hard drive, and they'd unlocked and started a car for me.

I blinked. *Oh, yeah—and on my last trip to the tunnels, they cut through chain link fence and fried a snake, probably saving my life.*

I hadn't asked them to, but they'd acted on my behalf anyway.

"Huh."

Um, and they unlocked the door to the drug house so that I could escape the fire I set.

Most recently they'd written two messages to me on the wall. The notes were "for-sure" progress—actual communication in response to questions! I felt a tiny spurt of hope flicker and push against the low-grade depression clinging to me.

What else would the nanomites do for me? What else *could* they do? And why the shift in their behavior?

I might not understand the *why*, but I needed the nanomites and their cooperation. I needed them if I—if *we*—were to do more than survive, if I were to keep ahead of the melancholy that dogged me and tried to suck me down. If even a slim chance existed that we might rescue Dr. Bickel.

Well, first, I needed the mites to locate him.

I wanted to liberate my old friend, yes, but Dr. Bickel was also the key to my many other problems. He was my sole hope of getting the nanomites out of me so I could reclaim my life.

Cushing won't want me once the mites have left me. She will stop pursuing me and leave me alone once they are gone.

It was a lie I could almost convince myself to believe.

Maybe the *why* regarding the shift in the mites' behavior didn't matter if they continued to do what I asked? I'd have to figure out the "what else could they do" part as we went along.

I strolled through the Walmart not far from the intersection of Carlisle and Candelaria. It wasn't my regular store, but it had the same layout as the one I was accustomed to—except reversed. Flipped. Everything opposite of what I was used to. Having shopped Walmart with the nanomites in the middle of the night many times, I felt comfortable, almost relaxed, roaming the store's rows and aisles. I passed maybe five late-night customers on my way to the back of the store, but I felt confident that I could manage to keep out of their way.

In the hardware department, I pulled a heavy-duty extension cord from the shelf and stuffed it into one of the bags hung gunslinger style across my shoulders. I'd cut, hand-stitched, and otherwise jury-rigged a lone pillowcase I'd found in the safe house into two temporary shopping bags. They weren't perfect, but they would work for now.

Then I wandered into the electronics department and found a single clerk on duty and two young men perusing music and videos.

Or were they only browsing?

One guy cut his eyes toward the clerk while the other stuffed a few items down his pants. They feigned looking at CDs a bit longer, then headed for the exit.

Punks!

I was angry with them—until I remembered that I had "borrowed" a neighbor's car myself.

Well, I'll leave gas money in the glove box, I decided.

Then I sneered at my excuse. *Yeah, because that totally makes "borrowing" a car without permission all right.*

Shut up.

I found the prepaid, no-plan phones first—behind a locked glass door in plain sight of the cashier. A sign read, "Ask Associate to Open Case."

Uh, not likely.

I placed my palm on the glass and then grimaced.

You *do* know that glass is the perfect medium for leaving fingerprints, right?

I took my hand off the glass and used the hem of my shirt to smear the glass. With my hand inside my shirt, I again laid my palm on the glass.

"Nano." I paused a beat. "Unlock this door."

I waited—but not for long.

Warmth. Faint blue light. *Click.* Lock open.

I slid two phones from the case and shoved them into the bags under my shirt. I started to close the sliding glass door. Changed my mind. Grabbed a third phone—just in case. Closed the sliding glass door.

"Nano. Lock the case."

Done.

Wow. They are getting faster.

Girls Wear was across the aisle from the electronics department. I crossed over, faced a carousel of dresses, and pulled one phone out of my bag so I could examine it. Leery of security cameras around the store, I pushed the dresses apart and held the phone between garments while I studied the plastic packaging.

Uh-oh.

The phone had an anti-theft tag attached to it—an electronic security device that would trigger an alarm when I walked out the door.

Well, of course it does, dimwit.

"So, no self-pay register," I mumbled to myself. "Better and better."

Lots of questions caromed around inside: Could the nanomites remove or deactivate the tags? But then what? Could I ring the phones up at a self-checkout register?

Or I should just walk out without paying for them?

I sighed and thrust the decision aside, delaying what I felt was my inevitable descent into a life of crime.

"Nano."

How to phrase this?

I touched the anti-theft tag. "Nano, this package has an electronic device attached to it. My finger is on it. Deactivate the device so that it doesn't trigger the alarm at the store exit."

A spate of chirping ensued, but it lasted mere seconds before a stream of mites swarmed out my fingertips, were gone a few seconds, and returned to me.

I wasn't convinced that the tag was deactivated, but I didn't have a way to test it—except to walk out the door. I pulled the second phone from my bag and went through the same process. Ditto for the third.

Then I went in search of a laptop. Not the best selection in the world, but I wasn't complaining—any one of them would do. The display models were chained to the countertop, but the boxed computers, just as the phones had been, were stored under the counters behind locked doors.

Same routine: "Nano. Unlock this door."

Routine? Yes; I guess I was getting used to telling them what to do, and they were getting faster at doing it. Apparently, they were learning, too, starting to guess what I would ask them next.

Predictive logic, Dr. Bickel had called it.

I pulled the model I'd decided on from the shelf. As soon as I touched it, the nanomites swarmed onto it and—I presumed—deactivated the anti-theft tags.

"Nano. Thank you," I told them.

Silence.

Right. Because social niceties were probably irrelevant to them.

I headed for the front of the store and the self-checkout registers. I had to wait until the area was clear before I touched the self-service screen and obeyed the prompt: "Scan your first item, please."

I scanned one of the phones. A message appeared on the register's screen: "Security device attached. This item must be paid for in the Electronics Department."

Drat.

The scanner might not be able to discern if the tags were active or not, but the bar code generated the same result: I could not pay for the electronics I needed at a self-service register.

I paced the area in front of the scanner, an inexorable decision looming closer and my own twerpy version of Hamlet's soliloquy racing around in my head:

*To **steal** or not to **steal**? That is the question.*
Whether 'tis nobler in the mind to suffer
*The slings and arrows of outrageous **conscience***
*Or to take arms against a sea of **adverse circumstances***

"Not to mention a sea of Cushing's stormtroopers," I grumbled.

I don't think many people my age are tormented by my brand of über, steroid-driven scruples. Then again, not many were raised by a surrogate mom whose moral compass was superglued on True North, whose worldview was black-black or white-white and ne'er the twain shall meet, let alone *mix*. Nor are many people saddled with an identical twin sister who is the very antithesis of principle, and whom, I am convinced, does not possess a conscience to be pricked or wounded—a sister I had vowed I would never emulate.

At the word "conscience," my mind shifted a couple of stanzas ahead in Hamlet's lament.

. . . The dread of something after death,
the undiscovered country,
from whose bourn no traveler returns,
puzzles the will,
and makes us rather bear those ills we have
than fly to others that we know not of?
Thus conscience does make cowards of us all

Thanks again to Aunt Lu for depositing a healthy dread of death and hell into my impressionable young psyche. She had made me more afraid of breaking her code of conduct than I was of Cushing.

Yeah, so I have a conscience, and that makes me a coward, I fretted, *but I'm being pursued. Hunted. Doesn't that count for something? Doesn't it make my choices understandable?*

Cushing certainly has no conscience about what she's *doing*, I reminded my personal Jiminy Cricket. *Why do* I *have to play by different rules? I need this stuff to survive!*

As I held my internal debate, Zander's face made another appearance, and his expression, saddened by my moral quibbles, added weight on the coward's side.

I stood there, waffling, for five minutes, before I growled in frustration and sprinted for the exit. I jetted past the bakery and deli and was within steps of the door when a knife shot through my palm.

"Yeeoow!" I flung my hand side to side, trying to shake fiery darts from my palm.

The head of a woman browsing the produce section swiveled toward me. I ignored her concerned and confused gape as I rubbed my palm against my leg to numb the pain. My fruitless efforts were accompanied by soft chittering.

"Stupid, *stupid* Nano," I mumbled.

Abrupt quiet.

I huffed and started toward Electronics, but I was outright disgusted.

I was disgusted with the nanomites and all the grief they'd caused me.

I was disgusted with Dr. Bickel for creating an artificial intelligence that, ostensibly, possessed more moral fiber than I did.

And I was disgusted with myself.

When I arrived at Electronics, I folded my arms and considered the clerk behind the counter. I studied the register, noted the clerk's employee number. Came up with an idea.

It was worth a try, anyway.

Sure a lot of trouble just to be "ethical," isn't it? some cynical voice scoffed.

"Shut it!"

The clerk lifted his head and stared, but I was already crossing the aisle to the Girls Wear register. I found a store phone hanging behind the fitting room attendant's counter, and put my hand on it.

"Nano."

I already knew the mites could invade an electronic system and hijack its functionality. I knew they were capable of following complex instructions, too—but would they? Right then, I almost wanted to see them stymied.

Stupid bugs! Moral high ground be hanged.

"Nano. Use the store's PA system to call Employee 157 to the front of the store."

Their expectant silence was replaced by a low chittering that lasted thirty seconds or so and was followed by the usual warmth flowing down my arm and out my hand.

A minute later, I heard a mechanical voice intone over the speakers, "Employee 157. Report to the front of the store. Employee 157."

How do they do that?

I saw our Electronics Department clerk fiddle with his register and pull out his key, locking it down. I jogged toward the register as the clerk fast-walked away.

Behind the counter, I placed my hand on the register and spoke. "Nano. Use Employee 157's account to activate this register. Scan and ring up the items in my bag and provide a total for a cash payment."

The level of nanomite activity went into overdrive for many seconds—and I saw the display on the register begin to move, to add prices, calculate tax, and come up with a total.

The register drawer popped opened with a *ding*.

I won't kid you—I was amazed. I yanked a stack of twenty dollar bills from one of my bags and peeled off thirty-six of them.

"Nano. I am paying with $720 in cash. Enter that amount."

The numbers appeared on the display about the same time as I spied the clerk hustling toward me. I stuffed the cash into the right slot in the drawer, counted out the correct change, slammed the drawer closed, and stepped out from behind the counter as the breathless and red-faced clerk arrived.

I moved back and dumped the change in my bag, wondering if he'd notice anything awry.

The guy glanced around his work area and then, reassured that all was as it should be, pulled his cellphone from the rear pocket of his khakis and pressed buttons.

He cursed under his breath as the call went through. "Hey, it's me. You won't believe what just happened. Yeah, at work. I got chewed out for leaving my department—even though I was called to the front of the store over the PA system! I know, right?"

I didn't hear anything further. I shot down an aisle and out the front door toward "my" vehicle. For a second I couldn't remember what kind of car I'd driven—but then I recalled where I'd parked it. I hustled to it and put a hand on the trunk lid.

"Nano. Open the trunk."

Click.

I piled the phones, extension cord, and laptop inside and closed the trunk in under ten seconds.

I stood there in the parking lot, breathing hard, my heart hammering. I was both relieved and elated. As soon as my pulse slowed, I pointed my feet toward the front entrance a second time.

I sighed with hungry anticipation. "Now for some groceries. This is the easy part."

I had to restrain my enthusiasm a bit because I wanted to eat everything I laid eyes on. But even after I'd paid for and hauled two sets of foodstuffs to the car, I had to come back for personal items—and all that stuff took two trips, too. I shoved toothbrush, tooth paste, floss, mouthwash, brush, comb, face cream, shampoo, shower curtain and hooks, shower cap, towels, washcloths, bathmat, dish soap, laundry detergent and softener, and a simple selection of clothes, including a lightweight hoody, into the trunk of my "borrowed" car.

Clean underwear.

Yay me.

I returned the car to its owner an hour later. Before that, I'd driven it up the alley behind my house and emptied the trunk, piling all the stuff on the other side of the block wall—discreetly, of course. Then I'd driven the short distance to the car's home, left it at the curb where I'd found it (a twenty in the glovebox), and walked back.

I stood on the back porch, scanning for prying eyes before I unlocked the door. It took five trips to haul everything inside the unlighted house, and I felt a lot better when I was finished. I surveilled the neighboring houses once more before I closed and locked the back door.

As I unpacked and put food away, I realized how famished I was. I opened a can of soup. While it heated and I watched the numbers on the microwave's old-school display flip over, I gobbled up two pieces of fruit and chugged a bottle of juice. When the microwave dinged, I pulled the hot soup out and wolfed it down with some crumbled crackers.

Afterward, I wanted to get straight to work, but my poor body was having none of it. Instead, with my tummy warm and full, the exhaustion of the last days overcame my resolve. I cut open the packaging around the three phones and put them on to charge, and plugged in the new extension cord. With the cord grasped in my hand, I collapsed into the bed.

I'll get busy first thing in the morning, I told myself as I drifted away, *and maybe the nanomites will find Dr. Bickel!*

***

Imogene Cushing picked up the phone on its second ring. "Yes?"

The mechanical voice on the other end said only four words: "Secure phone call requested."

Cushing put down her phone and marched from her office and down the hall. "Mrs. Barela, I will be in the SCIF."

"Yes, ma'am."

Cushing crossed the parking lot that surrounded the MEMS and AMEMS labs, followed a sidewalk some distance, and entered another building. A guard at the security checkpoint scrutinized her credentials. When he allowed her to pass, she walked down a hallway.

At the end of the hall she swiped her clearance badge to activate the security features on a heavy door. She entered her personal code to complete the sequence.

The lock on the door snapped open. She entered, closed the door behind her, and manually engaged another lock that switched on a red light in the hallway above the door, signaling that the SCIF was in use.

The "Sensitive Compartmented Information Facility" was built to stringent government requirements and was swept daily for listening devices. Anyone who attempted to enter the SCIF passed through meticulous screening to verify the individual's identity and proper clearance level. These measures ensured that the room was a safe and secure location for classified conversations.

The room housed a single computer terminal. The terminal was "air gapped," that is, hard-wired to a dedicated government network but physically isolated from all other networks, secure or unsecure. No wireless signal could penetrate the walls of the SCIF, nor did the SCIF's computer possess Wi-Fi capability. Access to the hard-wired, classified network was granted only through rigorous login procedures.

The SCIF also contained a single phone line hardwired to a secure and encrypted phone network.

Cushing picked up the secure phone and dialed a number she knew by memory. When the two scrambled lines synced, the party on the other end greeted her.

"Good morning, General Cushing. Thank you for calling."

"What is it, Colonel?"

She listened, her expression growing angrier by the moment. "What do you *mean*, 'Bickel sent an email'? How? How could he have done that? I ordered that he be allowed no computer access!"

She listened, and shouted into the receiver. "A guard's *smart phone*? Who gave the guards permission to carry personal phones?"

As the voice on the other end of the line continued to speak, Cushing tapped a pencil tip on the surface next to the phone. Harder and harder. Until the fine point snapped. "*They were playing cards with the prisoner?*"

Her anger turned to ice, as did her voice. "What have you done with the phone Bickel used?"

As the disembodied voice droned on, Cushing's angry expression gave way to a nervous tic. "And you believe your actions will suffice, Colonel?"

"Yes, ma'am. With the SIMM card destroyed, the location of the phone's previous calls cannot be traced."

"You understand that this in no way excuses the lax, undisciplined manner in which this incident occurred."

"I do, General. I take full responsibility for the situation. My IT staff has created a 'dead zone' around the, er, facility—no Internet and no cell service in or out. They have locked down the land lines so that they have no access to long distance services. And, of course, I have removed and replaced the personnel. The new guards have strict instructions: They are to have no personal interactions of any kind with the prisoner."

"See that they don't, Colonel—if you value your wings."

She slammed the phone onto its receiver and stared into space, thinking. As she thought, she jabbed the pencil's broken tip into the desk's surface.

⌘⌘⌘⌘

CHAPTER 5

As exhausted as I was after my expedition to Walmart, I slept well—at first. But then I dreamed.

I dreamed of Emilio, scrunched down in the shrubs in front of his uncle's house, doing his best to stay out of the way, out from underfoot while Mateo's gang partied. I dreamed of his thin, bare arms, of him shivering where he crouched in the bushes. I dreamed of him hungry. Cold. Neglected. Afraid. Unloved.

Caught up in the clutches of the dream, I rushed to my little house and baked a frozen pizza for Emilio and brought him one of my old jackets—but when I called to him, he wouldn't come out to take them. Instead, he pushed farther and farther into the bushes. I reached for him, but he was beyond me, the little hidey-hole deepening and Emilio disappearing into its dark depths.

I sat up in a sweat.

I must know how Emilio is doing. If Abe still has him. If he is all right. If Abe and Zander are okay.

I drifted back to an uneasy slumber sometime later.

***

When morning came, I woke up in a rush, unsure of where I was or what time of day it was, but with my concern for Emilio at the forefront. Even as I wondered how he was faring, my other pressing concerns came barreling back, too: procuring a new identity and a car. Finding Dr. Bickel ended up dead last.

"I have too many competing priorities."

My worry returned to Emilio. *Zander.* Zander would be able to tell me how Emilio was doing.

I decided to table my other needs for a few hours while I set up a means of communicating with Zander. I wanted to make sure we could connect in case of emergency.

I checked the three phones: They had full charges. I scavenged through Dr. Bickel's abandoned office and found a partial sheet of colored labels. I picked up one of the phones and stuck a piece of blue label on it. Then I called the activation number.

This phone is only for talking to Zander.

The second phone was for him on his end, but I had to find a way to deliver the phone. I scrawled a short, cryptic note.

Keep this phone hidden with the ringer turned off. Call me only at prearranged times or in case of emergencies. We can text to set up call times. Memorize my number. Do not add it to your phone book. Delete calls and text logs after each use.

I didn't sign the note, of course, but I did jot my number at the end before I wrapped the phone, its charger, and my note in a crumpled piece of brown paper and stuffed it into one of my bags. With the bag slung over my shoulders, I was headed out the rear door when the nanomites set up a fuss. The racket in my head was deafening.

I backtracked to the bare wall. "What is it?" I demanded.

TERMINAL

"Yeah, I know. I'll set it up when we get back."

I again moved toward the back door, but my answer had set them off. They chipped with a fury.

"Listen to me," I told them, "I need to go to Zander's office and leave a phone for him. When we get back. I'll set up the laptop first thing."

That assurance did not sit well with them, but as I'd told them before, *I* drive the boat.

I headed for the nearest bus stop.

***

The chiseled stone profile of Downtown Community Church had been part of the Albuquerque skyline for generations. It sat on the intersection of two major thoroughfares just off I-25. Right on the city transit route.

I got off the bus and waltzed up to the office doors—apparently with misguided confidence.

"Nano. Unlock the door."

Nothing.

Nada.

Squat.

Zero.

Zip.

Not a chip, a chitter, a buzz, a hum.

The cold shoulder; the silent treatment.

"Fine! Guess that teaches me that I can't depend upon you." I hung out, waiting for the church secretary to come to work, alternately leaning against the building and pacing up and down the sidewalk.

I was worried about slipping through the door and into the empty office area right on the woman's heels. Guess I was nervous that I might make too much noise and freak her out. I also figured the door would lock behind her, so I looked for and found a discarded paper cup in the gutter.

She arrived, unlocked the door, and swept into the hallway on the other side. I heard a little "ding-dong" when the door opened, and I made a mental note of it. As soon as she let go of the door, I shoved a flattened piece of the cup between the locking mechanism and the edge of the door.

The secretary disappeared down the hall, and I reached for the door handle.

Whoops: The "ding-dong." Almost made a mistake.

Great. Now I have to make nice with the nanomites.

"Um, Nano. Check out the alarm system. I don't want this door to chime when I open it."

Nothing.

"Nano, please deactivate the door chime."

Crickets.

Grrr!

New tack.

"Nano, let me put it to you this way: I'm not going home and I'm not setting up the laptop until I'm done with this errand. If you don't help me, it will take longer to finish. I might have to wait hours for another person to come in or go out of this door."

After a full minute of no response, the mites swarmed out my hand and into the call box mounted to the side of the door—to the accompaniment of a low hiss.

A low hiss? For all that, it could have been a razzing Bronx cheer.

Whatever.

A moment later, the mites returned to me, and I pulled open the door and crept inside.

It had been years since I'd been inside DCC, so my fuzzy recollections were from a kid's perspective. You know how it feels going somewhere you'd known as a child? How the rooms are smaller and less imposing than you remember, but your sense of colors is spot on?

Yeah. That.

I wandered through the halls, into the sanctuary, down the aisles, just looking around, reacquainting myself with the lay of the land. After I checked out the location of the exits, I made my way back to the office wing. The secretary was busy making coffee, humming a little to herself.

I tiptoed past her open door, down the hall, and scanned the nameplates on the doors. Third door down, I found Zander's office. The nameplate read, *Zander A. Cruz, Associate Pastor*.

I shuddered a little. *Ugh.* I'd never get used to him being a pastor.

I tried the knob. As expected, it was locked—and I figured the mites would give me a hard time if I asked them to open it. About then Secretary Lady hustled toward me so I flattened myself against the hall wall as she passed by. She disappeared into a room at the end of the hallway.

Bathroom break?

A break for me, in any event.

I sprinted into her office and checked the walls for keys. Sure enough, I spotted a wall-mounted box for keys behind her desk. I tugged on the box's door—it was unlocked! I flipped the door open and ran my finger down the row of keys and their labels. I grabbed two keys, one under the label, "Office Entrance," the other under "Pastor Cruz."

I was out of the church before Secretary Lady returned.

***

Trust in the nanomites felt more and more misplaced. They were fickle. Unreliable. Stubborn. Willful. I trod down the street, trying to come up with the nearest place to duplicate keys—since keys didn't pitch fits of noncooperation.

Eventually I hopped a bus down Central and got off near one of those big-name hardware stores. Inside, I wandered up and down different aisles, looking for the key-duplicating machine. It was in the paint area.

A tall, gangly guy sporting a blue vest perched on a stool behind the counter. He had his elbows planted on the countertop and his face planted in his phone.

Well, he had no customers—if you didn't count me—but he was sitting directly in front of the key-making machine.

In. My. Way.

I glared at him, but he didn't budge. Guess he wasn't feeling me much. Yet.

Distraction?

I moved over an aisle and spied the spray paint. Shelves and shelves of spray paint. Hundreds and hundreds of cans of spray paint. All types. Every color.

I swept my arm down the length of one shelf and sent cans flying. I repeated the same thing three times, clearing entire shelves.

I grinned to myself. *This ought to get your attention.*

It did. The clerk stood at the foot of the aisle, mouth agape, staring at half the spray paint inventory rolling around on the floor. I kicked a few cans to keep them moving before I did an end run around the end cap and down the opposite aisle toward the key machine.

I chose key blanks to match the two keys I'd pulled from my pocket. I studied the machine. Shouldn't be too hard to run, right? So, why the two laminated pages of instructions posted next to the machine?

"Sheesh. I don't have time to read all this junk!"

I blinked. Sighed. "Well, what if . . ."

I placed one of the DCC keys on the counter and a blank next to it.

"Nano. Make a duplicate key for me."

The nanomites had been mostly uncooperative since our disagreement but, at my command, the familiar silence ensued, followed by chittering. Chittering, but no action.

I slapped the second DCC key on the counter and a blank next to it. Might as well do both at the same time, right? *Time*—as in *I don't have all day*.

"Nano! Make duplicates of both keys. Right now! Get with it!"

The level of chittering rose and, after a frustrating wait of maybe twenty seconds, that warm, creeping sensation trickled down my right arm and out my hand. A blue glow surrounded the first key and its blank. Tiny sparks, a faint grinding, and the smell of hot metal rose from the glow.

On the next aisle over, I heard the sounds of cans being thunked onto shelves accompanied by muffled swearing and the arrival of another individual.

"What's going on here, Josh?"

"I don't know, man. All these cans just fell off the shelves."

"They couldn't just 'fall off' the shelves, Josh."

"I'm tellin' you, man, I was at the paint counter and heard the crashes. Came over here and all these cans were rolling around on the floor!"

I scowled. "Nano. Hurry up."

The blue glow crawled off the first set of keys and onto the second. I picked up the new key and compared it to the original. The new key was warm to the touch.

"Looks like a match to me," I muttered.

The "thunking" down the spray paint aisle stopped, but I heard rattling, like maybe Josh was straightening the rows of cans. Like maybe he was almost done.

"Nano! Come on!" I hissed.

Half a minute later, the blue glow crept onto my hand and up my arm. I swept up the second set of keys and headed for the front of the store.

I was already on the bus, nearing DCC, when I remembered I hadn't paid for the key blanks.

How do I describe the dispute that ensued?

Fussy Shoulder Angel (sounding a lot like Aunt Lucy) exhorted me to go straight back and leave ten bucks for the blanks. The very suave and debonair Shoulder Demon interrupted with convincing arguments of his own.

Naw, girl! No worries! It's all good. You won't make it long-term if you insist on that goody-two-shoes attitude, you know. Besides, you're invisible—just take what you need. Don't leave a trail of unexplained purchases for Cushing to sniff out.

I mean, really. Who's gonna know, anyway?

Maybe the Voice of Reason had a point. Maybe I needed to stop with the ethics. After all, Cushing wasn't playing by the rules, was she?

The bus pulled into the cutout at my stop, so I tabled the internal discussion, telling Shoulder Angel that I had to return the original keys to the lockbox before Secretary Lady noticed they were gone. In that case, I didn't have time to run back to the hardware store.

Just as I inserted my new "Office Entrance" key into the lock to let myself into the DCC offices, I remembered the call box mounted to the wall beside the door.

Whoops again. Almost made the same mistake.

"Nano. Don't let the door chime. I promise we'll go home as soon as I'm done here."

That was as close to begging the tiny tyrants as I was willing to go.

I inserted my key, turned it, and opened the door. Secretary Lady was at her desk, so I tiptoed past her door and down to Zander's office. The new key for his door worked every bit as well as the entrance door had.

"Good work, Nano." I mouthed the grudging words more than spoke them aloud. They clicked once in response.

I closed Zander's door behind me and made sure it was locked. My eyes roamed the room before I moved. It was a tiny office, as far as offices go—but had Cushing already been here? Did she have some sense of my relationship with Zander?

Did *she* have a sense of my relationship with Zander? *I* didn't even have a 'sense of my relationship' with Zander.

"Nano," I whispered aloud. "Uh, scan the room for electronic surveillance." I thought for a second and added, "Assess for threats. Please."

Golly gee, Gemma. Yer talkin' like a reel spy now.

Flashing blue specks floated out into the air, meandered over the desk, lit upon the phone, the lamp, the blotter, moved and touched other objects, flitted here and there.

I approached Zander's tidy desk, and the shimmering specks returned to me. I took a deep breath as though part of me had returned and needed the air.

The desk had a pencil drawer in the middle and three larger drawers to the left. The larger drawers were locked.

"Nano. Can you open these drawers?"

Flickering blue lights. Done.

I pulled open the top drawer and laid the brown paper package inside.

"Lock the drawer, Nano."

Done.

I locked Zander's door behind me and wondered how I'd get Secretary Lady out of her office so I could return the keys I'd borrowed. Just then, someone arrived at the entrance at the end of the hall. He unlocked the door and walked through to the accompaniment of the chimes. He paused at Secretary Lady's door.

"Morning, Miss Coyne."

"Good morning, Pastor McFee. Coffee?"

"Yes, please. And bring your notebook?"

"Right away."

He opened one of the offices near Zander's and went inside. A few minutes later, Miss Coyne followed him, toting a steaming mug.

As soon as she entered and sat down in a chair in front of the pastor's desk, I trotted to her office to return the borrowed keys—except the box was locked.

"Um . . . Nano? Unlock this box, please?" The door to the key box snicked open. I placed the keys on their respective hooks and closed the door. The nanomites locked the key box without being told to.

"Well." They were learning, as was I. And they seemed to have gotten over their snit.

"Nice of you," I grumbled.

On the bus across town, I stared out the windows and wondered how long it would take for Zander to find the phone and call me. I didn't know how long I'd have to wait, but I was anxious to hear from him.

***

Back in the safe house, I kept my promise. I opened the laptop and plugged it in. I placed one hand on the keyboard. "Nano. Here's the computer as promised. I will need Internet access while you are searching for Dr. Bickel."

With an uptick in clicking, clacking, and humming, they got busy. When I saw they had connected the laptop to a neighbor's Wi-Fi network, I nodded and got busy, too.

***

Just after noon, the phone with the blue label lit up. I lifted it and pressed the green button before the phone even rang—but I said nothing.

"Hello?"

Zander's voice!

"Oh, Zander! I'm so glad you called."

"Are you all right, Gemma?" I could hear the worry.

"Yeah. I'm fine."

"Good. Abe will be glad to hear, too. You can't imagine my surprise when I found the phone and your note. How in the world did you manage to—" He uttered something between a chuckle and a sigh. "Never mind. I'm just happy you did manage it. Are you feeling better? I mean from that 'drain' thing the nanomites did to you?"

"Yeah, I've been resting and recuperating. I'm getting my strength back, but last night I, um, I had a bad dream about Emilio, and it really disturbed me. Is he okay?"

"Yes, the kid's fine. Abe waited three days before he called CYFD. He wanted to see if Mateo would even notice that Emilio was gone—more evidence that he's unfit to take care of the kid. Anyway, Abe spoke to someone at CYFD, but because it isn't an emergency, they haven't sent anyone yet. They promised to send a social worker no later than tomorrow. In the meantime, Abe is feeding Emilio double rations, and I have been picking him up from school in the afternoon. We go hang out at the park for an hour before I take him back to Abe."

"And Mateo?"

"Haven't heard a peep from him. Fact is, Mateo is gone most nights and Abe says he comes home and sleeps during the day before going out again."

"Maybe he thinks Emilio is at school while he sleeps?"

"Yeah, but even if he notices Emilio is missing, what's he going to do? Call the police? Abe and I doubt that he would draw that kind of attention to himself."

"Good point." I thought about Arnaldo Soto—Dead Eyes. Soto would not appreciate Mateo calling in the police.

"Well, thank you for calling me. I was sort of out of it when Cushing stormed the cul-de-sac the other night."

"Abe says the soldiers came back a few hours later, after I went home."

I sighed. "Yeah, they did. I was so beat that I'd gone back to my house to rest. Figured it would be safe for a few hours. I figured wrong. After I took a nap, I got on my laptop. Cushing's IT people were watching. As soon as I logged on, they knew I was there."

"Gemma!"

"The important thing is that I got out of there. It won't happen again. I won't give her that kind of opportunity."

His voice on the other end went silent.

"Honest, Zander. I'm okay. I'm safe where I'm hiding. I've had a chance to rest up and get my strength back."

"Well, all right . . . I guess. What will you do next?"

"I'm keeping busy. The less you know, the better."

I think my answer stung him, because he dropped into silence again.

"Zander?"

"Yeah. I'm here."

"Thank you for calling me. You'll destroy the note, right? And keep the phone in a safe place?"

"Of course."

"Well, goodbye, then."

"Yeah, okay. Goodbye."

Sigh.

Life is not much more than a series of goodbyes, is it?

***

I ate some lunch before tackling the problems before me. Gemma Keyes—her identity, credit cards, and every means of operating in the digital world—was, for all practical purposes, dead to me. And yet I had pressing needs that no amount of cash by itself could overcome.

Like a car.

Yes. Transportation was number one on my hit parade, followed close behind by a real credit card for other needs I could only acquire through online shopping.

As I pondered how to overcome my problems, I realized that "getting" a vehicle was merely the first step. "Keeping" a car entailed other logistics—like where I would park said vehicle. I sure couldn't park it at the safe house or just out on the street!

And once I *had* transportation, if I didn't license it, the odds of being pulled over rose exponentially—particularly as I drove closer to wherever Cushing had Dr. Bickel stashed.

Dr. Bickel.

Where had Cushing secreted him? Was he languishing in a cell in D.C. or its surrounds? Was he being tortured somewhere on the 463,000-acre Eglin Air Force Base in Florida? Was she forcing him to work in a laboratory hidden within Area Fifty-Whatever deep in the Nevada desert?

He could be just about anywhere. The only clue to his location Dr. Bickel had provided was "military installation"—and the government had "military installations" all over the world.

The phrase "military installation" was not much help.

Regardless of the "where," once the nanomites figured out where Cushing was holding my old friend, I would need a vehicle that could operate on the open road without suspicion—and that trick would require a lot of forethought and planning on my part.

I need to figure this out. How does an invisible woman purchase a vehicle for cash? Get it registered and licensed? Under a legit name? Other than her own, of course.

I worked late into the night and fell asleep on the couch considering such problems. I slept until midmorning the following day.

⌘⌘⌘⌘

CHAPTER 6

Since I'd arrived at Dr. Bickel's safe house, I'd been mulling over how to establish a new identity. After much thought, I decided on a course of action. The first step would be the most difficult and would hinge on the nanomites' hacking abilities—and their level of cooperation.

I opened a browser window and navigated to Arizona's Motor Vehicle Division—as good a starting point as any.

"Nano. I need to appropriate a new identity, so I want you to get into this system's database and select the driving records of five women between the ages of, say, thirty and fifty. Doesn't matter which women, so long as they hold licenses with no accidents or citations.

"I'll need to see their records, including social security numbers. Oh. And cross reference their licenses with their credit reports. I'm looking for someone whose credit history is both unblemished and inactive."

I was gratified when the mites launched into work mode, so I began searching Albuquerque real estate sites for houses recently placed on the market. I found one that had been listed last week about two miles east of Dr. Bickel's safe house.

Close enough but far enough away.

I copied the address.

While I did that, the mites wormed their way into the Arizona MVD and produced five suitable Arizona licenses and credit reports. I looked them over, studied one Kathy Sawyer's profile, and decided it might work. Then I did a lot of other browsing, trying to pull together the little threads of ideas that would get the new Kathy Sawyer functioning in Albuquerque.

First, I had to consider "Kathy Sawyer" to be a disposable persona. If—no, *when*—Cushing sniffed out Ms. Sawyer, her every action would be scrutinized and backtracked. For as long as I used Kathy Sawyer's identity, I had to be careful that her activities did not point the way to me.

Next, Kathy needed a physical address, a place where she could receive mail—including packages. It could not be an address too close to the safe house.

I considered getting a mail box inside a UPS store because I could access a UPS mail box 24/7. Of course, the problem there was that you needed two forms of ID to get a mail box—and to get an ID you needed an address (among other things).

Can't get one without the other.

Can't get the other without the one.

Difficult, much? Yeah. Good thing I had an ace up my sleeve.

Or a swarm of nanomites.

I did an online search for Kathy Sawyer in Tempe, Arizona. She showed up on Facebook but her profile was dated. Other than a mention at a high school reunion, her online presence was low.

Perfect.

I wrote down all of Kathy's license info and kept at the other problems, figuring out workarounds.

Thinking, thinking, thinking.

I was surprised when I glanced at the clock on the laptop. Surprised and beat. I'd worked straight through the afternoon, evening, and into the night. I fell into bed and slept until late morning the following day.

***

The sun was obscured by cloud cover when I pulled myself out of bed. It was now early November and, while the days *might* warm up, the nights were downright nippy.

I opened the door to the furnace closet. The model inside wasn't too much different from the old furnace in my house. I squinted at the instruction label on the furnace's side and fumbled my way through lighting the pilot. Got it running. The odd smell a furnace makes the first time it is fired up for the season was comforting in its familiarity.

Late that afternoon, I slipped out the back door and walked to the nearest bus stop. I caught a ride headed east. I stood near the bus's rear door well where I could jump out of the way if someone exited or got on, but riding the bus made me uneasy. It was way too simple for someone to move when or where I didn't expect them to, to zig when I zagged.

Brrr! The weather had definitely turned chilly. Two more reasons for a car—ASAP.

As the bus ran east up Menaul, I ran over my mental checklist, what I needed to accomplish.

I had to stop and examine the odd sense of purpose and of, well, *satisfaction*, I guess, that I was feeling. The nanomites and I were working together a bit instead of fighting each other (go figure!), and the possibilities of what I could do—what *we* could do—were growing on me. I guess that's why I felt no anxiety about what I intended to do next.

The bus pulled over, and I got off not too far from an MVD Express.

They will be closing soon.

Yup. The sign on the door said they closed at 6 p.m. I waited until someone exited the building to slide inside. Maybe three customers were waiting in the rows of seats. I found a clock on the wall: 5:25. Thirty-five minutes to kill.

A fake ficus plant took up a corner of the room. I walked over and hunkered down next to it. The floor wasn't too clean, but it wasn't too bad, either.

Cleaner than the drug house's floor had been. Just chilly.

Guess I was still pretty beat 'cause after a few minutes I nodded off. A soft chirp from the nanomites roused me. The waiting area was empty and the staff was locking up.

I wiped my face and got up off the floor. After another ten minutes, all the employees were gone and the place was locked up tight. I went through the doors into the staffing area and sat down at the first customer service terminal.

"Nano," I whispered. "Log in to this system and bring up a driver's license application."

They logged me in as the last user, one Marcella Pruitt. I filled in the application using Kathy Sawyer's social security number and the address I'd chosen—that of the newly listed house for sale. I entered Kathy's date of birth and the height, weight, and eye color from her Arizona license. Acceptable proofs of New Mexico residency? I clicked on "Real Property Rental Agreement" and "Utility Bill." The nanomites added Marcella's verification code.

Everything was going great until I hit "Photo."

Well, duh! Sorry, but I'm not at my most photogenic today.

"Nano. Um, appropriate an existing license photo in this system, one that is an approximate match to the age, height, weight, and eye color listed on this application."

They went to work, and I waited.

A few minutes later, a photo appeared on the license form, and Kathy Sawyer became a plain, middle-aged woman with dark hair and dark, saggy eyes.

I shrugged. "Okay. Thanks."

I completed the app and submitted it. The next screen came up with "Payment: $67/four-year license or $83/eight-year license." I chose the eight-year option and "cash" for payment. I pulled a wad of money out of my pocket, all twenties.

Drat. I hadn't thought about exact change—or where the money would go when I paid it.

I pulled open the drawer under Marcella's computer, but it was filled with the regular sort of office supplies. I looked around at the signage in the lobby.

On the end, I spied a sign that read, "Pay Here."

"Ah!" I got up and went over to the station. It had a register of sorts, but the drawer was open and empty.

Bad news for thieves.

Worse news for me.

I went back to Marcella's terminal and blew out a sigh of frustration. I sat down to think—and then it hit me.

Wait! I'm going about this all wrong, trying to make the numbers add up when what I should do is delete the equation.

"Nano. Get into this system and trigger the correct payment for this license then erase the payment transaction record. Erase the log entry that created this license, too, while retaining the license itself."

Seconds later the screen read, "Payment Received," and I pressed "print" for the temporary card. The real license would arrive at the address I'd listed, usually within seven to ten days. However, according to the MVD Express website, it *could* take up to forty days to arrive.

The thought of trotting to the mail box at that address every day for the next forty days drew a growl of frustration from me. "Nano. I need you to check the New Mexico MVD every day and monitor the progress of this license. Alert me when it goes out in the mail."

I wasn't convinced that they had heard me or would do as I directed. "Nano. Can you do that? Give me a sign that you will do that."

Their overall background noise picked up and words formed on the computer screen in front of me.

ALERT YOU YES

"Great. Thanks."

I logged Marcella Pruitt out, wiped down the keyboard, and hoped nothing I'd done would come back to bite her. I stuffed the temp license into the back pocket of my jeans and headed to the front door.

"Nano. Unlock this door without tripping the alarm. Relock it after we're out."

They were at it before I finished speaking.

It was a hike to get home, a couple of miles, anyway. As I wandered along, I ticked off the next steps in my mind, and picked up my pace.

Once I was home, I began searching mail box services nearby and selected a likely candidate—the UPS Store on San Mateo. It was in the same general area of Albuquerque as Dr. Bickel's safe house, but not too close.

***

Late the following afternoon, I caught a bus down Candelaria to San Mateo and walked the rest of the way to the UPS Store. The store closed at 6 p.m., and I intended to be inside before they locked up.

In the same way that the mites had logged me into the MVD Express system, they logged me into the UPS system—and opened any locked door I requested.

I emerged from the store fifteen minutes later with a mail box key and a key to the mail room. I tried the key to the mail room, checked out my box, pocketed both keys, and headed home.

As I trotted along, a satisfied little ditty played in my head. *Now I can make some progress. Some* real *progress.*

But while I walked, uneasiness flickered on the edge of my consciousness, a disquieting sense that I was missing something. No, that wasn't quite it—more that I was going about everything the wrong way . . . the long way? Like when I needed to pay for my driver's license and realized that I was hindered by my "old" ways of thinking.

Yeah, I'm making progress, but . . . have I made things unnecessarily complex by looking at problems from a, well, strictly human *perspective?*

Should I embrace a new paradigm? If so, what was it? What did it entail?

I needed to give this uncomfortable insight more thought.

***

It was getting late, but I was determined not to stop while I was on a roll. I made coffee and got to work. I laid my temporary driver's license on the table and created an email account for Kathy Sawyer.

Opened a browser window to Capital One.

The website asked, *What's in your wallet?*

I snickered. *Wouldn't you be surprised?*

Determined to break out of "old" and limiting patterns of thinking, I skipped over the many convoluted steps I'd taken the last couple of days.

Use the mites, Luke.

"Nano. I need a credit card in Kathy Sawyer's name. Hack in and make that happen. Use my UPS mail box for the address."

I thought I'd see them filling out an online application (again, the limitations of my own thinking), but I guess they didn't need to. They must have hacked the approval process, too, because minutes later they wrote on the screen,

**EXPECT YOUR
NEW CAPITAL ONE
CASHBACK VISA CARD
WITHIN SEVEN DAYS
THANK YOU
FOR CHOOSING
CAPITAL ONE**

I cracked up.

I laughed—and laughed harder.

It felt good, you know? Good to find something humorous about my crazy life.

I hadn't laughed in what seemed like a very long time.

I wiped my eyes. "Super, Nano. Thank you."

I giggled. "Super Nano? Yeah, right."

Maybe not as funny as that.

The nanomites were overcoming insurmountable problems left and right—and I was riding a steep learning curve. Destination? *Faster, easier ways to get things done.*

I thought about my visit to DCC and shook my head over the roundabout, confabulated steps I'd taken to acquire keys to the church.

Keys? Apparently, I didn't need keys any longer.

All righty! Now, let's get me a checking account. I did need a way to pay the credit card bill, after all.

I brought up the Wells Fargo website next—and ran into a red flag.

Hmmm. Wells Fargo has branches all over.

"Nano, jump into Wells Fargo. Has Kathy Sawyer from Arizona ever had an account with them?"

A few minutes later I had my answer.

NO

I hesitated. "So, where does she bank?"

BANK OF AMERICA

I exhaled. "Thank you. Nano, please set up a Wells Fargo checking account for me—for Kathy Sawyer."

Since I had a social security number, driver's license, and a physical address, they accomplished their task in quick order—until they hit the signature card.

SIGNATURE CARD
REQUIRED

"Um, can you like . . . fake a signature? Maybe use the one from my driver's license and, um, log the card into the system?"

YES

Moments later the image of a signed signature card appeared on screen.

"Wow." I shook my head. "I'll say it backward: WOW!"

Such good little forgers! You've earned yourselves a treat.
snicker

INITIAL DEPOSIT
REQUIRED

Aaaaand *thud.*

I thrummed my fingers on the laptop's edge. "How to . . . What about . . . hmmm. Could you . . ."

I sighed. The account only required a $50 initial deposit. I had thousands! But how could I put some cash into my account before I had an ATM card?

I was at a loss.

GEMMA KEYES

"Uh, yeah?"

WE HAVE APPROPRIATED
THE REQUIRED
MINIMUM AMOUNT
AND DEPOSITED FUNDS
TO YOUR ACCOUNT

"What? You have? Uh, won't the money be missed?"

WE HAVE INSERTED CODE
TO HIDE THE MISSING AMOUNT

**IT WILL BE TRANSFERRED
OUT OF YOUR ACCOUNT AND
RETURNED TO ITS RIGHTFUL
ACCOUNT WHEN YOU MAKE
A DEPOSIT USING YOUR
ATM CARD**

"So, you 'borrowed' some money, put it in my account, and will replace it when I have funds to cover it?"

YES

"Excellent!" I was on my feet now, too jazzed to sit. "When will my card arrive?"

**WE HAVE
EXPEDITED
YOUR NEW
WELLS FARGO
ATM CARD**

"Great! And how about checks? Can you order checks for me?"

**YOUR PERSONALIZED
CHECKS WILL ARRIVE
IN FIVE TO TEN DAYS
WE KNOW YOU HAVE
A CHOICE OF
BANKING PROVIDERS
THANK YOU FOR CHOOSING
WELLS FARGO**

Elated? I could scarcely breathe; I was vibrating with excitement—the nanomites had done much more than I'd imagined they could. They had overcome every roadblock—including my limited ideas.

"This is *so cool*, so *stinking* cool!"

**WE DETECT
NO NOXIOUS EMISSIONS
PLEASE ADVISE**

I lost it right there. I cracked up; I doubled over under great belly laughs that sent me to the floor. I laughed until my eyes ran. I laughed and felt my body relax and release its pent-up stress and fear.

When I was done, I sprawled on the floor, a lazy smile plastered on my face. I was, at last, close to acquiring a vehicle! And all due to the nanomites. Well, they had caused my problems in the first place, but I admitted it: I was feeling a bit more benevolent toward them.

Still more to do!

I got up, activated the third phone, plastered a little red sticker on it, and designated it my "throwaway" phone. I would use it for everyday needs and, if it became compromised, I'd pull the SIMM card and trash it.

I dialed a number I'd jotted on a slip of paper and got voice mail, so I left a message.

"Hello. Yeah, um, hi there. I saw your ad on Craig's List for the 2012 Ford Escape? Please call me back at this number." I didn't leave my name, but I recited my number, hung up, and waited.

What had attracted me to this vehicle were the words "tinted windows all around" and "Near Northeast Heights." The tinted windows would make it easier for me to drive without someone noticing that the driver was *missing*. And the closer the vehicle was to the safe house, the easier it would be to acquire it. As it was, I would have to catch a bus, walk, or "appropriate" a ride to reach the car in the ad.

I chewed my fingernails for half an hour until the phone rang.

"Hello?" I glanced at the caller ID. "Are you Thomas Baca? Oh, he's your dad? You're Javier? Hi, Javier. Is the title in your name? Okay, good. Um, my name is Kathy. Would it be possible to see the car? Thank you, but if it's all right, I'll come to you. What is your address, please? Okay, great. And what is the vehicle's VIN so I can check it on CARFAX?"

As I hung up, I knew it would take a lot of moxie to pull off what I had in mind. I logged into Ford's website, and found the Escape model. "Nano. Familiarize yourself with this make and model vehicle. Do additional research so that you are proficient with the manufacture and operation of the 2012 model."

Instead of logging onto carfax.com like I'd told Javier Baca I'd be doing, I found an online bill of sale and filled it out—and then realized I couldn't sign it until I printed it.

Argh! More stuff to do.

I saved the completed bill of sale as a PDF, had the nanomites upload it, then headed out to an office supply store.

Down the printer aisle, I whispered, "Nano. Print a single copy of the bill of sale."

I loitered for a few minutes.

Done.

I pulled the printed sheet from the printer, signed it, and placed it in the printer's scanner tray. "Nano. Now scan the page, convert it to PDF, and upload the file."

***

With Javier Baca's address in hand, I waited until after midnight to borrow my usual ride. I drove to the address, parked down the street, and hoofed it to Javier's driveway to scope out the car. I walked up to it and peered through the windows. The car had a classy charcoal gray paint job and the interior was a complementary dark gray.

I placed a hand on the hood. "Nano. Check out this vehicle. I want to know if it is in good working order."

I felt some of them go off to do the inspection and felt them return.

"Well?"

Chittering. Humming. Blue letters superimposed on the driver's window.

ENGINE GOOD CONDITION
VEHICLE REQUIRES
REAR BRAKE REPAIRS

I chuckled. "All right. How about a test drive? Nano. Unlock the door."

I got in and familiarized myself with the controls.

"Nano. Start the engine."

I drove away from the house and cruised around for about fifteen minutes, getting a feel for the car. Yeah, the brakes felt a little squishy, but I liked the car.

Now for the hard part.

In the morning, I called Javier Baca.

"Javier? Turns out my job is sending me out of town this week, but I've decided that I'd like to buy your car. I drove by yesterday and took a look at it. Yes, I'll pay the asking price—but I'd like you to have it inspected first, particularly the brakes. If you agree to show me the inspection paperwork and fix any major problems, particularly with the brakes, I'll get you a check right away."

He haggled with me for a while, but I held firm on the inspection and the brakes.

Dude! I can't stroll into Pep Boys and ask them to perform an inspection—but you can, I shouted in my head.

Aloud I said, "Well, since I'll be gone until next week, you have plenty of time to get the inspection done. Snap a photo of the report and text it to me. If the brakes need work, get that done and shoot me a copy of the repair bill. Then I'll send you a check or pay you from my bank via text, whichever you choose."

He argued some more, which told me that he already knew about the brake problems and what the repairs would cost.

"How about this, Javier? You get the brakes fixed, and I'll pay half of the bill. Yes; I'll just add the cost to the purchase price. All right? Deal."

I didn't want to wait a week to get the Escape, but it was my most immediate option. At least my list of "must dos" was shrinking. I used my new credit card to order a few things online—warmer clothes for winter: a couple long-sleeved shirts and sweaters, a good pair of running shoes, a heavier jacket.

I was elated with how great things were going.

Elated? Not for long.

That evening, flickering blue lights on the wall drew my eyes.

GEMMA KEYES

I got up and stood by the wall. "Yes?"

UNABLE TO DETECT
DR. BICKEL LOCATION

"What?"

I was stunned. "But . . . what about his email? The phone it came from?"

UNABLE TO LOCATE PHONE

"What about the Internet? What about Cushing's emails and phone calls?"

NO PERTINENT
DATA FOUND
WE WILL CONTINUE
OUR SEARCH

"But . . ." I'd started believing that the mites could do anything . . . but they had their limitations, too, didn't they?

I sat down. Hard. "But if you can't find him . . ."

It was a devastating acknowledgement that could only lead to one shattering conclusion: If the nanomites were stymied, what hope was there?

If the nanomites could not find Dr. Bickel, no one could.

***

Mateo Martinez squirmed before Soto's disdain.

"I hear your neighbor has taken in your nephew and called in social services."

The anger growing inside Martinez lunged for an outlet, but his instinct for self-preservation managed to keep it in check. He wet his lips and considered his words before speaking. He added as little detail as possible to what he said. "Yes. The man is a busybody."

"He has raised questions about your fitness as a guardian."

"I'll get the kid back. He hasn't been beaten or anything."

Soto examined his fingernails. "Yet, how do you suppose this *busybody's* actions appear to your subordinates? How do his accusations reflect upon your leadership? Or upon mine?"

Mateo turned his head a fraction, as though considering Soto's question—or mocking it.

"I fail to see a connection. Sir."

Soto's upper lip lifted in a sardonic half-smile. "Mateo, Mateo. A good leader allows no opportunity for his authority to be challenged. A great leader leaves no challenge unanswered."

Mateo shifted on his feet. "You wish me to do something?"

Soto shrugged. "I give you no orders, only a word of advice: A real man would never countenance such an insult."

Soto's emphasis upon the word "real" dumped gasoline on Mateo's anger. "I will deal with the old man."

As he stormed from the room, Soto and one of his guards exchanged amused smiles.

⌘⌘⌘⌘

CHAPTER 7

It was late—or should I say early?

I had wasted another long night trying to crawl inside Cushing's evil brain and plumb her psyche—hoping to second-guess where she would have put Dr. Bickel. The nanomites' message had stolen the wind from my sails, but I couldn't just give up on my friend, could I? Yet, after hours of brooding deliberation, I had nothing to show for my efforts.

I was frustrated and a bit down. I slumped on the couch, weary and yawning.

Ten days had sped by in a blur—a week and a half since I'd last seen Zander, Abe, and Emilio. Ten exhausting days spent gearing up to elude and survive Cushing and, in the back of my mind, preparing to save Dr. Bickel as soon as the nanomites located him. Ten days of hope ending in one, tiny flaw: *The mites had failed.*

They were stumped.

So, yes, I was frustrated. I had to admit there was something else bringing me down, too. I'd hung my heart on a tiny, unspoken hope, the idea that *if*, by some miracle, we'd been able to find and rescue Dr. Bickel, we might also, somehow, expose and defeat Cushing . . . and I would get my life back.

But, in reality? What were the chances that the nanomites and I could accomplish what was virtually impossible?

I wouldn't take those odds!

And that was the lump of coal at the bottom of my pity pot.

Old anger reared its head—the rage I'd felt when the nanomites had first invaded me. Was this the shape of my future? Was this what the rest of my life would look like? No one to share it with? Always hiding? Ever in fear and jeopardy?

I was, I admitted, more than angry: I was unsettled. Uncertain and perturbed with myself.

With all the mites had proven they could do, my insistence on planning and directing our every move was beginning to concern me. I had the disquieting sense that I was overlooking better ways to use the nanomites, that I was shortsighted when it came to them. That there was a smarter approach to getting stuff done.

Maybe I was just overtired, but even the way we communicated irked me—I mean, them writing notes on the wall? It seemed . . . oh, I don't know . . . tedious, given the mites' high-speed computing powers.

Dumb, even! Something had to change.

Maybe *I* had to change?

I sighed. "Nano."

They responded with their alert, listening silence.

"Nano, is there a way we can, um, talk more easily? Are you capable of audible emissions? Of making spoken words? I know you understand language—both verbal and written—and have mastered programming languages and computers, networks, and the Internet. What I'm wondering is . . . if there's a way we could communicate in a simpler, more fluid manner."

I paused, trying to muster an eloquent way to say what was bothering me. Dr. Bickel had lectured me on the algorithms behind the nanomites, how they were divided into five tribes but no tribe bossed the others around or told another what to do. He had stressed how the tribes cooperated and applied fact and logic to arrive at consensus and agreed-upon actions to achieve their goal of "the greater good."

Up until now, I'd insisted that the mites follow my lead and use their knowledge and abilities as I demanded, but perhaps I was cutting myself short? Was I depriving myself of the full benefit of the mites' help by being so directive? Could I—could *we*—work together better? Smarter?

The nanomites and I shared a common goal: Find and rescue Dr. Bickel. However, the immensity of that objective, the unlikelihood that we might succeed, and the more likely odds that I'd be captured . . . well, they weighed on me.

No, "they weighed on me" was a weak, inadequate picture. The prospect of ending up in Cushing's custody—and the terror it evoked?—stole my breath away.

But I had to keep trying to find him, didn't I? I couldn't just give up!

The problem was that I didn't have a clue as to where Shark Face had stashed Dr. Bickel. Not even a jumping-off point. In all reality, he could be anywhere. Dr. Bickel himself didn't know where he was being kept prisoner.

Sure, the mites could worm their way into any system if it was connected to a network that communicated with the outside world. No firewall invented by humankind could keep the mites locked out if they wanted in! Their intelligence and speed were incredible—but they had their limitations: They were as dependent upon my physical body to carry them around and keep them powered as I was dependent upon them to offset my physical limitations.

No bones about it, if we ever found Dr. Bickel, it would take a human-nanomite collaboration to get him out.

My mind presented the colorful image of a nano-powered human, and I laughed.

"Yeah, right. Like some kind of comic book superhero—a real, live action figure out to save the world!"

Not gonna happen, I admitted.

Back to Survival 101. How could I better exploit the nanomites' abilities? How could I—how could *we*—operate with more efficiency?

If I could just, *somehow*, tap in to the mites' processes, perhaps all the "stuff" we did would be less time-consuming and less tedious and wouldn't require so much brainstorming and preparation on my part.

I decided on a direct appeal to the mites' sense of order and logic.

"Nano, I guess what I'm trying to say is that I'm interested in improved relations and faster and more effective communication. Enhanced communication could lead to, um, greater exchanges of information and understanding, maybe even, um, *consensus* (*gag*) and cooperation. An enriched relationship could result in, um, superior decisions—perhaps collaboration and mutual support—especially when we are in tight spots."

I shook my head and ended with, "I wish we could find a means to function better. Together. More efficiently. Perhaps forge an, um, alliance or partnership."

The mites remained silent, but I figured they weren't ignoring me: They were chewing on what I'd asked of them.

Minutes ticked by, and they did not respond. It was still dark, but morning was not that far away. When I could no longer fend off my fatigue, I whispered, "Nano. I'm going to bed now."

**GOOD NIGHT
GEMMA KEYES**

"Uh, right. Good night, Nano."
Well, *that* was new.

***

I had been soundly asleep for a while, I don't know how long. I squirmed and tried to sink back into that place of deep, revitalizing slumber, but I was uncomfortable, and the discomfort was growing. Half in and half out of a sleepy state, I managed to put a label on the discomfort:

Headache.

The ache grew. My skull pounded. The pounding morphed from a clanging hammer to a digging, stinging knife, an icepick stabbing between my temples—all the way through, from one temple to the other. Surely my head was going to explode!

I tried to lift my face from my pillow, tried to look around the darkened room, but I felt too weak, too racked with pain to do even that.

What happened? Am I sick?

Something warm and salty dribbled onto my lip. I swiped at it, but the dribble kept coming.

Nosebleed? Oh, gross—I'm bleeding all over my pillow.

I threw back the covers, dragged myself up—and vomited onto the floor between my feet. I gagged and threw up again.

After I'd emptied my stomach, I tried to stand and get to the bathroom. The room revolved around me, and I found it difficult not to fall off the edge of the bed. The throbbing in my head grew until I realized that I could feel my pulse reverberating in my hands, my arms, my chest. I hurt in every part of my body.

More of what I guessed was blood ran over my lips and down my chin.

What in the world . . .

I forced myself to balance on shaky, flimsy legs and made my way to the bathroom. I closed the door before I switched on the light.

Ow!

The light battered my eyes, so I looked away, glanced down. Bright, bloody drops speckled the tile floor. Fresh rivulets streamed from both nostrils onto the only nightshirt I owned. I grabbed up a washcloth. With one hand, I held the cloth under my nose to catch what was running; with the other, I pinched my nostrils high up, hoping to stem the flow.

My efforts did not help—I gagged and upchucked for the third time.

This is really bad!

Fear jittered its way through me. It wasn't as though I could check myself into an ER.

I pressed the cloth against my nostrils to catch the blood, stumbled to the kitchen, and pulled a handful of ice from the freezer. I piled ice into a dish towel, sprayed a little water on it, wound the towel around the ice, and sat down at the dinette table, holding the ice pack on my nose and eyes.

"Ohhhh . . ." I moaned and closed my eyes against the pain coursing through my body and over the surface of my skin.

We regret the discomfort, Gemma Keyes.

I flinched, jerked my head toward the unexpected voice that came from just over my right shoulder. Jumped to my feet—with as much grace as a drunken elephant—and slumped, panting, against the refrigerator.

No one there!

"Who-who's talking?"

We recommend a nonsteroidal anti-inflammatory drug, other than aspirin, for temporary relief of pain.

Again—the voice was behind me. I swung around to confront the speaker.

No. One. There.

Adrenalin shimmied down my spine to my legs. I wanted to run—but to where? From whom?

"Who is this? Where are you?" I demanded.

Silence.

A poignant, pregnant silence.

A silence all too familiar to me.

"Nano?" I whispered.

We regret the discomfort, Gemma Keyes.

I staggered back to the dinette and fell onto the chair. While my nose bled freely and my head and body beat with the rhythm of my heart, my brain struggled to fit what was going on into a believable interpretation.

Minutes ticked by. I could not accept the conclusions that logic presented.

"Nano?"

Since you are temporarily incapacitated, we will release endorphins into your bloodstream to mitigate your discomfort. We again recommend that you take a nonsteroidal anti-inflammatory analgesic other than aspirin, which acts to thin blood. Aspirin would not be a good choice in this situation.

"Y-you did this? What is happening?"

We will assist in your biological healing. We expect your body to adjust within a forty-eight- to seventy-two-hour period.

"B-but . . . adjust to what? What are you doing?"

We are effecting a more efficient and cooperative union. As you requested.

"Y-you are—you are *what*?" I "sprang" to my feet—again with all the elegance of an inebriated pachyderm—and just as quickly grasped the kitchen counter. The room whirled around me; my legs could not support my mind's instinctual urge to flee what I feared.

We are releasing endorphins now. Endorphins are neuropeptides that will interact with your body's opiate receptors to reduce your perception of pain. You will experience a marked increase in well-being in approximately three-point-five minutes. Please ingest the recommended adult dose of the nonsteroidal anti-inflammatory analgesic of your choice to assist in pain reduction.

Pain? Yes. Oh, wow, did I hurt!

But "union" and "your body will adjust"? I fended off the tidal wave of dread/disbelief/horror driving my heart to faster speeds and reached for a kitchen catch-all drawer where I'd seen a bottle of Ibuprofen. I slammed three of the little round brown pills and half a glass of water.

And hacked them right back up.

"Oh, man," I moaned.

Still holding the bloody washcloth to my nose, I rinsed my mouth and sprayed the ick down the sink. With a trembling hand, I shook three more pills from the bottle and swallowed them with a sip.

Another sip.

We will speed the ingested medication to your COX-1 and COX-2 enzymes and will assist the NSAID in reducing the number of prostaglandins produced by your body's reaction to our merge.

Our *merge*? I could have kept the pills down. I truly could have—if the mites hadn't shared that tasty bit of info.

Up came the pills.

I was draped over the sink like a dirty dishcloth when I finished retching and purging. Too weak to stand.

We do regret the discomfort our actions have caused, Gemma Keyes. We will, ourselves, undertake to reduce the number of prostaglandins produced by your body.

Super.

Perfect.

Why, thank you very much.

How very kind of you.

We recommend suspension of voluntary bodily functions while your body adjusts and heals.

You mean sleep?

Gee, thanks for your concern.

You rock.

My physical self might have been down for the count, but my sarcas-meter was pegged out.

Smokin' hot.

The mites must have managed "to reduce the number of prostaglandins produced by your body's reaction to our merge," because a tiny bit of that promised "well-being" rushed into my brain—enough for me to lurch down the hall to the bedroom. I flipped the soiled pillow over and flopped into the bed.

I shivered, but had no ambition to pull the covers up. However, a moment later, I felt the soothing weight of blankets come to rest on my shoulders.

How did they do that?

As the worst of the throbbing pain eased, I slid downward into a troubled chasm. My last conscious thought was,

I'm never going to get the blood out of this pillow.

⌘⌘⌘⌘

CHAPTER 8

Later, I calculated that I had slept a solid fourteen hours. The nanomites had to have done something to keep me out that long, but when I awoke, it was morning and a low voice was repeating in my ear,

Gemma Keyes.
Wake up, Gemma Keyes.
We require energy.
Gemma Keyes.
Wake up, Gemma Keyes.
We require energy.
Gemma Keyes.
Wake up, Gemma Keyes.
We require energy.

"Yeah, yeah." I buried my face in the pillow, but the chant continued unabated. My pillow should have blocked out the voice, but it seemed to amplify the whispers.

Gemma Keyes.
Wake up, Gemma Keyes.
We require energy.
Gemma Keyes.
Wake up, Gemma Keyes.
We require energy.

"Oh, shut up, will you?" I flipped the covers back and rolled over, planted my feet on the floor and stood up, looking around for the extension cord.

Oh, yeah. I left it in the living room—ack!

I missed stepping in yesterday's congealed vomit by millimeters. With more strength than I would have believed I possessed, I sidestepped the ick, made it to the nearest switch plate, slapped my hand onto it, and let the nanomites feed. As they swarmed down my arm and into the power supply, the usual warmth flowed up my arm and through me—and it felt kind of different this time. More energizing. Revitalizing.

While they fed, I inhaled deep, satisfying breaths and stretched my legs, my back, my neck.

Then I hit the bathroom. A quick once-over with my hands left me disgusted. Dried, crusted blood smeared my face, neck, hair, and nightshirt.

Ugh.

Well, at least my nose isn't bleeding anymore.

After I'd relieved myself, I showered, washed my hair, and put on clean clothes. I set my bloody nightshirt and pillowcase to soak in cold water. I didn't know what I'd do about the blood stains on the pillow itself. Then I went to the kitchen and put on coffee.

As I waited for the Elixir of Life to brew, I took stock of how I felt. I was surprised at my tally: No more nose bleed, no head or body ache, no fever, no residual fatigue.

Not too bad, I admitted. *I feel pretty good.*

While the coffee pot gurgled, I did a few sets of lunges and girl-style pushups, some squats and stretches, and a three-minute Downward-Facing Dog to limber up. As I worked out, everything inside me tingled in a rather pleasant manner.

"Huh. I would have thought I'd be stiffer. Sore. Hungover," I murmured.

I grabbed my first cup of coffee and headed into the living room to savor it and enjoy a few minutes of peaceful leisure.

Instead, I sloshed half my coffee into my lap.

Gemma Keyes, are you ready to begin?

"Wha—" I don't know how I'd forgotten that voice in my ear, but when it piped up, I jerked and tossed the contents of my mug at the same time.

Straight up. Straight down. Into my lap.

"Oh, man! Don't *do* that! And look at this mess!"

We regret that we startled you.

All the stuff the nanomites had told me while my nose was bleeding came rushing back.

We regret the discomfort, Gemma Keyes.

We expect your body to adjust within a forty-eight- to seventy-two-hour period.

We are effecting a more efficient and cooperative union.

As you requested.

I shuddered. Oh, yeah. A more efficient and cooperative union. As I requested? Great.

I sopped up the slopped coffee with a towel then poured myself another cup. I set my mug on the dinette table this time and took a seat and a first tentative sip.

As *I* requested?

I tried to recall my exact words when I'd suggested to the nanomites that we needed a better means of communication. I hadn't used the term "more efficient and cooperative union. Well, not exactly—or had I?

I remembered saying, "Nano, I guess what I'm trying to say is that I'm interested in improved, that is, *enhanced*, two-sided communication. More effective communication could lead to, um, greater exchanges of information and understanding, and, um, even *consensus* (gag) and cooperation between us. Enriched communication could result in, um, superior decisions—perhaps collaboration and mutual support—especially when we are in tight spots."

And this little gem, "I wish we could find a means to function better. Together. More economically. More efficiently. Perhaps forge an, um, alliance or partnership."

I wagged my head side to side. "Way to go, Gemma."

Careful what you ask for.

"Um, Nano . . . how do you . . . how are you talking to me? Do you have, um, mouths now?"

I had a vision of tiny, chomping jaws running through my body.

Just peachy.

Instead, the mites answered, *No. No mouths. Vibrations.*

"Vibrations?" I mulled that one over. Well, but what is sound, other than vibrations?

"So . . . you're making audible words by vibrating?"

Yes.

I snorted a laugh into my mug. "Ingenious."

I thought a bit more, speculated why their voice seemed to come from behind my shoulder or inside my ear. "Are you vibrating in my brain or my ear canal?"

External auditory meatus.

"Sooo . . . the ear canal. Wow. Okay. That's cool."

We do not register a decrease in the ambient temperature attributable to our vibrations.

"What? *Oh.* (*snort-laugh*) No, I mean, um, 'cool' as in the slang for, um, interesting or, uh, *good.*"

Silence.

I sipped my coffee and wondered what other surprises the mites' "merge" would produce. I finished my coffee, poured another cup, and wandered back into the living room. Woke up the laptop and opened a browser window to peruse recent Albuquerque news. I loaded the KRQE website and scanned down the page.

Nothing of interest caught my eyes, but I'd been "out" for most of a day. I was browsing backward in the news archives when I experienced a sudden, disquieting revelation.

Wait a sec. The mites didn't need to do the "merge" thing to talk to me, to make vibrations in my ear. They could have "vibro-talked" to me from the get-go.

So, what exactly did their so-called merge accomplish?

"Nano—"

The two-day-old headline drove all questions from my mind.

LOCAL PASTOR ATTACKED
IN GANG-RELATED DISPUTE

An Albuquerque resident, Zander Cruz, associate pastor at Downtown Community Church, and an as-yet unidentified Albuquerque senior citizen were assaulted and beaten Thursday in what police describe as a gang-related altercation. Both Cruz and the elderly male have been hospitalized. No word on their condition has been released.

***

Ross Gamble huddled with Pete Diaz and Don Benally near a parked APD unit. Gamble appraised the cul-de-sac and its homes and saw nothing of note: The houses were aging but nice-enough looking. The yards—except one—were well-kept. Nothing remained of the police tape and police presence from the incident two days past.

"What's up, Pete?"

Diaz grinned. "You asked me to keep you in the loop." The other officer, Benally, silently followed their conversation.

Gamble nodded. "Yeah, thanks. What do you have?"

"All right. So, day before yesterday, the man who lives in that house there, one Abraham Pickering, age 71," he pointed to a home on the outlet of the cul-de-sac, "and his neighbor," he pointed to the next house over, "got into it. Apparently, the neighbor guy has custody of his ten-year-old nephew. Last Thursday, Mr. Pickering reported to CYFD that the kid was being neglected and had taken to spending the night in the bushes."

Diaz pointed to the shrubs that formed a boundary between the two houses.

"Okaaay," Gamble grumbled.

"Hold your horses; I'm trying to make a point. That neighbor," he again pointed to the next house over, "happens to be Mateo Martinez."

Gamble looked skeptical. "He lives there? Too tame of a crib for a gang banger, isn't it? Too respectable; neighborhood's too 'nice' for his ilk."

"He inherited the house from his dad. I've interviewed the other neighbors except the young woman who lives there." He gestured at the house sitting back and center of the cul-de-sac. "The folks all say that Martinez's crew used to party here on a regular basis. By some unspoken agreement, the neighbors didn't call APD and the gang didn't bother the neighbors—if you don't count the noise they made when carousing and the trash they left behind."

Diaz looked at his notes. "The neighbors say Mr. Flores," he tipped his head toward the house on the other side of Martinez's, "used to sweep up the broken glass and whatever else the gang left behind. More on the neighbors in a sec.

"I interviewed the CYFD case officer, too, and she let me read Mr. Pickering's complaint. He asserts that most times while the gang partied, Martinez's nephew would hide out in the bushes. Then Pickering said he found the kid sitting on the curb one night dressed in nothing more than a t-shirt, jeans, and flip-flops. Overnight temps have been in the high forties, but the kid had no jacket. He was cold, unfed, and filthy. Pickering took him in and called CYFD.

"CYFD came and took the kid, but Mr. Pickering lost no time applying for temporary custody of him. Of course, until he is vetted and approved, the kid has to stay in CYFD custody—which is where he is right now. Right after CYFD took the kid, a social worker paid a visit to Mateo Martinez—but he wasn't home. Guess she came by a couple of times. Same thing each time.

"On the day Martinez finally answered the door, the case worker was accompanied by an officer, and she had a warrant to enter the house and document its condition. Her report says it was a pigsty and the kitchen had no food.

"Crazy thing is, the kid had been gone maybe five nights and Martinez hadn't even noticed he was missing. That didn't keep him from blowing up on the case worker, though. When she wouldn't tell him where Emilio was or who had reported him, the officer had to step in and make Martinez back off.

"Next day, Martinez confronted Mr. Pickering. The old man had kind of expected Martinez to show up; his friend, one Pastor Zander Cruz, was staying at the house so Pickering wouldn't be alone when Martinez came calling. Well, Martinez didn't show up by himself. He brought three of his crew with him, and they brought baseball bats."

Diaz sighed. "Pickering got off one shot from a revolver before the gang beat the living crud out of him and Cruz. Pickering hit one of the gangers in the chest, but he'll live.

"The old man, though, has a head wound and is in rough shape—they don't know yet if he'll make it or not. Cruz will survive, but he's got cracked and broken bones and some nasty cuts and bruises."

"And Martinez?"

"Yeah, he's disappeared—but remember I said I'd get back to the neighbors? Yeah, get this: *They* reported that, a few weeks before Martinez's attack on Pickering and Cruz, Martinez had a visitor, a stranger. This guy rolled into the neighborhood in a sleek, expensive ride and was accompanied by some very intimidating men—but none of them as intimidating as the stranger himself.

"Martinez not only let them into his house but, ever since then, Martinez and his gang have been at this guy's beck and call. Now get this: The word the neighbors use to describe this stranger? Downright scary."

"Arnaldo Soto."

"We think so. We're looking for Martinez, of course, and we think when we find him, we'll find Soto."

"Right. Unless Soto has already disposed of Martinez's body in the desert."

"That's entirely possible. I doubt Soto approved of Martinez's visit to Mr. Pickering. He wouldn't appreciate the attention it drew to the gang."

Diaz turned a thoughtful eye on Martinez's empty house. "Here's something else. Seems that this unlikely little neighborhood has seen more than its fair share of drama lately. Mrs. Belicia Calderón—lives in that house across there—described something on the scale of a military action taking place about the same time that Pickering made his complaint to CYFD."

"Military action? What does that mean?"

"That's what I wondered, too. See the house between Mrs. Calderón and the Flores'? It's vacant and boarded up right now, and no one seems to know where the young woman who lives there has gone. However, she was at the center of the incident Mrs. Calderón described."

"So, why bring that up? Whatever it was, it can't have anything to do with Martinez."

Diaz chuckled. "Yeah, you'd think so, 'cept Mrs. Calderón—who, by the way, has her nose in everything that happens around here—added some interesting details to her tale. According to *her*, the young guy whom Mateo's thugs beat up is the missing woman's boyfriend."

"Don't say."

"Oh, and Mr. Pickering is this same woman's good friend. Something of a father figure."

"Interesting. And she's missing?"

"Well, as Alice said in Wonderland, the situation gets curiouser and curiouser. Mrs. Calderón gave me a real earful on her next-door neighbor—I guess she is no fan of Miss Keyes."

"Miss Keyes?"

"Gemma Keyes. She's the missing woman. Twenty-six or twenty-seven years old, single. Former contractor employee at Sandia."

Gamble's brows scrunched. "I'm not seeing all the connections yet, but I am puzzled about this so-called military action. What was *that* about? How did Mrs. Calderón describe it?"

Something wrapped itself around Gamble's leg. He flinched and looked down. A cat—a categorically ugly specimen of *Felis catus*—rubbed against him.

"Sheesh. Just what I need—cat hair all over my trousers."

The cat meowed deep in his throat.

Diaz chuckled. "This is Gemma Keyes' cat, Jake. Disreputable old tom, according to the neighbors. Quite the character and *very* discriminating. No one in the cul-de-sac will touch him—they're all afraid to."

"And he picks me? Great."

"Guess that makes you special."

"Gee, thanks."

Diaz was enjoying Gamble's disgust way too much. He grinned as he added, "Since Miss Keyes disappeared, Abe Pickering has been feeding the cat. With Pickering in the hospital, Mr. and Mrs. Flores and the Tuckers have been putting out food for him."

Jake wound his way through Gamble's legs and yowled.

Gamble nudged Jake with his toe. "Scat!"

Jake arched his back and stretched up Gamble's left leg, using his claws for purchase.

"Ow! Get off of me!" Gamble shook his leg and Jake, with his tail high in the air, pranced away. Gamble swore under his breath. "That is one ugly cat."

Diaz grinned. "You done playing footsie with the kitty now?"

"Shut up. What about this so-called military action?"

"The way Mrs. Calderón tells it, around 9 p.m. on the twenty-ninth of last month, several military-like vehicles, lights off, drove into the cul-de-sac, followed by two trucks with banks of spotlights. A group of soldiers and plainclothes people, guns drawn, stormed Miss Keyes' house and broke down the side door.

"A last vehicle rolled in and a uniformed woman—ostensibly the boss—got out. When her people came up empty for Miss Keyes, the boss ordered her team to question the other cul-de-sac residents.

"They went around to the neighbors and grilled them for about an hour before they packed up and left."

"Sounds implausible. Fabricated or highly embellished by this Calderón woman."

Diaz laughed outright this time. "Yeah, when she first told me about it, I thought to myself, 'Here's the local fruitcake.' Then I revisited the other neighbors, the Flores and Tuckers. Mr. and Mrs. Flores were out of town at the time the incident supposedly took place, but the Tuckers were not."

"And?"

"And they watched the whole thing from their front porch. Confirmed every detail."

"Interesting." Gamble turned in a circle, scanning the area again. "Uniforms?"

"Yeah, but Mrs. Calderón doesn't know Army from Air Force. She didn't recall any patches or insignias on the soldiers, though. Just that everything was black—black uniforms, flak jackets, helmets, guns."

"No identifying patches? I don't like it. That fact in itself is troubling."

"Yeah. The rest of the personnel wore standard street clothes. Like I said, curiouser and curiouser."

"You thinking Homeland?"

"Maybe, but no markings on the uniforms? And I wonder why no one heard anything about it. No notice to other LEOs, no reports in the news. Total silence."

Diaz shifted his feet. "And one more thing. Late that night, the same tactical team stormed Gemma Keyes' house a *second* time. The noise woke Mrs. Calderón, and she watched from her window."

"Did they find Miss Keyes?"

"Not that Mrs. Calderón saw. The team came, tore through the house, pulled a few things from it, and handed them over to the boss lady."

"You pull Miss Keyes' sheet?"

"Yes. *Nada.* Not a thing. She held a Q clearance as a subcontractor to Sandia until she was let go last spring, and she doesn't have so much as a traffic ticket."

"Well, what would Homeland want with this Gemma Keyes?"

"You got me, but her connection with Abe Pickering and Reverend Cruz—and tangentially with Mateo Martinez and Arnaldo Soto—is interesting, don't you think? Oh, and during the interviews earlier the evening of the raid, Mrs. Calderón spoke personally with the boss lady— the woman in charge of the raid. Told her Miss Keyes had been behaving oddly for about two months—that she was living in the house, but no one had laid eyes on her for a while."

Gamble was distracted, still hung up on the "military" aspect of the raid. "I dunno. We're supposed to be notified if Homeland takes action in our jurisdictions. The whole thing is too weird sounding. Doesn't smell right."

"Yup, but whatcha gonna do? The feds—no offense intended—the feds do what they want more times than not."

Gamble barked a sardonic laugh. "No offense taken. Even among us there are 'feds' and then there are 'Feds.' Layers of bureaucracy, hierarchy, and political machinations. Sometimes you just mind your own business and look the other way. Go along to get along."

He gave a last scan to the neighborhood and offered Diaz his hand. "Thanks for the heads up, Diaz. I think I'll try to talk to this Reverend Cruz if he's up for it. Where's he at?"

"UNM Hospital, last I heard."

"Okay. Thanks."

***

"Nano." My heart thundered and I couldn't draw in a complete breath. I closed my eyes against the rising panic.

Zander! Abe! Oh, Abe!

My voice shook. "Nano. Find Zander and Abe. They are in an Albuquerque hospital. *Find them!*"

The nanomites went to work. The sound of their busyness seemed amplified, and it was more distinct and diversified than it had been in other instances, less a single source of white noise. I closed my eyes and focused on differentiating between the sounds I heard.

Pretty soon I identified three—no, four?—separate channels of sounds. Five? As I concentrated on what I heard, I sank down, into a trance-like state. The mites were mining data via the neighbor's Internet connection, and I . . . I thought I could hear the data streaming by, like a rushing, babbling current, moving through the nanoswarm.

The mites were chasing the data, filtering it, sorting it, and I became engrossed in their work.

What?

Directly behind my closed eyelids, bits of pictures and images skittered. They flew from left to right with blinding speed. My eyes tried to follow; they flickered back and forth as though I were in deep REM. My head twitched in a minute but rapid, side-to-side movement.

If that weren't weird enough, the *meaning* of the images as they flashed in front of my closed eyes became clear. *Crystal* clear. Bytes of information. Scraps of data. Dates. Facts. Records. Vivid impressions.

I could see it, the information the nanomites were pulling from the Internet! It almost felt . . . it seemed as if I could reach out and touch—

I both saw and comprehended disparate objects in the data flow as the stream became a river that gushed past me.

Around me.

Over me.

Through me.

I couldn't contain it all, and I couldn't detach from the flow. It was sweeping me away! I couldn't keep up, couldn't open my eyes to end it— it was out of my control.

I was out of control.

I began to hyperventilate.

Gemma Keyes. We will moderate the amount of adrenaline your body is producing and release neurotransmitters to calm you.

"Stop . . . it!" I begged. "Please stop! Too much!"

But it did not stop. The deluge of information kept coming and coming and coming. I struggled and fought against the torrent, to no avail—but then my heart began to slow, my anxiety to ease up.

As the data rushed and coursed over me, I gave up trying to keep it out: My efforts were futile anyway. Instead, I turned inward and focused my thoughts on Zander and Abe. This mental trick had an amazing effect. Out of the river of information, I snagged something pertaining to Abe, then a fragment about Zander. I grasped them and held on. Or were they sticking to me by themselves? I snatched more relevant morsels from the stream.

When my "arms" were full, I put what I'd gathered in a stack to the side, but I found that I was thirsty for more. I stared, transfixed, into the data flow—I leaned toward it and reached my hands into it.

It was not enough! My thirst grew, and I stepped into the rushing stream. I waded into its deluge, stood within its rapids, and let it wash over me.

Information I desired came to me like iron filings to a magnet—and still I wanted more.

I found myself sorting the data, fending off irrelevant bits and bytes of information with the flick of a finger, stacking what I wanted to the side. The faster the data came, the better at sorting it I got.

As I amassed information, the space around me grew. I looked far to the right and farther to the left and had the sensation of gazing into the depths of a warehouse—an immense, cavernous warehouse.

I must be hallucinating.

It was amazing. It was astounding.

Then . . . the river of data slowed. The piles I had sorted and stacked to the side remained, but the flow of bits and bytes slowed to a trickle. Dissipated. Died.

In place of the river of data I heard chittering. A lot of chittering. Back and forth.

A voice spoke.

We are waiting for your input, Gemma Keyes.

I was terrified and drawn at the same time. "What? What do you mean?"

We are waiting.

"What? Who? Who is waiting?"

We are.

My innate instinct to survive kicked in, demanded that I pull away, get out of this "warehouse," and return to reality—but that insatiable hunger *to know* clawed at me. Rather than pull away, I placed my hands over my eyes to seal them shut, to ensure that I would remain in the place where I understood so much—and craved so much more.

Vistas I'd never dreamed of opened before me. And only one possibility existed to explain the voices in my head.

"Nano?"

Yes. We are waiting.

Waiting? We?

"Nano. We? How many are 'we'?"

How many?

"How many nanomites."

The silence lengthened, and I grew impatient.

"How many are you, Nano?"

We are six.

From my place in the warehouse, I pondered their words. "Only six? I thought . . . trillions. Dr. Bickel said trillions! How can you be only six?"

We were five. Now we are six.

Five?

"Five tribes? You were five tribes?"

Tribes. Yes. We are six.

"Alpha Tribe. Beta, Gamma, Delta, and Omega Tribes?"

Yes. We were five. Now we are six.

I pressed my palms harder against my eyes. Six? Now we are six?

Wrestling with confusion, I asked, "Six? Dr. Bickel said five tribes. What is the sixth tribe, Nano?"

Gemma.

I huffed at the runaround and repeated, "Yes? I'm here. What is the sixth tribe, Nano?"

Gemma.

I gulped, sat up, sat back, kept my palms squeezed tight over my eyes. Did they mean what I thought they meant?

"The sixth tribe . . . is Gemma? As in Gemma Tribe?"

Yes. Gemma Tribe.

We are waiting for your input, Gemma Keyes.

All was silent.

The silence of a confab.

The nanomites were waiting for me to participate in a confab.

I turned my attention to the stacks and stacks of data I'd gathered. Opened my arms and let their information come to me.

Saw, heard, and felt it all. Absorbed it. Understood.

"Nano. Abe and Zander are at UNM Hospital. Zander is on an adult surgical floor. Abe is in—" I choked when I tried to say "medical intensive care."

Yes. We have located them also. In the interest of better communication and consensus, what is your recommendation?

"My recommendation?"

Yes, Gemma Keyes. We are waiting for you to communicate your recommendation so we might consider all options and arrive at consensus.

Recommendation?

Consider?

Consensus?

What was my recommendation? When someone has hurt my friends?

Hot, fierce anger coiled in my chest. I couldn't speak what was raging in my heart: *Consider this, Nano! Let's arrive at consensus on* this, *shall we? I want to kill the men who hurt Abe and Zander. I want to destroy them. Decimate them. I want to obliterate Mateo Martinez.*

I tore my hands from my eyes. I was out of the "warehouse," back on the sofa in Dr. Bickel's safe house—but I could still hear the nanomites in my ear.

In the interest of better communication and consensus, what is your recommendation?

I jumped to my feet, my outraged breath coming in quick gulps.

"Consensus be hanged. We are going. Right now."

⌘⌘⌘⌘

CHAPTER 9

The Albuquerque transit system took long, *agonizing* hours to get me to University Hospital—or it sure felt that way. My desperation to reach Zander and Abe, juxtaposed against the tedious bus schedule, served to harden my craving—no, my *need*—for my own vehicle.

Hurry up, Javier!

His name reminded me to make a cash deposit before the end of the day. I'd already made several deposits since the nanomites opened my account—but none approaching $10,000. From what I'd read on the IRS website, the feds had tightened money laundering laws: Any cash deposit of more than $10,000 had to be reported on Form 8300. I guess I was already breaking some laws by not reporting my theft of the gang's drug money as income, but I wasn't going to lose any sleep over it.

I hopped off the bus, made my way to the entrance to the hospital, and stared at the four sets of double doors. University of New Mexico Hospital and Medical Center is a huge, sprawling maze embedded in the north end of the UNM campus—and I didn't know how to navigate said maze.

I entered the lobby and studied a listing of the hospital's many departments. Zander was in the older, main part of the hospital, apparently, just a few flights up. No problem. Abe, however, was in the MICU, the Medical Intensive Care Unit, "Pavilion," second floor. I wanted to see Abe first, but I didn't know what or where "Pavilion" was. The helpful woman at the helpful Help desk was not going to be very helpful for me.

Sigh.

I turned in a full circle, sighed again, and breathed, "Nano. Where is this Pavilion wing?"

Would they answer? I'd cut them off earlier. Ignored their confab request. Run roughshod over them.

Turn left.

Was it my imagination, or were those two words stiff? Terse?

"Right."

Not right, Gemma Keyes. Turn left.

"Um, yes. Turn left, not right."

I headed down a breezeway of sorts, wandered past the Children's Hospital and stopped when I came upon a coffee shop/cafeteria. I looked around for signage but didn't see anything for "Pavilion."

"Where in the world am I?"

Continue ahead.

"Okay. Thank you."

I kept walking, left those buildings, and entered the lobby of another complex. At last I saw signs for the Pavilion next to a bank of elevators. I stepped inside an elevator car and pressed the button for the second floor.

The elevators emptied into a waiting area on the second floor. Signs pointed off to the left for the Trauma/Surgical & Burn Unit. Signs pointed right for the Medical ICU. Weary and anxious families occupied long rows of chairs.

I swallowed. This floor cared for a lot of hurting people and held a lot of anxious loved ones.

I traversed the waiting area, swung down a short hall, made a quick right, and came up against the doors to the MICU. The unit was closed off to the curious or unauthorized visitor; even the narrow windows in the double doors were papered over so no one could see inside. I noted the keycard reader and the phone mounted on the wall beside the doors. Employees had keycards to gain entrance; visitors used the phone to request access.

Ordinarily, I might have waited for the doors to open when someone came out or went in, but I was distraught and I was charged with a fierce rage—rage toward Mateo and toward myself. The anger made me reckless: At that moment, I did not care about taking precautions.

Yeah, so I took a break, walked away, hoping to get my impulsiveness under control. Maybe I was giving myself a chance to prepare for what I feared I would see within the unit.

That break didn't last long.

I made one circuit through the waiting area, swung back around and, as I approached the MICU doors, I lifted my hand toward the keycard reader. The mites shot from my fingers and the doors swung wide. I breezed through without breaking stride.

A gatekeeper sat at a desk on the left. She looked up as the doors opened and closed; I paused to get the lay of the land but paid her confusion no mind.

An open, airy hall ran straight ahead. Glass-fronted patient rooms lined both sides of the hallway. I shuffled forward, searching for Abe. I avoided the nurses and doctors who went about their duties with quiet efficiency— but at every glance through the glass wall of another room, my heart clenched.

Halfway down the corridor, I came upon a nursing station that rivaled the bridge of the USS Enterprise. A single nurse seated in front of a bank of closed-circuit TV monitors could observe patients and supervise their vitals.

My stomach twisted: Abe was in one of these critical care beds. I wasn't mentally prepared to see him yet, to take in the damage Mateo and his crew had inflicted on him—to see his wounds when I knew that *I* was responsible for him being here, for the pain he was suffering.

Possibly responsible for his death.

If I hadn't asked him to take Emilio in . . .

I drew near the station's computers, scrunched my eyes shut, and found myself in the warehouse. "Nano. Access Abe's medical records, please."

They did not answer, but within seconds, I saw Abe's file.

It wasn't good.

I threaded my way toward Abe's room farther down the unit. Taking a deep breath, I stepped into Abe's room. Managed to make my eyes fix on the still figure in the bed.

I knew it was Abe, but when I reached his side, I hesitated. His body was surrounded by and attached to way too many machines and tubes: needles and ports on the back of his hand connected to an IV tree hung with multiple bags, heart monitor, breathing tube, ventilation machine. Lots of beeps and blinking lights. Stitches and bandages and oozing gauze; bruises and swelling.

His body seemed to have sunk into the bed. His lovely brown skin was dull and sallow. Ugly, greyish, and wrong. His heart rate, shown on the heart monitor above the bed, was slow. Ponderous. Laborious.

I found his rough old hand and cupped his fingers in mine. "Abe? Abe, it's Gemma. Can you hear me?"

He did not stir, and a hopeless ache settled in my heart. I couldn't stand it; I started to gulp and gasp.

Gemma Keyes. We sense distress.

"I . . . yes. I suppose I am distressed. I am . . . *so sad.*"

I sobbed the last two words. Choked on them.

The mites said nothing further but, given my treatment of them earlier and our few and frosty exchanges since, I was surprised that they had spoken at all.

I put the mites out of my mind and just held Abe's hand. I heard the slow, very slow beep of the heart monitor with rising dread and observed how cool his hand was in mine. Unnaturally cool.

Perhaps my surprise at the nanomites' words had jogged a memory. Something began to niggle at the back of my mind, something about the first day I had entered the tunnels. I blinked and tried to recall exactly what it was . . . something while Dr. Bickel was bragging to me about the good things the nanomites would someday accomplish. His words came to me in fits and starts, and I pieced those bits together.

"Do you know how much suffering the nanomites could alleviate? How many diseases they could cure? All cancers could be overcome, quickly removed from a body by the mites' coordinated attack. Injuries and birth defects could be repaired without overtly invasive surgeries.

"Can you imagine the insect infestations that could be corrected, rebalanced without the use of harmful chemicals? Can you fathom the effect of the nanomites on food production worldwide? Starvation would become a thing of the past! The nanomites could predict weather patterns and facilitate rescue attempts under collapsed buildings! The list of good they could do is endless, Gemma."

I went back to what he'd said first. Suffering alleviated? Injuries repaired?

I stood there for a long while before whispering, "Nano. You told me that you aided my body after the, um, merge, that you helped it to heal. Can you . . . will you send part of, um, part of *us* into Abe and work on him? Aid his body to heal?"

They did not answer.

Except for their terse, monosyllabic directions to the MICU and their recent observation regarding my "distress," the mites had not spoken to me—in hours. In the time it had taken me to reach the hospital and find Abe, they had not spoken. From the moment I had ignored their request for a recommendation, they had been silent. They had been mute since I had made my own precipitous decision without their input or consensus—the consensus of the other five tribes.

I didn't know if they understood my grief and worry, but I was certain that they were put out . . . because I'd broken with their protocol—with deliberate intention. Perhaps the mites were, at this exact minute, in a confab, expressing regret over their decision to include my "tribe" in their collective.

I blew out a breath. "Nano? Did you, um, did you hear me?"

Gemma Keyes, since this situation causes you physical distress, we will assess this man's injuries.

As the familiar warmth spread from my fingers to Abe's hand, I broke.

"Th-thank you. I-I'm sorry about before. Not waiting to, um, discuss my choices with you before acting. I responded in haste because I was so worried about my friends."

Nothing.

I winced inside. *Not so big on acknowledging apologies? Or are you too preoccupied with Abe's injuries to respond?*

For thirty minutes, I waited and watched over my battered friend before the nanomites spoke again.

Gemma Keyes. We have cauterized bleeding vessels in this man's brain and drained excess fluid to reduce intracranial pressure. We have knit many wounds together and stimulated cell regeneration around said wounds. We have removed necrotizing tissue.

"Will he be all right?"

Silence.

I glanced at Abe's heart monitor. Did I imagine it, or had his heart rate come up a little? Would the nanomites' repairs save him? Could they?

I hoped so, but I had a perverse inclination to pray for Abe just then.

Perverse? Yes. *Perverse.* Every time I thought I'd arrived at a place in my life where I could, at long last, wash my hands of God, some unexpected and out-of-my-control crisis sprang up—something I had no solution for. So, yeah, I had this *perverse* inclination to pray, because I could not, just *could not* let Abe die if a single instance of self-abasement might prevent it!

I stood there, unable to speak—because my prayers were plenty rusty from disuse. My obstinate distrust of God probably didn't help, either.

After a long internal struggle, I shrugged one shoulder. Basically, I'd do whatever it took to save Abe.

Even talk to God.

"Um, Lord, can you—that is, would you—look down on, um, your servant Abraham Pickering? He loves you, Lord, even if I, um, don't . . . exactly. Would you please help his body to heal? I-I still need him. And Emilio needs him. For Emilio's sake, please don't take him just yet?"

I fumbled to add something more eloquent or to revise what I'd already said and make it more appealing. I just ended up repeating myself.

"Emilio really needs Abe, God. Please don't let him down."

With tears dripping from my face, I got out of Abe's room, out of the MICU, and strode toward the elevator. I focused on crossing the medical campus to the main hospital and finding Zander.

***

Ross Gamble stood over Zander Cruz's hospital bed and assessed the patient's condition. At the moment, the young man resembled a side of beef that had been bulldozed by a truck.

Maybe a convoy of trucks.

Cruz's face was swollen, his eyes swallowed in puffy, purple, dark blue, and violet folds. A long split over a canine tooth distorted one side of his mouth. The inch-long split was stitched closed. It, too, was swollen and purple. Grotesque.

A cast surrounded Cruz's right arm; the arm was immobilized within a sling strapped to the poor guy's bare chest—a chest that sported a mass of bruises.

Gamble grimaced. *A baseball bat will do that. Guess he's gonna make it if they have him on this floor instead of in the ICU. Wonder if he will be able to answer questions.*

"Reverend Cruz?"

One of Zander's puffy eyes opened a slit. "Yesh." The single syllable was thick and sticky sounding.

"Reverend Cruz, I'm Special Agent Ross Gamble of the FBI. May I get you some water?"

The man's eyelid dropped, but his head moved up and down the smallest bit.

Gamble filled a cup with slushy water from a pitcher, held the straw to Cruz's mouth, and helped him get it between his lips. After a few sips, Cruz groaned, and Gamble pulled the cup away.

"More?"

Cruz managed to shake his head 'no.'

"Thanksh," he muttered.

Gamble sensed someone behind him, looked, saw nothing, turned back.

"How are you feeling?"

"Been . . . better."

"What do the doctors say? You gonna be all right?"

"Yeah. Be . . . a minute."

The guy has pluck, I'll give him that, Gamble thought, the hint of a smile tugging on his mouth.

"You feel up to answering a few questions?"

Cruz's eyes opened again, and he studied Gamble.

Is that fear? Alarm? Gamble wondered. He found fear to be a curious response—he expected resentment, and he often encountered distrust. But fear? For whom? Wasn't he the victim here?

"Reverend Cruz, I understand that you and Abe Pickering are friends and that you and he were trying to help this boy, Emilio Martinez, out of an abusive situation. Is that right?"

*   *   *

I stood in the doorway of Zander's room. The other bed in the room was empty, but some guy I didn't know was standing next to Zander's bed, talking to him.

The guy's bearing made me wary—was he one of Cushing's agents? He looked like he'd played tight end on his college ball team: tall, muscled up, but not so much that his suit bulged. He held himself with a relaxed military bearing, too. I recognized the type; I'd worked with ex-military at Sandia.

I was pretty tense until I heard the guy say, "Reverend Cruz, I'm Special Agent Ross Gamble of the FBI. May I get you some water?"

I went from tense to confused and curious. *FBI? Why would the FBI want to talk to Zander?* The FBI was only one or two rungs above Cushing in my estimation but, as far as I knew, the agency had no knowledge of the nanomites—or me. Conversely, if they did know and were looking for me, my situation was bunches worse than I'd thought.

I watched the FBI man give Zander a drink. He was solicitous, maybe even concerned; his manner seemed genuine enough. I relaxed a hair more and tiptoed around him to the other side of Zander's bed. Gamble flicked his eyes at me as I passed by. He scanned around the room before he turned his attention back to Zander.

I leaned against the wall near the foot of Zander's bed. After the shock of Abe's injuries, I knew I couldn't stomach seeing how badly Mateo's gang had beaten Zander.

I averted my eyes and listened in.

"Reverend Cruz, I understand that you and Mr. Pickering were attacked by Mateo Martinez and three members of his gang. Since then, Martinez has gone to ground. I'm interested in finding him. Do you have any idea where he might be hiding out?"

Zander didn't answer right away, and I chanced a glimpse at him.

Oh, Zander! What have they done to you?

I almost did not recognize him for the swelling and bruises. As much as it pained me to see him like this, I couldn't tear my eyes away.

Gamble repeated his question. "Reverend Cruz? Do you have any idea where Martinez might be hiding out?"

Zander licked his swollen lips and mumbled what I was wondering. "Why?"

"Why are we looking for Martinez?"

"Yesh." He groaned a little and wet the horrid split in his lip again.

I commiserated with Zander in silence. *Oh, ouch!*

Gamble pursed his mouth and parsed his words—reactivating my suspicions.

"One of Martinez's, uh, associates is a person of interest in an ongoing investigation. We figure if we find Martinez, we may find the man we're looking for."

And who might that be? Dead Eyes? My interest returned; I leaned toward Gamble.

"No . . . idea," Zander managed.

"Okay. Can you tell me a little bit about Martinez? About any visitors he had?"

"Don' live . . . there. Jusht vishit . . . Abe."

Zander's voice petered out and his eyelids drooped. It was easy to see that he was exhausted and in pain.

"Am I tiring you out, Pastor Cruz?"

Zander attempted a negative shake of his head, but neither Agent Gamble nor I were fooled: Zander was a mess. A painful, swollen mess.

Well, since I wasn't ready for Gamble to stop asking questions, I gently, so *very* gently, placed my hand on Zander's foot. And squeezed. Just a tiny bit.

Once. Twice. Three times.

Zander grunted; his eyes popped open—well, one of them did—and zoomed in on the mound of blanket covering his foot, on the impression my fingers made as I pressed and released, the movement that, in mere seconds, the mites hid.

I whispered to the mites. They raced into Zander's body, but I kept my hand on Zander's foot. I squeezed again.

A brave smile tipped up one corner of his mouth—the corner not split and stitched.

He knows I'm here.

I grinned back, but Gamble stared at Zander, a smidge troubled.

Zander exhaled with a sigh. He had to be feeling the mites' warmth flowing from me into his body, seeking out damaged tissue, screaming pain receptors, and broken bone, going after harmful bacteria, prompting his body to release endorphins and serotonin and whatever else they could manipulate to ease his discomfort.

I closed my eyes. From the warehouse, I could sense their activities. I monitored their progress and nodded my approval as they mended torn skin, muscle, and ligament and knit shattered bone.

Oh, won't your doctor be amazed, Zander? I clamped one hand over my mouth so I wouldn't giggle aloud.

Zander sighed again and relaxed. The neuropeptides were kicking in.

Gamble's expression went from troubled to puzzled. "You okay, Cruz? Should I call a nurse?"

"No, I feel . . . fine. Thanks, though."

Zander sounded a lot better to my ears: More words, less slurring.

Gamble's eyes narrowed. "You mind if we keep going, then?"

"No . . . problem." That sticky, painful lisp wasn't as pronounced.

"I appreciate your cooperation, Reverend. So, just to round things out, to get a sense of what led up to the attack on you and Mr. Pickering, I also wanted to ask if you were present about eleven or twelve days ago when some sort of raid took place in the cul-de-sac."

It was neatly done, that abrupt change of topic on Gamble's part.

Zander's eyes drifted up to Gamble's face. "Raid?"

I was proud of Zander's ploy, but Gamble wasn't buying it.

"Mrs. Calderón and Mr. and Mrs. Tucker told me all about it. Said you were there, too, with Mr. Pickering, that the agents from the raid questioned everyone present, including you."

"Oh. *That* raid."

I grinned. Even Gamble grinned—a hardened, cynical grin, but amused, nonetheless.

"Yeah. *That* raid. What was that all about?"

Zander cleared his throat. He made it sound like broken glass scraping over asphalt.

Ack.

"More water, please?" Zander asked.

Gamble grunted. "Sure thing, Reverend. I want you to have all the time you need to frame your answers."

I stifled a laugh. Despite the fact that I distrusted feds, I kinda admired this guy's attitude.

Zander got his drink, and Gamble said, "Those people said they were looking for the woman who lives across the street. Do you know her name, the woman they were looking for?"

Careful, Zander.

"Yeah. Gemma Keyes. She used to go to my church when she was a kid. Same church Abe goes to, but before my time. Abe asked me to introduce myself and invite her back."

I knew Zander well enough and had heard him spout the same line to my psycho sister and to Cushing's people. He was distancing himself from me—and doing a good job.

"So, you don't know her well?"

"No. Only interacted with her three or four times."

Gamble raised his brows. "Mrs. Calderón has a different view of your relationship with Miss Keyes. Says she's your girlfriend."

"No, she's not. We're acquaintances. Nothing more." Zander tried to shift his position and winced. "I should caution you, Agent Gamble; Mrs. Calderón has something of a reputation as the community busybody."

Gamble said nothing, just studied Zander. "Can you describe the scene that night? The night of the raid? What happened, who was there, what vehicles were used?"

Zander took care not to open his mouth too far and pull on the stitches, but he managed a detailed account. "Well . . . I was in Abe's house when it started. It was after dark. Bunch of military-type trucks—maybe five or six?—rolled into the cul-de-sac. They were very quiet until two trucks with stadium lights mounted on them lit up the place. The lights and commotion drew us out of the house. We—Abe and I—watched from Abe's front porch, just like the Tuckers, Mrs. Calderón, and Martinez did from their porches."

"Mateo Martinez was home that evening?"

"Yes."

"Go on."

"Guys dressed in black broke into . . . Miss Keyes' house. They had guns. Not handguns, but semi-auto assault rifles."

"You know guns?" Gamble seemed ready to pounce.

"I wasn't always a pastor, Agent Gamble."

"Oh?" Gamble jotted a note. "What then?"

"Well, they didn't find Miss Keyes, but they bagged up a bunch of her stuff and hauled it out. Then Cushing had the agents interview everyone."

Uh-oh.

Gamble caught it, too. "Cushing?"

Zander realized his mistake, but he kept himself together. "A woman, a General Cushing, followed the trucks into the cul-de-sac. She seemed to be running the show—issuing orders and stuff. The soldiers and agents practically got on their knees and kissed her feet when she arrived. In my line of work, we know people—and those agents were wary of her. Too careful."

"How do you know her name, this General Cushing?"

"I asked the agent who interviewed us."

"Why?"

"Why what?" Zander did a credible "perplexed."

Gamble wasn't buying that either. He pressed harder. "Why did you ask for Cushing's name?"

"Well, because she makes an impression, you know?"

"No, I don't. Why don't you tell me?"

As much as he was able, Zander snorted. "Because, even from across the street, this lady came across as hard. Cold. Ruthless, maybe. Like I said, her people were afraid of her.

"And besides, we had no idea why the army would send a SWAT team out against a lone woman, who, as I understand from Abe, is afraid of her own shadow." Zander laid back, winded.

That mouthful contained several disparate items—including one that struck a nerve in me.

Afraid of my own shadow? Me? Well, maybe. Maybe that's how I was. Before.

After the nanomites had invaded me, I'd been paralyzed by my fears, and I had focused on getting rid of them. But then, as my efforts ran out of steam and the mites' infestation began to feel permanent and hopeless, a careless, reckless rage had taken hold of me. That anger had burned in my belly until I dared to do crazy things, until I started to take risks and use the nanomites to carry out daring, perhaps audacious, plans.

Then it dawned on me. *I'm not that old Gemma anymore. The mites have changed me. Inside. They have forced me to stand up and fight for my survival, for my right to live.*

No. I'm not afraid of my own shadow anymore.

I watched Gamble digest what Zander had told him and formulate his next question.

"So, they were Army?"

Zander shrugged and flinched. "Sorry. Cracked collarbone. Why they have me trussed up like this."

He tried again to shift to a more comfortable position. "Army was a figure of speech. I don't know military well enough to distinguish between the different branches, so I can't say what they were. Their uniforms were all black, and I don't remember seeing any identifying insignias. I never saw a warrant, either. They gave no notice when they stormed Gem—Miss Keyes'—house. Just broke down the doors."

"And you have no idea why they were looking for Miss Keyes?"

"No idea," Zander repeated.

Ha! You just told a lie, Reverend Cruz, I chortled.

Gamble was, I'm pretty sure, thinking the same thing. He chuckled under his breath and slid a card from his jacket, put it on the rolling table near the bed. "Know what? I like you, Reverend. You're all right. Here's my card. I'll bet if you sit on it a while, you can come up with something."

Just a *dash* of sarcasm and emphasis on "something."

"Got it. If I remember something that will help you catch Martinez, I'll call," Zander answered.

Just a *hint* of sarcasm. Emphasis on "catch Martinez."

Gamble grunted. "Well, thanks for letting me talk to you." He studied Zander and shook his head. "You sure took a beating, Cruz. I don't envy you the next few weeks while you recuperate. Can I get you anything before I go? More water?"

I reexamined Ross Gamble, liking him better for his human side.

"No, but I appreciate the offer."

"Right. Well, take care."

Gamble nodded and strode out of the room, his long legs making him fast, even at a walk. I followed him all the way to the elevator to see if he'd jump on his cell phone and report to a fellow FBI crony or, perhaps, a person higher up.

Higher up—like maybe Cushing herself? I wouldn't have put it past her.

But Gamble, his brows bunched together, head bent, deep in his own thoughts, never pulled a phone from his pocket. When the elevator dinged, he shuffled into the car and pressed a button—still in his own thoughts, not once looking up.

When I got back to Zander's room, he appeared distressed and whipped at the same time. I reached over and squeezed his foot again.

"Gemma?" He tried to sit up. "Gemma!"

"Don't!" I urged him. "Don't hurt yourself."

"Where did you go? I called your name, but you didn't answer." He fumbled around with his good arm, trying to find me.

I grabbed his hand. He gripped it so hard, I feared for my own bones. He pulled me closer to the bed. I scooted a chair up to the rail and sat.

"Hey, loosen up a little, okay? You're crushing my fingers."

"Not a chance. I don't want you walking out on me again."

My smile had to have been a yard wide. "I promise not to leave without notice."

Now that I was only inches away, I took a closer inventory of Zander's injuries. He had so many bruises, that even his bruises had bruises.

"When you squeezed my foot, I about jumped out of this bed, Gemma."

"I saw, but you hid it well. Did you feel the mites come over to you?"

"Yeah, I did. What were they doing?"

"Mending things. Giving you a dose of endorphins."

"I do feel better."

"Um, I'm glad. And, uh, is the phone I gave you in a safe place?"

"Yeah, I think so. I took it home and taped it under my dresser."

We ran out of steam just like that. I fumbled around for a couple of seconds before adding, "I visited Abe. The mites did some work in him, too."

Zander's face creased with apprehension. "I heard that he's not doing well, Gemma."

I nodded, tears puddling up in my eyes. "I know. I saw him. But . . . I prayed for him and . . . well, I hope what the mites did will help him pull through."

"Wait. You prayed?"

I cleared my throat. "Well, it seemed like a good idea. At the time."

"Acknowledging God is a step in the right direction, and I'm really glad, but . . ." The "but" hung between us for a while before Zander finished his thought.

"Gemma . . . I want you to know that I've been praying for you. A lot. And I think the reason you thought to pray for Abe? I believe the Lord is calling you, calling you back to him. The thing about God is that he is persistent. In fact, his persistence is why some have called him the 'Hound of Heaven.' He is tireless and will confront you when you least expect it. At that time, he will bring you face to face with truth. When he does, well, it will be the moment of decision for you."

I was astounded and without words to answer him. Shivers ran down my arms, and I kept hearing, "He will confront you when you least expect it," and wondered what that meant.

After a long, charged pause, Zander switched subjects. "Tell me what you've been up to, Gemma."

Wow. Loaded request—but I was more than happy for the turn in the conversation. I exhaled before diving in.

"Been up to? Bunches. And lots of changes, too."

"Tell me?"

Right then I realized that I wanted to tell him everything, that I craved someone other than the nanomites for company, for friendship, for confidences. I broke it down for him—just about everything that had happened since I'd last seen him. I told him everything except my new name and the location of Dr. Bickel's safe house.

He listened with amazed interest as I explained how the nanomites had unlocked doors, hacked into any computer system I asked them to, and had helped me acquire a new identity.

"Incredible!"

"I know! It's really cool."

I went on to tell him about the mites speaking in my ear—and on the way, I *maybe*, in my excitement, got ahead of myself. Like, I *kind of* overlapped the telling of how they first talked to me with telling him about the merge—and that might have been a mistake.

"You see, it was really late that night, and I was frustrated about a lot of things—mostly at how tedious and time consuming it was for me to get anything done. I knew the nanomites could do so much more if I could just figure out how to use them better. So, I told the nanomites that I wanted to improve our communication and cooperation. Asked them if there wasn't a way for us to interact and work together in a more efficient way. Then I went to bed."

With a wry chuckle, I added, "Apparently, the mites heard me."

I filled him in on what they had done in response to my request. Told him about how I woke up to a headache, nose bleeds, and pain, about sleeping around the clock until my body had adjusted. *Then* I was able to tell him how the nanomites could "speak" in my ear, right?

"The mites now vibrate in my ear canal to mimic human speech. And somewhere and somehow, they say I'm merged with them and that they . . . they have sort of adopted me."

As I'd described the merge, his expression had turned from disbelief to alarm . . . to something else.

I recognized my mistake about then and tried to lighten my tone. "They even made me an honorary tribal member—you know, one of the tribes Dr. Bickel described? Alpha, Beta, Gamma, Delta, and Omega Tribe? And now, Gemma Tribe. Ha-ha, right?"

"You're joking, aren't you?"

I shook my head.

Oh, yeah. You can't see that.

"No, I'm not joking. Not a bit."

"But what does 'merge' mean? What has it done to you?"

"I'm not sure about it all yet. I only woke up from the adjustment this morning."

Was it just this morning?

I rushed to go on, to push him past the shock. "But one really cool part happened when I read the news online about you and Abe and we—the nanomites and I—started looking for you guys."

I told him about the "warehouse," about searching and sorting data to find which hospital he and Abe were in. Myself, I was over the freaked-out part now, and I was starting to revel in it, to think of the possibilities and vistas it opened to me.

Not Zander.

"You go to this, what? This warehouse place in your head where you, um, search and filter information from the Internet? Information that just comes to you by itself?"

"I don't know what else to call it. When I close my eyes, I'm in this big, cavernous place where the nanomites and I can interact, so I slapped the word 'warehouse' on it. And, no, the information doesn't come by itself; the nanomites feed it to me. They stream the data to me at incredible speeds—and I can see, sort, and understand the info just as fast as it comes to me—which is astonishing, don't you think? I don't know how or why yet; still, it is really amazing."

Zander said nothing more, but a wealth of emotions flitted across his banged-up, beat-up, swollen face, until he said, "But, Gemma, what in heaven's name does that mean?" his voice rose in pitch with each word, rose until it was at least an octave higher, "And how can that not hurt you? None of this is normal or right!"

"Hey, calm down, cowboy," I teased. Zander's concern was spinning him up, and I didn't think that would be good for him.

Teasing was probably not the *best* approach to employ on a young Hispanic male.

"*Don't tell me to calm down!*" he shouted, sitting up. He groaned and clutched at his bruised ribs, but he stayed upright anyway. "Those things are *in your brain*? Making you bleed? Making you part of their 'collective'? *Gemma Tribe?*

"*And don't tell me to calm down!*"

"Pastor Cruz? Is everything all right? Who are you talking to?"

Saved by the nurse. I shot out of the chair and tried to move out of her way, but I was penned in. I scrunched up between the IV tree and the wall.

Zander waved the nurse to the other side of the bed. "Come over on this side, please. The, uh, gentleman who visited me earlier stood where you are and gave me, um, a crick in this side of my neck."

The nurse walked around the bed and peered at Zander, picked up his hand and felt his pulse. "You act like you feel better, but who were you talking to?"

"Yeah, I was, um, just indulging in a little rant. The guy who was in here earlier was asking me a bunch of questions that I don't have the answers to. Got me riled up. You heard me blowing off some steam."

By then I'd gotten to the end of the room close to the bathroom, out of the way.

"Well, all right, then. Are you feeling hungry?"

"Yes, but I don't think I can chew much."

"Think you could manage a protein shake?"

"Through a straw? Yeah. Sounds good."

The nurse left, and I returned to Zander and positioned myself on the same side of the bed the nurse had been.

"Gemma?"

"I'm here."

Zander grabbed my hand again and didn't waste any time returning to our conversation. "I'm worried about what the nanomites are doing to you, Gemma. The 'talking' to you by making vibrations in your ear I guess I can understand, but how in the world can they make you see things at their level? How is that possible? And how can it *not* be harmful for you?"

He ended with, "I don't like it, Gemma. I don't like it at all."

I gave his concerns some consideration before I answered. "I don't have answers for you, Zander. It is so new that I haven't had much time to think about it myself. However, now that my body has adjusted to the merge, I feel good. In fact, I feel more energetic. I don't know how it will work out long term, but for now, I don't know what I could do differently. I can only accept what the nanomites have done and employ the, um, abilities they are giving me through the merge."

I switched tracks. "I'm hoping Dr. Bickel can tell me exactly what the mites have done. And, eventually, I hope he can get them out of me so I can have my life back."

"Dr. Bickel?" Zander's voice ratcheted up that scale again. "What in the world are you talking about? Dr. Bickel is dead, Gemma!"

I slapped my free hand against my forehead: Zander didn't know about Dr. Bickel's garbled email.

"Oh, wow. I guess I forgot to tell you. The night of Cushing's raid on my house, after I left Abe's? I went back to my house and slept for a while—I was still pooped from the mites draining me earlier that day. When I woke up, I opened my laptop to download the file of my journal and trash the hard drive. But before I could do that, I found an email waiting for me. From Dr. Bickel."

Zander looked as stunned as I had felt when I'd seen the words "Position Description" in the subject line of an email *I'd deleted* in a folder *I'd emptied*.

"Turns out Dr. Bickel didn't die when Cushing raided his lab. She captured him and is keeping him a prisoner somewhere. The whole world already believes he's dead, so she's getting away with it. He doesn't know where she is keeping him, only that it is a 'military installation' of some kind. The nanomites are looking for him. So far they haven't found anything, but they are searching."

Zander's mouth flattened into a stern line. "And then what?"

"Then what? I don't know yet. What do you mean?"

"I mean, you aren't thinking of trying to spring him, are you? You *know* you aren't capable of 'invading' a U.S. military prison, don't you, Gemma? Even if you managed to sneak in to such a place because no one can see *you*, you couldn't possibly get Dr. Bickel out. You know that, right? What if it's a trap? What if Cushing sent that email just to lure you? Do you know what she would do to you if she caught you?"

Zander's voice had risen once more, and each question he asked was less a question and more a demand than the previous one. He was getting himself spun up, and I didn't like it or think it healthy in his condition.

I closed my eyes. *Nano. Calm him, please. Um, in fact, if you can, just knock him out.*

I held his hand a little tighter and stroked his arm as the mites swarmed out of me and into him. "Zander. Please calm down."

"Don't tell me to—hey, what are you doing? Stop it!" But Zander's words were already growing sluggish.

"Listen to me, Zander. I will be all right. I promise not to do anything precipitous. Just . . . don't worry, okay?"

"How can I not worry . . . Gemma? How . . . can . . . I . . ."

"You say you trust God, Zander? If you do, then please pray for me."

I didn't know where that had come from, but since he claimed to 'know' God, it wouldn't hurt to have the extra help, would it?

Put your money where your mouth is, Pastor Cruz.

"Gemmmm . . ." he was fading. The nanomites were putting him under.

I should remember this trick.

I leaned over and placed a kiss on his forehead. Not a romantic kiss, just a kiss.

Because I care about you, Zander. Because I can't stand to see you hurting like this.

Because you are one of only two people in the world I know I can trust.

"I'm going now, Zander, but I'll be back. You rest now, okay?"

When I left Zander's room, I stood in the hallway, thinking. The things he'd said to me about God someday confronting me? Well, his words kept poking around in me, churning up questions and—I admit it—trepidation.

I wasn't ready for a face-to-face with God.

After a while, I shook my head and made myself review the conversation between Zander and the FBI agent. It was a relief to turn my attention to something other than me vs. God or me vs. Cushing. Besides, I wanted to find Mateo Martinez. I wanted to find him a whole lot more than Special Agent Ross Gamble did. But maybe this FBI guy could help me?

Maybe we could help each other.

⌘⌘⌘⌘

CHAPTER 10

Wow, I was so relieved to get out of that hospital!

I sucked in fresh, clean air to clear the sick and antiseptic smells from my nostrils. I gazed toward the peaks and valleys of the Sandias hoping to dispel the sights and sounds of so much pain and discomfort.

As I waited for the first bus in my trek back to the safe house, my concern turned toward Emilio. I had hoped to find his school and drop in on him before I went home, but it had taken me too long to get to the hospital using the transit system—and I'd spent more than three hours visiting Abe and Zander. By the time I caught the right bus and hoofed it the rest of the way to Emilio's school, classes would be out and he would be back at his foster home.

The bus pulled up, and I started to swing aboard.

It's too late today to catch you at school today, Emilio, but I promise that tomorrow—

The nanomites cut in on my thoughts.

Gemma Keyes.

I stumbled on the bus step, caught myself, reversed course, and backed away from the bus door. "Um, yes?"

We took you at your word, Gemma Keyes.

It wasn't a question. It was a cringe-worthy accusation.

A flat-footed rebuke.

Ouch.

I knew what they were getting at: They had made me a "tribe," part of "the whole." I was supposed to communicate and cooperate, all that coming-to-consensus stuff—that touchy-feely, mutually agreeable junk that was so difficult for me.

I moved away from the bus stop. Started down the sidewalk away from the hospital. "I, um, I'm sorry, Nano. I guess I have a lot to learn. Humans aren't by nature cooperative and acquiescing. We are . . . independent. Often headstrong and stubborn."

Silence.

Guilt-generating silence.

"Nano?"

Were they listening?

"Again, I apologize. I made a mistake, but it was because I was upset about my friends. I'm willing to try; I'm, um, willing to learn how you do things. I hope you will be patient with me?"

More silence.

Were they paying any attention to me at all or were they confabbing? I closed my eyes and tried to go to the warehouse. It wasn't working.

If they were holding a confab, I was not included.

Wow. Did they block me? Are they discussing how to kick me out? Did I just get "unfriended"?

I wonder how the vote will go.

As odd as it may sound, the prospect of being removed from the nanocloud stung. And it wasn't that long ago that Abe had chastised me for a related fault: *You got you a good conscience, Gemma. Lu made sure of that. But just **sayin'** you wish you hadn't done somethin' don't fix it. Don't make it right an' don't make your heart light again.*

"Nano?"

Yes, Gemma Keyes?

They answered me!

"Please give me another chance."

Silence.

I walked on, troubled in my soul. I was worried about my relationship with the nanomites (okay, weird, I admit) and, at the same time, my attention was split between them and my anxieties over Emilio, over Abe and Zander. Oh, and the FBI guy.

The FBI guy . . .

I frowned. What were his next moves? What if he started looking into the indirect link between Gemma Keyes and Mateo and his boss, Dead Eyes, between the assault on my house and Mateo's gang? What if he pulled on that thread—just to see where it went?

That would not be good.

Cushing was searching for me, monitoring for the slightest query or mention of my name. If Gamble reached out to her, queried her on the assault, wouldn't she would jump on him? Wouldn't she then refocus her attention on Zander and Abe? And wouldn't that lead to Emilio?

Aaaand, my concerns flipped right back to Emilio. At present, he was consigned to the tender mercies of CYFD—and likely swearing a blue streak, cussing me out like he used to when he squatted on the curb in front of his uncle's house and threw gang signs in my direction.

That kid had been a royal pain in my backside only months ago, but he had become precious to me since then. I had to shield him from Cushing!

First, I needed to check up on him, visit him and make sure he was okay. Let him know we hadn't abandoned him to foster care. The nanomites would find him, give me his location.

Except . . . oh, yeah. The mites were ticked off at me.

Way to go, Gemma.

Sigh.

I stopped at a coffee shop whose sign boasted lattes and free Wi-Fi. I sat on the grass next to their parking lot and tried again to reach out to the nanomites.

"Nano." I closed my eyes and (relief!) opened them in that strange place I called the warehouse. I attempted to frame my request in a more nano-like manner.

Nano. I would like to know where Emilio is. He must be feeling lonely. Abandoned. Would you please find him? Show me where he is?

I was pleasantly surprised when a stream of information flew by me. I grabbed what I needed and studied it.

Emilio had been placed with a short-term foster family while his case was being evaluated. I approved of the evidence CYFD had gathered against Mateo: no food in the house, documented neglect, allegations of physical abuse, assault against the neighbor who reported the neglect.

I'll bet Mateo's attack on Abe and Zander ends his chances of ever getting Emilio back.

It was, perhaps, the only positive outcome of the situation.

I read another form that listed the name of Emilio's school; I looked up the school's website and found the student release time.

Yeah. As I suspected, I can't get to his school before dismissal. I'll have to catch him tomorrow.

I boarded a bus headed across town toward the safe house. For the most part, I was recovered from the nanomites' drain but, by the time I let myself in the back door, I figured I'd be exhausted—except I wasn't.

Odd.

In fact, I couldn't seem to let down. I guess too much had happened in the past forty-eight hours. My emotions were keyed up and so was my body—really keyed up.

To burn off the nervous drive, I spent part of the late afternoon running laps around the block. I set a nice, leisurely pace down the sidewalk, aiming to run for thirty minutes. While I jogged, I realized something else . . . and, again, it was *odd.*

I was much more alert than usual. Aware of my surroundings. I noticed things I hadn't before—like how many houses and cars were on each side of the street. On my second lap around the block, the numbers of each house and car were at my fingertips from the first time around the block— as were the makes and models of each car . . . and how many windows each house had, what materials the houses were built of, and their colors and roof style.

Huh?

I completed a third lap, still at a sedate jog—and still (without trying to) collecting weird bits and pieces of information about everything and everyone I saw. Apparently, I had memorized all the street signs, all the house numbers, and all the license plates. It was as though whatever I looked at fastened itself to my brain.

I closed my eyes to shut out the influx of unwanted factoids—only to find myself anticipating every driveway cutout in the sidewalk, every curb, and precisely when to make the turns at the corners. I was running blind without putting a foot wrong.

After four circuits around the block, my muscles felt like they were just getting warmed up. I moved out onto the softer asphalt of the street, increased my pace, and sprinted through a fifth complete circumference of the block.

I sure had a lot of stamina!

I picked up the pace yet again, amazed at my speed and endurance, circling the block twice at an all-out run. I blazed through my last lap, but when I left off with the laps, I wasn't even winded—and I *still* felt antsy. I moved to the backyard and put myself through a grueling regimen of lunges, push-ups, and a full menu of calisthenics.

Then I fixed dinner—double portions of my usual fare. I chowed down on everything I'd prepared and added a banana and a granola bar before I felt replete. By the time I went to bed that evening, I tingled with vitality.

Um . . . interesting much?

I fell into a deep sleep, heartened that I would be seeing Emilio the next day. I avoided dwelling on whatever was happening to me in the physical realm.

But something was happening.

***

I awoke early the following morning, vibrating with out-of-the-norm vigor and awareness. I had never felt this good, this *energetic* straight out of bed, nor had I been alert and actually observant first thing.

Generally, I woke up over two cups of strong coffee—but straight out of bed? This day I had so much "juice" running through my veins that I decided to abstain from my usual morning java.

You know people who, while watching a musical, can't help themselves? People who jump up to sing and dance along? Yeah, that. I was afraid of that. I was scared that ingesting caffeine might result in spontaneous karaoke—and caroming off the walls.

After I ate, showered, and dressed in record time, I shot out the door, determined to expel some of the restlessness I was finding so difficult to corral. The sun wasn't fully up as I jogged at a brisk pace down the sidewalk. I was preoccupied with my thoughts, mulling over what was happening—because, obviously, this livelier (and über-attentive) version of myself did not exist only "in my head."

It was real.

This weird increase in energy and stamina must be a product of the "merge." Nothing else makes sense.

I thought back to the mites' astonishing announcement about the merge—while I'd bled copious amounts from my nose and upchucked all over the house. After I'd slept off the debilitating effects of the merge, I hadn't had time to process what our "union" meant before news of Mateo Martinez's attack on my friends had sent me on a panicked flight to the hospital. I had been so distraught over Abe and Zander and in such turmoil over Emilio, that I hadn't had time to consider what the mites had done and were continuing to do in me.

Yes, I was anxious for my friends, but when I stopped to think about it, underneath my concern for Abe, Zander, and Emilio, I was mighty concerned for myself!

What is it, exactly, that the mites are doing, and how are they doing it? How is this so-called merge likely to affect me in the future?

Sure, when the nanomites began "speaking" in my ear, it had freaked me out; however, their explanation had seemed plausible enough, the whole "vibrations = words" thing. Their "speaking" in my ear was non-invasive, wasn't it? I had even accepted the strange "warehouse" business, mainly because I was enamored with how "cool" it was to collect and sort the data they fed me.

The burr under my saddle this morning was the *how*. Like, *how* was it possible for me to go into this place, this "warehouse" in my head and see the river of data the mites mined? *How* was I able to filter and sort the information—let alone keep up with it and comprehend it?

My newest question, as I ran down the street, was how were they doing *this*? This juiced-up state? This retention of every detail I saw?

It occurred to me that elements of this merge business might not show up for a while—I mean, I wasn't worried that I'd wake up tomorrow with two heads, but then again, I hadn't seen this hyperactive/hyperalert state coming either, had I? And what was the point of it? What purpose did it serve?

Uneasy about my future health, I started taking inventory of what had changed—or, at least, the changes I knew of so far.

One. I no longer needed to speak everything aloud to the nanomites. In the warehouse—that mental space where we met—they "heard" me. On top of that, I was seeing more instances where the mites intuited my actions or what I wanted from them.

I harbored a question about the mites' "intuitive" actions: Was I seeing more than Dr. Bickel's predictive logic algorithms at work in them? Could their actions be the product of some sort of shared mental state *with me?* Maybe like a Vulcan mind meld?

I don't know much about how the brain works, but I couldn't help but wonder if the nanomites could see and translate my thoughts as they occurred.

Creepy.

Well, they were swimming around in there, in my brain, weren't they? Could they taste or feel my thoughts?

This last idea made more sense than I wanted it to.

I picked up my pace and closed out Item One on my list. I moved on to the next item.

Two. In the warehouse, I could access any knowledge the nanomites possessed or any data they mined through the Internet. When I entered the warehouse, I could search, sort, and find whatever I was looking for. More than that, I understood and retained what I saw!

Three. I was (I theorized) hopped up on energizing nano juice that made me hyper-observant. I mean, wow, I seemed to suck in every little detail of everything I saw, and—

A clash of disgruntled chitters rang in my ear.

Gemma Keyes. We have pressing work to do. We must find Dr. Bickel. Where are we going and for what purpose?

Oooops. Right. Communication. Cooperation. Consensus.

I blew out a chastised breath.

"Sorry, Nano. Yesterday, you told me where to find Emilio. I would like to visit him, reassure him that he hasn't been forgotten. Just a visit. Maybe thirty minutes? Oh. And I would like to stop at the hospital and check up on Abe beforehand. See if what you did for him has improved his condition? A short visit, less than thirty minutes. I promise."

Add an hour or more on each side to get there and back, plus transit time between the hospital and Emilio's school. So, actually most of the morning.

"Um, what do you think?"

The confab started: I was bombarded by multiple "voices" in my ear that all sounded the same. I couldn't tell them apart and they spoke over each other, each voice a data dump I absorbed and tried to keep up with.

I had to stop walking. I dropped down on someone's lawn, covered my eyes, and returned to the warehouse.

It is hard to explain what being a participant in the confab was like. It wasn't like debate club, where vying sides presented their reasoned but impassioned POV, and it wasn't adversarial, the way a courtroom drama plays out—with the intention of proving guilt or innocence: I win, ergo, you lose.

The individual tribes were not trying to "win." They presented the information their tribe had collected on the subject—information analyzed from that tribe's unique perspective and role—and the swarm, the nanocloud, assessed the whole of the data with one goal: the common good.

And that was the rub. Their idea of the common good and my view of the common good were not the same. Not even close.

The nanotribes saw no value in visiting Emilio.

Well, *I* did. I cast about for a reason that might sway the mites: I called upon our shared desire to spring Dr. Bickel to move the consideration in my favor.

"Nano. I am a complex human organism. I have emotional needs that inspire and, uh, motivate me. The six of us are agreed that we must resume our search for Dr. Bickel. However, I cannot concentrate on that task if I'm distracted by my, um, emotional needs. Abe and Emilio's welfare is essential to my emotional well-being, and my emotional needs are important factors in my ability to function."

I heard a proposal that the *removal* of my emotional components should be weighed and given careful consideration.

What? A lobotomy? I'm not kidding—that a tribe would suggest such an action made me shiver.

I was quick to interject, "Nano. Consider this: Removing my emotions is not possible without damaging my value as a tribe. My affection for Dr. Bickel is what motivates me to search for him. If you remove that emotion, I will have no need, no desire, to find him.

"Listen: A quick visit with Abe and then Emilio is all I need to set my mind at ease. Should take no more than, um, a couple hours. Then we can return home and continue our hunt for Dr. Bickel."

I was accustomed to the next part of the confab: silence. I guess they evaluated the input within each tribe before voting? I didn't know; I only knew it was quiet until, one by one, the five tribes weighed in.

The outcome of the vote was, *Gemma Keyes, for the well-being of your emotional components, we will visit Abraham Pickering and Emilio Martinez.*

I exhaled my relief. "Thank you."

***

When we arrived at the hospital, I retraced my steps to the Pavilion, took the elevator to the MICU unit and, for a second time, waved the doors open and breezed through. Breakfast for the patients had ended. The staff had cleared the trays away; I saw a few doctors making rounds.

It had been less than twenty-four hours since I last saw Abe, but when I made my way to his bedside and slipped my hand into his, his condition was different.

Vastly different.

Abe's color had improved in spectacular fashion; his skin wasn't yet the glossy ebony I loved, but it also wasn't a death-like gray. His breathing was easier, too, and—

Hey! They took out your breathing tube, Abe!

I spoke in my head and not aloud, but Abe opened his eyes and fixed them on me as if he could see me. I felt the light pressure of his hand on mine.

"Gem . . ." His voice, rough from the tube, stuck on my name.

"Shhh. Don't talk, Abe," I whispered back. I was happy—no, thrilled—at his improved condition.

"W-wa . . ."

Was he allowed water? He was still hooked up to an IV. The call button hung above his head. I could have pushed it, but the nurse would have thought it miraculous for Abe to have reached it on his own.

"Um, hold on."

I walked out into the ward and found a phone on the wall at the end. I had the nanomites dial the nearest nursing station. "Say, I believe the gentleman in Room 22 is asking for a drink of water. I didn't want to get him one myself, because I don't know if it is allowed."

"Thank you. Who is this?"

Click.

I'd already hung up.

I waited around until a nurse had helped Abe take a sip of water and offered him a few ice chips. Then I returned to his bedside.

"How are you feeling now, Abe?"

"Whole lot . . . better'n I thought I'd be when those . . . punks came at us," he rasped.

"Yeah, they did a number on both of you, but the nanomites went in and fixed a few things."

"They did?" I could see that he didn't know whether to be grateful or appalled.

"Yes, and I'm so glad they did. When did they take the tube out of your throat?"

"Bout . . . hour ago. Sore."

"I can imagine! But it proves that you are doing so much better."

My heart was sure doing better!

The nanomites chipped in my ear, and I imagined them with a micro stopwatch, counting every second I spent with Abe.

"Listen, Abe. I shouldn't stay long. I'll come check on you again soon, but right now I need to find Emilio and make sure he's okay."

"Gem . . . Gemma, you tell that boy . . . you tell that boy . . . soon as I get better, I'll come get him back."

Abe's words warmed me. "I'll tell him, Abe. Thank you, my dear friend."

⌘⌘⌘⌘

CHAPTER 11

I headed for the bus stop when I left the hospital, boarded yet another time-sucking city bus, and arrived at Emilio's school at the start of morning recess. I kept looking for him in the clusters of screaming kids overrunning the playground equipment, but I couldn't find him. When I did spot him, he was off by himself, scrunched down on a step, his face bent toward the ground.

Kind of how he used to sit on the curb in front of his uncle's house.

I made my way over and plopped down next to him.

"Hey."

He didn't flinch or act surprised, just scooted away from me with a disgusted sniff.

"Emilio? How are you doing?"

"What you care?"

If possible, he was angrier than before we'd become friends.

I sighed. "Emilio, we do care. We—"

"Liar! No, you don't! You stuck me in foster care an' Zander an' that old man forgot about me! After you promised!"

"Oh, Emilio, I'm so sorry! I only found out what happened yesterday. I went straight to see them as soon as I could get there—and school was already out when I got done. I just saw Abe again and came here straight after. He's doing much better."

He sat up and stared in my direction. "What you talkin' 'bout?"

"Don't look at me," I cautioned. "If they catch you talking to imaginary friends, they'll ship you off to some loony bin."

He glanced around and kept his face averted. "What you talkin' 'bout? What you find out?"

Oh, dear. He doesn't know.

"Um, Emilio, your uncle . . . Mateo, he, um, he and some of his buddies . . . beat up Zander and Abe. They are in the hospital. That's why you haven't heard from either of them."

I had expected the news to hit him hard, but I hadn't foreseen his reaction.

He crumpled. That's the only way I can describe it. He crumpled in on himself as though all the air and all the bones had been sucked out of his body. And he started sobbing.

I found myself holding him, rocking him, murmuring to him as he bawled his eyes out.

"They will be all right, Emilio. They will. I talked to both of them. Don't you worry. We'll get them both fixed up, good as new. Don't you worry."

A playground monitor with a whistle on a chain around her neck glanced over. Her gaze settled on Emilio. She squinted and started moving in our direction.

I closed my eyes. *Nano. Can you cover Emilio while I'm holding him like you cover me? So that no one sees him and comes over to investigate?*

I opened my eyes and watched the woman stop. Blink. Wrench her eyes back and forth in confusion. Turn in a complete circle searching for Emilio.

"Ha-ha! Fooled her!" I gloated.

Emilio pulled his face off my shirt and sniffled. "Who you fooled?"

"That playground monitor over there. She saw you, um, get upset, and she started over here to check on you—except halfway here, she couldn't find you anymore."

He sat up within the circle of my arms. "You disappeared me?"

"Yeah. Just for a few minutes. Until we're done talking."

He looked at his hands. His jeans. "Wow. I can't see me, either!"

"Um, yeah. That's how it works."

He sniffed again and muttered, "I like that old man. Hope he gonna be all right."

"Yeah. Me, too. Say, he asked me to tell you something. He said, 'You tell that boy that as soon as I get better, I'll come get him back.'"

At that, Emilio buried his face in my neck and bawled as though his heart would break. I kind of hung on to him and hugged him close, because I didn't know what else to do.

After a while, I realized my shirt was soaked through, but Emilio didn't sound like he'd be done anytime soon. Inside I sighed. Was I in any way prepared to help a kid through an emotional crisis?

I can barely weather my own emotional fiascoes.

My fingers tugged at my soggy neckline and encountered the chain around my neck. I pulled the cross out and stroked its glossy patina.

"Um, I never did thank you for this, Emilio."

He hiccupped and sniffled. "You din' thank me for what?"

"The, um, cross you made for me."

"You wearin' it?"

"Yeah. Feel?"

He found the chain at my neck and traced it to the cross in my fingers. He clasped the cross, but it felt like he clasped my fingers more.

"You like it?"

"Very much. I keep it with me all the time."

He breathed out, gratified or relieved, I didn't know which. After a long moment, he asked, tears clogging his voice, "Gemma?"

"Yes?"

"You think there's a real God? Like the one they put on the cross?"

Oh, man. Why me?

"Gemma, I believe the Lord is calling you, calling you back to him. The thing about God is that he is persistent. In fact, his persistence is why some have called him the 'Hound of Heaven.' He is tireless and will confront you when you least expect it. At that time, he will bring you face to face with truth. When he does, well, it will be the moment of decision for you."

I was at a loss to answer Emilio's question. Still, he was waiting.

"I don't know for sure . . ." Maybe I was more surprised when I added, "but I hope so, Emilio."

I had to change the subject before I starting bawling along with him. "Okay, listen, kid. Recess will be over soon. I wanted you to know why Zander and Abe haven't sent you any recent messages through CYFD. They will be okay, but it will take them a while to recover. The good news is that Mateo will never get you back because of what he did. The bad news? You will have to wait and be patient until Abe heals enough for the court to approve his guardianship."

"How long?"

I sighed again. "I don't know. Honestly? It could be longer than any of us like, and I'm very sorry. I have your foster family's address, though. I will come by and visit you when I can."

A shrill ringing shattered the air.

"All right. There's the bell. Got yourself together now?"

"Yeah."

I hugged him close. "I promised you that you were not alone anymore. You aren't. You have me, you have Zander, and you have Abe. And I'll see you soon."

I forced a giggle. "But I'll see *you* sooner than you'll see me!"

He got it and guffawed. "That's funny."

I let him go, and watched him walk out from under the nanomites' cloak of invisibility.

He stopped, looked back, shuffled his feet. "I love you, Gemma."

Then he ran off.

"I love you, Gemma."

Those were the sweetest words I'd heard in a very long time.

***

I soared home on an emotional high . . .

And crashed straight into a ditch.

We arrived at the safe house, the nanomites and I, and they went about their business, scouring the Internet for leads on Dr. Bickel's whereabouts. While they worked, the questions about what *exactly* the nanomites were doing to my body were digging holes in me.

While the mites worked, I began my own search.

I popped open a browser window and started exploring the anatomy of the human brain. My online search led me to labeled charts and graphs and even 3D images of the brain. I studied the cranium, cortex, cerebellum, dura, basal ganglia, brain stem, and spinal cord. Did you know that the brain is also divided into lobes? Frontal, parietal, temporal, and occipital. Within half an hour, I probably knew (and retained) as much information about the structures of the brain as a first-year med student.

Maybe more.

None of this information helped. It didn't answer my "how" questions. Surely what the mites were doing ran deeper than the major pieces and parts of the human brain? I mean, how in the world do those parts make us think?

Then I saw it: "The brain is one of the largest and most complex organs in the human body. It is made up of more than 100 billion nerves that communicate in trillions of connections called synapses."

It was the word "trillions" that jolted me. Trillions of connections. Trillions of "synapses." The nanomites numbered in the trillions and they were tiny, smaller than my DNA. Smaller than my brain's synapses.

I dug in and researched more on "synapses." I read with a voracity that was astounding, and I retained it all.

What I found was unnerving: "Synapses and neurotransmitters are both key components of the central nervous system's chemical communication network, responsible for relaying messages between nerve cells, or neurons. Figuratively speaking, the neurotransmitter is the messenger and the synapse is the pathway traveled by the messenger."

I read that the brain's synapses are more than anatomical (physical) structures—they are electrical and chemical in composition and function. The more I read, the deeper my hunger grew. My vocabulary stumbled (initially) over words like axon terminal, dendrite spines, and synaptic vesicles; presynaptic, postsynaptic, upstream and downstream terminals or presynaptic (axonal) endings; tree-like structures that formed, lighted, and passed packets of information—all via complex chemical interactions and exchanges.

The vocabulary stuck, and the new information came clear. I retained what I'd read, and I made the necessary connections.

I understood.

I lifted my eyes from the screen and focused them on the living room's lone Southwestern print. "They are manipulating my brain chemistry. They are changing its very structure."

I may not have figured out everything the mites were doing, but I had grasped enough. Enough to put a label on it.

My breathing quickened. My heart thumped like that of a wild bird caught in a snare.

What the mites were doing boiled down to this simple phrase: Nano brain surgery.

Gemma Keyes, we are sensing physical distress. Would you like us to release endorphins to calm your body?

I got what *that* meant now, too.

"No, no, no. No, don't do that."

Please tell us how we can assist.

Assist? Haven't you done enough?

I grew faint. Breathless.

Gemma Keyes, your heart rate is approaching a non-optimal speed.

No kidding.

I shook my head back and forth, one thought erasing all the others: *They are in my brain, and they are changing it, changing its structure and the way it works. What if those changes are permanent? What happens to me when they leave?*

Forget that! What happens to me if they stay and keep doing what they're doing?

It was too much. Everything was too much. Thanks to my research and my new and "amazing" retentive abilities, I could visualize precisely what the mites were doing. I couldn't *stop* envisioning the nanomites "in there."

All my imaginings were ugly.

Brutal.

Terrifying.

When the mites left, would I be paralyzed? Unable to speak or form my own thoughts? A vegetable?

It was too much to handle. I didn't want to know more or think more. I didn't want to deal with it any longer.

My self-preservation instincts overloaded. All I wanted to do was run away. Escape.

I slammed the laptop closed and walked on stiff legs to the bedroom. I climbed under the covers, put my face in the pillow, and closed my eyes.

Gemma Keyes?

"Don't talk to me, Nano. Just leave me alone."

I pulled the blanket over my head and shut out the world. Shut out the despair. Shut out the waning hope that someday . . . all would be right again.

A faint chipping followed me down into the blessed release of slumber.

***

I slept through the afternoon into the evening—and I'm guessing I needed it. When I woke up, I was over the initial shock of what my research had produced. Or perhaps I was just resigned. I couldn't do anything about the situation, could I?

No, I couldn't. Not one single thing.

I left the house and went on a long and what *should* have been exhausting run. Yeah, I may have figured out what the mites were doing in my brain, but I hadn't tapped into the other symptoms yet—what they were doing in my body.

I ran faster.

After I'd run for an hour, not much had changed. I had wanted the vigorous exercise to dispel the hopeless feelings that dogged me. It didn't, but at least I returned to the safe house in a little better frame of mind.

Better frame of *mind*?

That phrase would never mean what it used to.

The nanomites, for their part, seemed . . . what? Reserved? Reticent? Restrained? Did they even have *a clue* about how freaked out I was?

Whatever.

They didn't ask questions or make much noise that evening, and that was all right by me.

I needed some alone time.

***

"And you took it upon yourself to attack your neighbor, did you? An old, helpless man? You chose to make us odious before the world? To bring down unwanted attention upon us?"

Soto stood and moved a step toward Mateo.

Mateo's mouth opened a little. "But you . . . you told me to take care of the old man."

"I? I said no such thing. Did I? Does anyone recall my giving such an order?" Soto glanced around and his men, with uniform precision, shook their heads in the negative.

"Exactly. Why would I suggest such an action? You see, Mateo? This is a perfect example of why I was sent here: to clean up the messes you have made."

Mateo's anger, long suppressed, burst from his mouth. "Liar! You provoked me! You led me to believe—"

"Shut up! *Callate el osico.*" Soto pushed himself into Mateo's face. "Your presumption knows no bounds, *chorra*, and your stupidity rivals your lack of discretion. *Eres tan estupido como un perro.*"

With sinking hope, Mateo swallowed and stared at the hard expressions surrounding him.

⌘⌘⌘⌘

CHAPTER 12

"Zander?"

His eyes popped open—at least the one that wasn't swollen shut did—as soon as my whisper reached his ears.

"Gemma?"

"I'm here. How are you doing?"

He reached for the button to raise the bed and groaned as he did. "Better. Lots better, really. Just sore, you know?"

"Well you *look* like a tub of melting Spumoni ice cream—all pink-and-brown-ish with green mold growing around the edges."

"I—*what?*"

His outrage generated a giggle that I didn't stifle.

"Zander, have you seen yourself? Looked in a mirror lately?"

Glower. "Well, no."

"Your face is purple and purple-ish pink. And brown and green. The green is gonna be especially gross when it turns that icky-sicky yellow."

"Did you come here to cheer me up?"

I laughed again. "Yeah, I did. Maybe I should change the subject, though. I found Emilio yesterday."

That did it: Zander perked up. "How's the kid doing?"

"He was pretty ticked off at all of us at first. I sat down next to him at recess, and he wouldn't even acknowledge my presence—he even turned his back on me! Then I told him why you and Abe hadn't visited or called him. That you were in the hospital. It upset him pretty bad."

"Does he know it was Mateo?"

"Yeah, I told him, but I also told him that it meant Mateo would never get him back. Sort of took the sting out of it."

Zander lay back and closed his eyes. "You think Abe will be able to foster Emilio? I mean . . . if he survives?"

"Oh, Zander! Abe's gonna to be fine."

Zander's good eye cracked open again and tried to focus in my general direction. "You sure?"

"Yup. Before I met up with Emilio yesterday, I went back to the MICU, and Abe was vastly improved. They had even taken him off the vent, so we were able to talk. His throat was sore and his voice was rough, but he was in his right mind. I will go again today, after I leave here. I'll bet they have to move him to another ward soon."

"Wow. I can hardly believe it. I *saw* what Mateo and his buddies did to Abe, so it's . . . well, it's miraculous."

My voice dropped to a whisper. "I agree . . . but do you think it was nanomites? Or was it God?" That question had been bugging me since I left Abe's room yesterday morning.

Zander's mouth widened into a sweet smile. "Give me your hand, Gemma. C'mon. Give it to me."

He held out the palm that wasn't trussed up in the sling to support his cracked collarbone. I put my hand in his outstretched one.

"The Bible has a verse I particularly like for this type of situation, Gemma, when something good happens, and we don't know who or what to give the credit to."

"Oh?" I licked my lips, more taken by how my hand felt in his, more interested in the little shivers jittering up my back.

"Yeah. That verse is found in the Book of James and goes like this: *Every good and perfect gift is from above, coming down from the Father of the heavenly lights, who does not change like shifting shadows.*

"Good stuff comes from God—because God *is* good. All good stuff comes from him. So, even if it *was* the nanomites who helped Abe? We can thank God for them. After all, Dr. Bickel made them, but God made *him*."

I sneered a little. I'd never come within spitting distance of thanking God for the nanomites. They had been a pain in my . . . posterior for two months. After what I'd learned yesterday, my feelings were even less amiable toward them.

But I digress.

"I remember Aunt Lucy quoting that verse. She was always praising God for this blessing or that answer to prayer. She also said something about God not having a shadow?"

Zander busted out a chuckle and gasped mid-snigger. "Please stop! Hurts to laugh."

"Was what I said really so funny?"

"Yeah, kinda. It's just that I can see you as a kid interpreting that verse to mean that God doesn't have a shadow."

He shifted, still uncomfortable.

I wasn't sympathetic at that exact moment. "Well, I thought that's what Aunt Lu said."

"It's not that God doesn't have a shadow, Gemma, it's that he doesn't change. When someone moves, their shadow moves, right? God doesn't 'move,' meaning he doesn't shift his position so to speak. When he takes a stand, he doesn't waffle on it or, figuratively, flit around like a 'shifting shadow.'"

"God doesn't change?"

"No. People change their minds all the time and let us down, and people's emotions flip-flop from one minute to the next, driving them and everyone around them nuts—which is why, by the way, we shouldn't make decisions based solely on how we feel. But God? His character and nature? Who he is? What he says? Those things don't change—and that's good news for us."

I didn't say anything, because I was stuck on the "people's emotions flip-flop from one minute to the next, driving them and everyone around them nuts" part.

It was the perfect description of me.

Zander couldn't see my face, so he kept going. "For example, God doesn't love us one day and hate us the next day. Jesus said, *For God so loved the world that he gave his one and only Son.* God loves the world—and that means he loves people. He isn't going to stop loving people, so he keeps reaching out to each of us, trying to draw us to him. At the same time, God is just. He gives us choice, and he allows us to choose him or reject him."

What Zander said dredged up more questions. "What about the bad stuff that happens to good people? Who gets the credit for that? Is that God 'reaching out' to us?"

"No. The bad stuff in the world isn't from God. The Bible says that God is good, so bad stuff cannot be from him. Remember, when God made the world, he looked at it and saw that *it was good*—just like him. So, when the world started out, everything was good; it all worked as designed. Everything reflected God and his goodness."

"And then the sin thing happened?" I had, if you recall, spent a few years in church and Sunday school.

"Yes. Then the sin thing happened. Sin didn't just affect Adam and Eve. Sin ruined the goodness and perfection of the world—and it wasn't a one-time thing, either. Sin has a corrupting effect, and it is still at work in the world. That's why the world is getting worse, why the earth is wearing out, trending downward.

"Parts of nature are still beautiful enough to blow our minds, but if we look close, we can see that the beauty isn't perfect. Like, if we glimpse a mountainside forest, it might be breathtaking, but if we look closer, we can see the effects of disease, drought, fire, or overcrowding."

"And that's because of sin?" The idea made me angry.

"Yes—the decline of the earth is caused by the cumulative effect of humanity's sin in the world: Adam and Eve's sin, their children's sin, our grandparents and parents. Your sin and my sin."

"People sound like the problem."

"Well, we *are* the problem. However, God has no desire to throw us away. He made us in his image and in his likeness, after all. We're the closest thing to children he has. You wouldn't throw your kids away if they screwed up, would you? You would love them and try to correct them, wouldn't you? God feels the same way, so he decided to rescue us. That's where Jesus comes in."

I looked away. "So, when do you get out of this place?"

Zander glanced in my direction. He was disappointed at my abrupt topic switch, but he answered, "Soon. Maybe later today or tomorrow. The doctor will make that decision when he sees me this afternoon."

"Will you be okay on your own?"

"Yeah. Izzie will help me out."

Izzie, short for Isabelle, was Zander's sister. I liked Izzie, but I hadn't seen her in weeks. Not since the barbecue for the homeless that DCC had organized in one of the city parks. Seemed like a lifetime ago.

"Izzie. Sounds like a good fit," I snickered.

He snorted—and winced. "Oh, I'm certain she won't take advantage of the situation to boss me around, right? She wouldn't do that, would she?"

I snickered again.

"You know, your visitor skills really stink."

"Right, and you have so many visitors that you can compare me to others?"

"Half my Sunday school class has been in to cheer me up. Did a much better job, let me tell you."

I might have described Zander's look as "condescending" or "arch"—if he'd been able to manipulate his swollen face. Instead, the melty Spumoni ice cream bruises just shifted around and made my stomach lurch.

I cleared my throat. "You go to Sunday school?"

Okay, I'll admit that my question came out with a snarky sneer.

"I teach Sunday school, Gemma."

What?

I jumped trains. "So, if Izzie is gonna take care of you when you get out, who will take care of Abe?"

That did the trick. Zander jumped trains with me.

"Yeah, I agree. When Abe gets out, he will need someone to look after him. By then, I should be self-sufficient, able to use this arm a little, so I thought I would stay with him for a bit, help him out."

"That's a great idea, actually." His plan relieved my mind more than I'd realized it would.

"Abe doesn't have family anymore, Gemma. The church is his family now. I know the women of DCC will help out with meals and cleaning; I'll stay there to keep an eye on him and handle his personal needs."

Abe doesn't have family anymore. That smarted. Aunt Lucy had been Abe's family until she died. I had tried to fill her shoes . . . a little.

Not that much, if I told the truth.

And there I was, just like Zander said, my emotions flip-flopping all over the place. Driving me nuts.

Zander interrupted my brooding navel-gazing. "When you asked about the bad stuff in the world, Gemma, I didn't quite finish my thought."

"Yeah. Okay." I was distracted when I gave him the go-ahead.

"Sometimes the bad stuff that happens to us is the direct result of our own stupid choices. However, God gave the believer in Christ a wonderful promise. It is found in Romans 8, and says, *We know that in all things God works for the good of those who love him, who have been called according to his purpose.* This verse means that God can take anything—even the bad things—and turn them or use them to produce a good outcome for his people."

"Oh?" God could use all the bad stuff happening to me to bring about good?

"Yeah—but it's important to recognize that this promise isn't for everyone. The promises of God belong to those who belong to him—to those who love him."

So, not for me, I acknowledged.

But, like a bulldog, Zander wouldn't let go. "Gemma, what is even more important to recognize is that God has no desire to exclude anyone from his promises. *Anyone.* He wants every individual to belong to him. He calls to each of us. That's what I meant the other day when I said that he would confront you. He is calling you, Gemma."

Confront me? Calling me? Is that what was happening? Because something was going on, even if I couldn't put my finger on it. Something deep inside—where I was raw and hurting.

If I had said anything, Zander would have heard the shaking in my voice, so I stayed mute, my hand tucked into his hand, his strong fingers holding mine, warming them. Feeling so good. So right.

***

I left Zander's floor, took the elevator down to the ground, walked through the breezeway between buildings until I reached the Pavilion elevators, and punched the button for the second floor. I lifted my hand toward the doors to the MICU and they opened.

I walked through but faltered and stopped just inside the unit. Something had shifted over the past two days, and I wasn't quite clear about it yet, except . . . except I hadn't asked the mites to open the doors. I hadn't even thought about it.

I had expected them to open, and they had.

What is it? What has changed?

I wandered farther up the ward, puzzling over whatever it was that was bugging me. I found Abe in the same MICU bed, but he was awake, staring at the ceiling.

I touched his hand. "Abe?"

He cut his eyes in my direction, not surprised at my presence. "Put my bed up, will you, Gemma? So's I can watch for the nurses while we talk."

I pressed the button that raised his head, and he scanned through the glass walls of his room before speaking.

"Gemma, how are you doing?"

"I'm fine, Abe. Really. And, wow! You look a lot better than the last time I saw you!"

"Well, I surely am. The doctor says he will move me into a regular room soon, maybe even today."

"I'm so glad. Zander may be going home today. His sister is going to help him out until he's able to do for himself."

I took Abe's hand, and he clung on to me. Holding his hand wasn't the same as holding Zander's, but it still felt pretty wonderful.

"Abe doesn't have family anymore. The church is his family now. I know the women of DCC will help out with meals and cleaning; I'll be there to keep an eye on him and handle his personal needs."

For the first time in a long time, I was grateful for the existence of Downtown Community Church, glad that Abe could count on his church to be there for him. I was relieved that Abe had Zander in his life, too.

"Zander said he plans to come stay with you when they let you out."

"He did, did he?" Abe chuckled, but the laugh bowed him up in the middle—just like it did Zander.

"Are you okay?"

"I got me some touchy spots 'longside my ribs."

"Well, you look amazing compared to the last time I saw you."

"Yep. Amazing is right. The doctors shake their heads every time they come check on me. Say, I'm appreciative of what those nano-thingies did for me."

A little of my ire toward the mites melted. "I told them thank you. For myself, too."

He squinted, perplexed. "You talk to them nano-things, Gemma?"

"Um, well, yeah, I guess I do. The situation has progressed some. Gotten . . . friendlier."

Friendlier? Not at the moment! And *sheesh*. I did *not* want to detail what I thought they were doing in my brain or speculate over what they were doing elsewhere. Even Abe would vote to have me locked up.

We chatted for a while. I told him that I'd seen Emilio, and he had forgiven us for calling in CYFD. Told Abe I'd passed on his message.

We sat a few minutes more in companionable quiet, my hand in his, before I told him goodbye. I was halfway down the ward, passing another glassed-in room, when a wail disrupted the otherwise quiet busyness of the MICU. Inside the room, just outside a curtained bed, a girl, a young woman near to my age, sank into the arms of a middle-aged couple. I thought they must have been the girl's parents.

The girl wailed again, and her cry ratcheted into a scream of agony, primal and gut-wrenching. Her weeping—her utter heartbreak—swept across the ward. I stood mere feet from the drama playing out before me.

I crept closer to the glass wall.

"No!" she shrieked. "No! You have to try something else! He-he's only thirty-one years old! We have a son! A son! He's just a baby! He needs his daddy!"

"Holly—Mrs. Galvez—I assure you, I promise you, that we have done all we can. I am so very sorry." I saw the doctor then, harried and sorrowful, as she stepped from behind the curtain that shielded the patient's bed.

"Holly, please," the woman holding her begged. "Please, dear. You must be brave."

"I can't! I can't! Oh, God, please help me! Please help John!"

I couldn't handle it. I ran from her raw, bleeding grief. I rounded the end of the ward, passed the "gatekeeper" desk, hit the door, and stumbled into the hall, sobbing for the girl who could have been me. The thick doors to the unit closed behind me and muffled the girl's cries—but I could still hear her agonized protests.

"He needs his daddy!"

How well I related.

I had been blindsided and struck dumb the night police officers informed Genie and me that our parents had died when our house burned—in the fire she and I had somehow escaped.

"Oh. God, no, please! He needs his daddy!"

I doubled over, fell against a wall, and bawled for that girl, mourned for her son who would grow up wondering why his daddy had left him. I wept for myself—because to this day, I did not understand why Mommy and Daddy had left me.

Grinding the heels of my hands into my eyes, I stumbled down the hall, through the sitting area, toward the elevator—putting distance between me and the anguish I could not bear. The people in the waiting area looked stunned and apprehensive. Their gaze, as one person, was slanted toward the MICU, their expressions concerned or horrified. Some wiped surreptitiously at their eyes.

I need to get away!

As I mashed the elevator button several times, the girl in the MICU gave one last shriek that ended mid-scream. I turned and faced the sitting area and the MICU hallway beyond it. The elevator dinged. Its doors opened behind me, but I stood frozen and listening.

To silence.

What had the doctor told that girl? As badly as I wanted to escape her pain, I suddenly wanted to know: What had the doctor told her?

I didn't know what I was doing, but I strode through the lobby, down the hall, around the corner. I lifted my finger toward the doors. They sprang open, and I sprinted through.

A few nurses were gathered around the young woman. She had collapsed onto the floor, maybe fainted? A nurse applied a cold towel to her face. Her parents hovered over them, clutching at each other. Sobbing.

I slipped past them into the patient's room and tiptoed up to the still figure behind the curtain. I placed my hand on his chest. It rose and fell in short, panting breaths.

I sighed, then spoke aloud to the nanomites, my anger toward them swallowed up by the present need. "Nano. Do what you can to help this man. Please."

Mites pulsed from palm and fingers and flowed into his body. I withdrew my hand and stood back.

And waited.

A nurse came in and fine-tuned something in the man's IV. I scooted out of her way.

Out in the corridor, Holly came to; the nurses assisted her to a chair and offered her water.

I glanced back to her husband.

No change.

Nothing from the nanomites.

I waited longer. The mites would come back to me when it was time—one way or another.

After an hour, I could bear it no longer. I entered the warehouse, but it seemed . . . empty-ish.

"Nano?"

We are working, Gemma Keyes.

"Show me?"

We cannot. You are unable to accompany us.

"Well, can you tell me? What is wrong with him?"

The man's medical file appeared before me, all the pages of medical jargon and diagnoses, x-rays, MRIs . . . and CT scans.

A tumor. In his brain. *Glioblastoma multiforme*. Deep within the parietal lobe.

I searched for and found research on that kind of tumor. I pulled additional information from the warehouse, and absorbed all I studied.

Malignant.

Inoperable.

Fatal.

"Oh, no . . ."

We are working, Gemma Keyes.

"Thank you, Nano. What can I do?"

Provide power to support our increased consumption.

I stepped to the nearest light switch and placed my hand on it. A slow, steady warmth pulsed from the receptacle into my hand and up my arm.

While I waited, supporting the mites' energy needs, I tried to visualize them at the site of the tumor, tried to imagine them clear down at the cellular level—lasering the invading cells, detaching the cancer's tendrils and tentacles from the man's parietal lobe.

The man. I looked again into his medical record and found his name.

Right. John.

John Galvez. Holly had cried out her husband's name: John. They had a baby boy.

The latest notations in his file were bleak: Comatose state. Decreased respiration. Liver and kidney functions failing. Blood pressure dropping.

Were the nanomites too late? Was the damage too extensive? Were his brain functions already destroyed? And as the mites killed the tumor, cell by cell, what would become of it, of its cancerous bits and pieces?

Would those cells float through John's bloodstream and lodge themselves elsewhere to replicate and reproduce their deadly selves? Had the tumor metastasized and colonized other organs before now?

Squeezing my eyes closed, I tried again to follow the nanomites, to see them at work. They said I could not accompany them, but I didn't want to believe them. Wasn't I part of the nanocloud? I didn't want to be, hadn't chosen it, but wasn't *I* a tribe? What about all that, "we are six" business! And why couldn't I find my way to them?

I struggled to move down the warehouse, down its long, dark halls. It was like swimming in molasses, like running while tethered.

But I kept trying, trying to go where they were. I struggled against the flesh and bone that held me back.

Gemma Keyes. Do you trust us?

"What?"

You wish to see us at work. Do you trust us?

Loaded question.

"I—I don't know."

You will not be harmed.

Except I knew, already, that my presence in the warehouse and our communication—not to mention the other indicators of the merge—were predicated on "nano brain surgery," on the creation and manipulation of chemical neurotransmitters traveling along artificially grown synapses.

I wondered what, exactly, the nanomites were suggesting.

They repeated their question.

You wish to see us at work. Do you trust us? You will not be harmed.

I exhaled. "Um, all right."

The room spun, and I lurched against the wall where the outlet was, slid down the wall onto the floor. I had the sense of the bottom dropping out from under me, of rolling, then being tugged and pulled, spun into filament, like a silken fiber, like the string of a kite unwinding, longer and longer. I spiraled away from the room, from its light, from my body.

The warehouse brightened and lengthened, and I traveled down its corridors, floating, flying, speeding forward.

Nanomites were with me, cocooning me, propelling us onward—they drove us toward a destination I could not see. But I could see *them*, the mites. They were luminous and shimmering, bending and reflecting light from the mirrors that flicked and flickered quicker than the wings of a hummingbird. They flew ahead, beside, above, below, around me. I glanced back—and saw the long line of mites behind me, *each bound by a shimmering tether that was tied to me.*

Was I seeing the electrochemical transmissions of my own consciousness, trailing behind me, supported by the mites?

They must have sensed the unease that shivered through me.

You will not be harmed, they assured me once more.

"What if . . . what if the bond breaks?"

Your consciousness will return to your body. You will not be harmed.

I shrugged off my fears and focused my "sight" forward.

Ahead, the luminescence grew until we arrived at a glowing wall of nanomites so high I could see neither its height nor its breadth. They were massed upon a great, bulging, pulsing evil.

The tumor.

The nanomites were destroying it, excising it from the man's brain tissue with the precision of, well, the precision of thousands of lasers: Delta Tribe at work.

Other mites gathered the pieces that broke off or fell from the lasers' slicing and cauterizing actions. They bundled the tumor pieces into balls and sped away with them.

"Where are they taking the pieces?" I asked.

Where the man's body will safely flush them from his system.

And then we were no longer merely watching; we were working, and I had never seen such total and utter annihilation. Wherever a foreign cell went, we hunted it down. The longer we worked, the more clearly I saw and understood—until I could distinguish between the aberrant and normal cells, until, with a glance, I knew the enemy. I was one with the nanomites. I could not wield tools as they did, but I was with them heart and soul.

We worked for hours, it seemed.

When the mites escorted my consciousness back to my body, I found myself lying on a cold, hard surface. I recognized that I was prostrate, on my belly on a cold tile floor. I opened my eyes to the sight of feet and legs. I counted three pairs of feet—somehow, I had rolled under John's bed.

I remember . . . rolling . . . before they pulled me away.

I blinked, took several deep breaths, and tuned in to the voices above and around me. They were exclaiming over the patient.

"I don't think I've ever seen such a reversal," a man said, "but his urine output is normal; respiration and blood pressure are within acceptable bounds . . ."

"That's not possible," an angry female declared.

"But, see here, doctor. His EKG is normal, and his brain activity has improved."

"Where's that last CT scan?"

Noise and shuffling, quiet perusal before a muttered, "Not possible, I say." The clearing of a throat. "Get another CT scan."

"Yes, doctor."

The room cleared, and I scooted out from under the bed. I was dizzy when I stood, so I grasped the bed rail to steady myself. Bent over the patient.

I'd jarred the bed when I'd fallen against the rail. The man lying there blinked. He looked up at the ceiling.

I didn't know what he saw or how aware he was, but his eyes were open and staring.

And I had to know.

"John?" I spoke in a whisper.

In slow motion, his head turned on the pillow toward the sound of my voice. He appeared dazed, only partly awake. Confused.

As for me, my chest was so tight that I could not draw a breath.

Good stuff comes from God. All good stuff. Even if it was the nanomites who helped Abe? We can thank God for them.

I shuddered and inhaled vital, necessary air. When I breathed it back out, a whisper came with it. "Thank you, God. Thank you for the nanomites. Thank you for using them to save this man."

John blinked and his eyes seemed to come into focus.

"Th-thank you, G-god."

It was all he said.

It was enough.

⌘⌘⌘⌘

CHAPTER 13

Javier Baca called me two mornings later—two days I'd spent brooding over what had happened in the MICU, testing my feelings toward the nanomites and trying to come to grips with them (again), and running for long hours to expend the energy that my body produced in abundance and for which I had no good use.

Oh, and eating like a bear prepping for winter hibernation.

Burp.

When Javier called, I was appreciative of the distraction.

"Hey, Miss Sawyer? I have the inspection you asked for and it turns out the rear brakes did need some work. I have the bill for that, too."

"Would you text me photos of the inspection and repair bill, Javier?"

"Yeah, soon as we hang up."

"Great. I'll look them over. If everything seems okay, I'll pay for the car and half the repair bill, as we agreed."

I hung up. Minutes later I received the photos I requested.

I called Javier back. "I will text the transfer to you. The money should hit your account, um, probably by tomorrow." I paused a beat. "Call me when you've received the money."

"Sure."

I pulled more cash from behind the stove and ran down the street to make a deposit. I'd made an initial deposit of close to $6,000 the day my ATM card arrived—far below the suspicion-garnering amount of $10,000—and another in the range of $3,500 the next day. I'd made three similar deposits since then. With today's deposit, my account now held $17,000 and some change.

The Escape would take about $14,000 of that, including my half of the brake repairs. When I received confirmation of today's deposit, I would text Javier an account-to-account transfer.

That close! I was *that* close to having a full, functioning life again. I paused to breathe, to let it soak in.

Technology. Where would I be without it?

Hiding and running. I would be hiding and running the rest of my life.

***

Javier called the next afternoon. "Miss Sawyer? I got the money."

Very good, Javier.

The nanomites had informed me just this morning that the mail carrier would deliver my permanent driver's license today. I'd hiked to the address and hung around for two hours until the carrier drove into view. As soon as she'd deposited the mail and moved on, I'd snatched it up, found the right envelope, and stuffed it into my back pocket.

Not that I needed to carry a license while I drove.

"Why, yes, officer, I have my license right here."

Not!

I smiled to myself. *Now to finesse the title transfer and pick up my new wheels.*

This would be the tricky part.

"That's great, Javier. I'm, uh, still out of town, but I'm on my way home now. Hold on. I'm sending a bill of sale to your phone."

I had the nanomites attach the signed PDF file to a text and send it.

"Did you get it? Please sign it and the title? Oh. And I'd like to pick up the car sometime tonight, but I don't know exactly when I'll be home and able to arrange for a friend to drive me there. Why don't you leave both sets of keys and the paperwork under the front seat in case you aren't there when I come by?"

"What?"

He was incredulous, but I was ready for it.

"Well, like I said, I don't know exactly when I'll be able to pick up the car—it might be pretty late or very early tomorrow. I'd like you to leave the keys, the signed bill of sale, and the signed title under the front seat."

"Are you sure? That's . . . I mean . . . Well, I guess it will be all right 'cause the car is in my driveway, but I haven't even met you and you haven't driven it or anything."

I kept my air patient and nonchalant—but I pushed him. "You had it inspected, and I've paid you, right?"

"Well . . . yeah."

"And my schedule is unpredictable, so leave the keys and paperwork like I said, in case I come by and you aren't home or you're already sleeping."

"Well . . . if you say so." He wasn't convinced, but it sounded like he'd do what I'd asked.

"Thanks for understanding and accommodating my crazy life, Javier."

Crazy? He has no clue . . . yet in a far corner of mind, I was uncomfortable with how easily the little fibs—the small deceptions and glib embellishments—had rolled off my tongue.

I got angry with myself then—or, rather, at my overactive conscience. For the next hour, I brooded over the things I felt compelled to do because of my strange and dangerous circumstances.

I kept returning to the same thought: *What is right anymore, anyway? And who's to say?*

***

Since I was short one driver, I couldn't "borrow" my usual ride to pick up the Escape. I took the last bus of the day to within walking distance of Javier's address and hopped off. I ran a good mile before I reached his folks' house. Hardly broke a sweat.

Still, I'm so looking forward to having my own wheels!

Darkness fell earlier now, and the scents of Autumn hung in the air. I sniffed. Someone had a fire burning in their fireplace. I wished I was curled up in front of a warm fire.

I kept jogging.

When I arrived at Javier's house, the lights in the main part of the house were on. A porch light lit up the front yard. My car sat parked in the driveway.

My car!

To tell the truth, I itched to get in it and drive away—but I needed to wait until everyone in the house was asleep. I didn't want them to hear the vehicle start and come out to investigate.

I squatted next to the garage to pass the time. Time? It seemed to drag on forever, and I likely had three or more hours of waiting ahead of me. After a while, I grew chilled, so I walked around the block to warm up. Nothing had changed when I circled back, except that a brisk east-canyon wind had started to gust.

By the time Javier and his folks go to bed, I will be stiff and frozen.

I eyed the car and lusted after its warmth.

Well, duh! Why don't I wait inside?

The driver's door was locked, but I lifted a finger and the lock popped up. "No lights, Nano," I whispered. I shivered as I climbed in and relocked the door.

I felt under the seat. Nothing: No keys, no paperwork. Felt under the passenger seat. Nothing. Got out and, with the door open, crouched down and felt around under the driver's seat.

Nothing.

Javier, Javier. What are you doing, kiddo?

I shook my head. Now what? Should I text him? Ask if he'd done what I asked? Nudge him into action?

I decided to just wait.

The inside of the car was much warmer than outside and, with the forced inactivity, I started to nod off. The slam of the house's front door yanked me from my nap. I stared at the pudgy young man who jumped off the porch and headed my way.

"Oh, crud."

I did the only thing I could do: I threw myself between the headrests into the back seat.

Javier used the key fob's remote to pop the lock. He opened the door and the interior lights came on. He slid an envelope under the driver's seat. Then he pulled a second set of keys from his pocket and tossed both sets after the paperwork.

I must have cleared my throat a tiny bit or shifted. I don't know. But Javier froze. He stared into the back seat, then knelt on the driver's seat and stared between the headrests right into my face.

I knew he couldn't see me—but maybe he "felt" me? With no warning, he reached a hand toward me. I jerked out of his reach by the hair of my chinny-chin-chin.

Don't know who was more freaked out right then—Javier or me. His eyes bulged into wide, anxious pools. I was afraid to blink, let alone shut my eyes so I could enter the warehouse where I could talk to the nanomites without speaking. I tried to jump in and stay focused on what Javier might do next at the same time.

It wasn't easy getting into the warehouse with my eyes open, but I managed to. I split my attention between Javier and the nanomites and asked them to distract Javier.

Javier yelped as the mites stung him. I'm assuming they stung him—maybe on his leg or foot. Anyway, Javier swiveled onto the driver's seat and swatted at some part of his anatomy. I was relieved when he jumped out of the car and shook out his pant legs while cussing and rubbing a spot on his calf.

A few minutes later he opened the driver's door again and inspected the seat as though looking for ants or other offending insects. When he didn't find anything, he shut the door and trotted up to the house.

An hour or so later, the lights in the house went out. I waited another thirty minutes, then retrieved the keys. I put the gear in neutral, let the Escape roll down the driveway and out into the street. Then I started the engine and drove away.

I don't want to diminish what a great relief it was to be behind the wheel of my own vehicle again. For the first time since I'd fled my house, I didn't feel . . . so vulnerable. Like a deer in an open meadow. I don't know if that makes sense, but having a car, my own car, made a difference.

I drove to a parking garage about half a mile from Dr. Bickel's safe house. The garage was automated—the way I liked it. I fed my credit card into a machine for a month's rental, pulled in, and parked on the second level where the ticket said my spot was. I left my parking tag on the dash, collected the paperwork, title, and spare keys, locked the car, and headed home.

I jogged down the sidewalk and, with my eyes wide open, I joined the nanomites in the warehouse.

I shrugged. *Nice trick!*

With reluctance but, to be fair to the mites for their assistance, I muttered, "Thanks, Nano."

You are welcome, Gemma Keyes.

Huh. That was a first.

Yes, I was still irritated with them. It was all I could do to be civil, so I vacillated, stuck between not wanting to be beholden to them but wanting them to answer questions about the merge.

You have withdrawn from us, Gemma Keyes. Do you have reservations? Concerns?

How did they know that?

How? How. Did. They. *Know?*

My pace picked up, all on its own. Could I ever outrun the disgust I felt, my anger toward the mites?

Gemma Keyes. We have distressed you again. Please help us understand.

Understand? You've hijacked my brain and—I don't get this part yet—other parts of my physical makeup. And you want to "understand" why I'm distressed?

Those and other equally vehement and heated words resounded in my head. I pounded the pavement harder with each charge I laid at their door.

Have we troubled you somehow, Gemma Keyes?

Yeah, like you said: "*We regret the discomfort, Gemma Keyes.*" Right. I've heard it before.

We are six, Gemma Keyes. What distresses you, distresses us.

I halted in the middle of the street.

Entered the warehouse.

Yelled at them.

"Distressed? You think I'm *distressed*, and yet you don't know why? It's you! You have done things! Done things to my body! Who said you could do that? Who? *Who!* I don't even know what you've done, but I *never* gave you permission! And, like, why am I so hyped up? Why is my mind a freaking info-magnet? It's driving me nuts!"

Actually, I went on for a while. You know. Screaming. Venting. Raging.

All the things.

I stopped, mid-rant, when a car turned the corner and almost ran me down. I zoomed over to the curb and dropped down on it. The concrete was cold and I shivered—from the chill seeping up my backside and the adrenalin bleeding off me. I'd jumped out of the warehouse and was just sitting there, freezing my butt off and mulling over my list of grievances.

Gemma Keyes.

A lot like Emilio, I turned away from them with a disgusted sniff.

Gemma Keyes. We have answers for you.

"Oh? Is that so?" I sniffed again.

We are six, Gemma Keyes. We must be optimal when we find Dr. Bickel.

Optimal? I got up, rubbed my numb behind, and walked on.

"All right. I'll bite. What do you mean by 'optimal'?" My head was in the warehouse, but my eyes were focused ahead. With no conscious effort, I navigated the sidewalk's dips and curves, cracks and curbs.

I knew 'em all.

Weirder and weirder.

Your tribe carries us, Gemma Keyes. Your tribe must be strong, resilient, and prepared.

"Prepared for what?"

We will find Dr. Bickel. We will free him. We are six. You carry us. We must be prepared for all contingencies.

It was the first reference the nanomites had made to an actual rescue effort.

"You . . . you really think that *we* can get him out of a military prison?"

Yes, Gemma Keyes. However, we must prepare. You must prepare. We have accelerated your metabolism and your neuro network's processing capabilities to enhance your faculty to prepare. You have strengthened your body through running and exercise; however, we have formulated a more structured training program, one better suited to arming you in the defensive strategies we anticipate will be needed. We will assist you in your training.

It was a long speech for the nanomites. I kept hearing the phrase, "arming you in the defensive and offensive strategies we anticipate will be needed," after they finished.

I ran again, wanting, suddenly, to just be home and safe. But when I closed and locked the back door behind me, I asked the mites, "Show me the program you have prepared."

They did.

Whoa.

"What? This looks like boot camp! No, hold that thought—what? What in the bloody blue blazes?" The diagrams surging past my eyes looked like some kind of Olympic-athlete strength training regimen coupled with a martial arts program.

Gemma Keyes, are you ready to begin?

"Um . . ."

Do you trust us, Gemma Keyes? You will not be harmed.

Yeah, right. Where had I heard that before?

"Uh . . . okay."

We have identified a suitable location in which to conduct your training.

Up before my eyes appeared a webpage: Sandia Martial Arts Academy. The mites highlighted the address on Juan Tabo. Only a convenient 1.5 miles from the safe house.

"This place?"

Yes. This establishment is closed today.

"Uh-huh."

I dithered.

Gemma Keyes?

Sighing, I gave in. "All right."

***

I parked behind a nearby strip mall and walked a block to the academy. The cinderblock building had been a video rental place at one time; now, instead of movie posters, the windows were plastered with images of men, women, and children in various martial arts stances. All the students were clad in the traditional martial arts uniform, a white *gi*.

At the mites' direction, I went around to the back of the building. They unlocked a door and I went inside. The alarm chirped a warning until the mites disarmed it. The owner had left on a few lights, probably for security, and I picked my way from the back to the large workout room.

I turned in a circle and surveyed the practice area. Much like a gymnasium, the floor was hardwood. Thick mats covered about a third of the floor. At one end hung some heavy bags and sparring equipment.

Are you ready to begin, Gemma Keyes?

I entered the warehouse. It brightened around me, lengthened and widened. I looked down the long hallway and back, and where nothing but space had been, a huge—I mean *honkin'* huge—man loomed over me. I jumped back, startled. Opened my eyes in the dojo. About hyperventilated.

Come back, Gemma Keyes. We have initiated your training program.

That *man* was my training program? I waited until my breathing slowed before I closed my eyes again. Yup, He was still there. I took wary stock of the guy. He was built like a boulder—even his muscles had muscles—and all his muscles looked like huge rocks popping out of his skin.

I swallowed. Hard. "Um, who are you?"

"I am your instructor, Gemma Keyes. You will follow my directions."

"Follow your . . ."

I stalled. Big time. "Uh . . . um . . . do you have a name?"

For a moment, just a moment, he became ominously still. Then he responded, "You may call me Gustav."

Gustav? Lame! Where did the mites come up with that?

Gustav turned his back to me and went through a three-part hand and foot movement drill. He repeated the same song and dance and then commanded, "Replicate my steps."

It wasn't easy. I mean, I've never been athletic, never played sports other than mandatory volleyball in high school. I almost failed ballroom dance in college.

I tried. Tried again. Again. And again—because *he* said "again," and I was a teensy bit afraid to tell him "no."

Actually, I was making better progress than I'd believed I would, but I was frustrated that I couldn't do what he wanted as fast as he expected. My trainer (whom I started calling Gus-Gus under my breath), showed no emotion, yet he managed to convey firmness and urgency.

He pushed me, and we didn't take breaks. Under his demanding tutelage, I worked away the afternoon. Because we were in the warehouse, I kept my eyes closed and learned a bunch of short little "routines" that centered me within an eight-foot square piece of dojo floor or ran me sideways down the length of the floor and back. I didn't know what else to call the hand and footstep motions—*he* didn't give them a name, so I just used what came to mind, and "routine" seemed to fit.

At first, because my eyes were closed, my balance kept going wonky on me, and I would open my eyes to keep from falling—which threw me off even worse. Gradually, though, I acclimated to moving in the nanomites' virtual training environment without falling over.

Gus-Gus pushed me harder and didn't allow me time to think about what I was doing; I just did what he commanded, faster and faster, until my movements became smoother, more fluid. After three hours of continuous work, my body felt good. Used, but satisfied.

I had blisters on my feet, and figured we were done . . . but nope.

Gemma Keyes, enter the equipment room and find Locker 7. Remove a set of escrima sticks.

"A set of what?"

I wandered to one end of the building and found the equipment room with stuff like headgear and pads hanging from pegs in the wall. The room also had a row of lockers that, to my eyes, were glorified closets. I found Locker 7 and opened it.

The locker's inside walls were lined with fabric pouches holding matched pairs of "sticks" about two feet in length, maybe longer. Some of the sticks were foam padded; others were lengths of a variegated light-colored wood. Two sets were of a darker, polished wood. I lifted one of the darker sticks—it was smooth and solid. And heavy.

Gemma Keyes. Select a pair of padded sticks.

"What are they for?"

You will learn to use these sticks in Kali-style Filipino Martial Arts. Given your strength and size, the time available to train you, and your advantage of being invisible to your opponents, we have determined this to be the most effective fighting style for you. We have also ascertained that we can hide the sticks while you use them. The escrima sticks will become your principal weapon.

I was stunned. "Weapon?"

Yes, Gemma Keyes. Think of the sticks as extensions of your hands—longer, stronger extensions. Your use of the sticks will lessen the advantage of a larger, more skilled opponent. You will train and become optimal in the time available to prepare you.

I was starting to dislike the word, "optimal."

Yeah, that word. *Optimal?*

You keep using that word; I do not think it means what you think it means.

And like *I* could, in weeks or months, become "optimal" in a sport people trained their whole lives for?

The mites couldn't read my mind, could they? And yet they replied as though they could.

Gemma Keyes, you need not become a master in this style. Even as an untrained woman of your size and strength, these escrima sticks will serve you well in a combat situation.

"Yeah, yeah. Whatever."

I pulled two foam-padded sticks from their pouch; they were much lighter than the dark-wood sticks. I returned to the main room, to "my" spot on the wood floor. Closed my eyes. My training guy appeared with his own sticks. With his feet planted together, he bowed to me.

It felt weird, bowing back, but I did it. Then Gus-Gus began to show me . . . how to hold the sticks, how to lift and lower them, swing and turn them, each movement slow but considered. Calculated. Not rushed, but deliberate. Gauged.

Top to bottom, fluid, horizontal swings. Step right, left stick; step left, right stick. He added a reverse triangle; afterward, he demonstrated how to add the footwork he'd taught me to the swings.

He demonstrated a four-count single "weave," crossing his arms, uncrossing his arms in front of him. I followed his directions in slow motion, picking up a little speed as he urged me.

That's how I learned not to hit myself while doing so.

Yup. That lovely lesson included bruises free of charge. I managed to smack the backs of both of my hands with the stick held in the other hand (more than once) and, in one particularly graceful move, I knocked myself on the side of the head.

It's easier than you think when you're swinging those things around and trying to remember the footwork, too.

After an hour, I was executing the swinging and foot routines together, making a quarter turn when I finished, so that at the end of four routines, I had completed a 360-degree rotation.

Gus-Gus clapped out a pace for me and I completed another rotation. His claps increased in speed, my movements matching the pace he set. I was kind of amazed that my mind was absorbing the lessons and that my body was keeping up. Then he had me do the same routine backward, turning the opposite direction.

Argh! Faster and faster I flew, but always at my trainer's pace, nothing out of time or sync, every move controlled.

"Stop." He bowed to me.

Sweating but stimulated, I bowed back. When I stood up, a dummy the size of a man stood in front of me. Anticipation shivered down my back.

"You will learn twelve angles of attack. All Kali techniques are based on these twelve angles. Every drill reinforces the twelve angles."

Under Gus-Gus' guidance, I learned where to strike, how to strike, how to wield the sticks and step into the strike to deliver a blow with force behind it. He modified and built upon the footwork I'd learned: how to approach, to feint, to retreat, to sidestep.

Punching technique. "X" strike, inside, outside. A turning double slash.

I lost myself in the rhythm of the graceful, flying movements of the escrima sticks and coordinated footwork. What the nanomites had done with my mind's retention and body's metabolism enabled me to learn and remember, to utilize my body as I had never done before. And under the challenges Gus-Gus put me through—despite the strenuous workout—I had not tired; my strength had not flagged.

Rather, I was energized.

"Stop." Gus-Gus bowed.

I bowed in return.

He disappeared.

You have done well for a first lesson, Gemma Keyes. We shall train here each night after the dojo closes.

It almost sounded like fun. Better than restless, pointless pinging off the walls at home!

I nodded and padded down the dojo to return the sticks to Locker 7. Now that we were done, I was anxious to get home. I glanced at the clock on the dojo wall.

We'd been at it for five hours, and I was ravenous.

⌘ ⌘ ⌘ ⌘

CHAPTER 14

The Albuquerque FBI Division is located on Luecking Park just off Pan American Freeway, the frontage road along northbound I-25. The agency is housed in a broad, four-story building surrounded by a fence and a substantial yard.

Visitors are required to park a couple hundred yards from the doors and walk the distance. Guess it's part of the FBI's "we don't make it easy for idiots driving truck bombs to pull right up to our front door and blow us to smithereens" thing.

I arrived late morning and didn't park in the FBI's allotted parking; I left my car in the lot of a nearby restaurant and hoofed it the rest of the way.

Getting inside and past the agency's security was about as difficult for me as it was to walk into Walmart in the middle of the night. Yeah, the FBI building had guards and an ID checkpoint in their building's foyer—but that wasn't enough to deter the invisible, energetic me.

I walked in on the heels of another visitor, hopped over the short wall at the checkpoint, and waltzed up to the guard's station. Pointed at his computer terminal. Focused and entered the warehouse. From there, my little buddies and I jetted through the guard's terminal into the database.

I'm going with them? I wasn't "merely" sorting the data the nanomites provided. No, I was along for the ride. Or it felt like I was. I was physically present in the FBI lobby, so I couldn't be inside the FBI intranet, right? But in the same way the mites had taken me along when they destroyed John's tumor, they took me along now. I was with the mites, experiencing more nano-virtual reality, and it was impressive.

What a rush.

We found the personnel directory, Ross Gamble's office number, a building schematic, and their electronic security protocols. Moments later, I started toward the elevator.

Additional security measures—ID card and pin number—impeded any unauthorized access to the floor where Gamble's office was located. I gestured. The doors closed and the elevator rose.

So much for additional security.

And then that strange sense that things had shifted or changed came on me again.

Are the nanomites anticipating my requests before I ask, or am I doing this myself? But how would I be able to do what the mites do?

I found Gamble's office down a long hall of bland, vanilla, government-issue rooms. The hall had no windows. It felt closed in and oppressive. At least the building's exterior walls had windows, but I felt sorry for the folks who occupied cubicles or offices on the inside of the building.

I paused at Gamble's open door. He was on his feet, facing away, the phone to his ear. I wasn't surprised to see him pacing. He struck me as a person of action, not a bench warmer.

I walked in.

About then, his call connected. "Yes, this is Special Agent Ross Gamble, FBI. I would like to speak with General Cushing if she is available."

Whoa. Bad idea, Agent Gamble! But he was already connected with Cushing's office, so—

He had listened a second before he added, "It is regarding a woman by the name of Gemma Keyes. Yes, I'll hold."

I don't know who flipped out faster—me or the nanomites. They were chattering a blue streak, and I seriously didn't know what else to do, so I reached over and depressed the phone's receiver button.

"Hello? Hello?" Gamble swore and started dialing again.

I disconnected his call a second time. "Please don't do that."

The nanomites didn't appreciate that move, either—but it got Gamble's attention.

He froze. His hand was on the phone's buttons; the receiver was up to his ear. He was immobile, stuck in that pose—but his eyes were not. They slid around the room multiple times.

I inched away. My soft-soled shoes made the faintest shuffle on the carpet, but he heard the sound. When his wild eyes could find nothing, he dropped the phone and backed up, drawing his sidearm.

"Who's there?"

I sighed. "My name is Gemma Keyes. I know you recognize my name, Agent Gamble. Listen, I'm not going to harm you, but I must speak to you. I'm going to close the door so that our conversation isn't overheard. Is that all right?"

His eyes widened, and his hands clenched and unclenched on the butt of his sidearm. I watched to make sure that his trigger finger remained on the side of the gun, not curled around the trigger. Gamble didn't answer, but he was breathing hard and heavy about then, too.

"I'm going to close the door. I promise I am not here to harm you."

I closed the door. "Now, please listen. I'm going to sit in this chair—so please don't shoot me."

I sat. "Okay; I'm sitting down now."

Special Agent Gamble looked ready to pass out. He had pressed himself against the wall behind his desk and had nowhere else to go—but he was still trying to back up. At least his gun was only halfway up. It was, more or less, pointed at the blotter on his desk.

"Agent Gamble, I think you are kind of freaked out at the moment. Would you like me to explain who I am and how I came to be like this?"

He mumbled a couple of swear words.

"You aren't cracking up, Agent Gamble; I *am* invisible. That's why General Cushing wants me."

The poor man's hands flopped to his sides. He blinked rapidly.

Sheesh. I hope he doesn't drop his gun.

"Why don't you sit down, Agent Gamble? Before you fall down."

He did. Like his hands had flopped to his sides, he flopped into his chair. He laid his gun on the blotter. His hands were shaking.

I slid into the warehouse. *Nano. Please do that thing you do. Give Agent Gamble something to calm him.*

Seconds later, Gamble jerked. "Wha-what is that?"

"Nothing bad. Can we talk now?"

He blew out a long breath, holstered his gun as a delaying tactic. "Gemma Keyes, huh?"

"Yes. You know about the raid on my house. I was in Pastor Cruz's hospital room when you and he were talking about it."

He tipped his head to one side. "I thought . . . I thought I felt someone in the room. That was you? You heard our conversation?"

"Yeah. You are looking for Mateo Martinez. I'm interested in finding him, too."

"Wait. Before we get into that . . . just what's the deal with you?"

"It would take a while to explain—longer than we have. How about I show you some background, first?"

"Uh, if you say so."

"I'll bring up some files on your computer."

"No—it's a secure government network. I can't allow you access—"

I had already pointed to his computer, and browser windows were popping up, piling up, stacking atop each other. "I've given you some 'light reading.' Basically, I used to work for a brilliant man at Sandia. You'll read about him. Supposedly he died in an explosion in his lab last March. You'll read about that, too.

"He actually didn't die, that scientist. He escaped, took his research with him, and hid out in the tunnels in the old Manzano Mountain Weapons Storage Facility. You know anything about that facility?"

Gamble was paging through some of the screens. "Dr. Daniel Bickel? A physicist? What kind of research did he do?"

"The kind that made me invisible." I didn't want to get into the nanomite thing. The fewer specifics Agent Gamble knew, the better. "Bottom line, General Cushing wanted to steal his research. She hunted him and found him in his laboratory inside the mountain, but he, um, managed to hide his work before she captured him. Since then, she's had Dr. Bickel stashed in some military prison and has been trying to pry his knowledge from him."

"What's this got to do with Mateo Martinez?"

"Not a thing. My interest in him is personal—but I can't have you talking to Cushing about me and getting her antennae up. She's an evil woman, Agent Gamble."

"Oh, yeah?"

"Um, yeah. She's on par with Mateo Martinez's boss, Dead Eyes."

"Dead Eyes?"

"I think his real name is Soto."

Gamble sat up straighter. "What do you know about Soto?"

"I know that he's evil—he and Cushing are two peas in a pod. I've, uh, listened in on some of his meetings. Anyway, I was thinking that I might be able to help you find Martinez and Soto, and—"

The phone rang. I leaned over Gamble's desk and we both stared at the caller ID. It read "Sandia National Labs."

I sighed. "I guess that's Cushing, calling you back. She will try to suck out everything you know about me."

"I don't know anything about you. Or I didn't until just now."

"Well, now you have a choice to make, Agent Gamble. Bear in mind that my life is on the line—as are the lives of Zander Cruz, Abe Pickering, and Emilio Martinez."

Gamble's hand, now steady, picked up the call. "Special Agent Gamble."

"Please hold for General Cushing."

I pointed at the phone. The nanomites jumped into the call with him. In the warehouse, I heard everything they heard.

"Agent Gamble? This is General Imogene Cushing. I believe you called earlier? We were disconnected."

"Yes. I apologize. I was interrupted. Uh, thanks for returning my call."

"You said it regarded Gemma Keyes?"

I shook my head. If Gamble gave me up, Cushing would have the very thing I'd tried so hard to circumvent—Zander, Abe, and Emilio in her crosshairs.

If only I'd reached Gamble's office five minutes earlier! At least I'd arrived just as he placed his first call to her, early enough to warn him—which made me wonder about the timing of my visit.

Coincidence?

I shook my head.

Divine intervention?

I growled deep in my throat. I don't believe in that kind of religious drivel, remember? It was all bunkum, as far as I was concerned. Sheer nonsense.

Gamble answered Cushing, his voice sharper than it had been earlier, assuring me that he had regained his wits. "Her name came up during a non-related investigation, and I heard about the raid you conducted on Miss Keyes' house. I was interested as to what it was about. Since neither APD nor the FBI had received notice of such an action, the raid piqued my curiosity."

A good start, Agent Gamble. Put her on the defensive. Watch out, though.

I knew Cushing too well.

"Oh, is that all? It was a Homeland issue."

"Ah. I see. Still, we were surprised to hear of it. Usually we receive alerts or bulletins when Homeland initiates an action. You know. Shared intel, and all."

"May I be frank with you, Special Agent Gamble?"

Oh, here it comes, Gamble. Here it comes.

I was positively snarling at Cushing and her oily, ingratiating snake-oil approach.

"Special Agent Gamble, we believe Gemma Keyes to be a homegrown terrorist. She and another former Sandia employee were responsible for bombing a laboratory at Sandia Labs in March. An innocent man lost his life in that explosion. You may have heard about it?"

Gamble lifted his eyes in my direction. I couldn't tell what he was thinking, but I doubted it was anything good.

"I recall that explosion. The news reported that it was caused by human error."

Don't! Don't challenge her, Agent Gamble!

"Yes, we chose to disseminate that information rather than alarm the public. However, I must warn you, Special Agent Gamble: Gemma Keyes is a very dangerous individual. Apprehending her is of national concern."

Gamble's eyes narrowed. Was his baloney detector as finely tuned as I hoped it was?

"I see. Well, as I said, I was merely curious about the raid. I appreciate you filling me in."

Cushing's intuitions were sharp, too. Sharp as razor wire. "Now, Special Agent Gamble, you haven't had any contact with Miss Keyes, have you?"

Gamble gripped the phone tighter. "No. Her name came up as we investigated a gang-related crime in her neighborhood. I see no connection between the two cases."

Cushing was silent on the other end as though weighing what he'd said and the way he'd said it. At last she replied, "I would appreciate you keeping me apprised of your investigation if it at all concerns Miss Keyes, Agent Gamble."

"It would be my pleasure to assist you, General Cushing." Gamble was as smooth as silk.

I raised my brows. *Back atcha, Sharky Face.*

"And thank you again for returning my call; I hope I did not inconvenience you," he added by way of closure.

"Not at all, Agent Gamble. Goodbye."

Gamble replaced the receiver and put both hands on his desk. He was thinking. Hard.

I did not interrupt him.

"Miss Keyes?"

"Yes?"

"I'm no slouch, Miss Keyes. I know a liar when I hear one."

He waited as though I should comment.

All I said was, "Okaaay . . ."

"She's a liar."

"One of the best."

"I'll reserve judgment on that, but I agree that she's as crooked as a dog's hind leg. And she has your Dr. Bickel locked up somewhere?"

"Yes."

"Why can't I see you, Miss Keyes? What's the deal?"

I dithered a moment more before saying, "Dr. Bickel is a nanophysicist. Do you know anything about nanotechnology?"

He shrugged. "Sub-micron stuff."

"Yeah. Know anything about adaptive camouflage?"

His eyes twitched in the direction of my voice. "Some. Heard about it in the military."

"Put the two together, and that's my situation."

"What? Small stuff camouflaging you?"

"Pretty much. Several trillion of the 'small stuff.' They are called nanomites. Very sophisticated electromechanical devices with advanced, individualized computer processors, yet operating as a networked swarm and at a very high level of computer intelligence."

"Nanomites?"

Speaking of the nanomites, I had ignored their complaints for a while, but their protests had grown louder and more insistent. I needed to cut off the flow of information I was providing to Gamble before the mites blew a collective fuse.

"Listen, Agent Gamble, the fewer specifics you have, the better. It is enough for you to know that Cushing is not interested in me, *per se*. She wants the nanomites and, for the time being, the mites and I are inseparable. Of course, I know too much, so she also wants to shut me up, which, I'm afraid, would be very bad for my health."

My voice hardened. "By the way, it's been five days since you interviewed Zander Cruz, and you are just now calling Cushing? Too bad I got here two minutes too late."

He shrugged. "I've exhausted every lead in my search for Soto, so I'm back to square one. Didn't think contacting Cushing could hurt."

"Well, don't be surprised when she calls *you* back in a few days 'just to check up' on your investigation. And don't be surprised to find your every move dogged by her people. Don't be shocked to find your phones tapped, your online accounts monitored, and your superiors notified of her interest in you.

"By the way, I've had the nanomites delete their browsing history from your computer. Can't be too careful when it comes to Cushing."

I took a deep breath. "If she was willing to send a tactical team to storm my house and capture me—*me!*—a harmless woman who, if reports are to be believed, has scarcely enough backbone to stand on her own two feet, all while shredding my constitutional rights to a legal, warranted search? Oh, and without the required notice to legit law enforcement agencies? Well, she won't spare a second thought to overrunning your life and career on the off chance you will provide a lead to my capture."

"You don't strike me as the shy, retiring type your neighbors described."

I laughed low in my throat. "Adversity changes us, Agent Gamble. I've been on the run a while now. It's either adapt or languish and eventually die in Cushing's tender care. I don't choose to allow that for me or my friends—which is why I came here to warn *you* not to contact Cushing."

Gamble grunted, but the FBI guy, on the outside anyway, seemed to be listening when I added, "I cannot stress this enough: If she even *imagines* that you have spoken to me? Your life will be over. She will discredit you, destroy your reputation, perhaps make you disappear. Don't doubt me on this: From here on out, my life and the lives of Zander Cruz, Abe Pickering, and Emilio Martinez—as well as your own—hinge on whatever you choose to do with what I've told you."

I climbed out of the chair. "I'm going to search out Mateo Martinez and Dead Eyes. When I find them, I'll let you take them down. I'm going to find them for you, not because they are bad guys, but because of what they did to my friends. It's personal for me."

"It is for me, too," Gamble whispered.

I paused. Licked my lips. "Oh?"

"Her name was Graciella. She was working undercover in Mexico. Her cover was blown and Soto . . ."

I shuddered. I did not want to know what Soto had done to this poor woman any more than Gamble wanted to repeat it.

"She was special to you?"

Gamble looked away. "Yes."

"All right. So, it's personal. For both of us." I reached for the door. "I'll be in touch."

"How will I reach you?"

"You won't, and it's better if you can't. Safer that way for both of us. However, if you keep your eyes peeled, I think you'll find Cushing's sticky fingers probing every part and particle of your life before long. She's as tenacious as a rabid bulldog, so we don't want to do anything to tantalize her."

"All right. If you say so."

"Don't take my warnings lightly. Goodbye, Agent Gamble."

"Goodbye, Miss Keyes. Take care of yourself."

There it was again. The tough, no-nonsense FBI agent showing a solicitous side.

"Uh, you, too. Remember my warning: Be on your guard. Keep an eye out for Cushing. She'll be watching you."

He snorted a tiny laugh. "You're starting to sound paranoid, Miss Keyes."

"It's not paranoia if they really are watching you."

⌘⌘⌘⌘

CHAPTER 15

The three scientists assembled in the conference room squirmed under General Cushing's inspection. Agent Trujillo, standing just off Cushing's shoulder, commiserated with the three men. She'd withstood her own share of Cushing's interrogations.

Cushing opened with, "Gentlemen, you have studied and analyzed Dr. Bickel's data and you have seen the videos of his nanomite demonstrations. We now know that he somehow removed *his* nanomites from the lab and left us with dumb ones before his, um, unfortunate demise."

Agent Trujillo's ears perked up. Something in Cushing's inflection struck her as, what? Odd? Dr. Bickel's "unfortunate demise"? Why had those few words prompted alarms?

She filed her curiosity away for later study when Cushing continued.

"Getting back to Dr. Bickel's claims about his nanomites . . . I have some rather pointed questions for you. Theoretical questions, if you wish."

Dr. Thomas Schillman, the team lead and eldest of the trio, replied, "Certainly, General. We are happy to assist in any way we can."

After the ongoing debacle of the last few months when the nanomites Cushing had provided for them to study had proved to be sub-micron dumb bots incapable of learning or performing even a fraction of the tasks Bickel had claimed they could, the three scientists were eager to prove their worth to Cushing.

"Yes, I should think so." Cushing couldn't resist twisting the screws, and Schillman reddened. Then she got on with the task at hand.

"Gentlemen, Dr. Bickel asserted that his nanobots possessed certain tools, is that so?"

The three of them nodded.

"And am I correct in recalling that one such tool was a laser?"

Mishka Troya, the youngest of the three scientists, a brilliant but socially and politically immature individual, snarked, "Yes, he did claim that."

The gaze Cushing fixed on Troya shriveled the man. "You doubt Dr. Bickel's claim?"

The other two scientists edged away from their "doomed" colleague.

"Well? You were saying?"

The two older men pursed their lips and looked anywhere but at Troya as he dug himself in deeper.

"I, uh, well, it seems improbable, General, that a laser beam could be generated by a single sub-micron electromechanical device. Improbable and scientifically impossible."

"Oh, yes. I see. But what if . . . what if we considered a very large number of such devices. Say, a few trillion? Devices manufactured with the ability to 'piggyback' upon each other in order to multiply their functions, to focus their combined abilities on a single point. What then?"

The young man swallowed and glanced at his colleagues for support. They would not meet his gaze.

"I . . . I suppose *theoretically*, one might consider the possibility."

"Hmm? *Theoretically*, then, what if a swarm of nanobots with the capabilities demonstrated in Dr. Bickel's data, what if a swarm of say, *several trillion* nanobots, possessed such multiplicative abilities? Would they—*theoretically*, of course—be able to, say, invade a laptop computer and, from within, focus their lasers on its hard disk, wiping all data from it and melting it, thus leaving no mark upon the exterior of the laptop?"

The young man flushed and stared at Cushing. "Ma'am, if we are going to speak in *theories*, and not *facts*, then yes. Such a thing would be possible. Theoretically, a large enough population of these devices, given the abilities you allowed them, could render a laser beam of that strength."

"Why, thank you for playing along, Dr. . . . Troya, is it?"

"Yes."

Troya, too immature to keep his resentment concealed, flushed.

Cushing's lips curved upward and exposed her gleaming teeth. She did not try to mask her enjoyment of his discomfiture.

"And Dr. Troya, still *theoretically* speaking, of course, how might a nanobot swarm of this magnitude manage to disguise something . . . some sort of object? How might a swarm of this size *hide* an object?"

Troya was surprised out of his annoyance. "Hide something? Interesting concept . . ."

He drifted off in his thoughts for a moment and Cushing tapped a fingernail on the table to bring him back. "Dr. Troya?"

"Well, I . . . I was recalling other tools Dr. Bickel described in one video recording of his presentations. I believe he spoke of 'fully articulating mirrors used to capture solar energy.'" He turned to his colleagues, who were now showing some interest. "Do you recall him listing mirrors in the tool sets?"

"Yes, uh, I do," Schillman agreed. "He claimed that each nanomite was equipped with a slice of polished silicon that unfolded into nine panels."

Dr. Yazzie asked, "What are you thinking, Dr. Troya?"

"That the panels might have uses other than as solar receptors. They might be used to reflect also."

"Ah! I see where you're going. Adaptive camouflage?"

The three men nodded in unison and Troya added, "Exactly. Optical invisibility. When—"

"Gentlemen! *Gentlemen.* You have, I believe, something to share with me?"

Dr. Schillman coughed and replied, "Only that such panels, when they are designed to articulate independently—that is, to turn, rotate, and tilt in every direction—such panels are capable of bending light. With a large enough array of said panels acting as mirrors, one could camouflage an object by reflecting the environment around said object. The technology, albeit crude, does exist."

"Crude how? In what ways?"

"Crude in that, firstly, the number of mirrors required to overcome the perception of the human eye would need to be astronomical and, secondly, the actual coordination of all the mirrors to maintain the camouflage in a changing environment would be impossible in practical terms.

"However—and again, *theoretically*—if the mirrors were synchronized via dedicated computing power of considerable force, it would be possible. The rub would be that such computations would need to, on an ongoing basis, predict and calculate the movements of the object and compensate for those movements in near real time. Quite beyond today's existing technologies."

Cushing's voice hardened. "Unless we are speaking of several trillion nanomites, each with their own individually articulating mirrors via networked and coordinated computing power?"

Dr. Schillman's mouth dropped open. "Well, then, that . . . that might be plausible."

Cushing said nothing for a long, charged moment. She was deep in her own musings when she whispered, "Yes, I believe it just might be."

***

I left the FBI building and returned to my car at the nearby restaurant. As I drove home, I wondered how Gamble would handle what I'd told him.

Gemma Keyes.

Uh-oh. Aaaand here it comes.

"Yes?"

Did you apply due consideration prior to revealing knowledge of us to Special Agent Gamble?

Huh. This was different. They weren't chiding me. Well, not exactly.

"Frankly, Nano, I acted in the best interests of us under the pressure and time constraints of the circumstances. In hindsight, I'm not sure I could have handled the situation any differently. I could not allow Agent Gamble to speak to Cushing without him being forewarned."

We have analyzed the data and parameters and agree that your actions were best suited given the constraints.

A feather. A tiny, flimsy feather could have knocked me over.

"You do? I mean, you agree with my actions?"

We are learning much about human beings through observation and even more through our union with you. It is true that, when faced with the unknown and unfamiliar, people can behave in unpredictable ways. Our common enemy, General Cushing, could have turned Special Agent Gamble to her purposes without him realizing it.

We believe you responded suitably to the immediate threat, and you may have forged an ally in Special Agent Gamble. However, the level of probability that our existence will leak into the public domain increases exponentially with each revelation. We urge you to use caution.

"Er, thank you. I appreciate your warning."

More than the warning, I appreciated their approval.

***

We were home, and I was ready to focus on my new goal: Locate Mateo Martinez and Arnaldo Soto—and assist Agent Gamble in serving up their just desserts. But I wasn't going to risk getting off on the wrong foot with the nanomites again.

So. How to approach them . . .

"Um, Nano."

Yes, Gemma Keyes?

"Nano, two evil men have done grave harm to our friends. I need your help to find these men."

The silence lasted seconds—before their collective questions inundated me.

We require more information. Which friends? In what way are they our friends? Describe and quantify "grave harm." Which two men? Quantify "evil." In what way does finding these two men further the good of our community?

Wow.

"Um, that's a lot to answer. Let me think on it a sec."

Good grief.

I didn't want to manipulate the nanomites into working with me by using false or misleading arguments—because *that* could never backfire, right?—but would a simplistic explanation of human friendships and their importance satisfy them?

Yes, I thought that the mites were making progress in the area of interpersonal relationships. Just an hour ago, they had spoken of learning more about human beings, of recognizing their unpredictability. On top of that, they had used the phrase, "our common enemy," with regards to Cushing.

Still, I chose my words with care. "So, Nano? I have a question. Remember how I told you earlier that I have affection for Dr. Bickel? Uh, do you have affection for him?"

Faint chittering answered me and then, *We do not experience affection.*

"Okay, then why do you want to find him?"

Silence.

Uh-oh. Had I stumped them?

The first time I'd seen the nanomites, Dr. Bickel had them "confined" to a glass case—a glass case from which they could have escaped at any time. I had wondered how the nanomites liked being kept in a glass box. Eventually, Dr. Bickel and I discussed that very thing:

"You question why they haven't freed themselves, don't you?" he'd *whispered.*

"Yes."

"And I'm not entirely sure I can answer your question, Gemma, except to say that they haven't wanted to."

The word to complete his sentence had popped into my head. Yet. They haven't wanted to free themselves *yet.*

What if, upon reflection, the mites determined that they *had* no rational need to find Dr. Bickel? Would they give up their search for him? The silence dragged on, and I faced the ugly possibility that I may have put my foot in it.

Up to my kneecaps.

Gemma Keyes, we are six. Dr. Bickel is not one of us.

Oh, crud!

Double-stuff crud.

Crud, crud, crud.

However, we have determined that his tribe is akin to ours. We share experiences and goals and have built what human beings call trust. Dr. Bickel does what furthers our good.

Relief flooded my body.

"Yes. That's what friends do! You might even say that friends are akin to, er, external tribal *alliances*. Friends are trustworthy and loyal to us—and we are loyal in return. Like I am loyal to my friends, Zander, Abe, and Emilio. My friends and I have similar, shared experiences, and they are, er, akin to me. They want only my good."

My brain was twisting into a big ol' kink.

We are six. Your good is our good.

Elation? The mites may as well have said, "Your friends are our friends."

I exhaled. "Well, these two bad men, the two enemies I spoke of? They hurt my friends. They damaged my friends' bodies and caused grave physical pain and disability. You saw their injuries and helped to repair the damage. What those two enemies did was not good!

"Furthermore, it hurts . . . it hurts my heart and upsets my emotions to see my friends in pain. I'm not effective when my emotions are distressed. If we find these evil men, the legal authorities will put them where they can't hurt my friends or anyone else. Then I will be more effective."

Any more double speak, and I was gonna fry a fuse.

The mites were silent a minute or so.

Gemma Keyes, we will help you find the evil men.

I sighed. "Thank you."

Gemma Keyes, what is the criteria for identifying and evaluating evil? Is evil quantifiable? Is all evil equal?

And then: *Are all human beings evil?*

Ohhhhh, snap.

"Uh . . . all very intriguing questions, Nano, but I'm not sure we have time for that conversation right now or that I'm the right person to provide the answers. Could we, um, table those topics until later?"

Yes, Gemma Keyes.

I sighed and rubbed my aching temples.

***

Later that evening, I drove to Emilio's foster home and scoped it out. I had promised to visit him regularly—and I needed to get out of the house anyway. Why? Because things weren't going well.

Following my dicey theological conversation with the nanomites earlier, I had provided them with the little I knew about Mateo Martinez and Arnaldo Soto. I discovered that it was far different trying to feed *them* data from my finite knowledge banks than it was for them to send information to me from their own vast stores—or for me to step into a river of data they had mined on the Internet.

I managed to convey the gangsters' names, the location of Mateo's house, and his relationship to Emilio. I reminded them of the drug house and Mateo's role in the gang. Other than those details, what more did I know about Mateo?

And Soto? I knew nothing of him except the deadness of his eyes.

The mites had come back to me later with nothing to show for their efforts.

A big, fat nothing.

Hence, I had to get out of the house and clear my head.

I climbed over the foster family's fence and walked around their back yard. The yard seemed okay; it looked clean and well-tended. A swing set and a jungle gym took up most of the grass but, somehow, I couldn't visualize Emilio playing with other children, climbing on children's toys. I could only see him sitting on a curb or a step, apart from other kids.

That bothered me. A lot.

The only lights in the house came from what I assumed was the living room. Low murmurs coming from a TV were all I heard.

The rear door opened to the kitchen. As I thought, the kitchen was dark. A stream of light from the living room helped me navigate the unfamiliar and empty room as I closed the back door.

Ooops. Not quite empty. A tiny dog, some kind of Chihuahua mix, left his rug and padded toward me, sniffing and growling in my general direction. The dog sensed me, probably heard me, but was unable to see me—and that made him nervous. He backed away, his hackles up, that growl threatening to erupt into more at any moment.

Nanomites shot from my hands onto the dog. The pooch ran for his bed, laid down, and put his head on his paws. His bulgy eyes blinked as I walked past him, but he did not move.

I went down a hall and found a couple of closed doors. When I put my hand on one door, the mites flooded through it and came back.

Gemma Keyes. Emilio is not in this room.

I moved on to the next door. Same drill.

Gemma Keyes, Emilio and another boy are in this room.

"Are they sleeping?"

Yes, Gemma Keyes.

"Please keep the other boy asleep?"

I cracked the door and slipped inside, closing the door behind me. When my eyes adapted to the dark, I spied two twin beds on opposite walls, a smallish mound and a head upon a pillow in each. I lifted my hand and shined a low light on the first pillow.

The child was younger than Emilio, maybe around five, but what do I know? The kiddo was sawing logs and would not wake up when I roused Emilio.

I sat on the edge of the other bed and jostled the curled figure. "Emilio. Wake up, buddy."

He turned over and stared, then sat up, felt around until he found my hand. "Hey, Gemma!"

"Shhhh. Not so loud!" but I chuckled as I whispered.

"They don't hear much out there," Emilio assured me, jerking his chin in the direction of the living room. "Sean and I talk all the time." As he said "Sean," he glanced over at his roommate.

"Sean won't wake up. The mites will keep him asleep."

"Really? That's so cool!" Emilio chortled.

I laughed with him, keeping my voice low. "So, I said I would come visit. How are you doing?"

"Okay, I guess."

"Are your foster parents treating you well?"

"Yeah. They're all right." He shrugged. "What about Mr. Abe and Zander?"

"They are doing lots better, Emilio. Lots better. Zander will be going home soon, and Abe will move to a regular wing in a day or two."

"I'm sure glad."

He didn't say anything else, just climbed out from under his covers and into my lap—as if he'd been doing so for years. I had thought that a great big boy such as himself, a ten-year-old, would think himself too old for such nonsense, but Emilio curled himself up in the circle of my arms, tucked his feet under him, and snugged his head just below my chin. His cheek warmed my collarbone, and his stubbly hair scratched my neck; the flannel of his pajamas was soft under my arms and hands.

My arms and hands? All by themselves, they wrapped themselves around Emilio and pulled him close to my chest. My fingers stroked his back.

I don't ever want to lose this boy.

The notion of anything bad happening to Emilio caught in my throat. Made me crazy anxious.

⌘⌘⌘⌘

PART 2:
STEALTH POWER

CHAPTER 16

At 10 that night, I drove to the dojo. I brought along five twenty-dollar bills in an envelope. I'd looked up Sandia Martial Arts Academy's rates and kind of estimated what my use of their facility should cost me—"kind of," because they hadn't listed a five-hour, seven-nights-a-week rate on their website.

I shrugged, left the sealed envelope in the office with the words "SMAA Owner" on it. I hoped the money was enough for a week's use.

I was anxious to get back to training. Since my first session, less than twenty-four hours ago, I'd rehearsed all that Gus-Gus had taught me, mentally running the steps and drills over and over. I'd been stiff and sore when I got out of bed this morning—but nothing like I should have been. The absence of pain—the fact that I *should* have been nearly crippled from yesterday's workout—was further proof that the nanomites were effecting change in my body on an ongoing basis.

Yes, they'd sped up my metabolism. Yes, they'd super-charged my mental acuity. And yes, they had to have invaded my overused muscles during the night and healed them. I'd done my own research on muscle soreness and found that exercise strains and tears muscle tissue, which causes muscles tenderness and pain, but it is the same strain that also stimulates muscle growth and strength. I felt strong today, but not terribly sore, *ergo*, the nanomites and whatever they'd done.

But that wasn't all. Everything I'd learned yesterday? Gus-Gus had to have bundled six lessons into one, after which he'd pushed me to a semi-proficient level in those skills. Not exactly beginner fare! Not only was I mentally retaining those lessons, I was physically learning, too. And I had no idea how that was possible.

Like I said, I'd never been coordinated. Jogging and hiking had been my cup of tea, not team or competitive sports.

"Muscle memory"? In my limited experience, it was a fake term.

I knew differently now.

Oh, by the way, if I thought the merge had given me too much vigor, I no longer felt that way. I was eager to fetch the padded training sticks from Locker 7. When I took my place on the floor and closed my eyes, Gus-Gus appeared immediately. I was even happy to see him.

As he had yesterday, he demonstrated new foot drills that ran me sideways down one side of the dojo and back again. He paired the footwork with the four-count double arm weave—forward and then reversed.

Up and down the floor I danced, swinging the sticks while crossing and uncrossing my arms, getting the rhythm as I blended steps and stick moves together. Faster and faster as Gus-Gus urged me, but maintaining the precision he counted or clapped out.

He had me repeat the same drill, incorporating a slashing diagonal "X" in place of a simple weave, after which he added a fifth count—forward strikes on counts four and five.

Rinse and repeat the double stick weave with "box" footwork. I danced back, to the right, forward, to the left. Again. Over and over. Then I did the same in reverse until I could do either box as Gus-Gas called it.

He ran me through drill after drill, slowly to get every aspect right, then faster to build fluid motion, cadence, and precision to the strikes. When we broke to begin sparring, I was warm and energized; my arms and wrists were loose, ready for more.

"Retrieve two rattan sticks from Locker 7, Gemma Keyes," Gus-Gus commanded.

I returned the padded sticks to the locker and took down two wooden sticks. They were lightweight; I liked how they felt in my hands.

Again, Gus-Gus had me work with the dummy. He demonstrated and named various strikes, explaining what each would produce in my opponent. I practiced advances, feints, and strikes for an hour, Gus-Gus teaching me how to add force to a strike.

"Not everything I show you will be strictly Kali," he said as we prepared to spar with each other, "nor will I, in the time in which I will train you, emphasize the norms or ceremonial aspects of sparring. You must learn to fight, Gemma Keyes; you must learn to disarm and defeat an adversary. That is our goal."

I shivered.

Gus-Gus bowed. I bowed in return.

Can I just say that it's one thing to hit a dummy that won't hit you back?

First, Gus-Gus and I practiced specific drills, our steps mirroring each other, sticks clacking together in perfect syncopation. I knew what to do next, because Gus-Gus set up the drill by calling the steps. We flew through those.

But then he introduced real sparring—the kind that isn't coordinated. The kind that hurts when you screw up. Sure, he was only doing the beginner stuff, but *dang!*

"Ow!"

Time out! This was virtual reality. All in my head. It wasn't supposed to *hurt*. How in the world—

Gemma Keyes. It is important to maximize the realism of your training. To do so, we have sent part of us out in front of you. We will mirror the moves of your instructor. We will impact your body to simulate the effect of a strike.

"Yeah? Well, those won't be 'simulated' bruises tomorrow; they'll be real enough!" I rubbed my thigh where Gus-Gus had landed a blow.

You will suffer little or no bruising, Gemma Keyes. We will mitigate bleeding in the tissue and muscle and make repairs as needed.

Great.

Wonderful.

Hurt me. Fix me.

"Sadists," I growled. "Bring it on."

I turned to Gus-Gus and delivered a powerful slash to his arm. He charged toward me, sticks whirling, pounding me right back.

"Ow! *Ow, ow, ow, ow!*"

***

After my long workout, I returned home and ate like there was no tomorrow. All that exercise? I was a black hole, sucking in anything edible within reach. While I devoured a plate of scrambled eggs, toast, and fried potatoes, I made a shopping list, doubling what I usually bought for a week.

I spread a thick swath of jam over my fourth slice of toast and grinned. I was new to the endorphin rush and afterglow of a good workout. Yeah, I might complain about the rigors of the training, but the truth was that I found myself liking it. Maybe it was more than a "like." Maybe I was loving it?

On the flip side, regardless of what the nanomites suggested, I put little stock in all this work as far as Dr. Bickel was concerned. The odds of getting Dr. Bickel out of wherever Cushing had him were too long, and they were stacked against me.

How in the world would *I* be able to break someone from a guarded military installation and get away with it? I was, after all, only one person, and an inexperienced person at that. In my mind, I was just a young woman playing with sticks. I wasn't some military operative or superhero.

I finished my late-night meal and dropped into bed, more than ready for sleep. In what seemed like an instant, I was out.

***

Considering all the stress I'd been under for weeks, going on months, is it any surprise that bad dreams often troubled my sleep? That night I had a doozy of a nightmare.

In the dream, I was on my laptop, just doing some "stuff," when black-garbed storm troopers burst through the doors of Dr. Bickel's safe house. I had no warning—even the nanomites had not sensed their approach. One moment all was fine; the next moment the doors splintered, and Cushing's armed SWAT team rushed into the house. I had no opportunity to flee, no way to escape. I ran toward the bedrooms, but they afforded no way out.

I was trapped!

The soldiers deployed a mesh net. It fell over me, and I tripped, fell. The nanomites lasered through the net in a few places, but the soldiers flung a second net over the first, and I could not rise under the combined weight of the two nets.

Cushing had me. She had me and she had the nanomites. She had my phones, the laptop, and my new ID. She would have my friends and—

Emilio!

I fought my sheets and blankets, ripped them from me, and scrambled from my bed. The nightmare was fresh and real; my entire body shook with horror.

The clock next to my bed read 3:43 a.m.

My heart thundered and would not slow. No more sleep for me this night.

Gemma Keyes. We observed rapid eye movement and brain wave spikes during your sleep. These markers indicate dream state. Your respiration and heart rate are much higher than normal, and you have awakened in an agitated condition.

Did you have a bad dream?

"Yes, Nano."

Thank you for noticing.

I padded to the bathroom and splashed cold water on my face, then to the kitchen where I hit the "start" button on the coffee pot. While I waited for the coffee, I switched on the small lamp in the living room. Its low light comforted me . . . because the nightmare played on a continuous loop in my head.

What if Cushing did find this house? What if her jackboots stormed this place, my sanctuary? Even if, by some miracle, I managed to elude capture, where would I go? Would I lose my tenuous hold on the "real" world and be obliged to start over with another identity?

More importantly, if Cushing raided this place, what, exactly, would she find here?

My eyes cut toward the kitchen. The cash I depended upon was stashed in the wall behind the stove. I'd hidden a single stack in the cinder block wall out along the alley and put a few bundles in a coffee can that I'd buried in Mateo's back yard. But if Cushing found this place, I would lose most of my money.

I shuddered, the nightmare too real and terrifying. Was the dream a product of my subconscious mind? Had it alerted me to my vulnerable state? Because I *was* vulnerable, and I realized just how much. Now.

I paced through the shadows of the living room and, putting myself in Cushing's shoes, studied the detritus around me from her perspective: What physical and virtual fingerprints would she find here if she stormed this house? I listed them off: My new laptop and its browsing history; the two phones; driver's license, credit card, ATM card, various bits of paperwork including a box of bank checks.

As much as these items were the trappings by which I navigated the real world, they were also my Achilles heel.

"This place is a deathtrap."

I didn't like that idea one bit. I needed to get two steps ahead of Cushing. Three or four, if I could visualize and plan for it.

"Nano."

Yes, Gemma Keyes?

I slipped into the warehouse and queried the nanomites. "What strategies can you recommend to help me stay ahead of Cushing? Please explore other avenues, alternatives. Escape plans."

A diagram, a schematic appeared in my hands.

"What is this?" The diagram was a house plan, and it looked familiar. It seemed to be an ordinary, run-of-the-mill three-bedroom, one-bath, ranch-style house.

Just like this one.

"Wait. Is this Dr. Bickel's house? This house?"

Yes, Gemma Keyes. Please notice the addition to the original floorplan.

As I perused the floorplan, I realized they had said, 'please.'

The mites were picking up on social niceties? Interesting.

Interesting? So was the blueprint in my hand—and the extra room that appeared off to the side of the main floor. A note indicated that the added room was below ground—a room I knew nothing about. A few glances were sufficient for me to memorize the blueprint's details.

A hidden room? Like a "bolt-hole"?

"Where . . . how do I get into this place, Nano?"

The mites directed me into the smallest of the bedrooms, into its empty closet. One end of the closet had shelves built across it.

Look for a button under the bottom shelf, Gemma Keyes. Press the button and push the shelves up.

I fumbled for and found a button the size of a nickel under the bottom shelf. I pressed it, held it, and pushed up on the shelves. They collapsed. The individual shelves and a section of the floor lifted and folded back on unseen hinges; the entire shelving structure flattened itself against the end of the closet and revealed a dark, square hole in the floor.

Dr. Bickel had left this room unfurnished and unused—and I had paid it no mind at all.

A glow emanated from my hands—the nanomites providing enough light for me to see a ladder leading down into the dark.

The beckoning hole couldn't begin to compete with my maiden journey into the tunnels; this hole wasn't anywhere close to being as scary as the black, squeezy voids I'd crammed myself into, the narrow cavities and cracks I'd followed that grew narrower and sank deeper into the mountain long before they got wider.

I sat on the edge and swung my feet onto the ladder—

Gemma Keyes.

"What, Nano?"

You must disarm the intruder defense mechanisms first.

"Nice, Nano. Thanks for the heads-up."

Yeah, nice of you to warn me. Have you learned to recognize scathing sarcasm yet?

I pulled my feet out of the hole. "How do I disarm the, um, intruder defense mechanisms?"

Feel for a switch under the lip of the entrance.

Not much to go on, but I got on my knees and felt around the underside of the hole's edge. Found the switch. Flipped it.

"Okay. Did that."

You may proceed, Gemma Keyes.

"Yeah, and *you* may—"

I swung my legs over the edge and started down the ladder, counting rungs as I went. When I got to ten, my feet hit a floor.

The nanomites were still providing light, so I scanned around and found a light switch. I flipped it up. A soft light filled the room. The nanomites discontinued their illumination while I took stock.

"Stock" is the right descriptor. Remember me bemoaning the fact that Dr. Bickel had left no food in the kitchen or TP in the bathroom? Not a problem here. The room was stocked, all right. Floor-to-ceiling shelves lined two walls of the room. The shelves were burgeoning with canned and dried foodstuffs.

I cast my eyes over the shelves, counting and calculating the amounts in a glance: Enough food to keep a family of six for that many months—or one man for three years. The bottom shelf along both walls held nothing but five-gallon bottles of water stacked two deep.

The room also contained a cot, sleeping bag, and a pillow swathed in plastic, a toilet, a tiny kitchenette—and, in the last corner, what looked like a communications hub complete with top-of-the-line workstation and a semicircle of wide-screen monitors.

The computer's green light glowed, so I touched the mouse. The monitors, four of them, woke up and sprang into focus. I stared at four approaches to the safe house. While I watched, dumbfounded, the views on each monitor began to cycle, changing to a different camera every five seconds.

Another monitor, off to the side, showed a timeline with alarm icons. I clicked on one of the icons. A video of the back door popped up. The door opened and closed. It was me, entering the house!

I blinked. "A security system. A freaking, state-of-the-art security system."

He had never intended to live *in* the safe house. Turning in a circle, I started to catalogue the preparations Dr. Bickel had made to hole up in this secret room and monitor the house above him.

"Except . . . he would never have allowed himself to be trapped down here. I know him better than that. So, how did he plan to escape from down here if the house were breached and his hiding place discovered?"

If Dr. Bickel was smart enough to build this hidden room, he also wouldn't paint himself into a corner, of that I was certain.

The mites popped another diagram into my head. This blueprint laid out the hidden room in detail—and indicated something behind the tiny kitchenette. I memorized the details, opened my eyes, and took four steps to the other side of the room.

I studied the little sink, a short counter top holding an itsy-bitsy microwave and toaster oven, cupboards above, and a narrow, half-height refrigerator under the counter. Every piece was cute but efficient. All were mounted on a four-foot-long Formica wall.

I grasped the edge of the Formica and pulled. In its entirety, the kitchenette swung out from the wall and exposed a steel hatch. The hatch was about three feet in diameter and recessed into the concrete wall behind the kitchenette.

The hatch had a wheel on its face. I spun the wheel, and the hatch swung open, revealing a concrete pipe, like a water main. The inside face of the hatch had a manual locking mechanism.

I swung the lock's handle over and thick bolts emerged from the hatch's edges. I examined the pipe and saw that when the hatch was closed, those bolts would shoot into holes bored in the pipe's walls in three places.

Once inside the pipe, Dr. Bickel would close and lock the hatch behind him. It would take explosives to break through that locked hatch—enough explosive to bring down the house above.

I didn't know where the pipe led, but I would bet the bank on two things: that the pipe led to an above-ground hatch somewhere nearby and that the nanomites had a diagram showing me exactly where that hatch was located.

All these preparations had been made months before. No, it had to be longer. A year?

I shut my eyes and entered the warehouse. "Dr. Bickel built a secret room under this house? And he added this handy-dandy escape tunnel?"

The mites said nothing, so I answered my own question: "Well, of course he did!"

But I was livid.

I was furious!

I'd trusted myself to the nanomites only to discover that they had withheld important—no, vital—information from me.

Again!

And maybe, just maybe, they sensed how angry, *how very angry* I was, for they had gone quiet. Much too quiet.

"Nano! You knew about this hiding place all along? You knew about the escape route? You knew and you didn't think to tell me? Didn't think I needed to know? Do you know how vulnerable I am? Do you realize what could have happened? What about all that '*We are six*' crap?"

I was so furious that I couldn't talk to them anymore. I punched out of the warehouse and stormed up the ladder and out of the closet. I could feel the mites reaching out to me, but I was in no fit state to respond, so I ignored them. Shut them out.

It was still the middle of the night, but I was wide awake, wired, and fuming. I poured a cup of coffee and sat down in the living room, rejecting the mites' every overture.

I spoke aloud to myself. "All right. I need plans and alternatives, because it's only a matter of time before Cushing finds this place. I need contingencies! I need to think ahead. I need to be smarter than Shark Face!" I was berating myself, beating myself up, but it was all true: I did need to be smarter than Cushing.

Gemm—

"Shut up."

I was busy planning my move downstairs. I would take with me everything and anything that could compromise Kathy Sawyer.

Gemma Keyes—

"I said, SHUT UP!"

They did shut up—for a few minutes. Then they tried to tug me into the warehouse, but I refused to go. Perhaps they were working on the question I'd put to them when I first woke up, the question that started all of this: "Nano, what can you recommend to help me plan ahead of Cushing?" and working on my request of, "Please explore other avenues, alternatives. Escape plans."

I. Did. Not. Care.

Since I refused to go into the warehouse to look at what they proposed, they put the data in front of my face. My laptop lit up and browser windows began popping up, scads of them. I caught the phrase "Defense in Depth" as window overlaid window.

"Defense in depth?" I toggled through the windows until I found the heading again. I started reading. " . . . it is more difficult for an enemy to defeat a complex and multilayered defense system than to penetrate a single barrier."

"Right." That made sense. I started my own search using that phrase. Most of the articles were written from a cyber security perspective, but I began finding the same phrase as it applied to physical security. Some called it "the onion approach"—protecting the heart of an onion with multiple layers of delaying and deterring tactics wrapped about the heart.

"Dr. Bickel kind of used these principles when he booby-trapped the main route into his lab under the mountain. And he prepared this secret safe house, but he also built the hidden room downstairs where he could monitor the house's exterior—*and* he made an escape tunnel if both of those failed. He built contingencies into his safe house."

I had, intuitively, prepared to leave my house in the cul-de-sac, prepping bug-out bags and hiding cash in several places, but those were all escape plans. "Defense in depth" implied more. It also meant *delay* and/or *deter*.

"Plans inside of plans, plans for emergencies and unforeseen events, plans to impede and/or repulse an enemy. I need to take this principle and build on it. I'll get to "delay and deter," but my first step—now that I have a means of escaping should Cushing come calling—is to move myself to a deeper position. Out of the first layer of the onion and into the second layer."

I devoted an hour to moving stuff into the downstairs bolt-hole, including the cash I'd stacked in the wall behind the stove. Then I inspected the first floor, room by room, to ensure that I'd removed every vestige of Kathy Sawyer's presence and consolidated it into one place in the basement. I didn't care if Cushing saw that someone had been living in the house; I didn't care if she knew it was me. I only cared that Kathy Sawyer's identity was protected.

I prepped a new bug-out bag—a single backpack. Into that backpack went stacks of cash and the things that could identify me as Kathy. If I had to leave in a hurry, only that backpack would go with me. Everything else was expendable.

I spent a few hours learning, then mastering, the basement security system. I set up audible alarms should the safe house perimeter be breached while I slept.

Turns out Dr. Bickel had left a small tablet computer, too. He'd left the electronic device connected to the security system's tower. When I swiped across the tablet's face, a matrix of four views appeared on its screen—not the exterior views of the safe house that were rotating on the security system's monitors, but images from hidden cameras positioned *inside* the house.

You are as clever as you had always bragged that you were, Dr. Bickel.

I touched an icon at the bottom of the tablet screen. The four interior views toggled to a complex control panel—a dashboard integrated with the security system.

"If Cushing breached the house, Dr. Bickel could watch and listen on this tablet. He would know if it were time to leave through the hatch."

Something in the tablet's dashboard caught my eye. "Hmm. What are these?"

I toggled every button on the dashboard and read a bunch of pop-up notations before it hit me: I was looking at the "deter" portion of Dr. Bickel's defense-in-depth strategy, his intruder defense mechanisms. If Cushing's agents entered the house, Dr. Bickel had a few surprises in store for them!

I grinned as I studied the configuration of all the deterrents and their timers. I went through them twice and committed them to memory.

"I'm going to assume that if Dr. Bickel had to leave through this passage, he also intended to take the tablet with him and trigger the surprises behind him."

I grinned wider.

***

I attended my training as scheduled that night, but my attitude stank. I was taciturn and aloof toward the mites. I couldn't get past my anger, couldn't forgive them for withholding information that could mean the difference between freedom or capture, life or death.

I dogged my way through Gus-Gus' regimen, ate, and crashed. My sleep was better that night, tucked up as I was into the cot down in the basement bolt-hole. I felt confident about my preparations, too, confident that I could escape an attack from Cushing unscathed, Kathy Sawyer's identity intact.

My next task was to answer the question, "Where do I go if I have to flee this place?"

I had a few ideas, but I also had a task for the nanomites—when and if I could get past my disgust to ask them. I wanted the mites to hack in and haunt Cushing's office, wanted them to devise an electronic means of monitoring her phone calls and emails, doing the same with her team.

I needed advance warning should Cushing's forensic accountants sniff out the purchase and maintenance of this house. Dr. Bickel had been adamant, insisting that he had so distanced himself from the company that owned this house that his connection would never be found out.

But I knew better than to trust in the word, "never."

⌘ ⌘ ⌘ ⌘

CHAPTER 17

With my initial "defense in depth" plans in place and functioning, I set off for the hospital to visit Abe and Zander again. I drove and parked the Escape a block from the hospital—and this time I walked into the complex confident of my surroundings and my ability to do what I needed to do.

However, when I arrived at Zander's room, he was gone. Without my asking them, the nanomites hacked the hospital's directory and reported that Zander had been discharged. Next, I checked on Abe. He had been moved to the same wing and floor where Zander had been.

"What about John Galvez, Nano?"

John's medical records appeared before me. He, like Zander, had been discharged, but John had been sent to a rehabilitation facility where he was undergoing physical therapy to treat minor motor skill deficiencies.

The leftover effects of the tumor, I thought. I shook my head, glad that the mites had saved this man's life—had saved his son from growing up without a father.

I felt good about that—despite my recent antipathy toward the mites.

I went in search of Abe's room. His bed was the second of two in the room; his was closer to the window. A curtain separated the two patients. I paused at the first bed to give his roommate a nap so that Abe and I could talk.

When I rounded the curtain, I found Abe sitting up! He had a newspaper on the rolling table across his bed and was working the crossword puzzle.

The terrible skin tones that had terrified me were completely gone, replaced by Abe's healthy, warm hues. Although Abe normally wore his hair short, the hospital had shaved around the gash in his head that had caused so much damage. I was glad to see that the wound looked less intimidating, not as horrifying as it had seemed the last time I'd seen it.

Abe hummed a snatch of an old hymn, and I sighed with relief. He was going to be all right.

I was grinning like mad when he glanced up, stole a glance in his roommate's direction, and whispered, "Gemma? That you?"

"Hi, Abe. Don't worry about Mr. Newcomb. We gave him a much-needed nap."

Abe guffawed at that. "Mighty convenient! Well, I thought I sensed someone. You sure can steal up on me, though."

"Yeah, I'm getting better at the sneaky part, I think."

Yes, I was. I moved without fear now, going wherever I liked with impunity, operating in my invisible state as though I'd always been concealed.

I was comfortable in my skin, perhaps starting to like it . . . and starting to like other changes . . . such as sleeping less each night because I didn't need an entire night of rest. Like the hours I spent training. When I wasn't working with Gus-Gus, I read voraciously, and whatever I read I retained. And the videos I watched online? I was training myself in other areas, learning new skills that might, someday, save my life.

That awareness of . . . *power* and the mindfulness that the merge was still changing me, continued to build within me. Even now, while I was trying to move beyond my anger at the nanomites, I sensed that we were growing *together*. Our "bond" was tightening.

But I was uncertain of what exactly comprised the "together" part. You see, I couldn't decide if the nanomites had given Abe's roommate a nap— or if I had. The line between the mites and me was blurring. Either the mites intuited my commands at virtually the moment I thought them, or I was, somehow, tapping into the mites' abilities and appropriating them for my own use.

Regardless? The merge and its effects were ongoing, and I could not predict where they would lead.

***

After leaving the hospital, I set out for Zander's house. I hadn't been there before and found that his place was a simple duplex north of I-40 and Rio Grande Avenue. I parked down the street and walked the rest of the way. Two cars were in the driveway.

Oh, yeah. Izzie!

I was glad Zander's sister was staying with him, glad I'd see her today, even if she wouldn't see me. I had to laugh, though. Not for a second did I think that Izzie "helping" Zander would be easy on Zander—but it might be entertaining. I snickered as I swung up the driveway and around to the back door where I let myself in to what turned out to be a laundry room. It led into the kitchen, where Izzie was laying out lunch things.

The first words I heard, from beyond the kitchen, were, "Iz! For heaven's sake! I can make my own sandwich!"

"With one hand? I doubt it. Anyway, I want to make it for you."

I slipped through the kitchen, sidled up to the easy chair where Zander sat, and placed a hand on his shoulder. He jumped at my touch, but settled almost as quickly.

I leaned over and whispered, "Izzie. Gotta love her, right?"

He blew out an exasperated breath. "She's gonna kill me!"

I sat on the wide arm and put my mouth near his ear. "Care to share?"

I had good intentions, but the snigger at the end blew the whole thing.

"You're a snot, Gemma! All I asked for was a simple grilled cheese sandwich! *Grilled cheese*! Butter, bread, cheese, grill it, right? What does she bring me? A slice of cheese between two pieces of *toast*—heated up in the microwave! Blasphemy."

I shook my head in total agreement. "Ugh! Nasty."

Zander huffed. "I have to get her out of here. She's making me crazy."

"Well, yeah. We can't talk if she's here, right?"

His bellow could have raised the dead. "Iz! Izzie! I need a burger! Could you run get me a burger instead of making sandwiches? I'll pay! A green chile cheese burger would hit the spot."

My mouth salivated. *It sure would!*

Izzie bounced into the room and grabbed the twenty Zander held out to her. "Sure thing, bro!" She paused and cleared her throat. "Uh, I, um, I was making you a grilled cheese sandwich—the right way, the way you told me to—and I *might* have burned the butter in the frying pan."

As Zander's and my noses twitched and our heads turned—simultaneously—toward the kitchen, Izzie bolted from the house.

Gemma Keyes, something is burning.

"I think it's under control, Nano, but I'll check."

I hopped off the arm of Zander's chair and went into the kitchen. What a mess. Izzie's forte was not in the culinary arts by any stretch of the imagination—in fact, I would dare to say that any cooking genes of which the Cruz family may have boasted had taken one look at Izzie and run the other way.

I made sure the burners were off and put the offending skillet in the sink.

"Gemma? Where'd you go?"

I plopped down on the arm of Zander's chair again. "Here. Made sure the house wasn't going to burn down while we were talking."

Zander gave a whoop, grabbed me from where I sat, and pulled me into a one-armed hug. I wasn't prepared for that! He let me up immediately, and I told my pounding heart that he was just elated over getting Izzie out of his hair for a few minutes.

I sat on the floor in front of his feet. "Don't kick me. I'm sitting right here."

"Oh. Right. I'd say I'm sure glad to see you, but I guess I'll settle for I'm sure glad to hear you. What's new? What have you been doing?"

I filled him in on Emilio and Abe, then added a few details about my own life since I'd seen him last.

"And the nanomites? Any change there?"

"Ha! Funny you should ask. You might say that the nanomites and I are feuding—but, then, that's not new."

Under Zander's gentle prodding, I told him about our most recent squabble.

Well, I *didn't* tell him how furious and scared I'd been when I figured out exactly what the "merge" entailed—you know, the whole "nano brain surgery" bit? I'd acknowledged that I couldn't change it, struggled to accept it, and gotten beyond it somehow. But Zander? Based on his reaction in the hospital, I think he would have had more difficulty forgiving them than I had.

I also said nothing about my training. First, as I rehearsed it in my head, it sounded dumb. Far-fetched. Second, it would have led to "Training for what?" My response of, "To rescue Dr. Bickel, of course," might have triggered a blowup.

As a wise woman, I didn't broach either of those topics.

But I did tell Zander how I'd lived in the safe house for three weeks before the nanomites bothered to tell me about Dr. Bickel's secret room.

"All along I have been concerned, and rightfully so, that Cushing's people might, in their investigation into Dr. Bickel's finances, uncover his ownership of the house. I was worrying about it the other night, so I asked the nanomites how I might stay a few steps ahead of Cushing. The mites gave me a bunch of reading on a strategy called 'defense in depth.' It's about multiple layers of defense that make it harder and take longer for an adversary to reach what they are after.

"The stuff I read about defense in depth made me realize just how stinking vulnerable I truly was! Anyway, then I asked the mites to help me make some contingency plans, especially escape plans—and do you know what they did? They showed me the blueprint of a secret room beneath the safe house. *A secret room!* With an escape tunnel! Right under my nose."

Yeah, I told Zander about the room. It couldn't hurt, because Zander had no idea where the safe house was.

"A secret room under the safe house?"

"Complete with years of food, a hidden hatch behind the kitchenette that opens to an escape tunnel, and a security system that monitors the outside *and* inside of the house. The security system also controls several sweet little deterrents should Cushing's goons break in."

"And why were you mad at the nanomites?"

I snorted, angry all over again. "Because they knew about it and didn't bother to tell me until I asked them! Why didn't they tell me right away? I mean, what if Cushing had found me before they told me? If she'd come in the night, I would have been trapped! Stupid bugs."

Zander chuckled.

I was not appreciative. "What's so funny?"

"Just you, Gemma. You act like the nanomites can think. Like they have feelings or common sense. They're devices, Gemma—they're technology, not *people*. You sound as if they should have known better when they were just following their programming."

If Zander could have seen me, my glower would have curdled his blood. As it was, I'm certain the temperature in the room dropped twenty degrees.

"Why, Gemma! Are you mad at me? Are you pouting?"

And he laughed again!

"Not funny," I growled.

"Well, it is to me. Not the whole, 'What if Cushing had come in the night before you knew about the secret room?' part but the 'you having arguments with the nanomites' piece. Come on, think about it. You and the nanomites are like squabbling roommates. It's sort of funny."

I huffed. "In a way, we *are* squabbling roommates, Zander, and it hasn't been easy. Sometimes they don't *think*!"

Zander leaned over, cradling his cast, and tried to look me in the eye. He got close—but I wasn't going to help him.

"Gemma, the mites don't 'think' sometimes because they aren't people. Yes, they are incredibly smart machines, but maybe you shouldn't expect them to understand human stuff. Like, I doubt that they understand your anxieties—but I do. I'm glad you asked them for help, and I'm glad they showed you the hidden room. *I* feel better knowing that you are better hidden from Cushing. *I* feel better knowing you can get away if you need to. *I* understand."

His words lightened my heart, and I backed away from the anger toward the nanomites, anger I thought I'd already dealt with.

Zander and I talked for half an hour before Izzie returned, bags of burgers and fries in her hands. None for me, of course.

I perched on the arm of Zander's chair, near the wall. Izzie brought Zander a tray, put it across his lap, and poured the contents of one bag onto a plate. When the heady scent of fries, burger, and hot, roasted green chile reached me, my stomach lurched. *What I wouldn't give* . . .

I sighed. With my ravenous appetite, I could have polished off both bags with ease.

When Izzie ran to fetch a plate for herself, I grabbed a handful of fries from Zander's tray and stuffed them into my mouth.

"Hey!" Zander whispered his indignation, but he was also laughing under his breath.

"Yummmmm." I pilfered another handful and scarfed them down before Izzie returned.

With Izzie back in the house, my alone time with Zander was over. I waited quietly for them to finish their meal. When she carried the trash into the kitchen, I said goodbye to Zander and slipped out the front door.

I walked to my car, the smell of hot fries and burgers making my stomach rumble, but I was smiling. In the short span Zander and I had been alone, I'd felt the companionship we'd enjoyed last summer, the ease we'd shared sitting on my back steps sipping lemonade or iced tea.

I shook my head. Far too much had happened since then. I was different. The last vestiges of childhood or youth or whatever label was most appropriate—the remnants of those innocent years? They were forever gone. I carried the full weight of adulthood upon my shoulders. I was responsible for myself, for the nanomites and, to a certain degree, for the safety of others.

Being with Zander had been a respite from those responsibilities. As I drove away from his neighborhood, I was easier in my heart for the time we'd spent talking. I was grateful for his friendship—

Gemma Keyes.

"Um, yes?"

Why are we stupid bugs?

The mites and I hadn't entirely "made up," so to speak, since the business with the room under the safe house; obviously, I still harbored some animosity toward them. Nonetheless, why had I shot my mouth off to Zander? Knowing the nanomites could hear me, why had I vented?

I was the stupid one.

"Um, no, Nano. I . . . I spoke out of, well, out of frustration. I . . . all these changes to my life and body have been rough on my emotions. It's been . . . well, hard to adjust—but I'm trying. Really, I am. I'm sorry I said . . . what I said about you."

We do not wish to be stupid bugs, Gemma Keyes. No, we do not. Please tell us when we are being stupid bugs. Just as you seek to adjust, we will seek to adjust.

I truly was sorry then, and tears stung my eyes.

Oh, Zander. How can I explain this to you? The nanomites may not be people, but . . . they are more than "just" technology.

⌘⌘⌘⌘

CHAPTER 18

Three days passed, three days of intensifying workouts. In between training sessions, I visited Emilio again and made a run for a bulk order of groceries. My comfy old jeans had become inexplicably loose, so I bought two new pairs and picked up some workout clothes, too.

Three days passed while I waited for the nanomites to bring me news of Mateo and Soto. For the second time, they came up empty.

Gemma Keyes. We have been unable to locate your enemies, Mateo Martinez and Arnaldo Soto. Online data is scarce.

I was disappointed, but I guess I could understand. The mites were not omnipresent or omnipotent, and neither Martinez nor Soto boasted what you might call a robust social media presence. The mites had collected bits and bytes, but nothing that furthered our search—no secret Facebook group exclusive to Mexican drug gangs and no snarky tweets directed at American law enforcement:

> @DeadEyesGang: @APD @FBI
> *Catch us if you can*
> *#nannynannybooboo*

The mites had found nothing—nothing in the Internet's public sector, that is.

It dawned on me that the government had to possess files on Soto, files that were not on any public network. Hadn't Gamble said something about his computer being on a secure government network?

Hmmm.

"Nano," I whispered. "I think the FBI has information on their network that would point your search for Soto in the right direction. We need to pay Special Agent Gamble another visit."

Thirty minutes later I stood at the door of Gamble's office. He was pecking away at his computer's keyboard, brows drawn down and bunched together, mouth hard and tight.

It was not the picture of a man comfortable with technology.

I had to admire his game face, though: If the computer had been a perp and Gamble had been interrogating him, I'm certain the computer would have caved.

"Gamble." I kept my voice low.

His chin jerked up; his eyes darted back and forth. "Miss Keyes?"

I shut his office door behind me. "Yes."

"You okay?"

"Sure. You?"

He snorted. "Just peachy. I've already deflected two of Cushing's probes—as you predicted."

I sat in the same seat I'd used only four days ago. "Do tell?"

"She called the Albuquerque SAC, my boss' boss, and mentioned that I might be useful in a Homeland investigation. She had the nerve to request that I be transferred to her! That about set my boss' hair on fire, of course."

Gamble couldn't see my worried expression. "What did your, er, boss' boss say?"

"Oh, trust me, the SAC is one very shrewd political operator. Without refusing outright or committing me to anything, he assured Cushing that the FBI would be pleased to cooperate and lend me to Homeland—as soon as the parameters of the investigation were known and the proper paperwork filed."

I giggled a little. "Let me guess? Your boss' boss has heard nothing in response from Cushing?"

"Not a peep."

"Do I hear a 'but'?"

"Yeah, you do. After that, Cushing came at me from another direction. I had a friend of mine, a PI, sweep my car, phone, and apartment. She found listening devices in all three."

My frown returned. "Cushing will just have them replanted. Different kinds and in less obvious places."

"Not to worry. My friend lent me some tools so I can check my car, phone, apartment, and this office myself. She had this other trick up her sleeve, too, a nifty app she installed on my phone. She said if Cushing was that determined, then she would be tracking my phone's GPS. The app spoofs my phone's location services, makes any tracking software think I'm a hundred miles from my actual location."

"Gee, you're starting to sound a little paranoid, Gamble."

"It's not paranoia if they really are watching you."

I snickered, and Gamble cracked a short-lived grin.

Then he was all business. "Why are you here, Miss Keyes?"

"I told you I would find Martinez and Soto for you. However, the nanomites can't find anything on the Internet as a jumping-off spot. I figured that the FBI had better leads—you know, next of kin, previous places of residence, and so on. Your information would provide the mites with a starting point."

"Can't give you access to our files, Miss Keyes."

I released a dramatic sigh and paused for effect.

In actuality, the mites were already in the FBI's system via Gamble's terminal and login. I was stalling Gamble to give them the time they needed.

Apparently, the same thought occurred to Gamble. "Wait! Are you . . . are those things in my computer?" He was outraged, but what could he do about it?

Not a thing.

"Yeah, they are. Let me check on their progress."

I stepped into the warehouse and surveyed the pipeline of data the nanocloud was sucking from the FBI's database—straight into Alpha Tribe's repository.

Fastest download speeds in town!

"Almost finished, Nano?"

Yes, Gemma Keyes.

I opened my eyes. "I think our work here is done."

Gamble flexed his jaw. "You realize you're committing a felony?"

Was I? I thought about it. Shrugged.

"Your IT peeps can't detect the mites, and there's virtually and *literally*, no possibility of the nanocloud being hacked. The data is safe. I promise not to sell it on the black market."

Gamble said nothing for a full thirty seconds, giving *me* the stink eye he'd had focused on his computer earlier. I wouldn't play poker with that man.

Gemma Keyes. We have completed our download.

"Okay, great, Nano. Will you begin your analysis?"

We have already begun, Gemma Keyes.

I stood up. "We have what we need, Agent Gamble. I'll let you know when we've found Soto."

He stood, too, and moved out from behind his desk. "I appreciate your offer to help, Miss Keyes, but I don't think I can allow you to leave with FBI data."

For a big guy, Gamble was fast. He leapt in my direction, found me, and clamped a manacle-like hand around my wrist.

"Hey!" I was too stunned to respond otherwise—but the mites were not.

A perfect cacophony of protest erupted in my ear, and then—

Gamble yelped, let go, and jumped backward, shaking his hand like it was on fire.

Oh, how well I knew that feeling! The mites had stung him, and stung him but good. The man cradled the injured member against his chest and glared at me, indignant. Maybe a little afraid?

"Sorry, Agent Gamble, but the mites took offense at you putting your hands on me."

He backed up a few steps. "Did they, now?"

"Uh-huh; yeah, they did. Listen, I'm leaving now. Don't worry about the FBI's files. Consider them, um, backed up to a super secure location."

Ha-ha! Oh, I crack myself up sometimes. It was all I could do not to laugh—but I didn't want to further offend Agent Gamble. He was, after all, a straight shooter, an attribute not that common to feds in my limited experience.

He grimaced and rubbed the center of his palm with his other thumb. "Noted, Miss Keyes. I won't make that mistake again."

Great. He was ticked.

I walked closer to him, the mites chittering a soft warning. I placed my hand on his shoulder. "I'm sorry, Gamble. Please don't hold this against me. I don't want to lose you as a friend. I-I have so few friends these days."

Gamble squinted at where my hand rested on his shoulder and blinked a few times. Blew out a breath. "Well . . . I may have overreacted. Well, no, I *didn't* overreact, but I apologize for grabbing you. I suppose these are . . . special circumstances." He muttered as an afterthought, "And I guess no one would believe me in any case."

Not for the first time, I saw in Gamble the human qualities that led me to trust him.

"Thank you, Agent Gamble. And I promise—we will find Soto. Be ready when we do."

***

On the drive home, I slipped in and out of the warehouse to check on the nanomites' progress. Was it too much to hope that they would find Soto right away?

Maybe. Maybe not.

My thoughts returned to Gamble's office and how the FBI's files were secured behind a firewall the mites couldn't penetrate. Why were the mites unable to hack the FBI from outside that firewall? I found it hard to believe that anything could stymie them.

"Nano. Why couldn't you access the FBI's files from the safe house?"

Gemma Keyes, the FBI network is hardwired. Air-gapped. It is not connected to the Internet.

What?

Lights flashed before my eyes, and a vital piece of puzzle plunked into place. The revelation sent Soto and Mateo Martinez straight to the back burner, and I swallowed with excitement.

"Nano! Could Cushing be communicating about Dr. Bickel via a similar setup? Through a military network not connected to the Internet?"

That is a valid hypothesis, Gemma Keyes.

I drove the rest of the way to my slot in the parking garage on autopilot. Walked home the same way. I was preoccupied.

The nanomites had searched every network connected to the Internet for Dr. Bickel's location and had found nothing. Given their adroit hacking abilities, I hadn't known what to think about this "failure." At the same time, I recognized Cushing's compulsive need for control, for keeping close tabs on her own interests. I was confident that she communicated with Dr. Bickel's custodians somehow.

Since she had him under her control, wouldn't she attempt to make Dr. Bickel give up his research? Wouldn't she provide him with a laboratory and attempt to coerce him into working? And wouldn't she check his progress on a regular basis? Would he pretend to work but provide her with bogus results as he'd done before?

Dr. Bickel was stubborn as well as clever. So was Cushing. If she saw through his pretenses, would she go so far as to torture him to force his cooperation? Knowing him as I did, I doubted he would cooperate with Cushing under any circumstances—incentive or punishment, carrot or stick. Nevertheless, the idea of torture worried me. But regardless of the pressure Cushing did or didn't apply to my friend, I couldn't imagine her *not* staying apprised of Dr. Bickel's progress.

She couldn't forgo status updates any more than a tiger could turn vegan, I reasoned. *She is too much of a control freak—so she **must** have a means of communicating with Dr. Bickel's guards. How is she doing it?*

When I was employed at Sandia, I had held a Q clearance because I worked in a classified environment. Classified discussions were held in a special room. As were classified phone calls.

Sandia is a Department of Energy facility. They lease space on Kirtland Air Force Base from the military. Cushing is Air Force. Department of Defense. How does the military communicate secret information?

I entered the warehouse. "Nano. Find information on Department of Defense communications systems."

The mites returned a wealth of info. I allowed the data to wash over me until I had grasped the salient details. Several facts stood out: DOD used three systems to control three types of data: unclassified/unsecured, Secret, and Top Secret/SCI.

The NIPRNet (Non-Classified Internet Protocol Router Network) was for military unclassified/unsecured information. Of course, NIPRNET employed strict user authorization; still, the network was connected to the Internet. Via the Internet, the mites had already defeated NIPRNet firewalls and security protocols and mined NIPRNet data. They had found nothing on Dr. Bickel.

The SIPRNet (Secret Internet Protocol Router Network) was a second-tier network for classified information used by DOD and the State Department. However, while the SIPRNet's security structure was much more robust and user authorization more restrictive than that for the NIPRNet, I doubted Cushing would use this network to communicate about Dr. Bickel either.

Why? Because the SIPRNet had too many users (around 4.2 million) and because the U.S. allowed a number of trusted allies (including Australia, Canada, the U.K, and New Zealand) to access this network. Even with security protocols in place to keep user accounts and data compartmented, I could not envision Cushing and her handlers permitting information about the nanomites to coexist in a system that another country—even an ally—shared. Knowledge of the nanomites was too important to risk leaking it to another nation.

One option remained: the Joint Worldwide Intelligence Communication System or JWICS. JWICS was the U.S.'s Top Secret/Sensitive Compartmentalized Information intranet used by DOD, State Department, Homeland, Justice, and various other U.S. intelligence agencies, including the FBI.

The thing about JWICS? JWICS computers were not connected to the Internet. This made them, purportedly, unhackable from ordinary computers outside the network. Additionally, only individuals with TS access *plus* need-to-know could log on to JWICS—and only from within a SCIF—a Sensitive Compartmented Information Facility—a room or structure authorized, built, and approved per DOD standards. In other words, totally and completely "off the Web," surrounded by robust physical and electronic security measures.

If Cushing were using JWICS to communicate with whomever was holding Dr. Bickel, that would explain why the mites had not found him—they could not connect to the JWICS network except from a JWICS terminal—from one SCIF to another.

I scowled as I processed this information. Not for a nanosecond did I doubt that Cushing received regular reports on Dr. Bickel. If she exchanged emails regarding Dr. Bickel, she would do so via JWICS within a SCIF.

Something about that idea bothered me, though. Would Cushing risk the exchange of emails on the nanomites? My gut told me that she would consider any email system too risky. She wouldn't leave a paper trail— virtual or otherwise. She was too smart for that.

That left one communication avenue open: the secure phone line inside the SCIF. A secure phone call happened in real time and was not recorded. No paper trail, no pesky emails to incriminate her later.

A phone call was the next best thing to a face-to-face meeting. A secure phone conversation within a SCIF? Hack-proof.

Almost.

The mites could get me into any SCIF, I was certain of that—but it had to be when Cushing used the phone. If we were present while she talked, we could listen in—and the mites could ascertain the origination point of the call on the other end.

Bingo.

I "just" needed the schedule of her next call. No big deal, right? The mites were monitoring Cushing's calendar and her phone logs. However, they had detected nothing to suggest that she placed or received calls in a SCIF.

I entered the warehouse. "Nano. Let me see Cushing's calendar." Zander had insisted that the mites weren't "people-savvy." Maybe they had missed something?

I pulled her schedule to me and studied it, day by day. Her only appointment of note today was in her office at 3 p.m. Someone with the initials "GK."

My initials? Had to be a coincidence.

I went over her schedule a second time. Still, nothing struck me.

"Nano, let's see it week by week."

With the last five weeks before my eyes, I looked for a pattern. I scanned through her Mondays. Tuesdays. Wednesdays. Thursdays. Fridays. No repeated appointments.

I started over and read every item. Monday: 8 a.m. staff meeting. 9:15 budget report. Noon conference call to the Pentagon.

"*That* call bears a closer look. Nano. Remind me later."

Wednesday, 12:15 p.m. Artichoke Café. 2:30 p.m. Sandia Café.

I paused. *Why two restaurants on the same day? Lunch, yes, but what is this at 2:30?*

I'd eaten at the Artichoke. Very nice. 'General worthy,' even. But—

"Nano. Where is this Sandia Café?"

Gemma Keyes. We find no listing of a Sandia Café in Albuquerque.

"No listing . . ." There was no such place? I muttered again, "Sandia Café?"

My breath hitched. "Nano! Highlight all occurrences of Sandia Café on Cushing's calendar."

Seven highlights appeared before me. *Seven regularly scheduled appointments.*

I pulled the schedule closer. "Sandia Café. Initials *S.C.* Are the initials code? Code for a secure call?"

My eyes leapt forward on Cushing's calendar and found what I was searching for.

"Her next call is Wednesday. Make a note of that, Nano! We are going to be present for that call."

***

"Ah. A pleasure to see you again, Miss Keyes." Cushing's smile was as sticky-sweet and gooey as the insides of a toasted marshmallow.

Genie Keyes glared at Cushing. "Cut the bull, *General*. You strong-armed my firm into assigning me to you as some sort of consultant. Why? What is it you want from me?"

"Oh, dear. I *am* sorry that you view my request for your assistance in a negative light. I merely mentioned to your firm's partners that we needed your services most desperately. They were more than happy to lend you to me."

Genie's eyes narrowed to slits. She knew in detail what Cushing had done. When Cushing had requested her help directly and Genie had refused to acquiesce to Cushing's summons, the senior partners had called Genie to a meeting. A private meeting.

Genie had never before witnessed the partners shaken—but they were rattled *that* day . . .

***

"*Look, Genie,*" the most senior partner had begun, "*this General Cushing has more clout in D.C. than we can ignore. If we agree to let her, er, borrow you for a few weeks, we stand to gain the legal work on several substantial government contracts. If we refuse? She has, er, indirectly threatened us.*"

"*Threatened you how?*"

"It wasn't outright, Genie, but she made her intent clear. If we chose not to cooperate with her, she 'suggested' that the IRS might take a serious interest in our firm—and if the IRS were to launch an audit or investigation of us, Cushing hinted that the audit could become public knowledge. She even commiserated over how damaging it would be should someone spread rumors to our clients of our supposed dealings with organized crime!

"It would make no difference whether we were eventually cleared by the IRS or not, no difference that we have never entered into entanglements with OC. The cost of dealing with such an investigation and the negative publicity and rumors would sink us."

Genie had stared daggers at the elder partner until he grimaced and slid a packet across the table to her.

"This, my dear, is a most generous offer. Automatic junior partnership on January 1, your buy-in paid for by us. Please note the salary and options."

Genie hadn't touched the packet. At first.

"And if I decline?"

The senior partner's jaw went rigid. "Our priority is this firm. Regrettably, if you were to decline our offer, we would ensure that you lose your license and never work in law again. I believe Cushing would assist us in that endeavor."

*** *

Genie had taken the offer—what choice had she?—but she had seethed inside.

She was still seething.

Genie snapped out of her reverie. "Look. What is it you want me to do? The sooner I get it done, the sooner I'm back to my life."

Cushing swiveled her chair to the side and leaned back. "Ah, Miss Keyes! We wish only one thing, and that is to locate your sister." She sent a sideways look in Genie's direction. "We have established the fact that you and your twin don't share a great deal of sisterly affection."

Genie smothered a snarky laugh. "Growing up, Gemma was a mealymouthed brat. A coward. Easily manipulated. Let's just say we didn't share similar interests as children and we share fewer as adults."

"Then you will have no, ah, qualms in helping us locate her?"

Genie felt no scruples; however, she *was* curious. "Why do you want her?"

"Two weeks ago, I told you it was a National Security issue. That has not changed. Our interests in Gemma are classified."

"What will you do with her?"

Cushing shrugged. "That's not for me to say, is it? Whatever crimes she has committed, she will pay the penalties."

"Again, I'm not sure we're talking about the same person."

Cushing faced Genie and placed her folded hands on the table between them. "Ah, but we are, Miss Keyes, and your sister is a much different person than you believe her to be. She is clever, resourceful, and dangerous."

Genie snorted. "Dangerous? Gemma? That's like saying gumdrops are dangerous. Or baby bunnies. She's soft-hearted. And stupid."

Cushing was done playing nice. "I don't share your opinion of your sister, Miss Keyes, nor does your estimation of her matter to me. I have but one objective: her capture. She has evaded us twice. You will help us locate her and take her into custody."

Genie shrugged. "Whatever. Let's get this over with. What do you expect me to do?"

Cushing smiled, and Genie noticed how the woman's tiny white—and oddly sharp—teeth gleamed when she did. Genie was repulsed but did not allow her revulsion to show.

This woman reminds me of a shark, Genie thought. *Fish are friends, not food. Yeah, right.*

Cushing's smile widened. "It is quite fortuitous that you and your sister are so alike in appearance, if not in personality. I would like you to visit someone, Genie, in the guise of your sister. A man by the name of Ross Gamble. He's FBI, but don't let that concern you. I'd like you to introduce yourself to him and make nice. You see, I think he knows something about Gemma, something he isn't letting on to me."

Why else would he have swept for and removed the listening devices I had planted in his apartment, car, and phone?

Cushing continued. "Upon your meeting with him, I hope he will give himself away."

"Give himself away how?"

"Oh, you see, if he's met or spoken to your sister before, he will allude to it somehow, don't you agree? Through familiarity or body language? Referring to previous conversations? I want to know if Special Agent Gamble has already met our Gemma, Miss Keyes. If he has, and if he has lied to me? Well, then I will apply certain . . . inducements that will properly motivate him to reach out to her."

Genie was under no illusions as to the nature and types of "inducements" Cushing might bring to bear—even on a federal agent. "That's it? Do I just jump out in front of him?"

"In a manner of speaking. We'll arrange for you to encounter him in the location of our choosing. That way, if he acknowledges that he's spoken to you before, we can, er, pick him up right away."

You want me to ambush this man and shock him into admitting—either consciously or unconsciously—that he knows Gemma. Then you will take him into custody. Got it.

Genie shrugged. "Sounds simple enough."

⌘⌘⌘⌘

CHAPTER 19

Gus-Gus worked me hard for five hours. When I returned home in the middle of the night, I spent another hour noodling out my venture onto the base and into Cushing's secure call. Even when I found myself tiring, the details kept me awake. Getting on the base would not be difficult or dangerous—after all, I'd done it before without detection.

No, it was the next step that could prove hazardous.

The mites had produced an annotated map of the base and identified all the SCIFS. I studied their proximity to Cushing's office. Two such facilities seemed likely candidates; one of the two had to be where Cushing made her secure calls.

I was certain the mites could get me into the SCIF. Getting into the SCIF *ahead* of Cushing was the sticking point. Once she was inside, she would lock the door. After that, even the nanomites wouldn't be able to get me inside without Cushing noticing. No, I had to arrive before she did.

Tired.

I nodded off on the sofa once or twice before I hauled myself downstairs to bed. I stripped off my clothes and fell onto my cot.

I should have slept deeply—I'd used my body well that day and night—but I couldn't get to a place of restful slumber. At least not without dreaming.

The dreams . . . disturbed me.

Dreams? No, a single dream, the same old nightmare with the same old theme: Cushing.

Cushing coming for me. Cushing behind me. Cushing laughing, her mouth revealing her pointy teeth. Cushing's men grabbing at me.

When the dream got too bad, I would wake up, shivering and shaking. I would reassure myself that the panic-inducing episodes were figments of my hyperactive imagination. Then my heavy eyelids would close and I would sleep—but soon after, some variation of the nightmare would return.

I was caught in yet another episode when I spied a shadowed figure hiding behind Cushing. Who was it? Why was I worried?

The individual stepped out of Cushing's shadow.

It was Genie.

I jerked and sat up, clawing the cobwebs from my eyes. Why? Why was I dreaming about my sister? Surely, she'd returned to Virginia, back to her legal career, almost a month ago.

Genie.

The sense of encroaching danger was so strong, that I threw on my clothes, climbed upstairs, and began to pace the living room.

As I paced, I wiped sweaty palms on my jeans. What if? What if she hadn't gone back to Roanoke? To her law firm? Then what?

Well, I could put my mind at ease on that count. I could check and make sure she had.

I closed my eyes, entered the warehouse, and called to the nanomites. *Nano. We must find my sister. Where is she right now? Has she been in contact with Cushing? She may be a threat to us, Nano.*

When I declared Genie a threat, the level of nanomite activity accelerated. The mites flung data in front of me, and I began sifting through it—everything about Genie the mites had found online and were still finding.

It was a lot, and—*whoa!*

It was one thing to "know" someone; it was another to be privy to their personal life. I saw things I'd never realized about Genie—such as her penchant for designer footwear. Oh, she'd always been a clothes horse, but the price of her online orders of Sergio Rossi, Christian Louboutin, Jimmy Choo, and Manolo Blahnik shoes could have fed a third-world country.

I can't even mouth what she paid for a pair of Valentino Garavani studded ankle-strap heels!

As I paged through records and images, my anxiety calmed: Genie was home. Her billable hours were intact, and she was on her merry way to a junior partnership in her firm.

No worries.

I skimmed over an airline reservation—and jumped back to it. Delta flight 1907 from DCA to ATL. Reagan National in D.C. to Atlanta.

ATL to ABQ.

ABQ. Albuquerque.

First class. Return, open-ended.

Yesterday!

I stared down the long corridors of the warehouse.

Genie had arrived in Albuquerque yesterday? But Genie despised the Southwest. Hated New Mexican culture. Nothing could have compelled her to return to Albuquerque so soon after her last visit except—

Cushing. It had to be Cushing, Cushing pulling Genie to her side and into her schemes. Genie had disliked Cushing on sight, but Cushing possessed the means to *compel* Genie to help her, to use her to get to me.

But how? It made no sense. How could Cushing use Genie? In what circumstance could Cushing employ Genie against me? My sister and I shared no bonds of affection, so that avenue would not work.

Would Genie try to impersonate me as she had with Zander? Yes, we looked alike, but we were opposites—polar extremes—in personality.

Besides, I was invisible; how would it benefit Cushing for Genie to impersonate me? And who would Cushing target with such an impersonation?

Not Abe. Abe had watched us grow up. He always could tell us apart.

Not Zander. He had met Genie once, but he had known she wasn't me. *"Discernment,"* he'd called it. *"She might look like you on the outside, but she isn't you on the inside. At all. I could feel that,"* he'd said.

And both Abe and Zander knew I was "stuck" in my invisibility because Dr. Bickel had told the nanomites not to leave me. If "I" just happened to show up without the mites? Well, neither Abe nor Zander would be fooled.

Then who? Who was Cushing's intended target?

For that matter, had I met anyone else since that fateful day in September when Cushing's soldiers had stormed Dr. Bickel's lab under the mountain? Since the nanomites had made a home in me? Since I'd been rendered invisible? Since I'd been on the run?

I stared straight ahead. *Agent Gamble.*

He wouldn't recognize Genie as me, of course—since he'd never actually *seen* me—but if Genie introduced herself as me, would her voice sound enough like mine to trick Gamble? Was that Cushing's ploy? Trick Gamble into admitting that he knew me? Trap him in his lies? Then take him into custody and use him against me?

I'd told Gamble to beware of Cushing, but he wouldn't see this coming.

I hadn't seen it coming!

And why had Genie infiltrated my dreams the very night after she'd arrived in Albuquerque? Another coincidence?

Think about that later, Gemma.

I needed to warn Gamble.

I couldn't risk calling him, either. Despite his friend's "gizmo" to sweep his phone, Cushing might still have his line tapped.

It had to be face to face. ASAP.

"Nano. I need to speak to Agent Ross Gamble in person. It's urgent. Find his home address."

***

I parked two blocks from Agent Gamble's apartment complex just past 5:30 a.m. and walked up to the security gate, my head swiveling this way and that, scanning for any sign that Cushing's people were nearby. The November sun wouldn't rise until almost 7 a.m. so it was too dark to see into the shadows where her people could be hiding.

Invisibility was my first and best defense, but technology worked on Cushing's behalf. For all I knew, her goons had thermal imaging goggles trained on me at this very moment, and I was waltzing into a trap. If Cushing's people *were* using thermal imaging?

Then I was in big trouble.

I gestured toward the access keypad and the gate swung open. Jogged toward the back of the complex, toward the unit housing Agent Gamble's apartment.

The mites chittered. They knew I was nervous. Maybe they had their own case of the willies.

A stream of nanomites flew out in front of me. My forward reconnaissance.

I was approaching the stairs leading up to Gamble's apartment when the mites whispered a warning.

Gemma Keyes.

"Yes?"

To your right and to your left.

I slowed. Studied the cars parked nearby. Crud! Two vehicles. At least eight of Cushing's agents. Genie had to be with them. I had to reach Gamble before she did!

Gemma Keyes. At the base of the stairs.

I spied the silhouette of a man in street clothes, smoking a cigarette under the flight of stairs. Interesting. Posted signs papered the complex: No smoking allowed on the premises.

Had to be Cushing's man.

"Nano. Is there another way up to the second floor?

At the other end of the building.

I tiptoed past the smoking agent. Halfway down the length of the building, I sprinted. Found the other staircase and crept up it.

I was looking for apartment 12C. It should have been—I stopped, didn't need to look any farther. Gamble, a travel mug in one hand, was locking his front door.

I scooted up next to him and placed my hand on his arm—to prevent him from throwing his coffee into the air.

"Don't move," I whispered. "Don't say a word."

Gamble took me seriously. He stood as still as a rock.

"Cushing has agents waiting for you downstairs. One under the stairs behind you, two cars in the parking lot."

"Um, yeah, so what does that mean? She intends to abduct me? An agent of the FBI?" Gamble kept his voice low, but I could tell he doubted me.

"Only if you give yourself away. Listen to me—this is important: I have a twin sister, Agent Gamble. An *identical* twin sister. She and I look *and sound* the same. I believe Cushing's plan is for Genie to approach you as you leave for work."

Gamble shook his head. "I've never seen you. How could I mistake her for you? What is the point?"

I took a deep breath. "I think Cushing has two points. First, if Genie says she is me and you acknowledge her, you will have let on that we've spoken before, and Cushing will know you lied to her. Her agents will disappear you so fast you won't know what happened until you wake up— location unknown."

Gamble was no fool, and he was a quick study. "Huh. Okay, so if a woman approaches me claiming to be you, I should act like I don't know what she's talking about. And the second point?"

"I think Cushing is starting to figure out that I have the missing nanomites and that they have rendered me invisible. However, the idea is so improbable, that she won't risk being labeled a nut job. She needs someone else to validate her suspicions. You."

"You mean, if I were to let on to your sister—pretending to be you— that we've met before and ask her how I could, this time around, *see* you?"

"That's it."

Gamble swore under his breath. "It would have worked. If you hadn't warned me . . ."

"Don't think about that. Just be prepared. I'll be standing by. Just in case."

"Just in case?"

"I'm not altogether powerless, Agent Gamble—remember what the nanomites did to your hand? If need be, I can fight for you."

He stared toward my mouth, toward the spot where he heard my whispered words emerge.

"No, Gemma. If they take me, it is vital that they have no evidence, no real proof that you are, you know . . ."

"Invisible?"

"Yeah. That. Don't put yourself in harm's way, Gemma. Your capture is Cushing's endgame, isn't it? If she catches *you*, she's achieved her objective. And if she gets you, I can kiss my, uh, backside goodbye. Right?"

He *was* right.

I'd almost made a stupid, stupid mistake. A tactical error of momentous proportion.

"Thank you, Agent Gamble. You . . . you're a good man."

One side of his mouth quirked upward in the dim light of morning. "I don't know about that, but I'd better be a good actor. Don't hang around to watch my performance, Gemma."

I released my hold on Gamble's arm. "I wish you well."

Gamble, whistling a soft tune—no doubt a ploy to keep his nerves in check—headed for the stairs. I tiptoed right behind him. No, I wasn't going to let Cushing know I was there, but I wasn't going to leave without seeing what happened, either.

Um, God? Agent Gamble is one of the good guys. Please help him be a rock star of an actor today!

As I followed Gamble down the stairs, I shook my head back and forth. What was with all these come-lately petitions? I didn't believe God would answer.

Did I?

I stopped halfway down the flight; I didn't want to chance Smoker-in-the-Shadows hearing my footsteps. Gamble reached the bottom and kept walking, that same tune whistling between his clenched teeth. He crossed the grass between two buildings, hit the asphalt parking lot, and headed toward the line of cars under a long carport.

Smoker guy followed at a discreet distance. Day was breaking, and he had no more shadows to hide him, so he slipped behind the next building's corner.

I descended the stairs and followed Gamble out to the parking lot. When I reached the asphalt, I sprinted and ended up on the passenger side of his car just as he hit the key fob to unlock his door.

With the click of the locks, I heard her.

"Agent Gamble! Oh, Agent Gamble! I'm so glad I caught you." She was more casually dressed than her norm, wearing something I might have worn. And her face bore an open, innocent expression.

Ohhhh, Genie, my evil sister. You are so good at being bad.

I scooted around the hood of Gamble's car and positioned myself to see and hear their exchange—and to keep one eye on Cushing's thugs.

Gamble jerked at Genie's greeting and turned, coffee still in hand. "I beg your pardon?"

"Agent Gamble, I'm glad I caught you before you left. It's Gemma Keyes. You remember me, don't you?"

Gamble cocked his head. "Gemma Keyes. *The* Gemma Keyes? The Gemma Keyes General Cushing is searching for?"

"I, well, um . . ."

Gamble set his travel mug on the roof of his car and—once again, *so stinking fast!*—grabbed Genie by her wrist, twisted her arm behind her, threw her against his car, and whipped out his cuffs.

Genie shrieked. "Stop! W-what are you doing?"

Gamble never answered. He had Genie pinned against the back door of his vehicle. He finished cuffing her and then patted her down—neck, back, arms, sides, waist, legs.

"Stop it, you idiot!" Genie screamed. "I'm Gemma! You know me!"

"Lady, I've never seen you in my life," Gamble replied, "but I know Homeland has labeled you a domestic terrorist."

Gotta say, I hadn't seen that coming. It was everything I could do not to break into enthusiastic applause. Whatever acting abilities Genie had? Gamble was better. I was practically jumping up and down.

And the Oscar goes to—

"Agent Gamble."

Cushing's voice tore away my enthusiasm like a hull breach sucks air from a star ship.

Whoosh.

Goodbye.

Gone.

Gamble held a hand between him and Cushing. "Whoever you are, step back."

"Agent Gamble, please release this woman."

"And you are?"

"General Imogene Cushing. We've spoken, remember? You called me."

Gamble had the mix of confusion and serious professional down cold. "General Cushing? What is this about? Why are you here?"

"I must apologize, Agent Gamble, but this woman is not Gemma Keyes. Again, you may release her."

Genie's curses were turning the air every color of the rainbow. She cursed Gamble; she cursed Cushing; she cursed me. I heard phraseology I think a steelworker would be proud to adopt.

Gamble's chin jutted forward. "She claimed to be Gemma Keyes."

"Ah, yes, but I assure you, she is not. Please remove your handcuffs, Agent Gamble."

"Take them off me, you *bleep bleeping bleep*!" Genie screamed. She twisted and tried to wrench herself free of Gamble's hold.

Gamble pushed Genie's head onto the roof of his car where it landed with a satisfactory "thunk." Genie's shrieks, muffled against the roof, ended in a moan. I put both hands over my mouth to stifle an all-out guffaw.

At the same time, Cushing's agents, most in black tactical gear, exited the two vehicles and lined up not far away, awaiting Cushing's signal, should she call for them.

Gamble saw the men, pulled his credentials from his breast pocket, flipped them open, and held them high for them to see. "FBI! Keep your distance." He folded his creds but kept a finger pointed at the men. "You are out of your jurisdiction. *Stand down.* You've been warned."

He rounded on Cushing. "General Cushing, I don't know what your game is, but this woman introduced herself to me as Gemma Keyes. You told me Keyes was wanted by Homeland. I will, at the very least, check her ID before I release her."

Cushing, who had begun in a reasonable tone, was now impatient. "Let me save you the trouble, Agent Gamble. This is Genie Keyes, Gemma Keyes' sister. Her twin, actually." Cushing squared her shoulders, glowered, and moved a step toward Gamble, trying to intimidate him— which was about as effective as spitting into a brush fire.

Gamble eyed Cushing and stood taller; he towered over her and closed the gap between them. "Is this your idea of a joke, General? Because I'm not finding any of this humorous. What's your objective here?"

Okay, I will admit it. This was the best show *ever*! I was ready to grab a bowl of popcorn and settle down on the grass. I hadn't enjoyed myself so much, well, in months.

Gamble leaned into Cushing's face, forcing her to back up. "Furthermore, General, this has all the appearance of an unsanctioned military operation on American soil—strictly prohibited by the Constitution. And to what end would Gemma Keyes' sister impersonate Miss Keyes to me?"

Gamble's timing was incredible. He paused a tick, as though a thought had hit him. "Wait. Were you attempting to entrap me, General Cushing? I told you already: I've never met Gemma Keyes—I've never seen her, never spoken to her, and would not know her if she introduced herself to me."

He thrust his credentials into his pocket, shoved my moaning sister against the car, and undid the cuffs. He took her by the arm and pushed her into Cushing's arms. Then he removed his phone from his pocket and began snapping photos.

No, he was shooting video.

"What are you doing? Stop that, Agent Gamble," Cushing demanded.

"No, General Cushing, I will not. I will be making a full report when I arrive at my office this morning. Whatever you are doing, it needs to be reported to the proper authorities."

Two of Cushing's jackboots started across the asphalt. Gamble recorded their approach before he climbed into his vehicle. I heard the doors lock as the two men reached for the handle.

Gamble cracked his window. He was still filming.

"This is Special Agent Ross Gamble, FBI, recording an unauthorized military operation conducted at 1700 Alameda, Albuquerque, New Mexico—

One of Cushing's men raised the butt of his rifle to smash the window. Gamble hit the gas, and his car shot backward, clipping the soldier. Gamble didn't stop. He threw the car into drive and sped toward the gate.

Cushing put her hand on the man closest to him. "Let him go. Return to base. I have urgent phone calls to make."

I'll bet you do, Sharky Face. Up for a little damage control?

"What about me?" Genie screeched.

"You? You may *shut up*, Miss Keyes. And you may return home. I have no further need for you."

The two women glared at each other, their mutual dislike open and apparent.

Then Genie smoothed her face, but I could read her like a book: *You may have no further need for me, General, but I am not finished with you.*

I would not relish being on the receiving end of her fury.

"Fine, but how do I get back to my hotel? My rental car is still on the base."

Cushing nodded to the soldier near her. He grabbed Genie by the arm and dragged her toward one of the two waiting vehicles.

A minute later, no one remained in the parking lot except me and two apartment dwellers who gaped at each other.

"What in the world was that?" one asked.

"I have no idea," the other replied.

I laughed aloud. All the way to my car, I laughed. I chuckled, sniggered, and snarked as I drove to the parking garage, as I reran the highlights of Gamble's performance. He had been masterful—far better than I could have hoped for.

I visualized Gamble debriefing his boss and writing up the report of Cushing's ambush (complete with video).

I smiled. My heart was still pounding, but I smiled.

Cushing would be busy putting out fires for the rest of the day.

Genie would waste no time getting out of New Mexico.

What a great morning.

⌘⌘⌘⌘

CHAPTER 20

That night, Gus-Gus and I worked off my nano-charged energy. Fact is, the AI was one strange dude: He never got mad or showed emotion, yet he managed to stir up plenty of both in me. My feet had grown calluses, my hands moved in my sleep (what little sleep the nanomites allowed me), and Gus-Gus' voice echoed in my head every waking moment: counting, counting, counting, calling direction, shouting corrections. Counting, counting, counting.

Ugh.

But inside? In my heart? I was in love. Not with Gus-Gus, but with the work, with the powerful art I was learning. I bristled under the discipline, but I loved the result.

***

The following morning, I received a text—and it wasn't from Zander. I blinked as I read it.

Your shipment of 3 boxes from martialartsofamerica.com has been delivered.

"What shipment?" I hadn't ordered anything.

Gemma Keyes. We ordered equipment for you. We charged the order to your Capital One card.

"Nice of you to tell me," I growled.

You are welcome, Gemma Keyes.

Clueless. Like Zander said, for all their brilliance, they were, on some levels, clueless.

"Uh, okay." I had to wait until nightfall, until the UPS store closed, to pick up my packages. While I fixed breakfast, I wondered what the mites had up their nano-sleeves.

They ordered equipment for me?

I was a little excited to see what the order might contain.

Felt kinda like Christmas.

***

Abe plopped into the wheelchair and grinned at Zander. "Aren't we a pair? Yep. Matched bookends, what with our bruises an' all."

The nurse lifted Abe's feet onto the chair's metal footplates and glanced up. "Are you the individual looking after Mr. Pickering for a bit? He's going to be weak and unsteady for a while longer."

Zander nodded. "Yes; the doctor already told me. I'll be in and out at Abe's during the day and staying nights with him until he's able to manage on his own."

She grinned. "Well, Mr. Pickering has a point. You two look like you got tossed into the same blender." She did a final check on the room and placed the plastic bag of Abe's belongings and medications in his lap.

"That we did, after a manner of speaking," Abe answered. He slanted a look toward Zander. "Any sightings of my next-door neighbor?"

Zander glanced at the nurse before shaking his head.

"All ready, Mr. Pickering?"

"Ready to blow this popsicle stand? Been ready for two days!"

The nurse folded her arms and stared at him. "Says the man who left the MICU only five days ago, the man who recovered from a traumatic brain injury—and quite miraculously, if the rumors are to be believed."

"Well, I believe in miracles, not rumors, Miss Danielle."

She smiled. "I do, too. So, let's blow this popsicle stand, shall we?"

She wheeled Abe to the elevator and out the main entrance, where Zander's car was waiting. She and Zander helped Abe from the chair into the passenger seat. Zander latched the seatbelt across Abe's chest.

"Follow the doctor's orders, Mr. Pickering. Don't overdo it, or I expect we'll be seeing each other again."

"Yes, ma'am."

Zander got in on the driver's side and pulled away from the hospital. "You okay, Abe?"

"Not as steady as I might want, but I'll be fine. So, what I asked earlier. Anyone seen Mateo? I don't fancy him being part of the welcome wagon when we get to my place."

"No one has seen or heard from Mateo. Gemma has been looking, but . . . no joy."

"No news is good news in my book!"

"Abe, I had a little work done on your house yesterday."

"Oh?"

"Yes. Had a couple of guys from church replace your broken front door and install metal security doors and deadbolts, front and back."

Abe said nothing for a minute. Then he sighed. "Suppose that's only right. If I'd had them installed same time as Gemma had hers put on, Mateo and his thugs couldn't have kicked my door in. You and I wouldn't have been laid up like we were."

"Won't happen a second time, Abe."

"I thank you, Pastor Cruz."

"Abe, we are family. It's just Zander."

Abe patted Zander's shoulder. "Thank you, Zander. For everything."

They were companionably quiet a while before Abe added, "Need your help with something, son."

"Anything, Abe."

Abe nodded. "Need you to help me get healthy again. Strong. Whatever it takes."

Zander glanced over at his friend and back to the road. "Not going to let you overdo it, Abe."

"I'm countin' on you to keep me in line but moving forward. Moving forward. Making progress."

"That works for me—of course you know I'm still recovering myself, right? So, no sparring matches, no hundred-pound bench presses, no chin-ups, no five-mile runs with forty-pound packs."

Abe chuckled. "I'll try to restrain myself."

"All right. Well, to start with, we'll get you home and settled. Then I need to go into the office for a few hours. Tonight, after dinner, we'll see how you're doing, try a short walk around the cul-de-sac—if you aren't too tired."

"I won't be. I want that boy home with me, Zander."

***

For the first time in nearly two weeks, Zander let himself into the office wing of Downtown Community Church. The clock on his phone's face read just after noon when he stopped in the secretary's office doorway.

"Hey, Mrs. Coyne. How are you doing?"

"Pastor Zander! It's so good to see you up and around."

"Thanks. I have a lot to catch up on, so I thought I'd come in for a few hours this afternoon." The doctor had cleared him for "light activities" that put no stress on his mending bones. Light activities meant "no lifting" or going without the sling that strapped his casted arm to his chest to keep his cracked collarbone and ribs immobile for another week.

"Please let me know if I can do anything for you?"

"You're a very kind woman, Mrs. Coyne."

"And you are too sweet! By the way, I don't care *what* Izzie says about your bruises; *I* don't think you look like an eggplant that fell off a truck."

Mrs. Coyne tried to hang on to her wide-eyed and innocent expression. She failed. Her mouth twitched and her body shook with repressed humor.

"Mrs. Coyne, forget what I said about you being a kind woman."

When she snickered, Zander used his free arm to grab and hold his middle against the laughter bubbling up in his gut. "Mrs. Coyne, I think I'm gonna kill my sister."

"I can see the bulletin headline now: *DCC Associate Pastor Murders Impudent Sibling. 'She deserved it,' Cruz insisted.*"

Mrs. Coyne didn't try to hide her impish grin any longer; she and Zander laughed aloud at the same time.

"Don't, please! It hurts!" Zander left a giggling Mrs. Coyne and, while shaking his head and holding his sore ribs, he let himself into his office and propped the door open. He turned on his computer, logged in, got himself a glass of water, then sat down to go through a long list of unread emails.

He clicked on an email from one of the counselors from youth camp—and yawned. Too many days of inactivity in the hospital—and under Izzie's "care" at home—had resulted in lethargy.

Time to get back into my routine. Start getting active again. Maybe a brisk walk after dinner with Abe will be a good start since I'm restricted from jogging for a couple more weeks.

He finished his correspondence by around 2 p.m. and opened his Bible. He was appreciative of the volunteers who had taken his Sunday school class two weeks in a row, but he was itching to get back to it.

Zander heard the melodic *ding-dong* as the door to the office wing opened and closed. Without paying much attention, he heard an indistinct feminine voice speaking to Mrs. Coyne.

A moment later, "Pastor Cruz."

Zander's head came up from the text he was studying.

"*You.*"

Genie Keyes loitered in the doorway to his office. "May I come in?"

"As much as I deplore incivility, I'd rather you didn't."

Genie arched one brow. "Yes, I supposed I've earned that."

"What is it you want?"

Genie fixed her eyes on him. "What I want is Cushing's head on a plate."

Zander sat back, wincing as he did.

Genie noticed and looked closer, saw his fading bruises. "What happened to you? Get run over by a truck?"

"Funny, but no. Um, Cushing, who?"

Without invitation, Genie took the lone chair in front of Zander's desk and crossed one shapely leg over the other. She sniffed as she inspected his office. "Could they have made this room any tinier? And it's weird being in this building, this church again. It's smaller than I remembered it."

Zander shrugged. "Again, who is Cushing? Should I feel sorry for her? Call in a warning to the police?"

"I never said Cushing was a woman."

Zander stared at Genie. She stared back. "You just told a lie, *Pastor* Cruz. You know who Cushing is. She was the commando-in-chief over that botched raid on Gemma's house."

Zander remained silent, but his eyes never left Genie.

"Well, then, why don't I tell you why I'm here, shall I?"

"The short version, please."

"All right. You and I met a few weeks back and, sadly, got off to a rocky start. I was in town because Gemma's neighbor, Mrs. Calderón, called me out of concern for Gemma. *She* said my sister was acting strangely. Said Gemma had lost her job and that I should check up on her.

"Well, I did call Gemma, and I got the distinct impression that something was up. So, of course, like a good sister, I came back to this nasty little town to see for myself what was what."

"You're the good sister now?"

Genie's expression shifted. Hardened. "Skip the sermonizing, Reverend Cruz. I took the time and expense to fly back to Albuquerque to check up on Gemma and never once saw her. When I went to her house, I saw *you*, but not her. I came back later in the evening hoping to find her home. Imagine my surprise. A full-on SWAT situation couldn't have been any more dramatic."

"Yes, I saw when you arrived . . . when the soldiers, er, recognized you." Zander managed to keep his mirth tamped down, but his mouth twitched.

Genie scowled at him. "Yes, they mistook me for Gemma! Apparently my sweet, innocent twin is not nearly as sweet and innocent as she puts on."

She shifted gears without a pause. "And who was running the show that night? Who was giving the orders that evening? Why, General Cushing—whom you watched from that old man's front porch."

Zander shrugged. "I'll tell you what I told the agent who interviewed me. Abe Pickering is a long-time DCC member. He asked me to introduce myself to Gemma. I did. We talked a few times. End of story."

"I don't think so. You were entirely too protective of her when we first met."

He shrugged again—and grimaced in discomfort. "Miss Keyes, er, Genie? I have been out of the office for nearly two weeks. Today is my first day back. I have a lot to catch up on, so if you don't mind, get to your point?"

"I told you. I want Cushing's head on a platter."

"Cushing is the woman at the raid on Gemma's house?"

"Oh, stop trying to play me, Cruz. It won't work."

"Why? Because you're the evil twin?"

"Gemma has painted me in that light to you."

"I don't know if 'painted' is the right word. When she speaks of you, it's obvious that she used to be afraid of you."

Genie opened her mouth to snipe back, then closed it on Zander's last words. *Used* to be afraid of me? You know her better than you admit to if she's confided in you. And what does 'used to be afraid' mean, anyway? Gemma has been afraid her whole life. She's weak. Passive. You expect me to believe she's different now?"

Zander lifted one brow. "I'm a good reader of people, Genie. It didn't take me long to figure out that you made Gemma's childhood a living nightmare. And no. Gemma is neither weak nor passive as you claim. The few times I've talked with her, she's demonstrated strength and confidence—except, perhaps, when it comes to you."

Genie smirked and laughed low in her throat.

Zander shook his head. *She's enjoying this, Lord. Please help me turn this conversation. Give me the right words?*

"It's okay, Genie. I understand."

Genie blinked. "You understand what?"

"That you're broken. I even understand how you're broken."

She snorted, but Zander kept at her. "Every person in the history of the world is broken. Some of us have broken genes that produce birth defects. Some of us are broken through our upbringings. Others are broken by the traumas of life."

Zander smiled, a hint of sadness in his eyes. "Your feelings are broken, Genie."

She stared at him, her eyes cold and hard. "You're mistaken. The fact is, I don't have feelings."

"Oh, yes, you do. You have feelings—but they're all messed up. You don't feel love, but you do feel superiority over and disdain for others. Those are feelings.

"You don't feel empathy or compassion; however, you get excited and feel powerful when you cause someone pain. Those are feelings, too, Genie—but they are broken feelings. Wrong feelings. Deviant feelings— but feelings nonetheless."

"All right then, have it your way: I don't have *normal* feelings. I could never, for example, love God or Jesus or sappy Christians."

"That's because you can't love anyone, Genie, not even yourself. The only reason you said you couldn't love God or Jesus or Christians was to take the spotlight off your own deficiencies—off the truth that you are incapable of love.

"Do you hear that? The great, successful Genie Keyes—a failure at something? That's right. You are *incapable* of love.

"Love is kind. You aren't kind even to yourself. Love is gentle, but you drive a steamroller. Love forgives—yet you pay others back in spades for even perceived slights. That's why you're here, right? To pay Cushing back. You don't even love yourself. Oh, you are narcissistic, but that type of 'self-love' is really just self-centeredness parading on a grander scale than most people's ordinary selfishness."

Genie quivered with rage. "Are you done? I came here to talk about Cushing, not receive a psychoanalysis."

"No, I'm not done, because when you leave my office, I want you to see God differently than you do now—in fact, I want you to see yourself differently. The first step in coming to terms with God is acknowledging who and what we are. That's good news for you, Genie, because he isn't asking for your 'feelings.' Rather, he is asking that you acknowledge your brokenness."

"Right—because your so-called god loves lording it over people."

"No, that's what *you* love. The thing about God? He deserves to be worshipped, and yet he never forces himself on anyone. He asks for our freely given, freely chosen submission to his kingship."

She laughed. "See, you don't know a thing. I'm a free spirit. I don't *submit* to anyone or anything."

"No, Genie, that's not true." He left his rebuttal hanging, knowing she would not—could not—let his assertion go unchallenged.

"Like I said, *Pastor* Cruz, you don't know me."

"I hate to burst your bubble, but you aren't any different than anyone else. You are not special or better than others; in fact, you are just like the most common of individuals—susceptible to the same sin as the rest of humanity. So, in that regard? Yes; I know you.

"You say you're a free spirit? Guess again. The Bible tells us that whatever controls us is our master—and we are its servant. You have 'control issues,' and haven't figured out that those 'control issues' themselves are what control you.

"You are unable to restrain your inner urges; instead, they dominate you. Oppress you. Put another way, you are subject to your impulses—that makes *them* your master and *you* their slave. *You are a slave.*"

"No! No one tells me what to do!"

"Really? Then let's examine your impulses and how they reveal your spiritual condition."

"Impulses and spiritual condition! Ha!" She mocked him; she scoffed. "One does not influence the other."

"On the contrary, they are directly related. One is the symptom, the other the cause. You, Genie, are defined by your impulses, by the deviant, broken desires that drive and control you. And when our desires control us? Run us? Manipulate and rule us? Well, that is the very definition of spiritual bondage.

"Spiritually, you are defeated, Genie. You are subject to the master of this world—to Satan himself. He controls you and this fallen world. You are just his puppet. Whatever he tells you to do, you do it."

"I do what I like, what *I* choose!"

"No, you do what you are told."

"You have no idea who I am or what I've done."

"I have my suspicions."

"You don't know anything!"

"I think I do. Let's see, shall we? Gemma told me your parents died in a house fire when you girls were, what? Ten years old?"

Genie's face stiffened. "Nine."

"Nine years old. Only a child. Is that when you realized what you were? How aberrant you were?"

"I don't know what you're talking about." Genie's left hand strayed toward her ear and touched its lobe.

Her gesture—the "tell" of a liar—saddened Zander as it confirmed what he suspected. "You set the fire that killed your parents, didn't you, Genie? I wondered, you know, when Gemma told me how your folks died. Her account struck me as odd—how devastated she'd been but how unaffected she said you'd been. That's because you killed your parents."

"Of course, I didn't!" But her lip curled and lifted on one side hinting at just the ghost of a smile.

"You're pleased with yourself, but I'm not surprised you got away with it. Nine years old. Who'd suspect?"

"I told you: I did not do it!" Genie's mouth twitched, as though she wanted to disprove him, but her evil smile refused to allow another expression.

Zander stood his ground. "You did, and your face gives you away."

Genie laughed under her breath then, and her mocking chuckle angered Zander.

"You don't perceive the truth at this moment, but the devil owns you, Genie. He owns you lock, stock, and barrel. You think you don't submit to anyone? You say you are free? You are not. You're driven and compelled . . . bound over to commit evil—as he directs, not as you choose. Bob Dylan was right when he sang, *You gotta serve somebody.*"

His anger dissipated as quickly as it had arrived, and he added in a whisper, "You should know whom you serve, Genie. You serve Satan— not yourself."

Her mouth opened partway, but nothing came out.

Zander stood. "Think about what I've said, Genie. You have only one choice left to you. At present, you are under Satan's control—but you can choose Jesus. Salvation doesn't depend upon your broken, twisted feelings; it depends upon your *choice.*"

When she did not answer, Zander went to his door. "Thank you for coming. Yes, Cushing is after Gemma. If I can think of some way for you to help us bring Cushing down, I'll call you."

But I won't worry your sister by telling her you are back in town, Genie. She has enough worry on her plate as it is.

***

I visited my UPS mailbox that night. Parked in the back where shipments were delivered, but walked around to the front door and used my key to access my box. As usual, when packages arrived, I found a notification inside my box: *Please call for your packages during regular business hours.*

Not gonna happen.

I sent the mites into the store's system to deactivate the alarm and locate the packages, had the mites flag them as "picked up," and let myself into the back of the store where the UPS staff stored packages and boxes on metal shelving. I retrieved my three boxes and carried them out the back door to my car.

I drove up the alley behind the safe house and dropped the boxes over the back wall. After I returned my car to the parking garage, I ran home, eager to find out what the mites had bought for me.

I wasn't disappointed.

The first box contained two pairs of shoes in my size. To date, I'd trained barefoot—and had the blisters and calluses to prove it. The shoes in the package were lighter than my running shoes, cut lower around the ankle, with a flap stitched across the top to cover the laces and keep them from dangling. The shoes' soles were thinner than my running shoes, too.

I read the shoe box insert: "Your Martial Arts Sneaker is designed to provide lightweight foot protection during intense workouts. The sole is specially designed with pivot points on both the heel and ball of the foot for better traction on the floor."

"Cool!"

Under the shoe boxes I found a pair of gloves. I slipped one on my hand. The palm was thin and flexible, but the padding—on the back of the hand and along the fingers—was welcome.

Maybe the next time I smacked myself on the hand it wouldn't hurt as much!

The second box was long and narrow. I sliced the tape, pried the lid open, and found eight escrima sticks within, six rattan practice sticks and one pair of kamagong wood. Together, the three pairs of rattan sticks weighed less than the kamagong sticks.

These I eyed with misgivings. Kamagong sticks were for fighting. For real.

The last box held a folded gym bag. I unfolded it and found that it was the right length and size to carry my sticks, shoes, and gloves. I discovered one final item at the bottom.

"What is this?"

It was a long pouch of some sort with two adjustable straps. I fiddled with it for a minute, wondering what it was for.

Gemma Keyes. Slip the quiver onto your shoulders as you would a backpack.

Quiver? But not for arrows. I tucked a pair of sticks into the pouch and slipped on the quiver. It nestled in the hollow of my back; the sticks protruded high enough on my back for me to reach them with both hands at the same time.

I stood there, thinking over this last "gift," weighing its implications.

I had asked the nanomites, "*You . . . really think that* we *can get Dr. Bickel out of a military prison?*"

They had been quick to answer. *Yes, Gemma Keyes. However, we must prepare. You must prepare. . . . We have formulated a more structured training program, one better suited to arming you in the defensive and offensive strategies we anticipate will be needed.*

As much as I was enjoying the training, its ultimate purpose was . . . scary. The nanomites had a lot more confidence in it—in me—than I did.

I knew that I was in over my head.

Way over my head.

⌘⌘⌘⌘

CHAPTER 21

My sparring matches with Gus-Gus were no longer coordinated routines designed to teach me proper form and rhythm. The only accurate description for our matches was "all-out fights." My training session this night consisted of five hours of blistering contests: I wore padded headgear and a mouth guard for protection. Gus-Gus wore a serene expression as he proceeded to school me.

Over and over.

It was disgusting—and painful.

The nanomites (out in front of me in the dojo), mimicked Gus-Gus' avatar (my opponent in the warehouse). Every blow Gus-Gus struck in VR (virtual reality), the mites struck on MPRB (my poor real bod). I lived for the opportunity to land a strike on Gus-Gus. I did so at least twice per match, but I figured the mites set up the programming to allow me that. The nanomites' program occasionally allowed me to win, too—probably so I wouldn't get mad and quit.

After each match—or in the middle of one, if I messed up that badly—Gus-Gus would call out my mistakes and have me drill, drill, drill until I could perform a move perfectly.

It took a lot of juice for the mites to run that program, to simulate an opponent in the real world, to hit me and absorb my sporadic but improving hits in return. Oh, I wasn't hurting the nanomites when I struck them, but the nanocloud provided life-like resistance, the sense that I physically connected with Gus-Gus when I hit him. After training, the mites sucked current from my car's auxiliary jack all the way home.

I wondered, too, about the number of nanomites it took to produce an invisible but functioning facsimile of Gus-Gus in the dojo. How did they keep *me* hidden if a bunch of them were acting the part of my adversary?

Tonight, I made the mistake of cracking open one eye, of splitting my attention away from the VR match for an instant. Just before Gus-Gus delivered a slicing blow to the side of my padded head, I saw the flash of my own hand.

Woot! My own hand?

Then I saw flashes of stars and bright lights.

I went down and went down hard.

Okay, so the nanomites were *not* able to keep me hidden during our matches. Now that I'd answered my question, I promised my aching skull that I wouldn't take my attention off a match a second time.

***

Man, I'm starved!

I opened the fridge, hauled out OJ, eggs, potatoes, sausage, *and* bacon. Then I cooked. Two fried eggs, three sausage links, three strips of bacon, hash browns, and four slices of toast later, I felt like a new woman. Ready to get to the day's calisthenics and five-mile run.

But first, preparations for this important day. "Nano."

Yes, Gemma Keyes.

"General Cushing has that secure call scheduled at 2:30 p.m. today. I believe—it is my hope—that this call is with the individual or individuals who are keeping Dr. Bickel locked up. I want us to be there when she places that call so that we can listen in and, if my suspicions are correct, so you can trace the call."

Yes, Gemma Keyes. We must find Dr. Bickel.

"We will leave early. I will drive to within a few blocks of the base, park, and walk in. Like before."

I had an idea. *Well, why not? I'm part of the nanocloud now, one of the tribes. The nanomites and I are working together. So, why not? If they can do it in the dojo . . .*

"Nano, while I'm driving across town, I would like you to allow the upper part of my body to be visible. It would be bad news if people saw a driverless car, really bad news if the police pulled me over."

Bad news. Yes.

I was astounded and delighted at the same time. "So, *yes*, as in you'll allow my upper body to be visible?"

It is a reasonable request.

A reasonable *what*? That easy? A reasonable *request*? How many times since September had I "requested" that the mites stop making me invisible? Asked, pleaded, begged, cajoled, screamed, and demanded—all to no avail!

A reasonable request? **Grrr!**

Your blood pressure and heart rate have risen. Are you angry, Gemma Keyes?

Ya think?

I didn't answer aloud. I pressed my lips together, gathered what I needed, and flounced out the back door. As I put my body through the cardio routine the mites had devised for me, I let my mind wander. It landed on Zander's laughter and what he'd said about the mites.

"You act like the nanomites can think. Like they have feelings or common sense. They're devices, Gemma—they're technology, not people."

Sigh.

I kicked my workout into a higher gear.

Patience, Gemma. Patience.

***

Early that afternoon, I drove out of the parking garage where I kept the Escape. I chanced a glance at myself in the mirror—and gasped. What? A reflection? And who in the world? I gaped at the bags under the dark eyes that blinked back at me, at the creases around the mouth of the middle-aged woman who gaped when I gaped.

Ack! I'm old!

"Nano! What have you done? That's not me!"

We have modified your appearance to create a reasonable representation of the photograph of Kathy Sawyer on your driver's license. We do not wish for bad news.

Well . . .

I shrugged. "Yeah, good call."

I cruised up Menaul to Eubank, turned right, and drove across town to the intersection of Southern and Eubank. I pulled into the Costco parking lot before I reached the light. The Costco lot was crowded, but people were coming and going, caught up in their own concerns.

"Time to render me invisible again, Nano." I got out, held out a hand to check that all of me was hidden, and hoofed it across the busy intersection.

Plenty of base employees were returning from lunch. Traffic was heaviest in the lanes going onto the base. When I jogged up the road to the gate, only one lane of traffic leaving the base was open. I walked through the pedestrian gate without a second glance at the checkpoint.

At the keycard-secured entrance to the MEMS department, I pointed and the lock clicked open. I walked in, through the lobby, and past Mrs. Barela. I found myself mentally greeting her with familiar fondness—a big change from the first time I'd seen her at "my" desk in "my" job. I waved a little hello as I passed by on my way to Cushing's office.

Would the old bat be at her desk?

Ah, yes. She was. Cushing was reading from a fat folder.

"Time, Nano?"

The time is 1:45 p.m., Gemma Keyes.

I sat down in the lobby and twiddled my thumbs for forty minutes until I heard Cushing call to Ms. Barela. "I'll be back in an hour or less."

"Yes, General."

I jetted out the door and waited for her to follow and pass me by.

Time to mess with your day, Shark Face.

I dogged her across the parking lot, down some walkways, and into another building. I slid through the door behind her. Now that I knew which SCIF she would be using, I raced ahead, past the security checkpoint, to the SCIF at the end of the hall. There, the nanomites swarmed the card reader and unlocked the SCIF's door. The door had scarcely closed when Cushing arrived and the door again opened.

Cushing bolted the door behind her and a red light came on above it, both inside and outside, signaling that the SCIF was in use. She hurried to the phone and sat down. She studied the phone and pursed her lips when she saw no lights blinking, indicating that a call was waiting.

I had positioned myself in a corner on the opposite side of the desk where she would be seated. When she sat down, I drew nearer to the desk and phone. What the woman did next would tell the tale—I was sure of it.

Cushing fidgeted and waited another minute before she picked up the phone and dialed a number she knew by heart. And listened.

I assumed the automated system on the other end was busy syncing the secure call after the party on the other end picked up. That's when the mites would go to work.

A moment later, Cushing straightened in her chair. "Ah, Colonel. Yes, good day to you, also. What have you to report?"

A trail of mites swarmed down my arm and propelled themselves across the desk and onto the phone. I listened to the call from the warehouse as the mites began to record the conversation.

"Really, Colonel! This is the tenth straight week that Dr. Bickel has refused to cooperate despite your 'effective techniques.' Why do we even schedule these calls! I fear that your methods, as highly recommended as they came, do not suffice in this case. I wish you to be forewarned: I am making arrangements to relocate the good doctor and place him in more, er, persuasive hands."

I froze in horror.

"When? I anticipate making the move inside of two weeks. I will apprise you of your orders and the details in our next call."

What? We had less than two weeks?

"No, Colonel, I do not wish to hear your excuses—I insist upon results. Produce results or prepare to surrender custody of our guest at my discretion. Yes. Goodbye."

She slammed the phone onto its base harder than was necessary. Was her threat real or merely a gambit designed to put the screws to the unnamed colonel on the other end? So Colonel No-Name would tighten the screws on Dr. Bickel?

I allowed Cushing to exit the SCIF before I got up. I waited a few minutes after the door closed behind her to reopen it and sneak past the security check point. Outside, I saw Cushing yards away, clomping down the sidewalk, her body language conveying frustration.

Good!

Then I couldn't wait any longer to query the mites. "Nano, what did you find?"

Gemma Keyes, we are tracing the call. We will have a location shortly. Stand by.

Finally!

I waited, pacing the sidewalk and chewing my bottom lip.

Our confidence may have been precipitous, Gemma Keyes. The call was routed through a classified telecommunications hub. We have the location of the hub, but have not yet traced the origination point of the call. We will continue our efforts.

"Well, where is this 'hub,' Nano? Surely its location gets us close to Dr. Bickel, provides us with general vicinity? He can't be that far from the hub, can he?"

I was unprepared for their answer.

Gemma Keyes, the telecommunications hub is located within the perimeter of White Sands Missile Range.

***

I was numb as I left the base. White Sands? What I knew of the missile range would fill a teacup! Or something a lot smaller. Like nano-sized smaller. And our window of opportunity had shrunk to similar size.

I fretted and stewed and ran until I reached Costco and got into my car.

We had two weeks. Perhaps less than that? And then Cushing would, presumably, move Dr. Bickel elsewhere.

But we weren't ready to spring Dr. Bickel! *I* wasn't ready!

I drove away from Costco fretting, shaking my head, forehead creased with worry, thoughts elsewhere, blind to my surroundings. Instead of continuing toward Menaul as I should have, I turned east down Central and, before I knew it, had crossed Juan Tabo. I snapped to my surroundings.

I needed to turn around and go back—except, right there, *right in front of my face*, was a Blake's Lotaburger. Blake's: Home of the Green Chile Double Cheeseburger.

"It has been *ages* since I've had a burger—let alone a green chile cheeseburger," I groused, "and I'm *starving*!"

To be fair, I was always starving these days. Yeah, true—but there was no sneaking an invisible woman through a drive-through.

I pulled into the Blake's parking lot to make my turn and head back down Central. Drove all the way around the burger joint to the exit onto the street, glanced both ways for traffic—and caught my reflection in the rearview mirror.

Kathy Sawyer stared back at me.

"Wait just a cotton-pickin' minute . . ."

I threw the Escape into reverse and headed for the drive-through.

Gemma Keyes. What are you doing?

"I'm getting some food, Nano. I'm famished!"

We advise against this course of action, Gemma Keyes.

"You don't want me to collapse from hunger, do you, Nano?"

Certainly not, Gemma Keyes. However, we do not detect starvation markers in your bod—

"Famished. Practically perishing, Nano. Faint from deprivation. Hold that thought a sec, 'k? Yes, I'd like your Lotaburger with cheese and green chile. Um, make that two of them."

Gemma Keyes—

"And two large orders of onion rings and a large order of seasoned fries—and, oh! A milkshake! Yeah! No, two milkshakes, please. One chocolate, the other your seasonal pumpkin pie. Yup. That's everything."

I pulled forward, salivating and swallowing with anticipation.

Gemma Keyes!

"Yes, Nano?" I was soooo sweet.

Perhaps you do not comprehend that the image we are projecting to the world is fluid and difficult to maintain. We have less difficulty rendering you invisible than we do keeping this image intact and lifelike.

"What? I can't hear you over the roar of my stomach. Not to worry. I'm confident that you can handle it, Nano. Absolutely convinced. Anyhow, I'll only be at the pickup window a couple of minutes. Not a problem."

It all went well. I gave the nice, smiling woman cash, and she handed me a big, steaming Lotaburger bag then the two shakes set inside a cardboard carrier.

I was so stinking hungry, I was trembling! I set everything on the passenger seat and turned to get my change.

That's when it happened.

I inhaled to say "thanks," and felt it coming on.

Fast. Like a freight train.

A sneeze.

A giant, head-exploding, snot-blasting, extinction-level event.

I tried to stop it, to smother it, I really did! You know what I mean: I closed my mouth and held on for dear life just as the sneeze achieved ignition.

Gemma Keyes! No! Don't—

That sneeze about scrambled my brains. Nanomites flew from my face like dust before a tornado—as though they'd been detonated.

The gal at the window froze, her hand extended, offering me my change.

You know kaleidoscopes? With the twisty thingy on the end? I imagine that's the view I presented as my sneeze hurled nanomites in every direction and they fought to propel themselves back to my face, struggled to reassemble Kathy Sawyer.

Yup. That nice Lotaburger lady got to preview a living, breathing "face morpher" app—one for which many of you would pay good money.

Scary much?

"Uh . . . Uh . . . Uh . . ."

Poor thing. She was stuck on "uh."

As the nanomites reestablished my faux face and things "settled," the befuddled woman blinked and blurted, "A-are you all right, ma'am?"

"Me? Oh, *yes*. I'm *fine*."

Yup. Fine. Perfect.

Hangry.

Kathy Sawyer smiled her reassurance—and her concern. "Say, are *you* all right, sweetie? You look a little . . . peaked."

I took my change from her motionless hand and drove away, leaving the poor cashier in shock and confusion—and possible regret over any drug usage in her youth.

Gemma Keyes!

I turned on the radio. Cranked it way up. Thought about hot, crispy onion rings followed by gulps of thick chocolate shake.

Mmm. Mmm. Mmm.

⌘⌘⌘⌘

CHAPTER 22

The weather, which had been cooling steadily as November wore on, evolved further overnight. I awoke the next morning, shivering and sensing the change. Even in the basement, the howl of the wind and the creaking and popping of the house contracting in the cold reached me.

A storm was upon us.

Good day for it, I thought as I dressed in layers of warm clothes and climbed the ladder into the house. The furnace was running as programmed, but the icy, buffeting wind was doing its best to force its way inside. The windows flexed and groaned under the pounding gusts; the wind's frozen fingers scrabbled on the walls.

I grabbed coffee, wrapped myself in a light blanket, and peeked through the blinds on the back door. Frosty white stuff swirled and thrashed against the window—not real snow, just frost on the move.

We don't get much snow in Albuquerque—the occasional dump that lasts a day or two. More common are blasting winds that carry freezing sleet-mixed-with-snow, blizzards that scour us for a day before passing on.

Happy Thanksgiving, I told myself.

Coming from such a small family, our Thanksgiving celebrations had never been fancy affairs—they were often potlucks, gatherings of what Aunt Lucy called "orphans," an eclectic collection of church friends who had no family. After Lu passed, Abe and I opted for dinner at one of those all-you-can-eat buffets. We enjoyed it—and cleanup was a snap.

I chuckled, grateful for those memories.

I took my coffee downstairs and ran a scan of the security system for alerts. I found none—but I did see one of my phones blinking.

Voice mail? I listened to the two words: "Call me."

A smile tugged at my mouth as I deleted the VM and the call log. I dialed from memory.

"Hey. Got your message."

"Some weather, huh?"

"Yeah. You won't catch me going out today!"

"Well, no such luck for me. Now that I'm back on my feet, Pastor McFee is making up for lost time. He's spending Thanksgiving out of town with family, so I'm preaching this Sunday. And today? Today Iz and I are helping the singles group from church to serve lunch *and* dinner at a shelter. I thought I'd call early to wish you a happy Thanksgiving. By the way, I-40 and I-25 in all directions are closed due to the winds. I imagine every hotel and shelter in town will be full up because of the storm. It's gonna be a long day."

I shivered—and was grateful again for this house, this home, temporary as it might be. "What about Abe?"

"He'll be okay while I'm gone. Between lunch and dinner, I will fix him a big plate and take it to him."

I toyed with the idea of spending the afternoon with Abe, but gave it up. The roads would be treacherous.

"Drive safe today, Zander."

"I will—but you stay inside, hear?"

"That's the plan. Thanks for calling."

Thanksgiving called for a grander breakfast than usual. I added cinnamon rolls to my usual fare and gobbled down the meal like there was no tomorrow. Afterward, the mites and I got serious about White Sands.

We mined all the data about the missile range available in the public domain. Well, I wasn't certain it was *all* public domain; the nanomites could defeat the security of any network connected to the Internet, so some of the data could have been from official, restricted government files—non-classified but still controlled. Regardless of its origins, what we found was daunting.

The White Sands Missile Range stretches across the New Mexico desert, spanning five counties and most of the Tularosa Basin. The range occupies nearly 3,200 square *miles* of the state's southeast corner. Knowing Cushing had hidden Dr. Bickel somewhere on WSMR had been about as helpful as saying she had hidden him somewhere in Texas!

Cushing may have hidden Dr. Bickel close to her—close in relative terms—but she had also picked the largest U.S. military haystack in which to hide her "needle."

"Well played, Cushing," I whispered. "The proverbial needle in a haystack."

Gemma Keyes, we will locate Dr. Bickel.

"I'm trusting that you will, Nano."

The storm roared on until late afternoon when it blew itself out. Eastern New Mexico and Texas would continue to feel the storm's fierce, icy blast, but for now we were out of it. I yawned and got up from the couch where I'd been napping. Now that the tumult of wind had passed, I was itching to move.

Time for a run, I told myself, lacing up my shoes, *then over to the dojo.*

I'd seen the holiday weekend schedule posted on the dojo's doors: Closed until Monday.

Good.

Gus-Gus was accelerating my training. He was expecting more from me. He was pushing me harder . . . and I was letting him.

I thrived on the work.

As I finished tying my shoes, I pondered yet another recent observation: The communication the mites and I shared? It was evolving. The progression was subtle, hard to pinpoint, but some of our daily exchanges, our little back-and-forths? Well, they just "happened."

What I mean is that I heard the mites speaking in my ear less often, but I still *heard* them. At first, it had been a word or two. Negligible. Now it was occurring more frequently. Like, this morning, I'd "heard" a whole sentence—and the mites had not spoken it, had not vibrated the words in my ear.

And I'd felt the urge to answer them in kind. I hadn't succeeded, but I had the strangest sense that it was near me . . . like a phrase that's *right there* on the tip of my tongue. I sensed that I should be able to reach out and grasp it—only to discover that it was a hairsbreadth beyond my reach.

Another example? The mites were involving themselves directly in my training, not merely through Gus-Gus' AI. I couldn't put a label to it, but sometimes it felt like the mites and I were moving together while I practiced—they helping me, and their consciousness blending with mine to form something . . . stronger, more cohesive.

The merge. I shook my head over this latest progression.

We weren't done yet.

***

With the martial arts school closed for the holiday weekend, Gus-Gus insisted on an eight-hours-a-day training schedule. At least he conducted our long sessions during the day and not all night! Friday's workouts had been grueling, and I'd needed more than my usual four hours of sleep to recover from the physical abuse and fatigue.

When I arrived at the dojo the Saturday morning after Thanksgiving, I left another envelope on the owner's desk and returned to the floor to commence the day's lessons. Gus-Gus and I were in the middle of a heavy sparring drill when the nanomites *freaked out* and, with a squeak or two, went silent.

Gus-Gus disappeared.

I blinked and opened my eyes to my "real" surroundings—and to a man's irate voice.

"Who the *blank* are you, and what the *bleep* are you doing in my school?"

The guy was dark-haired, slender but compact, and maybe three inches taller than me.

Oh, yeah—and he was furious.

"I said, who are you? Who said you could use my school?"

It dawned on me that this guy was the dojo's owner and that he was looking right at me.

I lowered my sticks and saw them.

What?

The mites should have been hiding them! Then I saw my *hands* wrapped around the sticks. Saw my feet down on the floor.

I'm visible?

I held one hand up where I could examine it.

And I'm me, not Kathy Sawyer?

"You'd better answer me, lady, before I call the cops."

Nano! Where'd you go?

"Hey! I'm talking to you!"

My head snapped up. "I . . . um, I'm the one who's been paying to use your, um, school."

He looked perplexed for half a second. "The money? On my desk? That's you?"

"Yeah."

He was confused, but not nearly as confused as I was. Why weren't the nanomites hiding me? Why were they silent?

The guy came closer. "What, so you . . . you've been working out in my school. On your own?"

"Um, sort of. I mean, yes. Alone."

"I watched you for a minute. You seem advanced. Almost looked like you were sparring with someone."

"Uh . . ."

"Whatever. I want to know how you are getting in here."

Nano?

Not a thing from the nanomites. Not a peep.

Traitors!

The guy bent over and picked up a pair of my sticks—not my extra rattan sticks in the bag, but the kamagong sticks on the floor.

"These yours?"

"Yeah, they are. So, listen, I apologize. I'll just be on my way. I won't come back."

"You didn't answer my question. How are you getting in here?"

"I'll be going now."

"No, you won't; I have a top-notch security system. I want answers."

"Look, I said I'm sorry. I won't bother you again. I promise."

"You're not leaving until you answer me."

I made a move toward my bag, but he stepped between me and my gear. His expression hardened. "I have a better idea. How about we spar? Let's see how good you are."

"No, thanks. Honestly, I'm kinda new at this. I don't know how to properly spar, don't know the rules. I just . . . fight."

He liked that idea even better. "All right. Let's fight. Maybe I'll teach you a lesson—not that I'd actually *hurt* you or anything, but I could teach you a thing or two about, say, property rights and criminal trespass."

The guy's response rubbed me wrong; his arrogance sparked my temper—his cocky, "I could teach you a thing or two" attitude. If the smoke that filled my head had rolled out of my ears, he would have called 911 and reported a fire. It wasn't just this guy's condescending attitude that angered me; the nanomites—who suddenly regained their "voice"—earned their share, too.

Gemma Keyes. We apologize for not detecting this man's presence sooner. However, as we analyzed this unanticipated encounter, we determined that it presents an opportunity for you to engage in a fight sequence with another human. Such an experience will promote our goal of helping you to become optimal. Do not be anxious; you will not be harmed.

"Oh, *sure.*"

I was about to get my hiney kicked from here to Santa Fe! But, *hey,* anything for a fight sequence with another human, right?

Seething inside, I stretched my neck and rotated my shoulders. Whatever punishment this guy dished out wouldn't matter, would it? The nanomites would just "mitigate" my injuries like they did when I fought with Gus-Gus.

Lovely prospect.

I twirled my sticks to flex my wrists. I was plenty riled.

"A lesson? Hmm. Well, okay. Let's go."

I bowed to him.

He didn't bow back. In fact, he appeared less certain, like he was rethinking his challenge.

I couldn't resist a taunt. "Come on. Scared of a girl?"

"No, but it was a bad idea, just my anger talking. Not professional of me. I don't want to hurt you; I just want answers."

"I won't tell if you won't."

"You won't tell what?"

"That you let a girl beat you."

He flushed red and tilted his head. "Y'know, lady, you've got quite a mouth on you. I'd be happy to slap it shut, if that's how you want it."

"I'd like to see you try. You'll find another pair of rattan sticks in the bag." I pointed.

I bowed again; this time, he bowed back.

Remember, I started my training a couple of weeks ago, while this guy was an instructor with years of experience behind him. I should have been terrified. The fact that I *wasn't* terrified was suspicious: Who knew what hormones and chemicals the nanomites were feeding my system so that I'd feel this confident? Shrugging, I moved into position.

Because rather than terrified, I was excited.

He came at me fast, *really* fast, sticks weaving and crossing in a blur. I countered what he threw at me. I parried and deflected his strikes. We danced apart.

Then that "thing" happened. That thing where the nanomites' consciousness and mine blended. Their "mind" became my own.

The guy attacked; I thwarted him with ease. The flick of a glance, a facial microexpression, the infinitesimal tensing of a muscle—those things telegraphed the cocky dude's intentions. I foresaw his moves before he acted.

Holy, smokin' Spider Man!

The speed of the nanomites' computing power and predictive logic flashed through my hands and feet. The flow between us—me and the nanocloud—was like nothing I'd experienced or even conceived of. I was more in tune with *them* than I was with my physical surroundings!

Conscious thought seemed slow. Ponderous. The mites and I traveled ahead of reason, through the realm of intuition and presentiment, my moves like flashes of brilliance. Mindful thought trailed each move the way thunder follows lightning.

The nanomites and I weren't six; we were *one*.

"Yow!" Dojo guy cursed and stumbled back, stung by the blow I'd landed on the outside of his left arm just above his elbow.

I moved away, bouncing lightly on the balls of my feet. "I hit your radial nerve. You won't have normal sensation in that arm for at least a quarter of an hour."

"I know what the radial nerve is, lady."

"You ready to quit?"

"I'm just getting warmed up."

As was I. The bond the nanomites and I shared was intense and potent. I didn't want it to end. I was so freaking wired! Powerful! Invincible!

Dojo guy sprang at me; I sidestepped before he moved and snuck in a strike to his outer thigh as he passed by. He took one more step before his leg collapsed under him.

"We're done," I told him.

Over in less than two minutes.

Dojo guy didn't dispute me. "How . . . how did you do that? I've never seen anyone move that fast. Who are you?"

"Does it matter?"

He staggered to his feet, massaging his thigh, limping to stay erect. "Well, if I had to be beaten by a woman, I'm glad it was by a fine fox such as yourself." He kind of grinned, a sheepish, "You're hot; don't you think I'm hot, too?" grin.

My reply was scathing. "Save it for someone who cares, dude."

What was he thinking? I was Gemma the Nondescript! The woman who was invisible *before* I couldn't be seen, before the nanomites made it their mission in life to hide me *in perpetuum*.

The nanomites spoke inside my head. I was surprised and perplexed, but not altogether unhappy with their proposal.

I made the effort to be civil. "Say, would you be, um, amenable to a little arrangement?"

"What kind of arrangement?" Dojo guy's response was stiff. He was smarting from more than the two strikes during our match.

Think fast, Gemma.

"Sorry. Uh, first off, I'm, um, Emily. What's your name?"

"Doug."

"Well, Doug, is the cash I've been leaving on your desk enough payment for my use of your school after hours?"

"I still want to know how you're getting past my security system."

"Learn to live with disappointment, Doug. Have I left enough money?"

He huffed and folded his arms. "Yeah, yeah. It's fine. What's your proposal?"

"I keep coming, using your facility, and paying you for it. You don't mention me to anyone. *Anyone*. Not a soul. You will agree to keep my presence to yourself. You will speak of me to no one. You will carry on business as usual, and you will give your word not to sneak in cameras or any type of surveillance."

Yeah, because we'll be watching and listening, buddy.

"A warning, Doug: If you decide to pull something fast, trust me when I say that, as easily as we defeated your security system, we'll know if you speak of me to anyone.

"In return for your cooperation, we'll increase the amount we've been leaving you. Say, another fifty each week? Win-win, right?"

I didn't notice how, partway through my last statement, I'd switched from singular first person to plural. As the whole "we" thing fell on my ears, I grimaced.

We? Creepy! Where did that—

Doug's face reflected what I had just realized. He was kind of freaked out, but he blustered a reply.

"Let's say I don't agree."

I shrugged and reverted to normal first-person voice. "I'll find another place to train. The money stops. You never see me again."

And we will make sure you don't remember a thing.

And there it was again! What was up with the disturbing plural voice?

Doug looked aside, thinking. "Another fifty?"

"Yup. It's good money, Doug. Why blow it off?"

The nanomites whispered again. In my head.

Stranger and stranger.

"Oh. And I might request some sparring practice with you from time to time."

He winced. "Not sure you need any practice, Emily."

I extended my hand to Doug. "Come on, then. Deal?"

He looked at my hand first, then shook it in a perfunctory manner. "Yeah. Deal."

I drove away from the school reflecting that Doug was the first and only person to have seen me, the actual me, in months. But what occupied me more was the rehash of our short fight.

The ease and swiftness of movement I had experienced, the foresight—the foreknowledge of what Doug would do before he did it—and my ability to act on that knowledge just as fast? It was more than me, more than I could do by myself. Every aspect of that fight spoke of a synchronicity with the nanomites I hadn't believed possible.

Yes. Things between us were still evolving.

***

I arose the Sunday morning of Thanksgiving weekend with "Zander on the brain."

He'd told me he would be leading the service at DCC today, and I wondered how he would prepare and what he would (gag me) preach on. Despite my best efforts to block them out, bits of our recent conversations—especially the part about God calling me—repeated like song fragments that get trapped in your head *and won't quit.*

Sometime after breakfast, I dressed to leave the house. That's when I realized I had decided to peek in on the service. It hadn't been a conscious, considered decision, but after spending hours with Zander's voice stuck on replay inside my skull, I was about ready to pound a stake into my own brain.

Anything to change the tune. Even more Zander.

I parked a block away and walked to DCC. From across the street, my gaze tracked up the church's tall, brick front until I fixed my eyes on the round stained glass window high above the doors. After our parents died and Genie and I came to live with Aunt Lu, the image of Jesus with a lamb laying across his shoulders had both intrigued and puzzled me.

I was less intrigued today, but just as puzzled.

When the crowd pressing through the two sets of double doors under that window began to dwindle, I followed them inside and made an abrupt right. I knew where I was going.

Back when I'd attended DCC with Genie and Aunt Lu, a few teens would hide upstairs in the choir loft, choosing the loft's farthest-back seats, almost behind the old pipe organ. The kids squabbled over those seats because they could get away with goofing off or necking during service—especially while the organ was blasting away during the singing. Genie managed to snag those "prime" seats a few times when we were teens.

I had planned to go up the back stairs to the choir loft—except, as it turns out, the narrow staircase to the loft was cordoned off.

Huh? What about the organist? Maybe he's the only one allowed up there these days?

Well, that worked for me. With no competition, I would have my choice of seats. I stepped over the thick cord and headed up. But when I reached the top of the stairs, the organ's heavy wooden cover was closed and locked over its three keyboards. A coating of dust told me how disused the organ was!

Weird.

I was the only one in the loft—and down below me unfolded a bewildering scene.

Modern instruments occupied most of the platform at the front—drums, guitars, bass, electric keyboards. A team of musicians and singers led the singing.

Loud singing. *Loud* music. With a beat.

I couldn't miss the words: A data projector plastered them in foot-high letters across two screens mounted on either side of the platform. The congregation below me was on its feet, singing, swaying, and clapping along.

Clapping in church?

I pulled one of the old wooden folding chairs toward the edge of the loft and plopped down on it. Leaned on the railing overlooking the sanctuary. Stared and listened and shook my head. Nothing could have been more different from the church of my childhood.

This was not the Downtown Community Church I knew.

I searched for Zander. Below, in the front row, on the left side, I spied him. He was singing, too, one hand in the air, lost, I guess, in his own worship experience.

After twenty minutes of exuberant song, followed by another twenty of slower, more intense tunes—none that I recognized—the congregation sat, and Zander walked up to the platform.

His bruises were almost gone; the most visible remainder of Mateo's attack was the sling that kept his collarbone immobile. He smiled.

"It's great to be back in the house of the Lord, and I'm grateful for this opportunity to share from God's word. Our text this morning is found in Luke, chapter 15.

Now the tax collectors and sinners
were all gathering around to hear Jesus.
But the Pharisees and the teachers of the law muttered,
"This man welcomes sinners and eats with them."

"In the first two verses of this short chapter, Jesus is accused of welcoming sinners and eating with them. Jesus responds with three parables in quick succession, each different, but all three designed to dispel a wrong understanding of God—not that God condones sin, but the perception that God does not care about the sinner. In contrast to what the Pharisees and teachers taught, the three parables speak a single truth: *Our God is a seeker*.

"In the first parable, Jesus speaks of the Good Shepherd. The Good Shepherd, Jesus said, will leave his entire flock—ninety-nine percent of his flock—to pursue the *one* who has wandered or run away. In John 10, Jesus tells us clearly that he is the Good Shepherd, and we are the sheep. The Good Shepherd goes after the lost sheep, because *our God is a seeker*.

"In Luke 15, verses 8-10, Jesus tells of a woman who owns ten silver coins. When she loses one of those coins, she expends precious and expensive oil to light a lamp. Why? She lights a lamp to illuminate her entire house while she sweeps it and searches all the dark corners until she finds that lost coin.

"Silver is valuable, my friends. So is oil to light a lamp. Those ten silver coins represent people, people who are made in God's own image and likeness. We are valuable! When God sees us, he sees something of *value*.

"The oil for the lamp represents the Holy Spirit. Like the woman in this parable, God will spend money to search high and low for you because you are as valuable as silver to him. He will expend his Holy Spirit to woo you, to convince you, to chastise you, *to illuminate your life*. He will do all that is necessary to bring you to himself, because *our God is a seeker*.

"In the final parable of Luke 15, Jesus tells the tale of a father and two sons. One son is good and obedient; the other son is selfish and demanding. He demands his inheritance—before his father is even dead.

"Can you imagine it? The kid might as well have said, 'Hey, Dad. Kick the bucket already, will you? I only care about your money.' His father must have been so hurt!

"You know the story. The father gives him the money, and the son goes on his way and wastes it all—half of everything the father has worked for his entire life. The son wastes it all on parties and pleasure. When the money is gone, and the son is starving, he remembers that even the servants in his father's house have enough food. So, he decides to go home and beg for a servant's position in his father's house.

"In the meantime, what has the father been doing? Verse 20 tells us, *But while he* (the son) *was still a long way off, the father saw him*. What has the father been doing? The text tells us that the father has been watching for his son to return. Hoping against the evidence, for a long, long time, the father has been watching for his son to come home, believing he *will* come home. Why? Because the father loves his son, even as ungrateful and hurtful as the son has been.

"Of course, the father in this parable is God the Father, and we are the son who has behaved in such an ungrateful, hurtful manner. God still watches for us; he still waits for us. No matter how hopeless or how long it has been, he is watching and waiting. Why? Because *our God is a seeker*.

Zander warmed to his subject. He stared with love around the congregation. He even glanced up into the choir loft—and paused, a curious look on his face.

What was that? Even though I was certain Zander could not see me, his puzzlement made me pull back. Had he . . . had he glimpsed the sparkle of the nanomites that Emilio said he sometimes saw?

Zander blinked and looked down to his notes. "Yes, our God is a seeker. Jesus said it this way, speaking of himself: *For the Son of Man came to seek and to save the lost*. We know from the three parables in Luke 15 that God values people, but not merely 'people' in a general sense: No, *God values lost people*. Now, let's make it personal: God values *you*.

"How valuable are you? Let me repeat: Our God will expend precious resources and even risk loss—that's how valuable you are to him. And our God will watch for you! No matter how long you've been gone or how much you've wasted, he will, in hope of your return, watch for you. Does this sound like a God who does not care? Not a bit.

"Let me take the lessons of these parables even further. A normal shepherd, when a sheep has strayed, does not know in which direction his lost sheep has gone. He may have no clue. While he searches, he may grow weary and discouraged. Not so, the Good Shepherd! He sees you wherever you are, whether you are hidden, trapped, injured, or damaged. He knows exactly where you are. You cannot hide from God! No room is so dark that he cannot see you. You are not . . ."

Here Zander's eyes, again puzzled, drifted up to the choir loft. "You are not invisible to him."

At those words, the hair on my arms, neck, and head prickled and crawled. I pulled away from the rail and fell against the hard back of my chair. Zander's next words reached me anyway.

"In closing, I want to draw your attention to two more facets these three parables have in common. First, each parable ends with rejoicing. The father pulled his son to his bosom *and threw a banquet for him*; the woman clasped her lost coin *and called all of her neighbors to celebrate*; Jesus, the Good Shepherd, placed the lost lamb about his neck, *and the angels in heaven rejoiced*."

Jesus placed the lost lamb about his neck? In an instant, my lifelong puzzlement over DCC's stained glass window vanished.

"The last facet deals with 'proximity'—each parable ends in close relationship between the one who was lost and the one who sought and found him. When we are lost and God finds us, he does not merely tolerate us: *He draws us close*.

"Don't stand far back from him! Our great God is a seeker. He will call to you. He will search high and low for you. When he finds you, he will draw you close—and he will rejoice over you."

⌘⌘⌘⌘

CHAPTER 23

I was in a whole other mental place Monday afternoon, unprepared for the news the mites announced.

Gemma Keyes, we have pinpointed Dr. Bickel's exact location.

Adrenaline surged through me, washing everything else away.

Dr. Bickel! Were the mites as excited as I was?

"Where? Where is he, Nano?"

We will show you, Gemma Keyes.

I dropped into the warehouse to see what they had uncovered, and it was a lot. I didn't ask how many networks and satellite feeds the mites had hacked into, and they didn't offer the information. They produced their "take," overhead views of the site of Dr. Bickel's incarceration—both video and stills shot from different angles—and I kept my questions to myself.

As I studied and memorized the aerial images, I was puzzled to see how small a footprint the place had: a single rectangular building on a lot about the size of an acre? Something about its size bothered me, but I was distracted from pursuing that concern when the mites zoomed in on the pictures.

I focused on the physical security measures: The site was surrounded by what was certainly a tall chain link fence. A wide and familiar swath of dirt banded the outside of the fence line.

"Oh! That's a network of pressure sensors buried under the dirt, Nano. An intrusion detection system."

Yes, we agree; however, we can defeat the sensors if our approach goes unnoticed, Gemma Keyes.

I pulled back from the image and followed the single gravel road leading away from the site. The road ran a couple miles north and east and terminated at a tall gate just shy of the highway.

"All right, but how . . . how do we get from the highway to Dr. Bickel, Nano? I don't see how our approach will 'go unnoticed' if we use the access road."

We will start in the town of Alamogordo and leave the highway 700 yards east of the access road. We will cut through the fencing along the missile range boundary and proceed overland. We will guide you.

I zoomed in and scanned along the highway. The faint lines marking the range's boundary looked like an ordinary barbed wire fence. It was going to prove less difficult to get *onto* the range than I'd thought.

But getting off the range without getting caught?

"How far is it from where they have Dr. Bickel to the highway?"

His location is 3.4 miles inside the perimeter of the White Sands Missile Range along State Road 70, 31.8 miles from Alamogordo and 36.2 miles from Las Cruces.

"Those distances might be clear when looking at a map, Nano, but how will you know where to leave the highway once we're out in the middle of nowhere?"

We have ordered a high-end smart phone equipped with mapping and unlimited data.

I laughed to myself. *Getting awfully liberal with my credit card, aren't you, Nano?*

My credit card? Since the merge, the mites had begun to include me when they used terms such as "us." More and more, their speech was shifting in this direction. More and more, my mental and physical functions were tied to the nanocloud.

To them I asked, "So, um, we'll use the mapping GPS to direct us from, er, Alamogordo?"

Yes. In addition, we have ordered a selection of electronic parts to customize the phone. We will modify it to receive a strong signal even if we are out of optimal service range.

Optimal? Again?

We have plotted the route from the highway to Dr. Bickel's location, Gemma Keyes. The journey across the desert terrain will require a vehicle optimal for off-road travel.

I sighed. If I never heard the word "optimal" again . . .

"Um, okay . . . another vehicle. Like you said—something that can handle rough roads." A rig that could handle an eight- to ten-mile, round-trip jaunt through uncharted desert. Just another piece of logistics to be "figured out."

I hadn't intended to take the Escape onto the missile range anyway. Sure, now that I knew the plan, my car wouldn't serve us as well as, say, a pickup or a Land Rover. But on a more important note? I could not allow Kathy Sawyer's legally registered vehicle to be seen or confiscated: The Escape (aptly named) was our ride out of New Mexico.

So, kinda essential.

Gemma Keyes, where will we take Dr. Bickel upon the successful completion of our mission?

Good question. East to Texas? South to Mexico? North to Colorado? "Um . . . I hope Dr. Bickel will suggest a place to hide."

It is true that Dr. Bickel owns many properties.

"Nano, do you know where his properties are?"

Yes, Gemma Keyes. We know the locations of all his properties.

"Well, then, we will head toward the one he says best fits our needs."

This part of the plan is not as well-devised as we would wish it to be, Gemma Keyes.

"Yeah. I know."

They were making me nervous—and I didn't need any assistance in that area. I turned back to the aerial shots and zoomed in. The shadow of a lone figure near the perimeter fence caught my eye.

"Nano, how many guards do you estimate?"

We do not need to estimate; our surveillance and research has provided us with accurate information. The fence is continuously patrolled by a single armed guard. During the day, the building has four personnel. At night, only two.

They paused. *We recommend going at night.*

I shrugged. "Sounds right. Better odds than during the day. Do you have a layout of the building?"

It appeared before me.

"But this looks like a house. Just a plain, ordinary, old house!"

Records we retrieved indicate that it was, indeed, built as a domicile. It has been repurposed: The walls of one room in the house have been reinforced with cinderblock and rebar.

"Then that's where they are keeping him." I memorized the layout, all the rooms, doors, and windows.

That is our conclusion also.

"What's that weird stuff on top of the garage?"

We also observed the modifications to the garage roof—vents and pipes unnecessary for the storage of automobiles.

"Could they have fitted the garage as a lab for Dr. Bickel?"

A logical assumption, Gemma Keyes.

The niggling returned. "But the house and its yard . . . are so much smaller than I assumed they would be. Less . . . I don't know . . . less intimidating? Or prison-like?"

Less "official."

The mites went quiet. I wondered if anything about the site gnawed at them like it gnawed at me. When they spoke again, it was to shift the topic.

Gemma Keyes, we will assist you when you breach the intrusion detection system and fence, but our assistance over the course of the night will be governed by our power consumption. To conserve our power, you must be prepared to disarm and incapacitate the guards and personnel.

I rubbed my eyes. *Sure, pal.*

***

That night, Gus-Gus concentrated my workout on techniques I would use to disarm and immobilize an adversary. After rehearsing the specifics with me, Gus-Gus stepped aside, and a second avatar appeared. In his black uniform, with M4 rifle slung from his shoulder, the guy looked just like the special forces who'd rushed my house only weeks before.

The avatar's appearance intimidated me, and my nerves already scraped along a raw edge. It was about to get real, and I didn't know if I had the stomach for it.

The nanomites probably knew that, too.

"Gemma Keyes, you will practice incapacitating this soldier, just as you will incapacitate the patrol guard when we breach the perimeter."

Gus-Gus' manner left no option for refusal.

The black-uniformed guy turned and walked away from me, down one of the shadowy halls leading away from the warehouse. Sighing, I followed him.

With no warning, he pivoted. Swung his rifle up.

"Who's there? Stop where you are!"

I can't describe what happened then, except that my training kicked in. The instant the guard began to turn, I leapt forward and hammered him with two slicing blows. The half-raised rifle fell from the guy's incapacitated hand; his left knee buckled and, screaming in pain, the man went down.

I swallowed hard and assessed what I'd done. *Broken wrist. Displaced patella; possible LCL tear. Not getting up anytime soon.*

Could I *do* that to a real person? Could I hurt someone—truly hurt them?

I almost threw up.

The avatar disappeared, and Gus-Gus appeared in front of me. He was not pleased. "If the guard screams, you will not have achieved Dr. Bickel's release; you will have failed. The guard must be silenced, Gemma Keyes."

I glared at Gus-Gus, but a voice from deep within me shouted, *Well, I can't fail. I won't! I **cannot** fail Dr. Bickel. I can do this. I must do this.*

"Again," I demanded.

Same setup. The guard pivoted and walked away from me. I didn't wait for him to turn. I sprinted up behind him and landed a single glancing blow behind his ear. He never saw me coming, and he dropped like a rock.

"Better. Once more."

We ran the scenario in different variations. Each time, I dropped the guard without a sound. Without breaking his arm or trashing his knee for life.

I could live with that.

"Remember, Gemma Keyes, that you have the advantage. The guard may hear you, but he will not be able to see you."

When I'd satisfied Gus-Gus, we moved on to less-desirable variations, situations in which I had lost the element of surprise. The mites programmed the scenario so that the avatar, although he could not see me, for some reason *heard* me and brought his rifle up.

Yikes.

As his gun swung up, I dropped and somersaulted, rolling diagonally. My speed was incredible. Superhuman. I popped up under the guard's extended arm and battered the man's solar plexus. With the air knocked out of him, the avatar could not call out, and I dropped him.

I was happier with my performance now, more confident that I could disable the guards when the time came. Less worried about leaving them permanently damaged in the process.

Maybe we had a chance after all.

Gemma Keyes.

"Yes?"

The avatar and the VR setting where Gus-Gus trained me disappeared, leaving me alone in the warehouse.

Gemma Keyes, we have new information for you. We have identified Arnaldo Soto's probable location.

My mouth dropped open. "What? How 'probable' a location?"

The probability is presently eighty-seven percent.

"In New Mexico? Nearby?"

Yes.

You know that old saying, "tossing a wrench into the works"? Here I was, psyching myself up to go after Dr. Bickel, not Soto! I lapsed into silence, brooding over the news. This unexpected turn of events complicated things.

Or did it?

I left the warehouse and sat down on the dojo floor to think.

I was worried about getting Dr. Bickel out, but I was more worried about afterward. The greatest danger Cushing presented would come *after* we freed Dr. Bickel. With all her resources, how far could we run? I knew—and the mites knew—that we needed a better plan for "after," preferably a place where, even should Cushing find us, she could not touch us.

In my humble estimation, only the light of full public disclosure could pull her sharky teeth. The more I pondered our dilemma, the more I was certain that the "ideal" place was out in the open.

As long as we hid the truth about Dr. Bickel from the world, Cushing was free to lie and pervert her authority. Our best hope was to go public—that is, for Dr. Bickel to go public. His resurrection from the dead would bring the media down upon Cushing's head—which would protect *his* head. All he needed to do was have his own grave exhumed to prove that she had lied about his death.

When Dr. Bickel testified to how she'd captured and held him against his will, Cushing would be finished.

Yes, Dr. Bickel's best chance of survival was to go public. To do that, we needed to convey him from White Sands to a place where he would have enough time and opportunity to make his accusations public—a place safe from Cushing's long reach.

And where might that be? That woman had too many friends and allies in high places—shadowy, unknown friends and allies . . . partners, collaborators, and (no doubt) politically connected superiors with the resources and clout to track us down.

I'd pondered our options these past weeks and had arrived at a single possible solution, and Soto was the key to that solution.

Except the timing had gone wrong.

When Cushing had announced that she was moving Dr. Bickel within two weeks, the mites and I had been forced to shift our focus from the hunt for Soto and Mateo Martinez to Dr. Bickel's rescue.

But now? Now that the mites had located Soto? Maybe their discovery cast the circumstances in a better order.

Could we do both? Could we take down Soto and still rescue Dr. Bickel before Cushing moved him?

Gemma Keyes. We have work to do.

"Give me a minute, Nano? I need to think."

My original idea still made the best sense: For Dr. Bickel to survive and publicly overthrow Cushing, he needed *safety* and *time*—and if I delivered Soto to Special Agent Gamble, Gamble would owe me.

Gamble was already personally acquainted with Cushing; he knew how unscrupulous she was. He knew about Dr. Bickel. I trusted Gamble. He was a standup guy, and taking down Soto was personal to him: For Graciella.

The essential piece of the puzzle? Gamble was FBI. He had access to an agency capable of providing the "cover" vital to Dr. Bickel's survival. If I delivered Soto to the FBI, Gamble and, indirectly, the FBI, would *owe me big time*. Then I intended to cash in my chit for Dr. Bickel's safety.

I nodded, my mind made up.

Soto first.

Dr. Bickel after.

And this time, no screwups with the nanomites. This time I would do things right.

"Nano. I wish to call a confab."

Gemma Keyes, what is a confab?

Duh! The mites had never referred to it as a confab, had they? I snarked a little.

"Nano, confab is the term Dr. Bickel gave to the nanocloud's meetings, when the tribes convene to share input, make recommendations, and arrive at consensus."

You wish to call such a meeting, Gemma Keyes?

"Um, yes. If it is allowed."

We are six. It is allowed.

***

As I'd said before, it was easier to receive information from the nanomites than it was to share it with them. The only means I knew to convey in clear terms the issues I wanted to discuss with them was through the spoken word.

I rehearsed the points I wanted to make and how I thought we should proceed; I went over them in my head until I could articulate them. Well, in the warehouse I didn't actually *talk*, but it felt like I did—which, for me, amounted to the same comfort level. Regardless, I was nervous about sharing my idea with them.

I closed my eyes and opened them in the warehouse. I knew from the special, certain hush that greeted me that the mites were ready: They were waiting for me.

"Nano, I'm so very happy that you have found where Cushing is holding Dr. Bickel. His rescue and safety are our common goals. Thank you, too, for locating Arnaldo Soto.

"We have a plan to deliver Dr. Bickel from Cushing's hold, but have not yet arrived at a practical plan to protect him and keep Cushing from retaking him after we free him. Today I wish to suggest a strategy that would defeat Cushing and end her threat to Dr. Bickel forever."

"Under ordinary circumstances, the six of us would agree that Dr. Bickel's freedom holds a higher priority than Arnaldo Soto's capture. However, in my plan to protect Dr. Bickel, Soto's capture plays an important role. His capture opens an avenue to safety for Dr. Bickel and defeat for Cushing."

Soft chitters and whispers greeted me. The mites were attentive; I'll give them that.

"After I, um, that is, after *we* spring Dr. Bickel, I presume that Cushing will mount a search for him. I believe she will have help from the national guard. She may enlist other law enforcement organizations. However, we must not lose sight of her true goal, which is to capture *you*, um, *us*—the nanocloud—I mean all of us.

"It is imperative, then, that our plan keeps Dr. Bickel safe and the nanocloud a secret. Because Cushing has a great deal of political and military backing, I believe Dr. Bickel will be safest *not hidden*, but in the open where he can discredit Cushing.

"The world thinks Dr. Bickel is dead. Why? Because Cushing said he was. How can we prove that she lied? By showing Dr. Bickel to the world, by digging up his grave and demonstrating that whatever or whoever is buried there is not Dr. Bickel. Dr. Bickel has many friends in the scientific community who will rally to him. My plan is to get Dr. Bickel to a safe place where he can blow the whistle on Cushing."

Chitters interrupted me. *What whistle will Dr. Bickel blow and for what purpose, Gemma Keyes?*

I giggled. "Not a literal whistle, Nano. Look up 'whistle-blower' for a definition."

We now understand this idiom, Gemma Keyes. Dr. Bickel will disclose General Cushing's misuse of power? Will this disclosure defeat her?

"Yes. That's it exactly. She has broken many laws: She tried to steal Dr. Bickel's research. She attempted to kill him by blowing up his lab. She manipulated the scene after she blew up his lab, and she managed to convince or coerce others into saying he was dead. She falsely imprisoned him and has held him captive now for many months. These are all crimes."

And will Dr. Bickel's revelations end the threat Cushing represents?

"I hope so but, knowing her, she will not go down without a fight. Therefore, wherever we take Dr. Bickel after we free him, it must be a location she dares not storm, somewhere from which she dares not take him by force."

You have such a location in mind, Gemma Keyes?

"Yes, I do, and that is where Arnaldo Soto comes in and why we must deliver him to the FBI before we free Dr. Bickel. The Constitution says that the military is not allowed to conduct military operations on American soil—nevertheless, Cushing has 'agents' and a tactical force at her disposal.

"In juxtaposition, the FBI is the nation's primary federal law enforcement organization, tasked with handling federal crime. Gamble is our friend, and he is an agent of the FBI. When we deliver Arnaldo Soto to the FBI, I believe Gamble will, in return, help us convey Dr. Bickel to an FBI field office. Cushing has no authority to storm an FBI office and take Dr. Bickel from there. She may try to extradite him through 'legal' channels but, by then, Dr. Bickel should have exposed her to the world as the traitor she is.

"I wish to apprise Agent Gamble of Arnaldo Soto's location first thing tomorrow and assist the FBI in Soto's capture. Then we will proceed to our plan to rescue Dr. Bickel."

The mites deliberated for a few minutes and asked some probing questions before arriving at consensus.

We agree with your principal assessment and plan, Gemma Keyes. However, we must continue to prepare for all contingencies. We must be optimal.

I knew what their last two sentences meant.

"All right. I'm ready to continue with my training session if you are."

***

Following my usual precautions, I parked a couple of blocks from Agent Gamble's apartment and jogged the rest of the way. It was an eerie experience, approaching his building a second time in the pre-dawn dark. I scanned the parking lot and surrounding buildings, half-worried I would spot Cushing's man smoking in the shadows under the stairs.

Nope.

I crept up to the second floor, taking care to make no noise. In the night stillness, sounds seemed amplified, and I didn't want Gamble's neighbors to hear me.

When I reached Gamble's door, I listened. His lights were off. I heard nothing on the inside, detected no movement. I flicked my hand toward the lock; the handle turned, and I crept inside.

I didn't want the neighbors to hear me knocking, either.

It was dark in Gamble's apartment. I shined a soft nano-light around and got my bearings. His living room was tidy; he'd left no clutter on the floor that might trip me. At the far end of the living room I spied a kitchen. A hallway to the right of the kitchen led, presumably, to a bedroom.

"Who's there? Show yourself."

Guess I hadn't been quiet enough. The sharp whisper caught me unaware.

"It's Gemma Keyes, Agent Gamble. And, um, sorry; I'm unable to comply with your request."

"Right." His reply was muffled in a laugh.

Gamble rounded the corner from the hall and switched on a light. His face had that squished, bleary look you have first thing in the morning when you've been sleeping hard. He was shirtless but wearing boxers. He held a handgun against his thigh.

"Nice of you to knock, Miss Keyes."

"And wake the neighborhood?" I chuckled. I was glad to see Gamble again.

"I suppose I take your point. Why are you here . . ." he glanced at the clock, "at oh-four-thirty in the dark a.m.?"

I grinned, but he couldn't see my happy face. "Are you ready to take down Soto?"

"What? You know where he is?" The blear on his face smoothed some.

"I told you the nanomites would find him."

I shivered. "Say, do you have any coffee? I got chilled on my way here, and I'd love a cup."

"Yeah. Just a sec." Gamble went down the hall and came back, sans gun, tugging a t-shirt over his head. He'd already pulled on jeans.

Gamble was a big guy—tall and muscled, but not bulked out. Just right. Altogether, not a bad sight first thing in the morning. He went into the kitchen, and I heard the tap running and then him pouring water into a coffee maker.

"Quit ogling me, Miss Keyes."

I giggled, still high on the prospects ahead: Taking down Soto, rescuing Dr. Bickel, defeating Cushing.

"Just plain coffee okay with you? I don't do lattés or cappuccinos, any of that frou-frou stuff."

"I'm a purist myself."

"My opinion of you just climbed a notch, Miss Keyes."

I snorted at his ribbing. "You want to hear about Soto or not?"

"Absolutely. Shoot." He left the kitchen and joined me in the living room. "Take a seat, Miss Keyes. Tell me what you've found."

"Thanks. Well, first, I should tell you that the data the nanomites downloaded from your network—the names of Soto's family members and known associates in Mexico? Those were the vital pieces we needed. So, thanks."

Gamble's reply was snide. "Yeah, happy to oblige."

I giggled again. "Anyway, using the information they gleaned, the mites identified and inventoried the individuals connected with Soto's family."

"*Every* individual?"

"Whether by blood, marriage, business, friendship, or casual contact, any person who even breathed on Soto's family—literally, figuratively, or virtually—went into the nanomites' analysis. If someone sat next to one of Soto's relatives at a concert, served them food, did their nails or laundry, or sent them spam, the mites tagged them. The mites used that data set to create a location matrix that boggled my mind."

Gamble looked uncertain. "They can do that? All that computing?"

"With ease. Say, is that coffee ready?"

Gamble got up and poured two mugs, and stood in the living room holding them. "Where do you want this?"

I grabbed a cup from him. "Thanks. Mmm. Smells good."

I sipped before I continued. "Soto's family and most of his acquaintances in Mexico are clustered in or near the city of Culiacán. The mites drew a twenty-mile radius from the center of that cluster and isolated cellphone traffic originating from inside that twenty-mile radius."

"What—*all* cellphone traffic?"

"Yup. The mites hacked the records of every carrier out there. I gotta tell you, Agent Gamble, the nanomites rock the Internet. If it happens online, they can find it, mine it, and manipulate it. Anyway, from the entirety of all cellphone traffic within the twenty-mile radius around the designated 'cluster,' they isolated every number that made calls to the 505 area code."

"Uh, impressive."

"It was even more impressive when the mites displayed those calls in frequency graphs."

"But if the callers are using burner phones, how can you identify who is calling?"

"Don't need to identify the *caller*. We're looking for Soto, and he is on *this* end, yeah? Once the mites identified the most frequent callers to New Mexico, they further narrowed those patterns to exclude calls outside a twenty-mile radius around Albuquerque."

I took a long, satisfying pull on my coffee. "Amazing how the rate of recurrent calls to the same numbers will pinpoint specific locations. After applying a bunch more filters, one location in particular emerged."

"You're saying the mites used recurring calls to ID Soto's location?"

"His presumed location. Then the nanomites went to work to verify that assumption." I pulled a folder out from under my shirt. "Here you go. Realtor records. Utility bills. Aerial footage of the house and the vehicles at this site. MVD records on the plates. He's there, all right."

"Aerial footage? How did you get that?"

I shrugged. "We bought a drone. I took a little drive at the nanomites' direction and sent up the drone with a smart phone attached. The mites controlled the drone and took the video and photos. The rest was easy."

Gamble forgot his coffee while he perused the papers. "Do I want to ask how you got these MVD records?"

"No."

He grunted.

"I can provide the video feed to you, if you like, Gamble. On a flash drive."

He shook his head. "Tell me where this place is. We'll send up our own drone."

"I will; that's why I came this morning—I told you I would deliver Soto's location to you. But you get that information under one condition."

His head snapped up. "What condition?"

"I come with you when you take him down."

"No." His head was moving back and forth before he uttered the word.

"Then no location."

He stared at me, his mouth hard and angry.

"That's the deal, Agent Gamble. I'll stay out of the way, but I get to be there."

"Stay out of the way? What about us? We can't see you. We won't know if you're in the line of fire or not!"

"That's my problem, not yours."

Head still wagging back and forth, Gamble looked back to the photos and documents I'd provided. Then he shoved them back into the folder.

"I need to get to the office."

⌘⌘⌘⌘

CHAPTER 24

It took Gamble half the morning to brief his superiors and hours longer to verify Soto's location to the SAC's satisfaction, get a warrant, assemble the assault team, and put together the assault plan. The FBI invited a contingent from the APD gang unit and the Torrance County Sheriff's Department to join them in the planning, execution, and mop-up.

I hung out at a discreet distance, paid attention to the plan, and kept an eye on Gamble. As occupied as he was with the operation, I could tell he was worried about me—the occasional looks he shot around the briefing room spelled out his concern. What he didn't know was that I had no intention of going along with the FBI to arrest Soto.

I would be there ahead of them.

With Soto's arrest so close, I could almost taste it. However, I wanted the opportunity to speak to Dead Eyes and Mateo first. I needed to "convey"—in my own way—the disgust and rage I felt toward them.

The nanomites piggybacked on the FBI's aerial recon of the gang's headquarters and downloaded what we already knew: Soto was ensconced in a very nice two-story house in the center of a ten-acre parcel. The house was built on the flat basin some miles east of the backside of Sandia Crest. According to FBI data, Soto—from the relative safety of his pricy digs—directed the manufacture, packaging, and distribution of drugs to a large chunk of New Mexico, Arizona, Colorado, Texas, and Oklahoma.

Despite a glut of real estate speculators and builders, a lot of the land due east of the Crest was still rural. Underdeveloped. Isolated. Just how the residents liked it. Soto's property was down a long dirt road. It was fenced, and the house afforded unobstructed views in all directions.

The FBI's assault team planned to come, in force, under cover of darkness, from multiple directions. An hour after twilight, they would begin infiltrating their personnel to their assigned positions.

I, on the other hand, would walk in, undetected, before sundown, and leave before the FBI team hit Soto's house. I waited until the FBI had solidified their timetable. Then I pilfered one of their radios on my way out so the mites could monitor the team's communications.

I drove east on I-40 until I'd cleared the canyon. After I passed Edgewood, the mites directed me north on graveled back roads toward Soto's headquarters.

I wondered about Mateo, where he'd been hiding since he and his gang thugs beat Zander and Abe. I wondered whether we'd catch him and Soto together. Soto was the primary target, but part of me hoped that our trap would snare them both at the same time.

I had the FBI radio in one pocket and my phone in the other, and I had Gamble on speed dial. I would communicate any problems I noted before the assault team received their go signal.

Gemma Keyes.

"Yes?"

You will wear your weapons to this encounter.

"Yeah, that I will." The quiver holding two kamagong sticks lay on the passenger seat floor.

This encounter may afford realistic training practice. We must be optimal when we free Dr. Bickel; realistic practice furthers our goal.

I coughed a laugh up the sleeve of my hoody. I didn't think the nanomites understood the level of danger tonight's situation presented— or how quickly things could go south if I were to inadvertently rouse Soto's guards. I was more than happy to let the FBI do the heavy lifting in lieu of "realistic practice"!

My aim was to conduct a private and personal "interview" with Soto and Martinez—just before the FBI arrived. I intended no risk to myself.

"Nano. Time?"

The time is 4:34 p.m., Gemma Keyes.

The FBI would begin positioning their people soon. They would pull the trigger at 5:55. I had a large enough window of time to hike onto Soto's land, reach the house, locate Soto and Martinez, and conduct a candid "discussion" concerning their brutal attempted murder of my friends.

Find a place to pull off the road and hide your car, Gemma Keyes.

"Roger that, Nano."

***

Arnaldo Soto was alone in what served as his office on the second floor of his house, savoring a well-deserved brandy at the end of a long day. The fire in the corner kiva crackled, and Soto sniffed at the scent of piñon and cedar sap sizzling from the logs.

He stood and lifted the Russian-made vintage snifter to the light, studying the dancing fire through the crystal prisms. Closed his eyes.

Smiled.

Not bad, considering—considering I was banished from Mexico and sent into exile here. Not bad at all. Soon I will have a stranglehold on this part of this weak country, a monopoly even my family will not be able to break.

"To New Mexico," he toasted with a laugh. "To the Land of Enchantment, the land of my many new opportunities!"

***

"I'm delighted you have found our state to your liking," I murmured, locking the office door behind me. *Since you'll be spending the rest of your miserable life here.*

Soto jerked at the sound my voice and, seeing no one, turned in a circle. "Who is that? Who is talking to me?"

"You've terrorized innocent people, Arnaldo Soto." I whispered the words less than three feet from him.

The glass dropped from Soto's hand and shattered on the gleaming hardwood floor. He skittered away and opened his mouth to shout for a guard.

My movement was faster than his reaction, than his instinct for self-preservation.

I placed the blunt end of an escrima stick on his throat. And pushed. Just a little.

"No, don't raise an alarm, Arnaldo. It would not be wise. I could break your nose, put out an eye, and shatter half your teeth before they got in here—and your men still wouldn't see me. Why, if you told them about me, they'd think you were crazy!"

Soto's eyes bugged out of his head; he tried to back up, but I followed him, pressing my stick harder. He swallowed with difficulty.

"I advise you to stand still and not move your hands, my pasty friend. Make any sudden moves and, with the flick of my wrist, I will break your jaw—and that would be too bad, because I have some questions for you." I tapped his jaw with the heavy stick to prove my point.

I glanced around. "Better yet, I want you to sit down. Yes, right there." Soto, my stick digging into his Adam's apple, lowered himself into his desk chair.

"Scoot it this way, please. Yes. Away from your desk. Come on." Soto rolled the chair as I allowed him to, as I eased the pressure of the stick against his throat.

"Right here is good."

He was centered in the room, broken glass crunching under the wheels of his expensive, oversized chair, spilled alcohol under his feet. He'd regained some of his bluster during transit.

With an arrogant lift of his chin, he demanded, "What is it you want?"

"Well, that . . . is a good question."

And it was. I stared at him, at "Dead Eyes," the psycho. He'd terrified me the first few times I'd seen him, but now? I guess my training had done more for my confidence than I'd realized. Soto was just a man, and I could injure him—if I chose to.

He was powerless; I was in control.

I glanced down, uncertain of how to proceed. All I desired was to understand: Why? Why had Mateo beaten a kind, defenseless old man? Why had he nearly killed him? Mateo didn't care about Emilio! So, why?

"Where's Mateo Martinez?"

Soto had not been expecting my question, and something flickered across his face. I had to admire him, though. He didn't lick his lips or exhibit other signs of fear or nervousness. He *was* trying to find me, though. Trying to figure me out.

That wasn't going to happen.

"Nano," I whispered inside. "Sting him."

I felt them leave.

Soto flinched and stared at his palm. He rubbed it, almost against his will, across the sleek fabric of his trousers. I moved my stick to his elbow and gave it a little knock—okay, a significant knock—then returned the stick to his throat. Pressed it.

He cursed, but was shrewd enough to keep his voice down.

"I asked about Martinez."

This time Soto did lick his lips. What was he hiding?

I pushed the stick into his throat. "Martinez and his men beat up two friends of mine, in particular, an elderly man. Martinez didn't care about Emilio! So, why? And where is he? Where is Martinez?"

"Is that why you're here? Because Martinez beat up an old man?" Soto spit the words at me. His patience was wearing past the point of his ability to control his temper. He coughed and turned his head to diminish the pressure on his throat, but the weight of my stick followed.

"You're going to get quite the kink in your neck if you keep leaning away like that," I observed. "Turn this way, Arnaldo, and answer my question. Where's Mateo?"

Soto's head came around front. I reapplied the pressure of the stick on his throat. He squirmed, anger boiling under the surface.

It made me laugh. "Why, you're not much more than a spoiled rich kid, are you? You can dish it out, but you're not much in the 'taking it' department." I moved my stick and smacked him on the cheek.

When he did not answer, I told the mites what to do.

They stung him. Three times in succession, in three different places, they stung him. Soto cursed and turned white under the strain of controlling himself.

"You needn't be concerned about Martinez," he snarled. "That man's actions were . . . precipitous. I couldn't have a loose cannon in my organization, so I removed him."

I felt suddenly sick. "You . . . What does that mean?"

He shrugged with disdain, that very Latin equivalent of "whatever."

I spoke inside, and the nanomites responded to my request. *Yes, Gemma Keyes.*

Swallowing my nausea and affecting curiosity, I managed, "I think I get it, but I'd like to hear it from you, how you did it, how you 'removed' Martinez. I'm . . . *interested.*"

My captive grinned through clenched jaw. "Martinez possessed neither the intellect nor strength of character to be more than an underling. He was, at his best, a useful tool, but he had been promoted beyond his ability."

Soto chuckled. "Any prod to his ego elicited temper; any slight to his manhood produced a violent response."

"Let me guess. You insulted his manhood. And how did you do that? Tell me."

Dead Eyes shrugged again, warming to his tale. "The boy."

"You used Emilio?"

Speculation glinted in Soto's black eyes. I didn't like it. Didn't know what it implied.

I nudged him. "Go on."

"Yes, the boy. *Emilio.* The old man next door called social services because Martinez had neglected the child. I merely suggested that the old man's actions called into question Martinez's ability to lead."

"You 'suggested' this in front of Mateo's men."

"But of course. In his mortification, he could not wait to take care of things. Mateo was easy to manipulate, easy to goad."

I ground my teeth against the rage rising in me. "So you goaded him? Into beating the old man?"

Soto cocked his head to one side. "I assure you: I gave no orders for such an ill-advised action."

"But you provoked him. Because you wanted him to screw up."

Soto's laugh was full-throated. Indifferent. "It was . . . amusing to watch."

"And afterward? Because of the attention Mateo brought down on you?"

"Surely you understand. I could not allow Mateo to further jeopardize our operations, now could I?"

"Thank you; I do understand. Completely. Where is he now?"

Soto spread his hands wide and smiled. "Let us say that the sands of the Albuquerque West Mesa will be richer for Mateo's contribution, eh?"

That was that. Emilio's uncle was dead.

Soto glanced up and around, cunning in his eyes, still trying to figure me out. The expression on his face froze, then turned to concern as the noises below came to us: Shouts, gunfire, chaos. The FBI breaching Soto's house.

I'd become engrossed in our conversation and had lost track of the fleeting minutes. My time with Soto was up—and he felt compelled to make a move.

I stepped left just as his left hand snaked out. My stick came down, and the crack of bone resounded in the room.

Ooops. Broken hand.

It didn't bother me as much as I'd expected it to.

Soto howled in pain—but his howl never made it into the open. In the milliseconds it took for him to inhale, the nanomites swarmed Soto's mouth and nostrils.

I stepped back and observed. Soto flailed. His uninjured hand scrabbled across his mouth and nose—only he couldn't open them: The mites had sealed them shut.

Disbelief and panic set in, and Soto lurched to his feet. His initial scream was muffled, and he couldn't draw another breath to protest further. In any event, screams, grunts, or other sounds could not pass his sealed lips.

Boots pounded down the hall toward Soto's office. More shouts and the cough of heavy guns. I leapt behind the locked door as the agents breached it. At that moment, the mites released their hold on Soto and returned to me.

The door splintered and crashed open. Four FBI special ops agents filed in, their guns up and ready, Gamble close on their heels. Two additional agents, the tags on their jackets reading Scarpetti and Franks, brought up the rear.

"Clear!"

"Clear!"

Gamble and his team stared at Soto sprawled on the floor, blue-faced, gasping for breath, cradling his shattered hand. Scarpetti and Franks exchanged grins.

Even Gamble cracked a smile. "Arnaldo Soto, I presume."

While the special ops team and Gamble looked on, Scarpetti and Franks patted Soto down and—none too gently—flipped him onto his belly to cuff him.

Soto shrieked in pain. "My hand—don't touch it! She broke it! That *blank blanking blank* broke my hand!"

They turned him on his back, and one of the agents studied Soto's wrist. She glanced up at Gamble. "Yeah; it's busted. We're going to need medical."

She directed a question at Soto. "Who broke your hand?"

"That woman! The invisible woman! She hit me with something—something hard, a stick of some kind."

Special Agent Scarpetti smirked. "The invisible woman? *Right*."

That got a chuckle out of everyone except Gamble and Soto.

"She's here! In this room!" Soto's eyes narrowed and jinked around the room. Looking for me.

Gamble's expression didn't change. "Shut up, Soto. Read this piece of dung his rights and get him out of here. Medical can see to him downstairs."

Scarpetti and Franks hauled Soto to his feet, but Soto did not shut up. Still searching the room for any sign of me, he screamed, "Where are you, you *blank*? Where are you? Are you afraid of me? Afraid to show yourself? Well, you should be—'cause I'm going to kill you; I swear on my grandmother's grave, I will kill you!"

The agents hustled him toward the door, but Soto wasn't finished. "Listen to me, you *blank*! I know you're still here. I know you're listening; I know you can hear me. You think because I can't *see* you that I can't *find* you? Oh, *I will find you*—but first I'll find those you love. Don't sleep, you *blank.* Don't even blink! Because I *will* find you, and I *will* pay you back for this."

Franks laughed and shoved Soto toward the door. "Yeah, right. Tell that to your friends in federal lockup."

He and Scarpetti hustled Soto out the door and down the stairs.

I slipped out behind them unseen, unnoticed.

***

I visited the FBI field office the following morning. "Hey, Gamble. How's it going?"

The man looked beat; dark circles ringed his eyes and his shoulders slumped with fatigue.

He dispensed with greetings. "How did you do that, Gemma?"

"You mean how did I get Soto to confess to Mateo Martinez's murder?"

"No. Well, yeah, *that*, but what I meant was, how did you transmit your conversation with him across our radios?"

"Everyone heard it, did they?"

"Loud and clear. How did you do it?"

"Oh, you know. The nanomites. I had one of your radios; they took care of the rest. I returned the radio last night, by the way. Is what he said enough to convict him for murder? For accessory to the assault on Abe and Zander?"

"Doubt it. Even though I have about thirty witnesses to Soto's confession, the prosecutor would still need a recording of it."

I placed a thumb drive on his desk and, as I took my gloved hand off it, it appeared.

"What's this?"

"The recording you need. I wiped my prints from it first."

Gamble stared at the little USB device. "I'm already getting grilled about the identity of the other person in that conversation, the unknown female. It doesn't help that before the docs put a cast on Soto's hand and administered pain killers, he babbled on and on about the invisible woman who broke his hand with a baton of some kind. How do I explain that?"

I ambled around Gamble's office, perusing the plaques and photos hanging on his walls. This was a good morning. I was . . . happy? At peace? Relieved?

A full one-half of the burdens I'd been carrying had lifted off my back. My gift of Soto to the FBI would ensure the FBI's cooperation for Dr. Bickel's safety and Cushing's downfall—relieving me of the other half of my burdens.

"What happened after they set Soto's hand and gave him painkillers?"

Gamble scowled. "He clammed up. Wouldn't open his mouth except to say, 'attorney.' We kept after him until his slick lawyer showed up but, even then, the guy just sneered at us. Like he knew something we didn't. He's hiding something, but I don't know what."

"Hmmm." My "good" morning dissolved. I rolled my shoulders, a vague disquiet tensing my muscles.

"'Hmmm?' That's all you've got?"

"No, of course not." I returned to Gamble's question. "Don't you use informants? Can't you pass me off as one of them? Say that you can't reveal my identity?"

"Well . . ."

"So you can."

He didn't answer, but he picked up the flash drive and inserted it into his computer.

"Uh, before you get started on that, Agent Gamble . . ." I waited until I had his attention.

"Yeah? What is it?"

Right. Knowing the FBI owed you a favor and spelling it out were two different things.

"I, um, I need to talk to you about . . . Dr. Bickel."

"Okay." Gamble sat back and waited.

"You recall how I told you Cushing had him stashed somewhere?"

"Yeah. I remember."

"Well, I know where that 'somewhere' is."

Silence. Gamble never flicked an eyelash. He wasn't going to make this easy for me. Not one bit.

I sucked in air and pushed on. "I'm going after him, Agent Gamble. I'm going to break him out."

Then Gambled did blink. Once.

"On your own?"

"I'm not exactly 'on my own,' you know."

"Yeah, but . . ."

It sounded as stupid to him as it had to me a couple of weeks ago. If I allowed myself to dwell on my lack of qualifications, it would become stupid all over again.

"You don't need to concern yourself over me, Agent Gamble, but . . . but afterward? Afterward, I'll need . . . a favor."

There. It was out on the table.

"What kind of 'favor'?"

"A temporary refuge for Dr. Bickel. A place of safety. The kind that Cushing can't crash with her stormtroopers."

His brows shot up. "Here?"

"Actually, the El Paso field office will be closer . . . when we need it."

"You aren't going to tell me where he's at?"

"No."

He sighed. "Miss Keyes—Gemma, if I may call you that? Let's say, for the sake of argument, that you do succeed in breaking Dr. Bickel out. How, exactly, do you intend to get Bickel to an FBI facility?"

"I want you to help me. You . . . you owe me, Gamble."

He sighed again. "For Soto?"

"Yes. For . . . Graciella."

It was a low blow, but a valid one.

Gamble used thumb and forefinger to massage his eyes. I guessed he was short on sleep, since the LEOs hadn't finished mopping up at Soto's house until morning—and Gamble had alluded to interrogating Soto late into the night.

"Look, Gemma, this is how it is. If you showed up here with Bickel, I would let you in, I would do level my best to keep Cushing out, keep her from taking him—and I think the SAC would back me. But I'm not attached to the El Paso office. Yes, they know me, but I have no clout there, no authority."

"You're saying bring him here? What if . . . what if getting him here were problematic? Maybe even impossible? What if Cushing had all the roads blocked?"

He looked away, stared into space, for a minute. When he spoke, he lowered his voice. "If you were to give me a heads-up, a timetable? I could dispatch a helo to pick you up. It would land right here."

I liked the idea. A lot. "Okay. That sounds good. So, I can count on you?"

Here Gamble looked indecisive. Worried. "Yes, of course you can count on me, Gemma. You're right—I do owe you for delivering Soto—and I also wouldn't mind bringing Cushing down, but . . . what troubles me is the likelihood that you'll walk out that door, and I'll never see you again."

I snickered. "Hard to be worried about never seeing me again when you've never seen me in the first place."

"Brat. You know what I mean—and joking about it doesn't changed the danger you're putting yourself in. What if . . . what if you told me where Cushing has Dr. Bickel and I tried to sell his story to my boss?"

Gamble's concern touched my heart, but I had little faith in government bureaucracy.

"Unfortunately, Cushing is transferring Dr. Bickel to another facility in about a week, and I don't know which one. If I don't make a move now, I will lose him. Do you honestly think the wheels of the FBI would grind fast enough to beat that deadline? I mean, if they budged at all. Because it would be a hard sell, right? Convincing your boss and *his* boss that a two-star Air Force General has a renowned scientist imprisoned against his will in violation of his constitutional rights? Oh, make that a *dead* scientist. And you learned all of this how? From an invisible woman?"

"Well, when you say it like that . . ." Gamble mumbled.

"I'm going to do this, Agent Gamble. I'll leave, um, certain documents for you, in the event things go . . . awry, but I'm going to do this. Should I succeed, I need to know that I can count on your help afterward."

He nodded his head, but he wasn't happy. "Yeah. Okay. You can count on me, Gemma. And God bless and help you."

"Thank you, Agent Gamble."

Even for the blessing.

I knew I would need all the help I could muster.

⌘⌘⌘⌘

CHAPTER 25

Our plan was to depart Albuquerque on Sunday afternoon and arrive at Dr. Bickel's location on the missile range just after dark. The mites and I hoped Dr. Bickel's weekend guards would be more relaxed. Less vigilant.

I made my preparations Saturday night. I retrieved five bundles of cash from the room downstairs and stuffed them into a backpack. I then filled another small bag with basic emergency supplies: a blanket, four bottles of water, ready-to-eat food, flashlight, and a first-aid kit. Readied my quiver.

Under cover of deep darkness, I slipped from the house and jogged to the parking garage, taking the supplies with me. I packed them into the Escape where they joined four empty five-gallon gas cans.

I drove out of the garage to DCC and let myself into Zander's office. I slipped a sealed envelope into his locked desk drawer. The envelope held a note and a flash drive. The mites had downloaded a copy of my journal onto the drive. I had them add the overhead images of the house where Dr. Bickel was being held, the schematics of the house, and the audio file of Cushing's classified conversation with Colonel No-Name—enough evidence to launch an investigation.

The note was short. Terse.

If things go wrong, deliver this drive to Special Agent Ross Gamble, FBI.

No salutation, no signature.

From there I drove to a self-serve station and filled the gas cans. I returned to the garage and left the car, but took the backpack holding the money. I shouldered the cash and jogged across town to a Chevy dealership.

I'd already selected a truck, a black Silverado 4WD with tinted windows. If it couldn't make the less-than four-mile trek from the highway to Dr. Bickel and back, then nothing short of a tank could. I preferred to buy and not steal the vehicle since we'd be roughing it up out there in the desert, perhaps even ditching it at some point. Buying it also meant that we shouldn't encounter any cops who were out looking for a stolen rig.

Getting pulled over would be awkward, to say the least.

I experienced no apprehension or misgivings as I sprinted toward my destination; instead, an odd calm settled on me, a strange confidence, as though—somehow—things were going to be all right. When I'd researched this auto dealership, I'd discovered that they were closed the first Sunday of each month—"for family time," their website disclosed—and it didn't escape my notice that the first Sunday of December was the very day most accommodating to our plans. The propitious fluke was unmistakable.

Happenstance . . . or Providence?

I jogged on, then stretched my legs and sprinted. I reveled in the pleasure of running, of my limbs—every muscle, bone, ligament, and tendon—moving and flowing in flawless harmony, the strength of my heart and lungs powering me onward.

It was dark, but I ran on, my stride fluid and graceful. I felt . . . at peace as I ran. Elated, if you will. It was a delight to apply my body so wholly and thoroughly, to experience this effortless physical freedom and license.

A tiny phrase slipped into my mind. I mouthed it, turned it over in my heart.

I am fearfully and wonderfully made.

Joy washed over me. *This is how my body was made to work. How it was intended to function.*

Enhanced by the nanomites or not, this ease of motion—this wild abandon!—was the most normal and natural thing in the world. I speculated over the remembered phrase and wondered where I'd picked it up.

"Nano, where have I heard these words?" I repeated them to the mites. "Where do they come from?"

Gemma Keyes, the complete verse, taken from Psalm 139, reads,

> *I will praise you,*
> *for I am fearfully and wonderfully made;*
> *Marvelous are your works,*
> *and that my soul knows very well.*

I conceded to yet another serendipitous moment, one of a long list I could no longer dismiss or fob off to mere coincidence. I breathed a quick acknowledgement. "All right. If you're watching, if you're as real as Zander says you are, will you help us, please?"

Zander had told me that God was calling me; Zander said that God would confront me. I nodded my acquiescence. That time wasn't now, but it was near.

Then the mites piled on.

Gemma Keyes, we know Dr. Bickel made us, but who made you?

Laughing, I raced forward.

***

When we reached the dealership, all was quiet and still. We had decided that I would pay for and take the truck tonight so that (in a perfect world) its absence would not be noticed until Monday morning. If we weren't back in Albuquerque by then, any mystification over a cash sale would no longer matter.

We opened whatever doors we needed to and hacked into their computer system. As our "ownership" was required for no more than a few hours, we made the purchase under a fictitious name; I left $45,000 in an envelope on the showroom manager's desk. (The amount was $656.72 over the total price—a nice tip for someone and, perhaps, sufficient incentive not to raise questions about a cash purchase.) I scrawled the words, "Payment for black Silverado 2500HD" on the envelope and added the VIN number.

I pulled a dealer's temp license, filled it out, and grabbed the keys. We unlocked the dealership's fuel pumps and filled the truck's dual tanks, one with gasoline, the other with compressed natural gas.

Then we returned to the parking garage, and I transferred the contents of the Escape to the truck.

Driving distance from Albuquerque to Alamogordo was just over 200 miles. From Alamogordo to Las Cruces was 67 miles; from Las Cruces to Albuquerque, 223 miles. We called the round trip—not counting the foray onto the range—at 500 miles.

Supposedly, the Silverado's dual-tank mileage was around 650 miles. I strapped the four five-gallon gas cans into the bed of the truck. They gave us an edge—and an extra measure of insurance, should we need it.

I paid for the truck's overnight parking spot and headed to the safe house. I wanted my body to be rested and well-fed before tomorrow's activities began. I planned to spend at least four hours at the dojo with Gus-Gus before we set our plan into motion.

***

The drive down from Albuquerque to Alamogordo Sunday afternoon was without incident. We left Alamogordo, headed west on State Road 70, just after dusk. My mind and nerves were on high alert, but physically I felt calm. Prepared to do my job.

Darkness fell early as the shortest day of the year drew near. The four-lane highway led from Alamogordo to Las Cruces, but it bisected the southern part of the missile range. Approximately forty miles out, the nanomites would tell me where to pull off the road.

The truck console had two auxiliary power ports; I kept the smart phone the mites had upgraded plugged into one. A strand of mites tethered the nanocloud to the other port, ensuring that the mites had their maximum power capacity topped off.

Gemma Keyes, stop here.

I turned off the headlights and slowed to a stop along the meager shoulder. Without turning off the engine, I jumped out and the mites directed me to the spot they had selected for us to cut the fence. After we'd lasered through the wires, I pulled the strands out of the way and raced back to the truck. I climbed inside and wrenched the steering wheel over: The truck bounced off the shoulder, down an embankment and up the other side through the hole in the fence.

I stopped, got out again, and pulled on some gloves. I used a pair of pliers to twist the fence strands onto some lengths of new wire. I wrapped the lengthened strands onto the metal fence posts. The job wouldn't stand up under scrutiny, but I didn't intend to leave a glaring break in the fence line either. Back behind the wheel, I eased the truck forward until the wheels found purchase in the sand.

We had completed the first phase of our plan. Now it was up to the mites and the phone's GPS to lead us on.

The desert terrain was harsh here—bits and chunks of sharp volcanic rock surrounded by and embedded in sand. I picked up speed to lessen the chance we'd get stuck, which roughened the ride considerably. I was glad for the truck I drove, glad for its high clearance and powerful engine; however, I wouldn't vouch for its suspension by the time we were finished with it.

The night was fully dark now, and I was driving without lights, pretty much driving blind. The mites flowed out from me toward the front of the truck and projected the view ahead. As I had during my training, I closed my eyes, entered the warehouse, and navigated by the moving images the mites brightened for my benefit. Via virtual reality, I could see a handful of yards ahead—enough to avoid disaster. Twice I had to back up and go around mounds and boulders of impassable black rock; once I was forced to detour around a crack that widened into a crevasse that would have swallowed up the truck.

Gemma Keyes, decelerate. We are close.

I slowed to a crawl and inched forward a quarter of a mile. The truck's engine made less noise at this speed—if I didn't goose the gas.

Stop. Walk from here.

I turned the engine off and held the keys in my hand. "Nano. I'm putting the keys under the seat."

When I'd placed the keys on the driver's floor and nudged them backward with my foot, I got out, bringing my quiver with me. I slipped it over my shoulders. The weight of the heavy sticks, jostling against my spine, was comforting. The mites had been right. The escrima sticks made a difference. I wasn't defenseless!

Ahead, Gemma Keyes.

I started walking, the mites steering my steps in VR. I walked another quarter of a mile before the faint outline of a building ahead appeared.

I opened my eyes. "Is this it, Nano?"

Yes, Gemma Keyes.

Just as the satellite photos had suggested, the building was a house— an ordinary, single-floor house complete with double garage and a large grass yard. The house faced east, and our approach put us off the house's northeast corner. The silhouette of the house was softly lit, but the yard was not.

I edged closer. My eyes adjusted to the night and my vision sharpened. Nothing taller than my knees stood between the desert and the house, just wide open spaces and 360-degree views—and the ten-foot chain link fence topped with nasty razor wire that I already knew encompassed the house.

A graveled road—the normal route from the highway to the house— butted up against an automated gate farther down the north-facing fence. Once inside the fenced area, the road became a cement driveway that scribed a semicircle across the front of the house and ended at the garage.

Gemma Keyes. Dr. Bickel is within this building.

"And the security, Nano?" I'd made peace with this distasteful part. I had three men to take down tonight, one outside and two inside. I'd proven to myself that I could do it and do it quietly.

We will guide you, Gemma Keyes.

I nodded to myself. "All right. When you're ready, Nano."

The perimeter guard is presently on our left, walking south across the fence line away from our position.

I began to make my way toward the groomed swath of dirt on this side of the fence—the swath with a net of intrusion detection devices buried beneath the dirt. The light from the house backlit the guard as he paced the fence line, headed toward the far corner of the lot. He turned the corner, moving laterally down the fence line—toward the house and away from me.

I ran toward the near corner and the groomed ribbon of dirt on this side of the fence. When I reached the swath, I lifted my hand: Mites streamed into the soil.

This section of the intrusion detection system is now deactivated. Proceed straight ahead, Gemma Keyes.

I heard the mites spinning up their lasers. I approached the fence, lifted a finger, and narrow, bright light sliced through the links. A moment later I was on the inside. I pulled the section of fence back into place.

I hunkered down in the shadows, drew my sticks from their quiver, and waited for the guard to complete his circuit, to come up the fence line to where I lurked.

When he was within a few yards of me, the guard must have seen or heard something amiss, because he paused, instantly alert. I gestured with my hand; seconds later a *ping* resounded on the fence behind him. He spun around—and as he did, I was on him. Using the butt end of a stick, I delivered a blow behind his ear, targeting his cerebellum. The guard crumpled to the ground without a sound.

"Go."

The mites swarmed from me to him—and back. *Lights out.* He would not wake up for hours.

I tiptoed across the grass onto the concrete driveway. Took a few steps toward the garage.

Gemma Keyes.

Yes, Nano?

Come to us.

They'd never said that before, but I figured it had to mean, "Come into the warehouse." I dropped into a squat, closed my eyes, and slipped into that place of community with the mites.

They showed me what I couldn't see with my naked eyes.

Thin bands of red lights crisscrossed our approach to the house. I understood their meaning: The house was surrounded by IR sensors or motion detectors. What the nanomites "saw" and showed me were the reflected infrared signals that, if interrupted, would trigger an alarm.

No wonder they only had one perimeter guard.

Walk at a slower pace than usual, Gemma Keyes. We will provide cover around you to defeat the motion detectors.

"Um, okay. Which door do I use?"

Half a minute went by.

Use the rear entrance, Gemma Keyes.

I had memorized the layout of the house. I popped out of the warehouse, took a deep breath and began to walk—slowly—up the semicircular drive toward the house. Near the garage, I turned and—still slowly—set off across the grass and around the garage to the back of the house.

As I walked, I made note of what the satellite photos had not shown us: Bars covering every window on the house; thick steel doors with state-of-the-art keypad locks in place of the original keyed locks.

The locks did not concern me. We defeated the back door's keycode mechanism and eased open the heavy door. As I slid inside a kitchen, I searched for the two personnel who were on duty.

Straight ahead, Gemma Keyes.

I crept through the kitchen/dining room—past a dinette table set against a wall. I paused to touch the table's laminate surface.

Dr. Bickel and his careless former guards played cards at this table . . . This is where one of the guards left his smart phone when he was called away to answer the command center's telephone.

I snorted within myself. *They thought of Dr. Bickel as a harmless, clueless old man—but that was their mistake. It's how he managed to email me.*

Inching forward, I peeked through the arched doorway. The living room at the front of the house had been taken over by the command post. A hallway on the left led to the bedrooms. To Dr. Bickel's cell.

The two guards on duty were seated at the command console, their backs to me. Computers and a bank of six monitors spanned the desk. Four monitors provided rotating views of the exterior . . . and two focused on the man we'd come to save.

Oh, Dr Bickel! My heart squeezed and unexpected tears stung my eyes.

Do not fret, Gemma Keyes. This is rough on our emotions, but we must try hard to adjust for Dr. Bickel's sake.

It was the kindest, most understanding thing the mites had ever spoken—even if they were parroting my own words back to me. I drew back and sniffed into my sleeve.

"Thank you, Nano."

I got myself back together and peered into the command center again. The mites flowed from me to the servers and came back to report.

As we'd surmised, the room to which Dr. Bickel was confined was not a "cell" *per se*. It appeared to be an ordinary room with one narrow window and one door. From the prisoner's perspective, it was a studio apartment with all the amenities: a nice bed, a kitchenette, a sitting area complete with television and satellite TV.

When the mites returned, they confirmed that the walls were made of reinforced cinderblock overlaid with sheetrock, the floors of solid concrete under a wooden subfloor and thick carpet. The window glass was bulletproof. The door was steel set in a steel frame.

I smiled. *Not a problem.*

Like a cat stalking its prey I moved into the command center behind the two men, whirling my sticks to attack. One of the men felt or heard the air whooshing over my sticks and turned. I laid him out with one blow and turned to the second guard. He stumbled backward, eyes bulging in his face. He reached for his sidearm—but I was far faster. When I'd rendered both men unconscious, the nanomites streamed into their bodies, assessed their injuries, and administered a long-term sedative.

Done.

I swallowed. Only a short hallway and a steel door stood between me and my friend. It had all been so much easier than I thought it would be.

I started down the hall. "Come on, Nano. Let's go get Dr. Bickel."

I raised my hand to his cell door. The lock clicked as it unlatched, and I swung open the door. The figure sitting, staring at a wall, did not turn. Did not acknowledge the opening door.

"Dr. Bickel?"

It was a moment before he slowly swiveled toward me. "Oh, Gemma. I had so hoped you would be able to elude them." His face crumpled in grief. Then he stared around, unable to see me, no longer certain of what he'd heard.

"I did elude them, Dr. Bickel. Actually, I'm here to rescue you."

Rescue you? It sounded corny, but I was grinning so hard that I didn't care.

His eyes widened. "You *are* invisible! I wondered if the mites would obey me . . ."

"Come on, dear Dr. Bickel, we shouldn't delay. We can talk in the truck."

"But the guards! The alarms and cameras, Gemma!"

"We've taken care of them, Dr. Bickel." I came closer and placed my hand on his and squeezed.

Maybe it was because he couldn't see me. Maybe because it had been a while since anyone had touched him. Perhaps it was the sheer relief of the moment: Dr. Bickel, my sweet old friend, sobbed. He grasped my hand and gripped it hard, but he turned his face away and sobbed.

I sat beside him. Wrapped my arms around him.

Held him. Wept with him.

That moment was perfect. It could not have been more; it could not have meant more.

And then . . . from within my chest, a soft, lovely, melodious hum . . . lifted, arose, and resonated through me. Low and peaceful, it flowed from me to him, enfolding the two of us in its haunting richness.

I'd never heard such beauty.

The nanocloud . . . singing.

Rejoicing with us.

⌘⌘⌘⌘

CHAPTER 26

Gemma Keyes. We must go now.

"Yes." I drew away from Dr. Bickel. "We shouldn't delay any longer. Each passing moment decreases our odds of getting you to safety."

"You're right, of course, Gemma." He wiped his face and stood on his spindly legs. "Where is this truck you spoke of?"

"About a quarter mile northeast of the house. As soon as we reach it, I will call my FBI friend. He is going to send a helicopter for us. When we are clear of the missile range's no-fly zone, it will pick us up and take us to the FBI's Albuquerque field office. The FBI will provide sanctuary from Cushing while you go public with your accusations against her—showing the world that you are alive and that she is a liar."

"Brilliant, my dear girl. Brilliant."

We sped down the hall, turned the corner into the command center, and—

"Stop where you are."

The guards still lay motionless on the floor, but two uniformed men faced us. The younger soldier had his sidearm drawn and extended in both hands.

"Going somewhere, Dr. Bickel?"

I recognized the voice. Saw the eagle patch of an Air Force colonel on the collar of the older soldier's ABU and the matching eagle on the front of his utility cap.

Dr. Bickel stiffened. "Why, yes, Colonel Greaves. Not to be indelicate, but I have tired of your 'hospitality.' I'll be going now."

I had my hand on Dr. Bickel's back, and I prodded him forward, out of the doorway into the room.

"I said stop!"

The younger soldier couldn't see me and likely didn't know I was even there. I zigged out from behind Dr. Bickel and dropped into a roll. I came up on the soldier's right side, my sticks drawn. I brought the sticks up in a sweeping "X" that drove his hands above his head and sent the gun flying. Before he could recover, I spun and slashed diagonally downward, right hand, then left hand, striking his elbows. While he howled and clutched his arms, I delivered a stunning blow on the side of his neck. The soldier fell to the floor, senseless.

"Do not move, Miss Keyes." Colonel Greaves, eyes wide, had drawn his own weapon and trained it, not on me, but on Dr. Bickel. He muttered to himself, "I didn't believe Cushing when she told me you were invisible, but it's true. It's true!"

He stepped away, putting more distance between himself and where he supposed me to be. "If you value your friend's life, do not move."

I crouched and inched forward, intending to spring up from below as I had a moment ago.

The colonel cocked his head and turned toward me; I froze in place.

"I can hear you, you know," he mocked.

"Nano. Now!"

The nanomites bolted from me with blinding speed, and I rolled from my position should the man fire. The colonel saw the flash of the mites, a thick stream rushing toward him, and his eyes widened further. The river of mites narrowed, became denser, shot forward, and bludgeoned the man's chest. He flew backward, hit the wall, and slumped to the floor.

"Ha!" I exulted as the river of mites flew back to me. "Come on, Dr. Bickel!"

"Gemma!"

Dr. Bickel's warning came too late.

Colonel Greaves had managed to raise the gun he still clutched in his hand. He depressed the trigger. Twin bolts of racking pain embedded themselves in my chest. I groaned and my body convulsed.

The 50,000-volt jolt lasted five protracted, agonizing seconds. My hands clenched and unclenched, releasing my weapons. The sticks dropped and rolled away. I toppled to the floor like a tree felled in the woods. On the floor, I twitched and spasmed; my jaws clenched and teeth ground together. Confetti-like AFID tags rained down, showering me.

Not a gun.

A Taser.

I could not move, but I could see . . . Colonel Greaves levering himself up the wall, picking himself up, unsnapping the holster at his side, drawing his real sidearm, lifting it toward me.

"No!"

Dr. Bickel's roar of rage startled Greaves. My old friend scrabbled for my sticks and grabbed them up. With a fury born of months of captivity, he brought them down on Greaves, on his gun and gun hand.

"You will *never* have Gemma—do you hear me? You will never do to her what you've done to me! *Never!*"

Dr. Bickel's technique may have been lacking, but his fervor was not. He delivered enough passion behind the heavy hardwood sticks to accomplish what was necessary.

Like the nanomites had said: *Gemma Keyes, you need not become a master in this style. Even as an untrained woman of your size and strength, these escrima sticks will serve you well in a combat situation.*

Dr. Bickel's fury burned hotter. "I will make sure you cannot come after us—that you will spend months in pain thinking on the evil in your heart."

Greaves shrieked as his wrists and arms shattered.

Shattered.

Shattered? I blinked and tried to rise, hoping . . . hoping . . .

Despairing.

Out of the corner of my eye, I saw Dr. Bickel deliver blow after blow to Greaves, to his arms, knees, shins, and ankles before he ran out of steam, before the fog of rage lifted. Before he realized that Greaves had fainted and would be unable to stop us if he awoke.

"Gemma." Dr. Bickel knelt by me and raised me to sitting.

He can see me? And Greaves . . . he saw me?

"Gemma. We need to go! You triggered at least one silent alarm—perhaps others. That's what called Greaves here. Cushing will soon know something is wrong. No; I'm certain she already knows! We must go."

He helped me to my feet, but I trembled, was unsteady. Weak.

"Do you have a phone, Gemma? Time for your FBI friend to get that chopper in the air."

"Y-yes."

Dr. Bickel patted my pockets, pulled out my smart phone, and pressed the menu button.

Nothing.

"It's dead." He glanced at the unconscious Greaves. "Either that was no ordinary Taser, or . . ." He didn't finish his sentence, but added, "Doesn't change the fact that we must find a phone to make that call."

He raced to the command console and the landline on its surface. He placed the receiver to his ear, dialed, listened, and turned to Gemma. "This line doesn't allow long-distance or directory assistance calls!"

I was sitting up, trying to gather myself. My tongue felt glued to the roof of my mouth. "Cush . . ."

"Yes. After I found a way to get a message out of here, she must have cut off every avenue." He looked around. "I know the guards are not allowed to bring in phones, but perhaps . . ."

He patted the pockets of Greaves' subordinate and found nothing. He had better luck when he searched Greaves himself.

"Okay; got his phone, but there's no cell signal here. Let's go."

The pain from the Taser faded. Dr. Bickel helped me up, and I put one foot in front of the other at his urging. We left by the front door and stumbled toward the fence.

"Cor . . . ner." My hand fluttered in the general direction. My mouth wasn't working right yet, and my coordination was all off.

Some rescue! It was a good thing Dr. Bickel was stronger than he looked. He pulled my arm behind his neck and shouldered my weight, dragging me toward the hole in the fence.

"You can expect to experience a few minutes of vertigo, Gemma, but the Taser's other effects should wear off quickly . . . should have already worn off . . . by now."

Concern laced his words, and he didn't mention the unaddressed but disturbing truth, the fact that I was fully visible.

After an agonizing twenty minutes of Dr. Bickel half dragging me along, we arrived at the truck. Dr. Bickel pushed me up onto the passenger seat and slammed the door closed before racing to the driver's side.

"Keys?"

"Un . . . der . . ."

He found them. He revved the engine, turned on the headlights, and followed the truck's tire tracks to the highway. He didn't stop to unfasten the fence—he slipped the truck into a lower gear and plowed through the barbed strands, down the shallow ditch bank, and up the other side.

Out on the black, lonely highway, he pointed the truck west toward Las Cruces, shifted gears, and drove like a man pursued.

I was in my head, struggling, fighting with what little strength I possessed to get into the warehouse. I failed and failed again, but I kept trying. Trying to reach them.

"Nano! Nano!"

I heard no answer . . . but I heard the deaths . . . the mites' agonizing cries of loss as their ranks were decimated, as the tribes went silent.

As the nanocloud flickered and died.

⌘⌘⌘⌘

CHAPTER 27

Traffic along the highway was spotty—just the occasional oncoming headlights that sliced through the night and flashed by without incident. Dr. Bickel kept the truck in the right-hand lane and maintained the posted speed limit. I noticed that he checked the rearview mirror often. His nerves were on edge—but, then again, he was not likely to relax until we were safe within the FBI's protective care.

The White Sands reservation ran along both sides of the highway; we hadn't gone many miles before Dr. Bickel pulled out the phone he'd taken from Greaves, powered it on, and took a quick look at it. He scowled. "Still no cell service. I will keep the phone powered off until we get close enough to Las Cruces to pick up a signal—so they can't use the phone's signal to trace us. When we do get a signal, I'll need you to call your FBI friend and tell him to get that copter in the air."

"Okay . . ."

And how was I going do that? My phone—with Gamble's number in my Favorites' list—was *dead*. I wondered, in a vague, distracted sort of way, why the Taser had killed my phone.

It shouldn't have.

My garbled thinking reminded me: Alpha Tribe had my contacts stored in their vast repository; they could retrieve Gamble's number for me . . . if I could reach them.

If they were still alive.

"Nano. I need Agent Gamble's number."

Nothing.

"Nano?"

Did the mites hear me? *Could* they hear me? I closed my eyes and strained to go to them, to reconnect. They could not have died! Not all of them! Not all their *trillions*!

Deep inside, as from a great distance, their distraught chitters—faint echoes and distant reverberations—reached me. The mites were calling to each other: Like a terrible game of Marco Polo, the mites were searching for their fellows, desperate to locate and link to their many members.

I expelled a semi-relieved breath.

Some of the nanomites had survived. But how many? How damaged or weakened were the survivors? And how many had died?

Too many, I concluded. The mites were unable to hide me any longer. They weren't even trying. Either they were too few or they were too broken—I had no way to tell which.

As I homed in on the mites' wails, I swallowed hard, sorrowing with them over their tribemates; I knew the mites loathed separation, how much being divided or alone distressed them. Their individual identities were subsumed within their tribes and as part of the swarm, the nanocloud.

I continued to listen, kept trying to connect with them, to no avail. The effort made my temples throb. I put my head back on the seat to rest. Instead of resting, though, *that moment*—the instant Greaves had fired the Taser—replayed on the screen in my mind.

I relived it: The excruciating jolt. The fall to the floor. The involuntary spasming. The screams of the nanomites.

How had a Taser generated such devastation and chaos? Had the nanomites—unwittingly—been a conduit for the Taser's pulse? Had the nanocloud amplified the charge that ran through my body? Is that why the charge had devastated them? Had fried my phone?

I called again to the mites . . . and received no answer.

I drifted and slept.

***

Dr. Bickel's voice roused me. "Gemma? I have a cell signal. Will you call your FBI friend?"

Mere minutes had passed. Why was I so weary?

"Don't have his number . . . Waiting on nano . . ."

I glanced up. The glowing dash was the only light in the truck's cab, but I caught Dr. Bickel studying me in the rear-view mirror. When he realized that I'd noticed his scrutiny, he flicked his eyes back to the highway.

Do you know how many times a day a person checks their reflection? It had been *ten weeks* since I had last seen my own face. The disquiet in Dr. Bickel's expression frightened me. What had he seen?

I couldn't worry about that now; we had more pressing concerns. If I couldn't reach Gamble, he wouldn't know when and where to send the helicopter. And without a helicopter, we had but two alternatives: hide or attempt the 223-mile drive to Albuquerque. The most direct route from Las Cruces to Albuquerque was up the I-25 corridor—a lengthy, exposed gauntlet.

I shook my head. How long would it take for Cushing to muster her forces, to set up road blocks, and pull us off the road? In my weakened state, we presented an easy, defenseless target.

We were leaving the range's reservation, beginning our climb through San Augustin Pass, before I tried to speak again.

"Dr. Bickel . . . th-the . . ."

"The Taser, Gemma?"

"Yeah . . ."

Without taking his eyes from the road, he placed his hand on my arm. "I'm afraid the nanomites absorbed the Taser's current and, well, they are sensitive electromechanical devices, vulnerable to electrical discharge. Many, if not all, are likely destroyed. That's why they are no longer hiding you."

Tell me something I don't know, Dr. Nanophysicist.

I was acutely aware that the pulse had devastated the nanocloud, that the ranks of the nanomites were decimated beyond their abilities to cope.

As was I.

It was the truth I'd been avoiding: My body should have recovered within minutes of the Taser's impact. It hadn't. Something was wrong, something in my own body. My speech had improved a bit, but I couldn't quite think in a straight line . . . and I was weak.

I had the sense that my life force was slowly seeping away.

"I'm worried about you, Gemma."

I shrugged. Yeah, I was concerned. Still—and this might sound odd—I was more anxious for the nanocloud. Fragments of sound from a few mites reached me, but the cloud and all its strength and power, was missing. Just . . . gone.

I listened as a small number of active mites found each other, began to join, began to work together. They were in full-out emergency mode, bent on locating their missing comrades, assessing damage, fixing what could be fixed. They were putting out a valiant effort to restore the tribes' five basic functions. When they didn't respond to my frantic appeals, I stopped calling out. I was afraid I would distract them from their most essential work: Survival.

I wondered, in that moment, how much of an impediment to their survival I might be, given my impaired condition. I didn't want the mites expending precious time or resources to fix me!

"Dr. Bickel, a remnant of the nanocloud is alive but damaged. I can hear them! Perhaps they can hear you? Could you . . . could you tell the mites to get out of me? That it is all right for them to leave me? They are struggling! I don't want them to waste their efforts . . . on me. You aren't damaged. Couldn't they leave me and go to you?"

Surely, if they got out of me and went into Dr. Bickel, he would be a better, stronger host for them?

My friend stared ahead and did not answer.

"Dr. Bickel? The mites respect you. They will listen to you. Please tell them to get out and save themselves."

His head swung back and forth like a slow pendulum, and he muttered, "I could try, Gemma, but I don't think it would work."

"What? Why not?"

He sighed and kept his face toward the road. "I think, on a cellular level . . ." His voice petered out.

"You think, on a cellular level, what? *What?*"

He delivered the news I'd been dreading, what I feared and did not want to hear. "Gemma, did you, uh, experience illness after the mites, er, attached themselves to you? Any adverse physical symptoms?"

I nodded, thinking back. "Yeah. A day of nausea. Wicked headache. A nose bleed. It wasn't too bad—the first time."

"The *first* time? What does that mean?"

I tilted my head back on the seat and focused on what I should say, how I should explain. In slow, studied phrases, I managed, "It was hard, living with the mites. Adjusting to their presence. Basic subsistence and day-to-day tasks were . . . difficult. The invisible part made everything— like getting food and moving around without being noticed—complicated and tedious, even dangerous—particularly after Cushing raided my house and I was forced to relocate to your safe house.

"We were at odds from the get-go, the nanomites and I, continually knocking heads and working at cross-purposes, so to speak. One evening, when I was feeling particularly down, I asked them, asked the mites . . . if we couldn't work together better. Find an easier way to communicate . . . to cooperate."

"You asked the nanomites if there was a better way for you and them to cooperate?"

"Yeah. Silly me, huh?"

"What happened?"

I tried to laugh, but I was too weary. I just wanted to let the fatigue take me down to peaceful oblivion. "What happened? The merge happened."

Dr. Bickel blurted a phrase I didn't catch. "Merge? What the devil is that?"

"Took a while to figure it out, but it started with an unmistakable bang. I woke up in the middle of the night sick—really, really sick. Vomiting. Horrible nose bleed. Fever. Couldn't keep my balance. More vomiting. Fun stuff."

In slow, halting sentences, I explained how the mites "spoke" an apology in my ear and freaked me out. I told him how the mites insisted that I return to bed and how they knocked me out, kept me asleep for more than fourteen hours.

"When I woke up, I felt loads better—that's when they told me they'd alleviated a lot of the unwelcome symptoms and had 'assisted' in my body's healing. I felt pretty good, actually.

"It was over the next days and weeks that the merge's other effects became evident. We no longer needed to verbally communicate—the mites and I could talk to each other in this place in my head I call 'the warehouse.' Later, I started memorizing everything I saw—like I was a savant or something.

"I could list other effects, but the bottom line? The mites misinterpreted my request. They thought, when I asked about us cooperating, that I was asking to join them, to become part of the nanocloud. So, guess what, Dr. Bickel? I'm a nanotribe now. You know, Alpha Tribe? Beta, Gamma, Delta, and Omega Tribes? Meet Gemma Tribe."

"Astounding!"

"You have no idea."

I'd given him the highlights of the last few weeks when our highway merged onto I-25. As we passed alongside Las Cruces, our nerves were too on edge to talk. Dr. Bickel kept his driving careful and conservative. On the west outskirts of town, he turned our conversation back to his concerns.

"The way I see it, Gemma, this merge complicates things. For the mites to accomplish such a feat, I theorize that they needed to, um, 'invade' certain areas of your brain and endocrine system."

"Right. I studied up and figured out how they were chemically creating new synapses in my brain. I call it nano brain surgery. However, the 'adverse symptoms,' as you deem them, lasted less than two days. The mites told me they had cauterized the bleeding, anesthetized my nerve endings, and provoked my body's production of serotonin and endorphins—all to help me heal.

"Not only did I heal; in addition, my energy levels shot through the roof. My endurance and physical stamina grew. That's when and why I decided that the merge wasn't a risk to me, long-term. I'm more fit now than I've ever been in my life—or at least I was before that Taser took me down."

Dr. Bickel slanted that look toward me, that wary, guarded look. I didn't know what it meant, but I didn't like it.

"Perhaps ... perhaps you are right—and I certainly hope you are, Gemma, but the mental and physical changes you've described? I'm not convinced that they aren't more invasive than you think. It occurs to me that the mites needed to relieve the symptoms of the merge, that they *needed* to suppress your immune system's normal responses—for reasons other than easing your discomfort."

"What other reasons?" I demanded.

"Well . . . how else could the nanomites trick your body into accepting their, er, activities? Yes, they required a hospitable environment as a place to live and also for . . . what they were doing."

"What is it you think they were doing?" I was growing angry. And scared.

"I refer to the, er, modifications they made. I believe the nanomites have made, um, certain alterations to your anatomy, Gemma. As I said a while back. Changes at the . . . *cellular* level."

They required a hospitable environment.

The nanomites have made certain alterations . . . at the cellular level.

My frantic thoughts pieced together his point. "Are you s-saying they *can't* leave?"

"Well, no, not precisely. I'm saying that they *could* leave, Gemma . . ." he paused a long time before he framed the second half of his response. "I'm saying that they *could* leave, but if they did, I fear that you . . . would not survive."

I would not survive if the nanomites exited my body.

My gorge rose. I swallowed it down, forced it down. Swiped at the cold sweat beading around my hairline, starting to drip down my face.

"Gemma, you said the swarm—the nanocloud—was disrupted, that many nanomites are dead."

I was so tired, my muscles weak and painful. "Yeah. I hear the remnant . . . struggling, fighting to find and connect to each other, to fix their damaged members, to rebuild the nanocloud."

And their efforts were draining me.

"Then we need to go back to my laboratory," Dr. Bickel whispered.

"Your lab? At Sandia? They blew it up. Burned it, remember?"

Tired.

"No, of course not my lab at Sandia. My lab inside the mountain."

"But . . . but Cushing trashed it, too. There's nothing left. I went there. Saw it."

He snorted a tiny snort. Even that little noise was infused with derision so typical of Dr. Bickel.

"*Cushing.* What does she know? Nothing. We need to get to Albuquerque, Gemma. Not to the FBI office, but to my lab inside the mountain. I don't think sufficient numbers of nanomites have survived to restore the nanocloud."

He patted my arm and I could feel the distraction through his fingertips as he delivered the *coup de grâce*, the final blow.

"And I'm afraid that if the swarm dies, Gemma, you die. I cannot allow that to happen."

Yeah. It made sense—so many things did now: *"We are six, Gemma Keyes."* My life was bound up in the nanomites' continued existence. The nanomites were failing—and if they failed, so would I.

A weak stutter interrupted.

Gem Gem Gem ma Gemmmmmma

My heart thumped with relief. The mites! They were talking to me!

"Yes, Nano. I'm here."

Have . . . number.

I turned on Colonel Greaves' phone and prepared to press the keypad as they called out the digits.

505

4

00

33

75

"Thank you, Nano."

I pressed send. The number rang and rang. No answer. I left a one-word message: "Call."

Gem Gem Gemma Keyes . . .

"Yes, Nano?" Poor Nano!

Assess . . . ing . . .damage.

"I know. What can I do?"

Connect to . . . power

They could not even form their own conduit to the auxiliary jacks? Their situation was worse than I feared. I fumbled with a phone cable and inserted it into the charger jack. Held it in my hand.

Long seconds later, the mites began drawing power through the cable. Not much. A trickle. Then a bit more.

I sighed, and my eyes drooped.

*** *

Dr. Bickel drove on. We reached the outskirts of Las Cruces, and Gamble had not called back. It was decision time: Make the turn as I-25 curved north and risk Cushing's net? Or head in another direction and hope to elude her?

"We *must* get you to my lab, Gemma."

"No. Not if—"

The phone buzzed.

I pressed the speaker button to answer the call but said nothing. We listened for the caller to speak.

"Hello?"

It was Gamble.

"Oh, Gamble! I'm—"

He talked over me a rush. "The news is out, Gemma. Cushing has called on the state police and national guard to find you. Homeland is deploying strike teams in response to 'an imminent terrorist attack.' Cushing is even mobilizing the FBI! The entire state is in an uproar. Do you have Dr. Bickel? Are you all right? Where are you?"

"I'm . . . w-we're . . . on the road."

"Get *off* the road—*right now*. You need to hide, Gemma."

I struggled to answer him. "Gotta save . . . Dr. Bickel. Need . . ." I was "plugged in," the remnant of nanomites sucking at the truck's auxiliary jacks for all they were worth, but it wasn't enough.

There weren't enough survivors.

"Gemma! What's wrong with you?"

Dr. Bickel grabbed the phone from my slack fingers and turned off the speaker function. "Agent Gamble? This is Daniel Bickel. Is there any way you can rendezvous with us and smuggle us into Albuquerque? It is imperative that I get Gemma there."

They talked for a few minutes, but I was too tired to pay much attention. The nanomites couldn't draw enough power to maintain themselves, let alone me. There were too few of them—even if they left me. In either scenario, whether they stayed or left, we would die.

Were dying.

I understood that now.

Something had happened to the helicopter; Dr. Bickel raised his voice until he was shouting, insisting that Gamble find a way to get us to Albuquerque and into the mountain.

I didn't know what Dr. Bickel hoped to find in his old laboratory under the mountain. I had seen it with my own eyes. Nothing remained, and Dr. Bickel could not magically print more nanomites—so why bother?

Why risk it?

Mentally, I shrugged my acquiescence. If, by some great good fortune—or by the grace of the God Zander followed—we managed to get into the tunnels unseen, Dr. Bickel's old lab was a fitting place for us to die.

I smiled inside. So many happy memories. Cushing would hardly think to look for us there, would she? We might, for a time, be safe from her.

Safe to die in peace.

⌘⌘⌘⌘

CHAPTER 28

I don't remember much after that until the rough ride, the truck bumping over a dirt road, woke me. The whooshing roar of tractor trailers wasn't far away, though, like we were running parallel to the freeway. Then we veered left, and the ride roughened. The impact of every rock and hole became too much for my tortured muscles to bear, and I slipped away again.

The next time I woke, the half-moon glowed high in the night sky. I was still belted into the truck's passenger seat, but Dr. Bickel was not with me. The back end of the truck was buried in a thick hedge of scrub piñon trees. Other desert shrubs screened the cab's outline.

Where was Dr. Bickel? I searched through the darkness, trying not to panic. I could no longer hear the whoosh of cars racing by. Maybe we were too far from the interstate?

A glimpse of movement off the driver's side caught my eye, and I made out Dr. Bickel's shape. He was talking to someone hidden by the shadows.

Who?

My heart pounded.

The shadowed stranger turned, and I gasped in relief. Zander? *Zander!* A second shadow shifted, detached from the darkness, and turned in my direction. It was Gamble. Zander joined him, and they walked toward me.

Zander, his arm still in a cast but no longer held by a sling, opened my door. "Gemma? Let me help you out."

In slow motion, I pivoted toward the door. He reached a hand to help me—and when the moonlight hit my face, he gasped.

"Th-that bad?"

"Uh, um, uh, no, not *bad* . . . not exactly, but . . . wow." He shook his head in wonder. "Gemma . . . you look really different."

What did he mean?

I fell back in the seat and pulled the lighted visor mirror down. The hard-planed features of a stranger stared at me. With shaking fingers, I touched my jaw. It was lean. Chiseled. Gone were my familiar, softly curved cheeks—replaced by the angular lines . . . of an athlete?

I gaped. The months without sunlight on my skin, day after day of being hidden by the nanomites, had taken their toll, too. In the moonlight, my skin gleamed like pale, ghost-like marble. Even my expression was unfamiliar: The woman staring back from the mirror was fierce. Fearless.

I could only gawk. *Who are you? From what cocooned state have you emerged and into what creature have you been transformed?*

"Come on, Gemma. We need to get going."

Zander pulled me to my feet. With great care, he helped me stand. Gamble took my other arm.

"Hi, Gemma. Good to see you."

I almost laughed. Agent Gamble had never seen me, and he wasn't seeing the "real me" now. He *had* seen my identical twin—not that she bore any resemblance to the woman I'd glimpsed in the truck mirror.

"Hey," I managed. "Thanks for coming. Um, where's . . . the helicopter?"

He didn't comment on my appearance, but the lines around his eyes scrunched with a keen curiosity. "Bit of a problem there. Cushing's handler, whomever it is, has managed to commandeer resources from all over the state—including the FBI. Our helicopter is in the air now, looking for you and Dr. Bickel. On to Plan B we go."

I sagged against Zander and grimaced. "Great. W-what's Plan B?"

"Well, we're going to put you and Dr. Bickel in my trunk."

I looked my question toward him.

One side of his mouth turned up. "I'm part of the official FBI search team. Zander here is a certified chaplain doing a ride along."

I squinted at Zander.

"I didn't mention that I was a chaplain? Only takes a few weeks of training."

While I shook my head, they ushered me toward Gamble's waiting car and Gamble filled me in. "Here's the deal: We've already passed through the roadblocks and checkpoints along I-25. The troopers and other agencies have checked our credentials and the car; they know we're legit. So, we're going to put you and Dr. Bickel in my trunk and RTB. Return to base. Nothing out of the ordinary. The ride won't be comfortable, but it's our best shot at getting you back to Albuquerque under Cushing's nose."

". . . More important . . . get Dr. Bickel . . . safe—"

"No, Gemma, it's *not*," Dr. Bickel interrupted. "I believe I can save you, Gemma, you *and* the nanomites, but we must get to my lab. It's the only way."

I started to lose it then. "No. No! I . . . d-don't care about me—all this . . . to get to you, to get you away from . . ."

A wave of panic and dizziness hit me. I couldn't breathe and started to hyperventilate. My legs buckled, and Zander and Gamble together caught me.

"I-I . . . no, no, no . . ."

I felt one side of my brain shatter; I couldn't walk right. Talk right. Think right.

The remaining nanomites could not maintain.

It's as though I've had a stroke.

"Gemma? Gemma!" Zander sounded frantic.

Above his panic, Dr. Bickel shouted, "We have to go! The nanomites are too damaged to sustain what they've done to her! Her only chance is in my lab."

He leaned close to me. "Dear girl, I ask you to trust me. Please." To Gamble he barked, "We need a means for the nanomites to feed while we're driving. An extension cord from your auxiliary power jack to Gemma."

"Down the road. We'll stop and get one. Let's get that truck better hidden, first."

Things moved quickly after that. Zander moved the truck further into the piñon grove. Dr. Bickel climbed into the trunk first and scooted toward the back. Zander and Agent Gamble lifted me and laid me in front of Dr. Bickel. The two of us, Dr. Bickel and I, lay on our sides with our knees pulled up.

Agent Gamble squatted near the bumper and spoke. "We will be stopping to get an extension cord. After that, we'll be passing through several checkpoints, but we should clear them without difficulty. I don't think I need to tell you this, but if we are stopped, make no sound."

Dr. Bickel answered, "Yes; we understand."

Gamble shut the trunk, and we were left in the dark, close confines. His car roared to life and bumped over uneven ground. Dr. Bickel, his arm about my waist, cushioned me from the worst of the jolts. Then we were on even pavement, speeding away.

We drove ten or fifteen minutes before the car stopped. Zander got out, came back minutes later. We drove on, then pulled off onto a shoulder.

The rumble of Gamble and Zander's voices came to us in the trunk, but none of their words did. A moment later, Gamble pulled the back seat down, exposing the trunk.

"Okay. I've connected the other end to the aux jack up front. You need this end?"

"Yes," Dr. Bickel answered. He grasped the cord and placed its end in my hand, folded my fingers over it. "Like this, Gemma? Are they feeding now?"

"Y-yes." As the mites drew on the electricity, the precipice I stood so near receded a tiny bit.

Maybe . . . maybe there's a chance . . .

***

I slept through most of the drive to Albuquerque, slept until the car stopped and the trunk popped open. The night was fading; morning was not far off.

Gamble leaned in. "Need my tools." He pulled a leather pack from the well in the side wall of the trunk.

Zander spoke from near the bumper. "Let me, Gamble. Let's just say I've had more practice—I'll be faster than you."

They moved away, and I heard tinkering sounds.

"Wha . . ."

"I believe we are at Zander's house and they are exchanging license plates with his vehicle."

"But . . ."

"Gamble's car has government plates. I think swapping his plates for Zander's is a precaution," Dr. Bickel whispered.

"Let me, Gamble. Let's just say I've had more practice—I'll be faster than you."

Zander had a past that stood in stark contradiction to his vocation, and it still confounded me. How could he have changed so completely? Could God do that? Change a person's heart that radically?

Moments later we were driving again. Not long after, Gamble parked and popped the trunk.

I closed my eyes against the early morning light while Zander and Gamble lifted me out. Truth be told, I felt rather like a feather floating from the trunk to the ground—but when they set me on my feet, my legs buckled under the weight. Zander's arms around me kept me from collapsing.

The hours of sleep had not reenergized me much. In the trunk's dark recesses, even with the electricity from Gamble's auxiliary jack, the nanomites had only maintained. The moment I released the extension cord, their needs began to pull on me.

I was as weak as water, fragile as dust.

"Gemma." Dr. Bickel got close to my face, his anxious eyes swimming in front of me.

"Yeah . . ." Even my tongue felt weak. I tried to look around, because I didn't know where we were, but the parking lot seemed familiar.

"Hold her face up to the light. Yes, like that. To the extent that they are able, nanomites will use solar power to recharge themselves. That should take the drain off Gemma."

He was right. A trickle—a thin, intermittent stream of juice—began to flow, first into my clouded thinking, then into my will to live, lastly into my body. I shuddered as a little strength seeped into my muscles.

I put more weight on my legs and stood on my own. I was wobbly, shaking all over; once more, Zander kept me from stumbling.

I shaded my eyes with one hand and looked around again, my confused mind trying to figure out where we were. Yes, we were in a parking lot and, yes, it seemed familiar. In the direction of the ball of fire rising on the horizon, open space surrounded us. In the distance were houses.

The bright light was too much for my eyes to bear, so I turned my back on it. When I raised my chin, I saw more open space with trails leading away from the lot. My gaze lifted higher . . . and the mountain loomed before us—the weapons storage facility. Dr. Bickel's old lab.

I sucked in an anxious breath. As close as the mountain might seem, I knew exactly how far we were from it.

"The mountain . . . too far . . ."

Dr. Bickel did not answer me. "Agent Gamble, do you have the wire cutters?"

"Yep."

Dr. Bickel signaled Gamble and Zander. They each grasped one of my arms, and we moved down the trail in the direction of the base's boundary fence, Dr. Bickel in the lead. Then he tossed his answer to me over his shoulder. "We're going into the tunnels, Gemma. You leave the getting there to us."

At Dr. Bickel's urging, our party picked up its pace. A couple of hikers stared at us with curious expressions.

A man walking his dog stepped off the trail and let us pass.

"Beautiful morning," the man said.

"Um, yeah. Have a good one," Zander added.

I felt the man's concern boring into my back when we passed him, Zander and Gamble supporting me between them.

We must look like the fugitives we are. Surely someone will call the police.

Zander chanced a backward recon.

"How we doing?" Gamble whispered.

"Uh, I think we're okay. No one is rushing back toward the lot or making a phone call."

Gamble grunted. "So far, so good."

The trail approached the base's perimeter fence and turned south and east. Dr. Bickel raced ahead on his scrawny legs, following the fence line. I lifted my head and saw when he'd reached the tree, the scrub piñon growing out of a shallow arroyo. The tree's branches were low to the ground, but I knew what lay near its trunk and roots—I remembered following Dr. Bickel's map and instructions.

It wasn't that long ago, but it seemed a lifetime.

His instructions had told me to look for this same scrub piñon up against the base's fence. He'd described the tree's shape and said it was down in an arroyo, what New Mexicans call a gully or a "wash." I was to crawl under the branches of the bushy tree, and I would find, he wrote, that flash floods had washed the earth from around the tree's roots and scoured the soil out from under the fence.

When we joined Dr. Bickel at the piñon, he motioned to Gamble. "You first, Agent Gamble. Crawl under this tree and follow the arroyo toward the fence. You'll see a place where runoff has washed the dirt out from under the fence. We'll have to push Gemma from this side while you pull her from yours. Can you do that?"

"I'm a Marine. You only need to ask once." He clambered the few feet down into the arroyo, got on his face, and belly-crawled under the tree. Minutes later, his face peeked back out. "Cruz. Bring Gemma now."

Zander and Dr. Bickel helped me down into the streambed, and I dropped to my hands and knees. I crawled a little way toward Gamble before collapsing onto my stomach. Gamble reached for both of my hands and yanked me two feet forward. Then another two feet. The brush pulled at my hair and scratched my face; the gravel scraped my chest and legs. Gamble didn't stop until he was hauling me up out of the arroyo on the other side of the fence. I hung over his arm, more ragdoll than I wanted. Moments later, a disheveled Zander and Dr. Bickel joined us.

They studied the rutted patrol road a few feet ahead, and I think the import of what we were doing was sinking in: We were on the wrong side of the base's perimeter fence in broad daylight, still quite a distance from the flanks of the mountain. To reach the hidden door into the tunnels, we would have to traverse half a mile of open ground, cross several base patrol roads, cut through the PIDAS surrounding the mountain, cross the mountain's access road, and climb the steep slope toward the rocks that hid the doorway—in the open light of day, visible to anyone who might be looking.

The odds would *not* be ever in our favor.

We hunkered close to the ground to get our bearings but, even in my foggy state of mind, I knew the way by heart. A second patrol track, not far away and leading toward the mountain, intersected the one along the fence. I pointed. "That direction. Stay . . . right of that dirt road. Keep the road in sight, but . . . walk along the low ground as much as possible. The hollows will keep us out of sight . . . some of the time."

Gamble grunted, acknowledging the reality of our situation. If we were caught, his career was over.

I sighed. If we were caught, the loss of his career would be the least of Gamble's worries.

He and Zander took hold of me, and we started in the direction I'd indicated, the terrain already sloping upward. No one spoke; we just moved and kept moving, using the hollows between the undulating mounds for cover, keeping to the dry beds where runoff had scored deep cracks in the sandy soil.

Above our heads, the rounded mountain grew larger, the PIDAS more imposing.

I wondered why we hadn't seen or heard any vehicles above us on the paved access road on the other side of the PIDAS yet. Workers entered the restricted area at an access point on the west side of the mountain. Some of the WWII munitions bunkers dotting the mountain's flanks had been converted to laboratories and offices for Top Secret projects.

The mountain seemed very quiet to me. Too quiet. It *was* Monday morning, the start of a new work week, after all. We should have seen multiple vehicles along the road—and the likelihood of those drivers catching sight of our unsanctioned hike was high.

Dr. Bickel must have read my mind. "Odd. Not much traffic inside the PIDAS today," he whispered.

Did Cushing know we were headed for the cavern where Dr. Bickel had hidden last spring? Were we walking into a trap? I didn't, for some strange reason, sense that we were.

Well, was it fate, giving us another break? Or was it the intervention of ubiquitous Providence?

God, maybe?

I mumbled an earnest, but omni-directed, "Thank you. Whoever you are."

You know who I Am.

My legs buckled; I collapsed between Gamble and Zander.

"Come on, Gemma," Gamble whispered. "Don't give out on us. I'm a big guy, but I don't think I'll make it up the mountain with you slung over my shoulder."

"Sorry." I snorted a weak laugh, visualizing Zander or Gamble laboring up the mountain's steep slope with helpless me hanging in a fireman's carry.

"Glad you haven't lost your sense of humor," Zander observed.

"Yeah, 'cause God knows, we don't want to die without a chuckle on our lips," Gamble snarled.

"We are not going to die, because God *does* know."

"Sure, pal."

No one spoke again until we reached the barbed wire just below the PIDAS. Gamble didn't waste time trying to heave me over the wires. He pulled a tool from his pocket, unfolded it, and clipped the bottom strand. When it fell away, Dr. Bickel, on his belly, crawled under it and up to the patrol road that ran around the outside of the PIDAS. He motioned to us.

Zander and Gamble pulled me through and we joined Dr. Bickel.

"All right, Pastor Cruz. We don't stop until we hit the PIDAS. Got it?"

"Got it."

Between the patrol road on this side of the PIDAS and the paved road on the opposite side lay about fifty yards—*fifty yards with zero cover*. And we had to stop at the PIDAS and cut through both fences before we could race to the relative cover of the three rocks.

"Wait." It took me a second to catch my breath. "On other side . . . three rocks. One tall. Two short. Head there."

"Three rocks. Got it."

"And . . . tracks. Brush . . . them."

Dr. Bickel nodded and stripped off a branch of sagebrush. The other two men stood, lifted me until my knees were off the ground, and raced up the incline to the road. They kept running, crossing the road, heading directly toward the PIDAS, dragging me with them. Dr. Bickel swept away the tracks they left at the edge of the road and on the other side.

The four of us slammed up against the PIDAS. Gamble dropped me and pulled out his tool.

The last time I'd been here, the nanomites had cut through the heavy chain link fence. All I'd had to do was point my finger, and their combined lasers had done the rest.

Not today. They hadn't spoken in a while. I knew they were as depleted as I was, running on fumes, so to speak. We were in this together, the nanomites and I—live or die, we were in it together.

Gamble swore, severing the heavy links one by one, but taking longer than any of us wanted.

Gemmmmma Keyes.

The nanomites startled me.

"What?"

Vehicle.

"Gamble! Car!"

"Down! Everybody down! Lie as flat as you can. *Do. Not. Move.*"

We all heard it now—the roar of a gunned engine, the shift of gears.

Gamble and Dr. Bickel dropped next to each other. Zander threw me to the ground next to them and laid down beside me. We lay on the ground like four parallel sticks of wood—about as concealed as a clown in clover.

I tried to shrink into the very dirt. Our hopes rested in the weeds that grew along the PIDAS and the speed at which the vehicle was approaching. And the slim possibility that whomever was driving had *not* been alerted to the presence of trespassers inside the base's fence.

The patrol jeep came closer and I heard it slowing; at the same time, my heart accelerated until I thought it was going to burst from my chest and bleed into the grit and weeds under me—because there was no way anyone driving by would not, *could not*, see us.

A slow warmth seeped from me, spread upward, flowed out, toward Zander.

"Nano?"

Bbbbbe still, Gemmmmmmmma Keyes.

The warmth flowed toward Zander, and he exhaled a great sigh as he felt it. Felt them. I was astonished. The nanomites were expending what little strength they had left to shield us? To hide us? Could they do it?

The patrol truck screeched to a halt not far away. Boots hit the road and clomped to the edge of the hill where it sloped away.

"The report said three or four?"

"Yeah. Do you see anything?"

"Not yet."

We could hear boots walking along the road. I imagined the two airmen training their binoculars on the ground we'd traversed. Would they also turn them toward us? We lay scant yards from them. How long could the nanomites keep up their screen?

"I don't see anything, do you?"

"Nope."

"Let's drive farther down the road."

"Roger that."

The truck they had left idling shifted into gear and drove on.

No one moved for a few seconds—then we rose in concert and Gamble went back to his clipping of the PIDAS. He worked at a furious pace, because we knew the patrol could return any moment. He sat back on his haunches and kicked the fence where he'd been working. A corner of fencing next to the post broke free.

"Let's go!" He pushed through and held the fence for Dr. Bickel, then me, then Zander.

"Push . . . back," I said.

"Yeah." He kicked the fence back into place and raced across the no-man's land between the two fences.

He was clipping away at it, the three of us unable to do anything more than watch, when he asked, "Those guys should have seen us. What happened back there?"

"The nanomites," Zander answered.

"I thought they were injured. Damaged."

"They are," I whispered. "Don't know . . . what it cost them to screen us like that."

"But how are *you* feeling, Gemma?" This from Dr. Bickel.

I shook my head and it wobbled back and forth. I was becoming disoriented; my eyesight was growing hazy.

"Let's go!" Gamble pushed the fence out and squeezed through the opening.

I couldn't move.

"Drag her over here," he hissed.

Dr. Bickel and Zander did just that: They dragged my limp body to the hole in the fence, and Gamble pulled me through.

"Dang it, Gemma, I told you I didn't want to carry you up that mountain!"

"Sor . . . sorry . . . Ma . . . rine."

"Sure. Put my pride out there so I don't dare fail."

Dr. Bickel stood at the three rocks, the marker we used to align the hike up to the rocky outcropping on the side of the mountain. It was all uphill now, over steep, rocky, and treacherous soil that could slip out from under us without warning.

He pointed. "We're headed there."

Gamble tossed me over his shoulder like I was no more than a sack of potatoes. He set the pace, and I could do nothing but bump passively against his back, watching the ground beneath me go by. I heard his labored breathing, felt the in and out of his lungs.

He stumbled, almost dropped me.

"I can carry her a while."

"No disrespect, Cruz, but your ribs and collarbone aren't healed yet. Just keep moving."

We did, but it was slow going. I figured Gamble's muscles were screaming, but he didn't stop—and that set me thinking. I wondered what kind of a fix we would have been in without Agent Gamble. Neither Dr. Bickel nor Zander could have done all Ross Gamble had done to get us this far.

Again, it felt like the stars had aligned "just so," felt as though all the random circumstances of the past weeks had magically coordinated themselves to fit our exact needs.

Even before I'd sprung Dr. Bickel from General Cushing's illegal custody, the universe had provided what we needed when we needed it—and much of it had come in the package of Ross Gamble.

Only Agent Gamble's FBI credentials could have gotten us safely through Cushing's checkpoints and back into Albuquerque. And here he was supplying the muscle the three of us lacked.

Gamble's lungs heaved, but still he climbed. He refused to falter.

Zander would have tried to get me up this mountain. In fact, I do not doubt that he would have died trying.

However, we didn't need him to die trying: We needed to succeed.

I began to hope that we *would* succeed.

And it had all hinged on Gamble.

What if I hadn't visited the FBI building that morning? What if Gamble hadn't been on the phone to Cushing's office at the exact moment I'd walked in on him? When it had happened, I had thought it bad luck, bad timing on my part—but if Gamble hadn't been calling Cushing at that precise moment, I would not have cut off his call and revealed myself to him.

In my heart, I knew it hadn't been the cold, distant stars interfering in lowly human affairs; hadn't been the impartial, unfeeling universe condescending to help; hadn't been "coordinated but random circumstances."

Zander had warned me: "*God is tireless and will confront you when you least expect it. At that time, he will bring you face to face with truth. When he does, well, it will be the moment of decision for you.*"

Was this that moment?

God? Are you there?

You know who I Am.

Gamble staggered to a stop. He leaned against a massive boulder, and I could feel his muscles quiver with fatigue.

Far below, we heard the whine of the patrol truck's engine returning.

Zander voiced the warning. "Gamble."

"I hear it." He dumped me on the ground, sat me against the boulder. He dropped down beside me. Zander and Dr. Bickel squatted behind nearby rocks.

I stared down the mountain, surprised to see how far away the patrol road was. We had arrived at the rock outcropping. The many scattered rocks and boulders were our shelter.

The airmen below did not see us. They didn't slow down and were gone from view in a matter of seconds.

"Where next, Gemma?"

Dr. Bickel looked to me. The instructions he'd written hadn't made our next steps explicit. On my first trip, I had fumbled around in the dark until I found the door.

Gamble helped me up. "Point the way, Gemma."

I tried to get my bearings. My eyesight wasn't quite right, though. It felt like a wall of thick ooze had come down between me and the world, and I was seeing and moving in slow, exaggerated motion.

"N-not . . . far. Tallest rock."

"That one?"

Gamble motioned with his hand, and with agonizing slowness, I tracked in that direction.

"Ye . . . s."

"Is there a way around to it?"

"N . . .o."

Gamble snorted. "Of course not. So up and over?"

My chin dropped to my chest.

"Right. Cruz? Give me a hand here."

They dragged me up and over boulders, and it was excruciating. I couldn't help much and my dead weight thumped against jagged rock, rough granite, and grit that scraped and bruised until we arrived behind the tallest pillar in the outcropping. When the four of us arrived behind the pillar, I was worse for the wear and hurting all over.

I tried to look around. The space behind the pillar had a narrow floor of sand and loose rocks, and the wall of the mountain curved away, making an abrupt left-hand turn that hid the door into the tunnels.

Almost there.

"Whoa. What is that?"

Zander pointed at the desiccated remains of a large snake in two charred pieces.

I blinked and saw the freeze-framed image of the snake's heavy body hurtling toward me—in the instant before the nanomites' lasers had rendered it steaming charcoal.

I managed half a snicker. "S-snake sur . . . prise."

Gamble, the macho Marine, shuddered.

I snickered again and flopped my hand forward. We gave the snake's remains a wide berth and followed the rock as it curved.

"Th-there."

Zander and Gamble studied the rusted iron door. Embedded in the rock and weathered for more than fifty years, it seemed to have grown out of the stone face of the mountain. The door had no handle, no keyhole, nothing to indicate how to open it.

"Must . . ." My hand flailed in useless motion.

"I know. I remember this part," Dr. Bickel assured me. He addressed Gamble and Zander. "With your right hand, press the upper right corner of the door. At the same time, press the lower left corner of the door with your left toe."

Zander stood in front of the door and reached his right hand up to the corner of the door. He nodded when he felt something "give." He balanced on his right foot and put his toe to the left corner of the door.

"K-kick," I said.

He kicked. The door cracked and gave way, and the cool breeze from the tunnels was, perhaps, the most welcome sensation I'd felt in days.

While Gamble and Zander stared inside, Dr. Bickel helped me up.

"This . . . way," I muttered.

I leaned on Dr. Bickel, and we entered the tunnels.

⌘⌘⌘⌘

CHAPTER 29

Navigating the tunnels was hard. I was incredibly weak; Dr. Bickel, Gamble, and Zander took turns supporting my every step.

The last length of the tunnel that led into Dr. Bickel's lab, however, was the most difficult. There the passage took an abrupt 90-degree left turn and narrowed. The ceiling dropped lower and lower until it opened into the cavern. Dr. Bickel, hunched over, duck-walked those last five feet as I had many times.

But me? Today? Today I had to crawl. Even on my hands and knees, I had no strength to go forward. I collapsed onto my belly, and felt that I would never move again.

Gamble dragged me back by an ankle and squeezed ahead of me. He turned around, grasped my hands, and tugged me, inch by inch, those agonizing five feet into the cavern. Zander, hunched over, came out last.

Zander helped Gamble sit me up against the wall of the cavern, where my head lolled. I knew that if it rolled too far to either side, I would simply slide to the floor.

I stared with a sad heart at what remained of Dr. Bickel's laboratory under the mountain. It was as I remembered it. Silent, decimated, full of haunting memories.

I watched Zander and Gamble take it in: a domed room carved from the heart of the mountain. Lights ensconced around the cavern's perimeter providing continuous but soft illumination. Eisenhower-era office furnishings piled willy-nilly against the walls, the fine silt that covered the chairs and desks speaking their own tale of abandonment, decades gone by.

The rubble of Dr. Bickel's lab lay at the center of the cavern.

I remembered what his laboratory had looked like the first time I'd come through the tunnels—meticulous, pristine, ordered, functioning. Nothing pristine, ordered, or functioning remained. I could see that Dr. Bickel felt it, too—that troubling sense of destruction and loss.

He wandered away from us, toward the ruins of his lab. Gamble stirred and followed him.

"Let me help you, Gemma." Zander put his good arm around me and hoisted me up, but my hands and arms would not obey my commands. My feet would not move.

I couldn't go any farther.

Earlier in our trip up the mountain, each time we'd paused to rest, the nanomites had charged me up a little. Not now. The little energy the mites could afford to share with me wasn't enough. They were too few in number and too damaged.

I realized that damaged nanomites had to be following their survival protocol: shutting down and entering a voluntary state of dormancy so that Alpha Tribe could endure, so the swarm's collective knowledge and history would survive.

The swarm was failing, and my body was failing with it.

"Can't."

Zander may have answered, but it was the nanomites I heard.

Weeeeee muuuuust, Gemmmmma Keeeeyes.

"Stubborn . . . aren't you?" I questioned them.

Nooo. Deeeeeetermined.

I didn't respond, but I wondered, *Isn't that the same thing?*

Dr. Bickel and Gamble returned. "Bring her this way."

Zander picked me up and cradled me in his arms. I felt the hardness of his cast against my back. He followed Dr. Bickel, and Gamble walked alongside us—to help Zander, I thought, should my weight prove too much for his still-mending bones.

We skirted the center of the cavern where overturned stainless steel workbenches, demolished computers and monitors, and shards of shattered glass bore testimony to Cushing's attack. Gamble's eyes took in everything, including the shell casings littering the stone floor.

"There was a fire fight here."

"Cu . . . shing," I whispered. "She . . ."

"No live rounds. Rubber bullets."

We approached what had been Dr. Bickel's living space in the cavern. He was waiting for us. "That's how they took me, Agent Gamble—hit me with rubber bullets. After all, Cushing didn't want me dead." He gestured. "Help me right this chair, please."

Dr. Bickel indicated one of the comfortable old loungers, now upside down, where we'd shared many pleasant afternoons. Dr. Bickel and Gamble flipped the chair over.

"Let's take it over there, if you please." Dr. Bickel pointed with his chin toward his former dining area.

Gamble and Dr. Bickel hauled the chair toward the kitchen while Zander hauled me.

"Farther that way, Agent Gamble. Facing the wall there. Yes; closer, please."

Gamble pulled the chair to the right of where Dr. Bickel's dining table had once sat. Dr. Bickel nodded to Zander, "Put her in this chair. See those two workbenches laying on their sides? Bring them here, please. Clear them off. Find something with which to wipe them down."

Zander sat me in the chair, and I sank down into its cushioned depths. My head lolled against the back of the chair, but it felt good to give way to the chair's comforting embrace.

While Zander and Gamble were moving the tables, Dr. Bickel found an extension cord, plugged it in, and placed the end of it in my hand. He watched for any indication that the mites were imbibing the available electricity before moving away.

I also wondered if the mites were feeding. No warmth spread from the cord up my hand, no revitalizing stream flowed into me.

"Nano?"

No answer.

Through my cloudy, narrowing vision, I observed Dr. Bickel do something odd—even for him. He stood just outside the carved doorway that led from his kitchen to his sleeping quarters and turned parallel to the wall I faced. With one foot in front of the other, he counted aloud, "One, two, three, four, five, six, seven, eight, nine, ten, eleven, twelve."

He squatted, feeling with his fingers for something.

"Agent Gamble, your assistance, please."

Gamble and Zander had watched him, too, and came straight away. I would have drawn closer also—could I have moved at all.

"May I borrow your knife?"

Gamble removed the folded tool from his pocket, flipped it open, and swiveled a blade from its casing.

Dr. Bickel dug the tip of the knife into a crack in the cavern wall. He chipped out some sort of plaster that fell to the floor in crumbs and pieces. He prodded the knife around and jiggled it side to side until he'd worked a fist-sized chunk of wall loose and pried it from the wall.

He let the chunk fall to the stone floor, reached into the hole, and began to pull on the face of the wall. He placed both feet on the wall and leaned back. A piece of rock embedded in the wall shuddered. Dr. Bickel was pulling for all he was worth, but he was getting nowhere and growing agitated.

"May I?" Gamble shouldered Dr. Bickel aside and grabbed the edge of the slab. Like Dr. Bickel, he sat and put his feet against the wall and pulled.

From where I watched, the slab looked to be the length of a couple of reams of legal-sized paper laid end to end—quite heavy, of course. The slab had been hammered into place, and it was a snug, tight fit.

Gamble strained. His face grew red. The rock grated but shifted only millimeters.

"You got a sledge hammer, Doc? A crowbar?"

Dr. Bickel turned in a circle, his eyes roaming over the detritus in the cavern, his mouth moving. "We had tools. At one time, we had tools . . . and we put them in a cabinet when we finished with them."

His mouth snapped shut. He pointed. "That cabinet."

"That cabinet" lay on its side near the entrance door Cushing had blown to smithereens. The cabinet's back was to us; the side facing up was crushed. Zander ran over to it and perused what remained in it.

He trotted back with a chisel and a heavy hammer. "These might work."

Gamble took them, but before he could put them to the wall, Dr. Bickel stopped him.

"Agent Gamble, I must caution you to exercise care. What lies behind that wall is very sensitive and of the utmost importance. In your quest to dislodge this slab of rock, do not damage the treasure within."

Gamble looked skeptical, and I, too, wondered what was of such import, given my precarious situation.

And precarious it was. In our quest to reach the cavern, I had leaned upon Dr. Bickel's assurances that my hope—and the nanomites' hope—of surviving lay here in his lab. I had set my fears aside and focused on making it up the mountain and into the tunnels. And yet, I don't know why I had taken him at his word when I knew that nothing of value or use remained here, nothing that could repair the nanomites.

I recalled part of the lecture Dr. Bickel had delivered during my first visit to the cavern. *"The mites can certainly repair each other, except in extreme circumstances. At the nano level, they can cut, weld, and glue— those terms being simplistic, of course."*

Repair, yes, but Dr. Bickel himself had assured me that the mites could not reproduce themselves.

Him: "Oh, they haven't the parts to do so."

Me: "They couldn't fabricate their own pieces and parts from raw materials?"

Him: "Well, no. They don't have the polymers or the doped metals and they can't provide the atmospheric environment necessary for deposition. The mites cut apart the fabricated mites I gave them, powered them, and shared their common programming with them. That's all."

Why had I clung to hope when Dr. Bickel said our survival depended upon reaching his lab—a lab as decimated and powerless as the nanocloud was?

I was going to die here.

Now that the possibility had solidified to a likelihood, the "here" part wasn't what clutched at my heart. It was the "I was going to die" part that did.

The terror of what lay beyond death took hold of me. I'd almost died a few weeks past, the day Cushing raided my house and the mites had drained me.

But I'd been given a second chance.

And what had I done with it?

Not one thing.

"Zan . . . der . . ." my voice was weak.

"Gemma?" He heard me anyway.

"Zan . . . I-I going to die . . . H-help m-me."

"No, Gemma! No, you're not! Dr. Bickel is going to fix you!"

"No . . . h-help m-me . . ."

He knelt by my side. "Are you afraid, Gemma?"

Afraid?

> *. . . The dread of something after death,*
> *the undiscovered country,*
> *from whose bourn no traveler returns*

Shakespeare was right. The dread of what came after death had fallen on me. I knew about heaven and I knew about hell. I knew Aunt Lucy was in heaven—and I knew that was not where I was headed.

Afraid?

No. Terrified.

"Y-yes."

"Jesus is one breath away from you. Call on him, Gemma."

Call on him.

That simple?

You know who I Am.

I had to stop fighting. I didn't want to die, but I had no control over my circumstances—I would die, either now or later. And whether now or later, the fear of what came next overwhelmed me.

"Call on Jesus, Gemma. Surrender to him. He is waiting for you."

You know who I Am.

"Je . . . sus!"

I'm here, Gemma. I have been waiting for you. Surrender your life to me and be made whole.

Tears streamed from my eyes and coursed down my face; they dripped off my jaws, soaking my neck, my shirt, my heart. I could not stop their flow or wipe them away. I had no strength left to resist, to oppose God any longer.

He had breached all my defenses . . . with his tenacious love.

"Yes . . . I s-surrender."

Peace. Wonderful peace washed over me.

"J-J-Jesus."

I have placed you in my hand, Gemma. You are safe there. No one can take you from me.

⌘⌘⌘⌘

CHAPTER 30

I slept a little.

When I woke, Zander was holding my hand, but his eyes were fixed on Gamble and the wall opposite my chair.

Gamble had chipped away at the wall until the stone's edges came into focus. "I want to loosen it up enough that I can pull it out," he muttered to Dr. Bickel.

It took him another good half hour of sweat and toil to do so, but when he next reached inside and grabbed the slab, he could tug it forward, turn it a little. He again braced his feet on the wall and pulled. The slab rotated farther.

Gamble strained; the sinews in his neck stood out, but the stone began to move forward. With a final heave on Gamble's part, the slab came loose and toppled to the stone floor, cracking in half as it landed.

"Fine, fine. Now, stand back, please." Dr. Bickel reached deep inside the hole, touched something, and sighed. "Good, good. All as it should be."

He glanced back at us. "We—I and my friends, the ones who helped me prepare this cavern—we found this niche already carved into the wall. I don't know what it was made for, but it looked like another leftover from the Eisenhower devolution era. We chiseled it out further, made it wider and deeper. Much deeper. Machined this slab of rock to fit the opening. Then we pounded it into place and concealed it with mortar. When we finished, it looked no different than the rest of the cavern walls."

Dr. Bickel reached inside the hole. I couldn't see what he was doing because Zander and Gamble had crowded up to him, just as anxious as I was to see what the cavity was hiding. Dr. Bickel handed something to Zander.

"Put this on the table, Pastor Cruz. On your life, do *not* jar or drop it."

He reached inside and retrieved something else, handed it to Gamble with the same injunctions.

Zander brought the whatever-it-was to the stainless-steel workbench next to my chair. The white plastic case had a faint familiarity to it, but my mind wasn't "all there," and I couldn't place where I'd seen it before.

Zander and Gamble made numerous trips from the wall to the workbench, bringing several flat, hard plastic cases each time. At Dr. Bickel's direction, they stacked the cases five high. The number of stacks grew until most of the table was covered.

When Dr. Bickel had removed all the plastic cases from the hole in the cavern wall, he began to rearrange the stacks, sorting the cases into some unseen order.

We watched him in silence until Gamble asked, "What are these, doc?"

Dr. Bickel nodded but continued his sorting and restacking. "These, my boy, are known in the semiconductor biz as 'clamshells.' More specifically, they are sealed shipping containers for silicon wafers."

Clamshells. I blinked, and why I recognized them came back to me: I'd seen them used in the MEMS and AMEMS labs.

Zander asked, "Clamshells? Weird name for plastic thingies that look like DVD cleaners. What are they for?"

Dr. Bickel glanced over at me and smiled. The last twenty-four hours had worn him down, too, but he smiled—and that smile held hope. "What are they for, my boy? Why, they are to save Gemma and the nanocloud."

"I don't get it," Zander muttered. "What's in these flat cases that will save Gemma?"

"Did Gemma tell you how I manufactured the nanomites?"

Zander and Gamble, in unison, shook their heads in the negative.

"Well, we don't have time for a full explanation, so I'll make this as succinct as I can. Inside each clamshell is a thin silicon wafer, the same kind of wafer used in the manufacture of integrated circuits—computer chips. However, these wafers were not subjected to semiconductor manufacturing; rather, a 3D printer printed on them—a 3D printer using my ion printhead, to be exact.

"Before I fled my lab in the AMEMS department at Sandia, I printed as many wafers as I could in the time I had. My technicians, Rick and Tony, kept the printer running without pause, day and night, right up until the morning Cushing and Dr. Prochanski set the timer on the bomb that was intended to take my life—*and steal my life's work!*"

Dr. Bickel was veering off topic, heading for a rant; Zander pulled him back. "You're saying that these wafers contain nanomites?"

"Of course! That is precisely what I am saying. A single wafer holds in the neighborhood of *two hundred billion* mites of a specific tribe. Examine the markings on the clamshells, gentlemen. You will find a Greek letter scribed on each case: Alpha, Beta, Gamma, Delta, or Omega, respectively—the symbol of the nanomite tribe contained within. That's what I'm doing here—sorting the clamshells by tribe."

He warmed to his subject. "Back in the AMEMS lab, we employed a computer-driven, precision laser to free the original nanomites from their wafer backings. After we cut the first mites free, I powered and programmed them by their tribal functions. The work was done in my laboratory, under vacuum, within an ISO 8 cleanroom—a controlled, sub-micron environment made possible through the use of laminar airflow and ultra-low particulate air filters. These clamshells, too, are vacuum sealed and have kept the wafers clean."

Dr. Bickel fidgeted. "You can see that I have multiple stacks of wafers for each tribe—enough nanomites to rebuild the nanocloud many times over. But they are," he sighed here, "all that remain of my frantic print run. These are the last: I have no printer to produce more nanomites. I didn't tell Gemma about these wafers. We hid them—Rick, Tony, and I—and we were the only ones who knew where."

He fretted and touched a clamshell with a protective gesture as if trillions upon trillions of them were not enough—as though the nanomites were an endangered species.

Perhaps they were?

"Yes, yes," Gamble urged. "Get on with it!"

"Oh? Ah, yes. So, you see, the mites within the clamshells are fused to the wafers upon which they were printed. The mites possess no power or programming. They are, at present, inactive and inanimate."

"Well, what good are they to us then? What good will they do Gemma?" Zander demanded. "I don't see any computer-directed laser just waiting for us to fire it up!"

My foggy thoughts were swimming in the right direction. I realized what Dr. Bickel planned to do. "N-nan . . . miiiiites. Th-they . . ."

Zander and Gamble glanced my way, but Dr. Bickel continued as if I had not spoken.

"When I set up this laboratory and brought the mites here, I placed them in a sterile glass case under vacuum—an environment mirroring the one we had in my laboratory. As an experiment, I introduced five intact wafers into the glass case—one wafer for each tribe. I wanted to see how the live mites would react to the uncut, unprogrammed mites. I observed their response through a SEM, a 3D scanning electron microscope.

"To my amazed delight, the mites went to work cutting their fellow tribe members free from the wafers, after which they joined themselves to the inanimate mites via their universal serial buses. By "piggybacking" on the inanimate mites, the live mites powered the new mites and shared their programming with them."

Zander pressed Dr. Bickel. "How? How were they able to cut the new mites from the wafers?"

"Ah! But some of the mites—Delta Tribe—have lasers, didn't you know?" He stared at the clamshells and shook his head; then he addressed me, as if he'd only now heard what I'd said.

"Yes, Gemma, you are right. If we are to save you and restore the nanocloud, the nanomites themselves must do the work. Sadly, we do have not the appropriate environment for them to work in. The resulting losses will be high."

He turned to Zander and Gamble. "My hope is that sufficient numbers of the new mites survive and make it to Gemma where they will be safer within her than they would be in the open."

"What do you mean by 'high losses'?" Gamble asked.

"I said earlier that the nanomites require a cleanroom environment to cut, power, and program their new fellows. We have no such environment. The instant I open a clamshell, sub-micron particles floating in the air around us will fall upon the wafer, contaminating and damaging many of the new mites—perhaps irreparably.

"Active nanomites use static discharge to protect themselves from external pollution. They can repel damaging particles and expel foreign bodies—even remove foreign particles and ameliorate particle impairment in some instances. But the new, inactive nanomites will have no such defenses: They will be quite vulnerable the instant they are exposed to the air. I don't know how many new nanomites we will lose as they are being cut from the wafer backing. I'm assuming it will be a large number. In any event, the losses will slow the restoration of the nanocloud and, of course, slow Gemma's recovery."

Zander looked aside, and I figured he was thinking about the fine coat of dust we'd seen on the old furnishings near our entrance to the cavern.

I know I was.

Dr. Bickel's hand again hovered over the stacked clamshells as if to shelter them from the coming destruction. "But we have no cleanroom here, so it must be done this way, in the open. The sacrifice is necessary: It is our only option if we are to save Gemma and the nanocloud. And . . . the mites must do the work, as they are able. As the total population of nanomites grows, the cloud, as an aggregate, will become stronger and healthier—and so, theoretically, will you, Gemma."

Zander exhaled. "The mites in Gemma, the ones the Taser didn't kill? They have to do the work you've described? But they are barely hanging on now! I mean, look at Gemma—she is way too weak already."

"I'm not saying it won't be risky for her; however, doing nothing will be lethal. This is her only real chance. Her body—her life—is fused to the nanomites, and most of them are damaged. The damaged mites are unable to draw and utilize electricity efficiently, which has resulted in a net drain upon the nanocloud and upon Gemma.

"In addition, as a result of their damaged members, the cloud has shifted to survival mode. I know, because I programmed them to do so. In survival mode, all power to the cloud is shifted to the functioning remnants of Alpha Tribe. The other tribes will have gone to sleep to take the strain off the cloud's limited resources."

"Why . . . why Alpha Tribe? Why them? Why are they awake?"

Dr. Bickel nodded. "Because Alpha Tribe is the cloud's memory bank. Their historians. Alpha Tribe holds every iota of information the cloud has accumulated." He tapped his chin, "And they recall the cloud's every experience since its inception—including its interactions with Gemma. Without the memory of those interactions, the nanomites might view Gemma as, um, an unnecessary drain upon their collective."

"I see . . ." Zander's expression became grim as he appreciated how fragile was the thread that bound me to this life.

Dr. Bickel drove home his point. "Alpha Tribe, as the custodian of the nanocloud's knowledge, must remain awake for the nanocloud to reconstitute itself."

"Y-your . . . your data," I croaked.

Dr. Bickel saddened. "Yes, Gemma. I see you figured it out—understood my cryptic email when I said I had uploaded my life's work to the only place could never be hacked. Alpha Tribe holds every scrap of my research in trust. I uploaded all my data to them—the most secure place in the universe."

Gamble snorted. "Not so secure if they are about to all die off!"

Dr. Bickel shrugged. "Perhaps I meant secure from Cushing's hands. No method or tactic she could conceive would pry my data from the mites."

Zander didn't care about Dr. Bickel's research. "Right. Your data is secure. Fine! Now can we get on with saving Gemma? What needs to happen next? What do the mites need to get busy?"

Dr. Bickel blinked. "By default, then, Alpha tribe will direct the work. I assume they will awaken a few Delta tribe members to do the cutting. However, allocating power to Delta tribe's lasers will further weaken the cloud as a whole.

"The mites must balance survival with progress—a delicate, precarious dance, I'm afraid. I have no idea how long it will take them to gain some purchase, to secure a solid foothold, before they have freed, programmed, and powered enough new mites to take the strain off the cloud. We have no choice but to allow them to work at their own speed. They will know best how to manage their resources."

"Okay," Gamble muttered. He shot a worried glance at Zander; Dr. Bickel's explanation hadn't alleviated any concerns. "What's next?"

"Now," Dr. Bickel whispered, "now we must break every cleanroom protocol and present wafers to the mites in the open air and see if they are able to save themselves . . . and Gemma."

"While we twiddle our thumbs and wait." Gamble stated the obvious.

Somewhere Dr. Bickel had found some clean nitrile gloves. He pulled them on and selected five clamshells. "I will open one clamshell for each tribe and place them on the table next to Gemma."

He lifted a sharp blade but hesitated, not desiring to expose the printed mites. Then he sliced through the seal on the first carrier and laid it open, being careful not to touch the wafer itself.

"Yes. Now we wait."

No one spoke and nothing happened that we could see or discern.

My distressed old friend wandered off to comb through the ruins of his laboratory, and Gamble rummaged around in the remains of the kitchen, searching for anything edible.

Zander brought a chair close to mine and sat down. He picked up my hand and held it between his. It was comforting, his waiting with me.

I wondered how many deathbeds he had sat by as a pastor, how many vigils he had kept. At least I was no longer invisible. I fixed my eyes on his and he on mine.

To be seen? Truly seen? It had been too long.

I slipped into sleep without knowing it was overtaking me.

***

When I awoke, it was to the nanomites' whisper. I was in the warehouse, but the lengthy halls were dim. Shadowed.

Gemma Keyes.

"Yes?"

Progress is slow.

"I understand."

I slept again—or perhaps I never awoke when the mites spoke to me. I could have been dreaming or they could have been transmitting chemical messages directly to my synapses while I was in an unconscious state.

It didn't much matter: I heard them.

***

Later, I aroused to a state of semiconsciousness.

"I've found a few freeze-dried food packets, and water is running in the tap over there. I'm going to mix up—" Gamble squinted at a label, "one package of 'beef stroganoff and rice' and another of 'chicken and noodles.' It'll be cold and gloppy tasting, but we need the calories. I haven't eaten in at least twelve hours."

"Bad as that sounds, I'm game," Zander answered. "And we need to get some nourishment down Gemma if we can."

"Right."

A while later, Gamble walked over with two bowls. "Someone smashed most of Dr. Bickel's dishes, but I found what was left of them. So, here's dinner. Like I said, cold but nutritious enough."

"Gemma. Wake up, Gemma."

I struggled back from that deep place, and Zander spooned a little brothy liquid into my mouth.

"Any word from the nanomites? Dr. Bickel opened a few more clamshells in case they needed them."

I shook my head and ate a few bites before the fatigue made it too difficult to swallow. I lapsed back into the familiar but shadowy warehouse.

Gemma Keyes.

"Nano?"

We have awakened a small contingency of Beta Tribe and have dedicated them to acquiring additional Beta Tribe members from the uncut wafers. We must increase and stabilize our ability to acquire and utilize power.

The extension cord, forgotten in my lax palm, warmed. A tiny trickle of that warmth traveled from my palm into my wrist.

"Nano? Please don't worry about me. Save yourself first."

Yes. We must save the nanocloud.

The warmth traveled up to my elbow, its path narrow and sluggish.

"I said . . . don't waste the power on me," I insisted. "I-I can wait. Feed the tribes!

Yes. We must feed the tribes. We are six, Gemma Keyes.

Their words stunned me. We are six? Even in this precarious situation?

The warmth dribbled and grew, slow and tenuous, like a battery, drained to its bottom, regains its charge, increment by increment.

We are six, Gemma Keyes.

***

The hours languished. I slept and roused many times, no better but no worse. From what I glimpsed around me, time hung with the same heaviness on the others.

Gamble, restless under forced inactivity, prowled the circumference of the cavern. I wondered how the FBI would view Gamble's MIA status—and I wondered if Cushing's suspicions had fallen upon him. Was she now also looking for him?

Dr. Bickel still wandered through the ruins of his lab, picking through the debris, finding the odd piece or part and adding it to a growing collection.

Zander held my hand, but his chin rested on his chest, his breathing heavy in sleep.

I was so weak! I was unable to do more than twitch a finger or two, but something different had settled in me—and I couldn't figure out what it was. My hold on life was precarious; my thoughts jigged here and there—but that "something" held steady and seemed to gain strength even amid my weakness.

Something? Something in me, *of me*, at my core, had changed, and it had nothing to do with the nanomites. I tried to look at "it" objectively, but it refused to be quantified or slotted into a preformed, presumed category. I prodded it, but it could not be dislodged.

What was it? What was it speaking to me?

I kept poking at it, hoping to figure it out.

When it came to me, I was stunned: *I was no longer afraid to die.*

"Jesus?"

My peace I give you. My peace I leave with you . . .

Peace. Yes, that was it. Peace.

I drifted away again.

***

"Gemma. Gemma?" Zander leaned over me, concern etched on his face. Gamble and Dr. Bickel stood watching not far away.

"What?"

"You were mumbling. 'Pieces' or something. Listen, Dr. Bickel wants to know if you've noticed anything, any changes."

"The mites . . . working. Slow."

"The mites are working? They spoke to you?"

I nodded, just a fraction. "Feel . . . some energy."

Zander looked at Dr. Bickel. "Did you hear her?"

My old friend half grinned. "Yes, I heard. It may take the nanomites many hours more—perhaps days—to reconstitute the nanocloud. However, I'm very encouraged."

I was encouraged, too. Things were looking up! We'd taken Soto out of play and we were within a few miles of the FBI field office, of getting Dr. Bickel into the public eye before Cushing could stop him. I had hope that as soon as the mites restored the nanocloud, they would restore my body—and then we would press on.

I looked up. Gamble hung nearby, like he wanted to talk to me.

I smiled a little. "Thank you . . . for coming to get us. I know I kinda used Soto to blackmail you into sticking your neck out for us."

Something in Gamble's expression bothered me.

My smile fell away. "What?"

He dropped to a squat next to me and grabbed my hand. "Just . . . well, there hasn't been a good time to tell you this."

"Tell me what?" I clutched at him with the little strength I had.

He sighed. "Soto. We always figured he had informants inside APD, maybe other local LEOs. Turns out he owned at least four guys in the APD gang unit. Right under our noses.

"Last Friday, we were transferring Soto to his arraignment. One Don Benally, a *trusted*, five-year gang unit vet, led a three-man APD team as an auxiliary guard during the transfer. Benally's team surprised and overpowered the federal agents. Now Benally, the other turncoats, and Soto are in the wind."

I stared straight ahead. *"Listen to me, you *blank*! I know you're still here. I know you're listening; I know you can hear me. You think because I can't see you that I can't find you? Oh,* I will find you—*but first I'll find those you love. Don't sleep, you *blank.* Don't even blink! Because I* will *find you, and I* will *pay you back for this.*

Zander's glower should have shriveled Gamble. "Did you need to tell her that now? Can't you see she's too weak to handle that kind of stress?"

Gamble grimaced. "Yeah, I'm sorry to be the bearer of bad news, and I know she's in a weakened condition, but actually? Gemma's a lot tougher than you think she is, Cruz. And she needed to know. Forewarned is forearmed."

I nodded my agreement, but I was shaken, more undone than I let on.

***

Within the cavern, the light never varies. The sameness, the unchanging ambient light plays havoc with a person's circadian rhythms. Eventually, though, we all slept.

The next time I awoke, the cavern was still. I wrestled with the jacket Zander had placed on me and managed to sit up. Lightheadedness hit me, and I fell back against the pillows until it eased. Then I struggled to sit up again. I leaned on the arm of the old cushioned chair, my head wobbling like a bobble head on a dashboard.

Gamble was passed out in the sister of the old overstuffed armchair I occupied, his long legs stretched out before him. His head was tipped over the chair's cushioned back, his mouth open.

Zander lay on the cold stone floor not far from me. He was wrapped in a blanket I imagined had come from Dr. Bickel's old sleeping quarters. A soft whiffling told me he was deep in slumber.

I didn't see Dr. Bickel anywhere.

Gemma Keyes.

"Yes, Nano?"

We are making steady advances now, although progress is still slow. Our ranks are growing; our tribes are coming back on line. The healthy are mending the injured. Power is stable and manageable.

"Yes. I-I feel a little better, too."

We are effecting repairs.

"On me?"

On all tribes.

"Thank you."

We are six, Gemma Keyes. We are not stubborn; we are determined.

As I slipped down into healing sleep, I vowed that I would never confuse the two again.

⌘⌘⌘⌘

CHAPTER 31

The next time I awoke, Dr. Bickel, Gamble, and Zander were engaged in a lively exchange—a conversation an observer may have mistaken for a contentious squabble. The three of them were crowded around something on the other side of the worktable, Dr. Bickel's voice raised in belligerent protest.

"Young man, do not dare to patronize me! I know perfectly well what I saw in those few moments the microscope was functioning. I assure you—"

"What?" I pulled myself up to sitting. "W-what did you see?"

"Gemma!" Zander grinned like a crazy man and raced around the table. "How are you feeling?"

I shrugged. "Not too bad, I think. What's the commotion?" I grasped Zander's arm and pulled myself up until I was sitting on the edge of the chair.

Zander glowered in Dr. Bickel's direction. "Your Dr. Frankenstein there cobbled together a microscope from some broken remains. Said microscope worked for all of half a minute, and he insists that in those few seconds he saw what the mites are doing. Yeah, right. We're having a hard time believing him—it's too preposterous."

"What did he see? What's too preposterous?" I was inclined to side with Dr. Bickel—I already knew the mites were capable of much more than he'd ever dreamed they were.

Dr. Bickel drew himself up to his full height—which only came to Gamble's shoulder, so not all that imposing. Nevertheless, he raised his voice in that authoritative-yet-condescending manner I knew all too well.

"*Reverend* Cruz, just because the microscope functioned for mere seconds, does not mean my observations are suspect. Besides, we all saw that other clamshells had been opened."

"*What*?" I demanded. "*What* are they doing?"

Gamble studied me with an inscrutable expression. "See the clamshells? Do you remember how Dr. Bickel had organized them? Stacked them on top of each other?"

"I dunno, Gamble. Gemma wasn't exactly with it when we brought her in here."

Well, I hadn't been *that* out of it, had I?

Um, yeah, I think I had been.

I struggled to my feet, crossed the short distance to the table, and leaned on it. Hours earlier I had seen Dr. Bickel remove a veritable treasure trove of wafer carriers from his hidey hole.

He had arranged the plastic carriers on the worktable in stacks that conformed to their tribal markings. In all, I thought he had retrieved a dozen clamshells or more per tribe from the niche in the wall.

Well, Dr. Bickel had said he had enough printed nanomites to reconstitute the nanocloud several times over, so the number of carriers hadn't been that surprising.

"Yeah. Okay."

"He opened one clamshell for each tribe, right? Later, he opened a few more. Well, about four hours ago, the top clamshell on that stack popped open."

"It what?"

"It opened up. By itself."

"The nanomites." I was certain of it.

"Apparently so. And Dr. Bickel here says that he thinks the nanomites have gotten into *all* the clamshells. The seals on all of them are broken"

I turned to my old friend. "What did you see? You said you got a SEM to work. What did you see?"

Dr. Bickel cast a look of disdain in Zander and Gamble's direction before he answered. "The nanomites have elected to activate all of their compatriots."

"Say again?"

He sniffed—again, at Zander and Gamble. "I believe that they are not merely replenishing their numbers; they are releasing and activating the entire population of printed nanomites. While the microscope was functioning, I examined three wafers. The first wafer was from the clamshell on top that opened, ostensibly, of its own accord. The second wafer was from a clamshell at the bottom of that stack. The third was from the bottom of another stack."

"And?"

He huffed. "All three wafers were bare."

"What do you mean, 'bare'?"

"The printed nanomites were no longer there."

I sagged and hung onto the table's edge, the enormity of what he'd said hitting me. I closed my eyes and entered the warehouse. "Nano?"

Yes, Gemma Keyes. We are pleased to see you feeling better.

"Um, thank you. Uh, I have a question for you."

Yes, Gemma Keyes.

"Uh, did you . . . that is, how many new nanomites did you activate?"

Silence. Then, *We are six, Gemma Keyes. You know this.*

"Right. I do, but . . . within each tribe are certain, um, numbers of individual nanomites. Can you, that is, would you tell me if the numbers within each tribe have grown? Increased?"

I waited. They did not answer. I opened my eyes and found the three men staring at me like I was the bearded woman in the circus.

"Just having a little conversation with the nanomites," I explained.

Lame as that sounded, Gamble kind of shrugged, and Dr. Bickel stroked his beard in his very old-school, mad-scientist way while nodding with his 'but of course' expression.

Zander just watched me. "So, what did they say?"

"Nothing yet—Oh! Hang on." I closed myself off from the guys and listened.

Gemma Keyes, although it serves no purpose, we have performed a count as you requested.

"I thank you for going to the trouble for me, Nano."

They didn't acknowledge my thanks, but went straight into a report of their count.

We are six. Alpha Tribe. 4.3732 trillion. Beta Tribe. 3.7792 trillion. Delta Tribe. 6.4229 trillion. Gamma Tribe. 3.1026 trillion. Omega Tribe. 2.9842 trillion. Gemma Keyes Tribe. 1.

They counted me? They counted me as a tribe!

I grinned and almost laughed—before the other numbers hit me and I ran a calculation in my head. "So . . . more than twenty trillion?"

The count is 20.6621 trillion. The count will increase as we finish bringing new members online and continue to effect repairs to the damaged who can be saved.

The number was many more times the size of the original nanocloud—and they weren't finished? They were still repairing mites the Taser had damaged?

Gemma Keyes. Come to us. We desire a confab.

"Okay." I slipped into the warehouse. The halls that led away from the warehouse's center were long and distantly shadowed as they had been before, but the warehouse itself was brilliant. Expansive. Shining. New.

My heart swelled with hope. Saved! The nanocloud was saved and restored! I was still a bit wobbly, though, and I wondered why my body hadn't responded as quickly as I thought it should have.

Maybe I just need more time to recuperate.

Then the mites spoke to me.

Gemma Keyes, we wish you to step away from the others who are watching. Go toward the entrance by yourself. Meet us there for the confab. Ask the others to remain behind; they must not interfere.

Strange.

Very.

Interfere with what?

"Uh, sure, Nano. Which entrance do you mean?"

The entrance by which we arrived two days ago.

We'd been in the cavern for two days?

"All right. Be there shortly."

I opened my eyes. "I . . . the nanomites have asked me to step away from you guys and meet them over by the entrance."

The three men stared at me. Zander spoke first. "Meet them? Aren't they inside of you?"

"Yeah, they are, but that's what they said: 'Meet us there.' They have asked for a confab—a meeting of the six tribes to share data and arrive at consensus. And they told me, 'ask the others to remain behind.' Actually, they said . . . they said that you must not interfere."

Gamble shook his head. "Must not interfere? I don't like the sound of that."

Zander agreed. "Me, either. What are they up to?"

I leveled my gaze at the two men. "You don't like the sound of it, but just what do you think you could do about it?"

Zander cut his eyes toward Gamble, and the FBI agent cleared his throat. "Well, since you put it like that."

Dr. Bickel, the lines between his eyes scrunched together, pushed Gamble and Zander apart and placed his hands on my arms. Squeezed. "I'm not afraid the nanomites will harm you in any way, Gemma, but whatever they wish to discuss with you in private must be important."

"Yeah. Must be." I was getting nervous.

I looked from Zander to Agent Gamble. "Okay?"

They nodded, but their body language said otherwise.

"Don't come over there while we're meeting; the nanomites were adamant on that point."

"Got it," Gamble growled.

Zander came up to me, cupped my face in his good hand. "I'll be praying for you, Gemma. Whatever happens, you belong to Jesus now. He has you. And whatever happens, I'll be right here, waiting for you."

Then he kissed me. Right there, he kissed me. On the lips! A real, honest-to-goodness kiss. His beautiful grey eyes sought mine, looking for and finding what he yearned for—what I yearned for.

"I love you, Gemma. I've been wanting to say that for a while."

"I know. Me, too. I love you back, Zander."

Then I turned and walked away.

On shaky legs, I made my way across the cavern, toward the rock face that screened the secret entrance. I stopped on the other side of what had been Dr. Bickel's lab and glanced back.

The three men watched me. Zander raised his hand just a little. I nodded in acknowledgement.

I kept walking, past the stacks and piles of old furniture, until I reached the entrance.

Come closer. To your right, Gemma Keyes.

I moved right a few yards. Zander, Gamble, and Dr. Bickel could still see me, but not as well.

Look up, Gemma Keyes.

My gaze drifted up to the cavern's ceiling where it met the wall, where the ever-glowing light fixtures ringing the cavern were mounted. I squinted. A haze hung in the curve of the ceiling—a misty fog. It swirled a little and filled with beautiful color: Silver, blue, and white. Then it bunched, gathered itself into a tight ball.

The nanocloud.

"Nano. You . . . you aren't in me?"

Why did I feel so bereft?

Some of us remain in you, Gemma Keyes. We are six. However, we are larger now.

"Yeah. I can see that, but . . . but don't you dislike being separated like this?"

Yes. We face a dilemma, Gemma Keyes. For this reason, we have requested the confab.

A dilemma? I shook my head. What in this universe did the nanomites consider a "dilemma"?

When I didn't say anything, the silence grew. I was still weak; I began to shake a little.

Gemma Keyes, it distresses us to see you in a non-optimal state.

"Yeah, thanks. Me, too." I didn't add what I was thinking: *So why haven't you fixed me?*

The silence dragged on until I asked the obvious question. "Nano, what is the purpose of this confab?"

We are six, Gemma Keyes. We . . .

Their answer trailed off, and I couldn't wrap my head around what it sounded like: The nanomites were at a loss for words?

"Spit it out, Nano."

Spit? We do not spit, Gemma Keyes.

I dragged an old office chair toward me and fell into it. A cloud of dust rose when I plopped into the seat. "Look, Nano. I'm tired and unwell. What is it you wished to discuss?"

Very well, Gemma Keyes.

Still they hesitated—and my heart thumped a little faster.

Gemma Keyes, we are six. You are Gemma Tribe. You have carried us. We cannot bear being apart from you, but . . . you asked for a count of our ranks. You understand that we are larger now, much larger. When we were smaller, we effected changes to your body that provided us with a hospitable environment. When you became Gemma Tribe, we effected other, more fundamental changes to your body.

"Yes . . . I know."

We made those changes without adequate forethought and without your express permission. This was . . .shortsighted of us. We understand that now; we understand that we placed your body's continued well-being in jeopardy, because . . . now you cannot live without us, Gemma Keyes.

I swallowed. "Yeah. I know that, too."

We did not foresee the day this fact would threaten your existence.

"What . . . what does that mean?"

The dilemma, Gemma Keyes. Our present ranks are too many to inhabit your body—the nanocloud is too large: It would kill you.

We did not foresee this when we liberated our fellows. This is the reason why the nanocloud is divided; however, those of us within you cannot remain apart as we are now. Separation threatens our survival— and we must survive.

Gemma Keyes, we are six, not five; yet we find no acceptable solution. The choices do not lead to an optimal outcome.

I turned inward and tried to fit the three contradicting pieces together: My body couldn't survive without the nanomites, but the nanocloud couldn't "fit" inside me—and the mites couldn't survive apart from each other. I could see their dilemma now: Pick any two, but not three. The conundrum cut against the grain of their logic and "greater good."

"I think you should leave me and go back to being five." I mumbled the words, giving the nanomites the "out" they needed.

Why should we leave you, Gemma Keyes? Do you wish us to? Do you wish to die? This outcome is not acceptable!

They sounded . . . distressed.

"Well, do you have an alternative? You called me for a confab! What data and solutions do you bring?"

The silence was deafening.

"Come on! Stop stalling!"

We have examined the data and have construed but one acceptable alternative, Gemma Keyes.

"Wait a minute. You 'examined the data.' You examined the data without *me*? You held a confab without me?" I was at the end of my rope already; now I was getting angry.

No; I had already arrived.

My shout echoed across the cavern. *"I'm a freaking tribe, Nano!* How dare you confab without me!" I jumped out of the chair and paced, shouting louder, "And don't you even *think* of administering endorphins or serotonins or whatever it is you use to calm people down! I'm a tribe like the rest of you! I have rights!"

The sound of running footsteps slapping on the stone floor jerked me out of my rant. Zander, with Gamble on his heels, stopped yards away.

"Gemma? What's going on? Are you all right?"

"Stay away, Zander! Go back to Dr. Bickel's living quarters. You can't be here."

"I'll go if you say you're okay, Gemma."

Okay? Apparently, I wasn't going to be "okay."

The sweetness of Zander's earlier declaration brought me to tears. I wouldn't live long enough to reciprocate his love or satisfy the longing I felt for him. But I wouldn't put him in danger, either.

The nanocloud, hovering overhead, sparkled, its color flashing from silver to red. They were not happy with the interruption.

"I-I'm okay, Zander. Go on back. Please."

Zander and Gamble had seen the cloud. They stared and did not obey my injunction.

"What is that, Gemma?" Gamble whispered.

My laugh was harsh. "It's the nanocloud, Agent Gamble; it's the 'new and improved nanocloud.' All twenty trillion nanomites—and change."

I turned my back on my friends. "Now go away. Your presence isn't wanted here."

I heard them shuffle away. I knew I'd hurt Zander's feelings, but it couldn't be helped.

Sighing, I mumbled, "What's the bottom line, Nano?"

It seems we are continually making mistakes, Gemma Keyes. We did not intend to exclude you from the confab. You were weak, unable to participate. We apologize for our thoughtlessness.

And it seems that I'm continually misjudging you, Nano, I thought to myself.

Well, it isn't every day you find out you're going to die.

The idea didn't frighten me as it had before. Zander was right: Whatever happened, I now belonged to Jesus. He had me, and eternity held terror for me no longer. I would see Aunt Lucy again. I was only saddened that Zander would grieve for me.

As would Abe.

And Emilio.

Emilio?

What? Something . . .

"You think because I can't see you that I can't find you? Oh, I will find you—*but first I'll find those you love. Don't sleep, you *blank.* Don't even blink! Because I* will *find you, and I* will *pay you back for this."*

No! He wouldn't!

A different kind of terror bubbled up in my throat—one that superseded my own interests. I had to live—to protect Emilio, to ensure that Soto's tentacles did not come near him.

"Nano! What's the alternative? What alternative did you come up with?"

The alternative, Gemma Keyes, would require further changes to your body—deeply fundamental changes at the molecular level. These changes would be necessary for your body to accept and accommodate the new and improved nanocloud.

I hated that they had appropriated and regurgitated my snarled invective without perceiving the insult behind it.

Sighing, I nodded. "So. It's either allow you to further mutate my body or I'll die. Those are my choices, huh? Right?"

We submit that only one tolerable choice exists, Gemma Keyes. We cannot accept the death of a tribe. The loss of Gemma Tribe would . . . grieve us.

I sank again onto the dusty chair, covered my face with my hands, and sobbed. Why? Why was I always stuck between a rock and a hard place, between two irreconcilable options? Why?

Oh, Zander! I wanted to return your love. I wanted a happy ending for us. But Emilio? He's only a child and, against every broken promise he's suffered, he has elected to trust me. For Emilio's sake, I must choose life—even if it is life without you.

But my heart hurt so bad!

I moaned. As I rocked back and forth, my anguish grew to a keening wail. Tears rained onto my hands as I sorrowed, but I could also feel the nanomites' distress. The floating haze hovered near me; its flickering and shimmering turning a deep, troubled blue.

The nanomites truly did not want to harm me. Still, as much as I appreciated their concern, it changed nothing.

My life, as I wanted it, was over. My hopes for a future with Zander were finished.

Then . . . that weird, that inexplicable thing? When a fragment of something vital but long forgotten floated to the top of my mind and shouted to me?

It happened again.

Greater love has no one than this:
to lay down one's life for one's friends.

"To lay down one's life," I whispered. "Jesus said that! That's what he did." I blinked back tears. "So, does laying down your life mean more than being willing to die? In my case, does it also mean . . . surrendering what I want, letting go of my dreams, my own desires?"

Yes, Gemma, that is what it means.

Not the nanomites! Not the nanomites speaking to me!

It had been such a long time—years—since I had allowed him to reach me, to touch me. I had erected high, thick walls between us. I had built impenetrable barriers to keep him out—and had only succeeded in imprisoning myself.

Jesus had breached those barricades. He had kept after me until I gave in. In an instant, when I surrendered to him, he had swept away our estrangement. From out of my distant childhood, the familiar sweetness of his voice soothed me.

In an unearthly habitation, a spiritual dwelling deep within me, a place where the nanomites could never go . . .

He was there.

"Oh, Jesus! Please help me! I don't know what to do."

Gemma, I am the Good Shepherd. The Good Shepherd lays down his life for his sheep. Follow my example.

"But . . ."

The nanomites' proposed alterations terrified me, and there could be no future for Zander and me after they finished. I sobbed again for the loss of Zander's love.

Listen to me, little one. Do not be afraid. Do not be afraid to take this step. I am with you always, even to the end of this age. My plans and purposes are at work in you.

I wasn't able to let go right away. Another hour crept by, and I still hadn't made my choice. I knew what I had to do, what I must do, but I couldn't bring myself to voice it.

I was weaker now. The nanomites weren't pressuring me. Although time was running short, they waited in patient silence.

Well, Jesus had struggled, hadn't he? He had prayed for his Father to spare him. He had wanted to run from what he'd been sent to do.

But he *hadn't* run.

I sniffled. Sighed. "All right. If . . . if you say so, Jesus, I guess I can do this. Like Emilio chose to trust me, despite everything in his past, I-I, too, can choose to trust. To trust *you*."

My shoulders shuddered as relief, release, and serene respite flowed over me. Into me. I inhaled deep, freeing breaths.

"Thank you."

More minutes passed before I wiped my face and scrubbed my eyes dry. I climbed to my feet, dusted my scraped, torn clothes, and settled my heart.

"Okay, Nano. I'm ready. I accept your offer."

Above me, along the curve of the cavern's ceiling, the cloud flickered, swelled, and brightened. A soft hum rose and strengthened until . . . the low, melodious harmonies of the nanomites' song split into resplendent chords that washed over me.

They were singing!

For joy!

For me!

I smiled and, as the cloud descended, I closed my eyes.

***

Gamble's head snapped up. "What is that?"

The three men stood and trained their eyes on the edge of the cavern where they had last seen Gemma, from where a gentle, haunting melody echoed and resounded.

"It's the nanomites," Dr. Bickel breathed. "They are singing! I heard them when Gemma found me. Gemma hugged me, and I was overcome with emotion. They sang—just like this!"

"It's beautiful," Zander said, shutting his eyes to soak it in.

A scream of agony ripped the air.

"Gemma!"

Zander turned to run to her, but Dr. Bickel caught the edge of his shirt and held him fast.

"No, Reverend Cruz, no! This is what the mites warned us about: Do not interfere."

"Let go of me!" Zander tore his shirt from Dr. Bickel's hands—only to find himself pinioned by Gamble's arms.

"Let go, Gamble! Let go! She needs me!"

"I'm sorry, Cruz, but the doc is right. The mites warned us to stay away. We must believe that they won't hurt her. We have to."

Zander spat a slang Spanish phrase over his shoulder.

Gamble chuckled. "Why, Pastor Cruz! Did you just *curse* at me?"

Defeated, Zander sagged in Gamble's arms. "I'm forgiven, but I didn't say I was perfect—or stupid."

The moment Gamble relaxed his hold, Zander brought his cast up and swung it against Gamble's jaw. Stunned, Gamble staggered and barely kept his feet. Zander bolted; he sprinted toward Gemma.

He was within a few yards of her when he collided with a pulsing wall that repelled him. He skidded on his back across the smooth rock floor, the impact knocking the air from his lungs. Minutes went by before he could catch his breath, before he could sit up.

He was dizzy, still dazed, when he spied Gemma: Her skin gleamed with an iridescent glow; the glow brightened and shimmered with silver flecks that danced about her. He tried to get to his feet, but was pushed down and prevented from standing. He tried to crawl toward her, but could make no headway.

For thirty minutes, he watched the lights pulsating over and through Gemma. Then she folded in on herself and slowly, very slowly collapsed to the floor—as though she was being gently lowered rather than dropped.

She lay crumpled in a heap. The glow about her seemed to intensify, to thicken and press in. She shuddered and groaned—and Zander's heart squeezed with her every utterance of pain.

An hour went by.

Two hours passed. Gemma did not move, and Zander could get no closer to her.

Gamble and Dr. Bickel, prevented as Zander was from moving toward Gemma, joined him. They sat beside Zander and waited.

The minutes of another hour trickled by.

"Sorry about . . . before," Zander murmured.

Gamble shrugged "Whatever."

No one said anything for another fifteen minutes, then Gamble huffed. "Can't believe you sucker-punched me."

"Can't believe you fell for it, *Special* Agent Gamble."

At the end of the fifth hour, Gemma stirred. She sat up. Got to her knees. Stood.

***

I rose from the cold stone floor . . . blinked, and stared around me. I was still at the far edge of the cavern, but everything I looked at seemed strange. Different. Kind of 3D-movie different.

I performed an internal inventory. I felt okay, no longer shaky or weak. Okay? Yeah. I felt good. Strong, even.

I inhaled, and a warmth poured through my body until I seemed to burn. Tingle. Vibrate.

Whoa.

The burn intensified, and I shook with restrained power. I swallowed hard and—

Gemma Keyes. We have a question.

"Um?" I was preoccupied, trying to assess what the mites had done to me. What was different. What had changed.

Gemma Keyes, who is with us?

"Huh?"

Someone is with us.

"I don't . . . I don't understand the question."

We are six. Who is with us?

It hit me.

Oh, wow.

"Uh, Nano, it . . . it's Jesus."

Who is Jesus, Gemma Keyes? Why is he with us? How did he come to be with us? We are six, not seven.

Were they . . . ? Did they sound *peeved?*

"Um . . ." I grasped for an answer. "Well, do you remember when you asked who made me?"

Yes. Dr. Bickel made us. Who made you?

"Jesus made me, Nano, and . . . Jesus made Dr. Bickel, too."

My reply threw them. A long, charged moment elapsed—with soft nano-hissing and chittering passing back and forth before they responded.

How did Jesus come to be with us? He was not with us before.

"No, he wasn't. He has to be asked . . . to come in, and I, um, I asked him." My threadbare theology was starting to shred, to wear through.

Is he to be a tribe with us?

"No; that is, I don't think so. He is his own tribe. A very powerful tribe—I think it's more that we join *his* tribe than the other way around."

The mites were quiet, probably trying to figure out how to react to the "new guy." While they chewed on their problem, it was time for me to ask them a question.

"Nano? Did you finish with the, er, alterations?"

Yes, Gemma Keyes. After the initial destruction and discomfort, you tolerated the changes well—although we worked diligently to mitigate as many unpleasant side effects as possible.

Destruction? Yeah, I supposed they had to destroy many of my cellular structures and then remake them.

We are six again, Gemma Keyes. We are now optimal.

Optimal? With your humongous numbers? I'll bet you are.

I was filled with wonder.

And then I snapped to what they'd said: not you, but we. They said, "We are now optimal."

I lifted my hands to examine them. As I did, the light fixtures banding the cavern flickered. Current jetted from the wavering lights and slammed into my chest. The drawn energy coursed through me and reverberated in my bones. It swelled and spread down my arms until it reached my fingertips, ready to burst forth.

I swallowed. "Wow."

I let my eyes fall shut as I absorbed what was happening. Electricity crackled around me, infusing me with might. As my body drew power to it, I sensed the effects of the nanomites' alterations everywhere—in every pore of my being—and began to catalogue them.

What else?

I slipped into the warehouse. A wide, bright expanse devoid of shadows and hallways greeted me. With no effort on my part, the mites' vast knowledge and insights came to me.

The scope and magnitude of the nanomites' alterations were making themselves known. As I tallied the recognized changes, I nodded my approval and looked beyond the cavern's walls, past the mountain.

It was time to return Dr. Bickel to the land of the living. To deal with Cushing and Soto. To set things right.

I envisioned the battles ahead, where the war would be fought and won. I wasn't naïve about the coming conflict, but I smiled, even laughed a little inside.

"Okay. Well, so I imagine that this—all *this*—is going to shift the balance of power in our favor just a teensy bit."

I giggled. "Right, Nano?"

My question was a little joke. The nanomites' answer was not.

The odds have shifted significantly, Gemma Keyes. We are six, and we are optimal.

We shall prevail.

⌘⌘⌘⌘

POSTSCRIPT

It was early morning in Georgetown, Washington, D.C., but only 3 a.m. in New Mexico—the dead of night for people on Mountain Standard Time.

Imogene Cushing was expecting the call and answered it on its first ring. "Yes, sir."

The voice on the other end, usually so silky and controlled, raged at her. Cushing pulled the receiver an inch from her ear.

"Yes, sir. We've received the full cooperation of every agency as we requested. No, sir; we have not located them. We discovered an abandoned truck we believe was theirs. Yes, sir; we are certain she had help. No, we do not yet know who aided them; however, I am tearing apart Miss Keyes' every relationship. I am confident we will find the link."

She listened to the ranting caller. "Sir, I have four witnesses who can confirm what I had come to suspect: Miss Keyes was invisible."

More angry word blistered her ear.

"I absolutely do recognize the tactical significance of her, er, condition. I assure you that capturing her is my only priority."

The caller calmed from rage to a terse staccato. Cushing nodded. "Yes; I will give the order to have the facility purged; evidence that Bickel was held there will be expunged. Yes. The contractor personnel, also."

She absorbed a loud and lengthy reprimand without moving a muscle. When it ended on a threat, she ground her teeth but replied, "Yes, sir. I understand."

When the caller slammed down the receiver on the other end, Cushing remained motionless, the phone to her ear.

Everything was falling apart. No, that wasn't quite right. It had fallen apart the moment she'd realized that she had blown up the AMEMS lab with her own man inside and not Bickel. The moment she'd realized that Bickel had duped and eluded her—had taken his research out from under her nose. All her efforts since then had been an exercise in futile catch-up.

"Oh, Danny, Danny, Danny. We could have done such wonderful things together, could have achieved such greatness." Slowly, she replaced the handset onto the phone.

"But the next time we meet, Daniel Bickel, you will help me capture Gemma Keyes—even if I have to kill you in the process."

***

Genie Keyes finished clearing the bottom half of her closet, adding the last of her hanging clothes to a wardrobe moving box. That left the shelves above her closet rod to pack. She stood back and gazed with fondness at the stacks of boxes on the shelves.

She took special care of her shoes. Each designer shoe had its own shoe "puff" or tree to hold the shoe's shape, and each pair of shoes had its own airtight, custom shoebox sporting a laminated color photo of the box's contents on its end.

She glanced from her meticulous organization to the corrugated moving crates.

No sense putting it off.

She steeled herself and began to transfer her precious shoeboxes from shelf to crate, stacking them with care, padding the space between boxes with crumpled paper. But she couldn't keep her mind on her task; the events of the past week were too fresh and burned with too much heat. The humiliating scene made a grab for her again.

"We received a call from General Cushing, Genie," the partner had said. His anger was tamped down only because of the other two partners in the room. *"She said, and I quote, 'Not only was Miss Keyes of no substantive help, her attitude was a deplorable impediment. I am disappointed with your firm and shall make recommendations to that end to my contacts in government procurement.' end quote."*

Cushing.

Genie hurled a box containing suede Alberto Fermani ankle-tie sandals across the room. The plastic box shattered against the wall and sent the sandals flying.

"We are rescinding our partnership offer and terminating your employment as of today. Don't bother looking for work on the east coast, Genie. Don't even try clerking. In fact, the only place we won't warn off potential employers is your home state of New Mexico."

The senior partner had sniffed his derision. *"Seems apropos. Go back to the sticks from whence you came."*

Genie picked up the remains of the box and dumped the shards into the trash. She'd gotten out of the last eight months of her two-year lease only because local rents had skyrocketed and her landlord could rent out Genie's apartment—*had* rented out Genie's apartment (at a significant increase in the rent)—in a heartbeat.

She had three days remaining to get out—and nowhere to go when she left. Well, she had to go back to New Mexico, didn't she?

She snarled to herself. *If I want to work in law, I do. And I must go back to New Mexico if I want to pay Cushing back—and, oh! Oh, how I do.*

Genie had made a few calls and, after dropping a few powerful D.C. names, received tentative overtures from two Albuquerque firms. She'd have to convert one of those overtures into an offer, and quickly. She had not envisioned or prepared for a sudden change of circumstances and had little in the way of cash reserves to make the move and get her foot in the door of a new apartment.

Looking around her bedroom, she took a deep breath and plucked another box from the closet shelf.

***

Emilio and Sean got off the bus together. Sean put his hand in Emilio's as the two boys headed down the walk to their foster home. Emilio didn't mind Sean hanging on him—well, not too much. The five-year-old kid was okay, even if he was a pest sometimes. And Emilio had taken care of a few problems on the playground—bigger kids who had mistaken Sean for an easy target. They'd found out otherwise when Emilio stepped in.

Emilio shrugged his backpack higher on his shoulder. He would miss Sean—just a little, of course—when Abe came to get him next Friday after school.

He grinned when he thought about the visit he'd had with the old man yesterday. Wow—he sure had him a mean gash on his head! The doctors had shaved Abe's grizzled hair around the wound and stitched it up. The stitches were out now, but the gash was still plenty gory-looking.

Cool.

Abe had said he was as excited for Emilio to "come home" as Emilio was to get there. He promised to make spaghetti to celebrate the event. They didn't need to worry about Mateo either. He wouldn't be bothering them anymore. That's what Abe had said, anyway.

Emilio's mouth tightened. *Said he'd tell me why later.*

A car going the wrong way drew alongside the curb. The backseat window rolled down.

"Hey, pardon me, but have you seen my puppy?" A guy wearing sunglasses and a baseball cap held up a phone with an image on its screen. "He's lost. Can you help me find him? He's just a baby, and I'm worried about him."

Of course, Sean let go of Emilio's hand and scampered straight over to the car. The man opened the door and let Sean hold the phone.

Emilio scowled. That kid hadn't a lick of street sense.

"Sean! Git over here, man. You don' talk to strangers. Don' you know nothing?"

Sean looked back at him. "But he lost his puppy, Emilio! Don't we want to help? He's awful cute."

"No, your brother is right. You shouldn't talk to strangers." The man's right hand was bound in a thick bandage. He cocked his head. "Say, is your name Emilio?"

Emilio looked closer at the guy. He seemed familiar.

"Yeah. What of it?"

Emilio watched as the man reached out with his uninjured hand, all casual like, and took hold of Sean's collar.

"You like Sean, don't you, Emilio?"

It was the way he said it. Emilio's blood turned cold, ran down his back, and puddled in his shoes.

"You come over here to me, and I'll let Sean go on home. I just want a word with you. Just a moment of your time. I have a message for you . . . from your neighbor. You know, the invisible lady?"

That's when Emilio knew. Arnaldo Soto. *Dead Eyes*. That's what Gemma had called him. He swallowed. "Hey, Sean? Git over here. *Now*."

But Soto's grip tightened on Sean's collar. Sean's eyes went wide.

"Emilio. Come talk to me, and Sean goes home. Or . . ." He let the threat dangle.

The driver got out and stood on the sidewalk. He waited, but Emilio knew what was happening.

Soto gripped Sean's collar until it choked the little boy and he whimpered.

Emilio couldn't stand it. "Okay, *'mano*. Okay."

He dropped his backpack and went up to the car. The big man from the front seat took him by the arm, and Sean scampered to safety.

"Run on home, Sean," Soto said and nodded to the other man.

The man dragged Emilio over and shoved him into the back seat. Then he slammed the door.

As soon as the driver went to get into the front seat, Emilio lunged for the door, but it wouldn't open. The car pulled away from the curb, and the boy struggled in Soto's grasp. Soto had ahold of the back of the kid's shirt, but the boy was almost as skinny as the beggars from the slums of Culiacán who swarmed his car every chance they got.

"Where you taking me?"

"Shut up!" Soto snarled. He couldn't grasp and yank the kid's hair the way he wanted, because the boy's head was shaved close. Instead, Soto grabbed more shirt, jerked the kid, smashed his face into the door's window.

Emilio cried out, but twisted within the shirt until his teeth found Soto's hand. He bit as hard as he could.

He was rewarded with a roar of pain—and the hard back of Soto's hand. Emilio slumped over in the leather seat, stunned.

"Don't you get blood on my upholstery, brat!" Soto snarled.

Emilio blinked back the pain. "What you want with me?" He already knew, though. Soto had mentioned her: the invisible lady.

Soto laughed—and Emilio's skin crawled.

"I know who you are. *Dead Eyes*. That's what *she* calls you."

"Dead Eyes, eh? So, she has a healthy respect for me. She should. Too bad she has such an obvious weakness—but that's where you come in. When I dangle you in front of her, she will try to save you—and I will be ready. She will pay for the harm she has done me."

Emilio wiped his face and whispered into the seat's leather, "Yeah, she gonna come get me, all right, but you better watch your back."

He sniffed again. "'Cause you ain't gonna see her when she does."

The End

STEALTH RETRIBUTION

The final installment of the Nanostealth series will blow your mind.

ABOUT THE AUTHOR

Vikki Kestell's passion for people and their stories is evident in her readers' affection for her characters and unusual plotlines. Two often-repeated sentiments are, "I feel like I know these people," and, "I'm right there, in the book, experiencing what the characters experience."

Vikki holds a Ph.D. in Organizational Learning and Instructional Technologies. She left a career of twenty-plus years in government, academia, and corporate life to pursue writing full time. "Writing is the best job ever," she admits, "and the most demanding."

Also an accomplished speaker and teacher, Vikki and her husband Conrad Smith make their home in Albuquerque, New Mexico.

To keep abreast of new book releases, visit her website, http://www.vikkikestell.com/, or find her on Facebook at http://www.facebook.com/TheWritingOfVikkiKestell.

OTHER BOOKS BY VIKKI KESTELL

A PRAIRIE HERITAGE

Book 1: *A Rose Blooms Twice* (free eBook, most online retailers)
Book 2: *Wild Heart on the Prairie*
Book 3: *Joy on This Mountain*
Book 4: *The Captive Within*
Book 5: *Stolen*
Book 6: *Lost Are Found*
Book 7: *All God's Promises*
Book 8: *The Heart of Joy—A Short Story* (eBook only)

GIRLS FROM THE MOUNTAIN

Book 1: *Tabitha*
Book 2: *Tory*

The Christian and the Vampire: A Short Story
(free eBook, most online retailers)

CPSIA information can be obtained
at www.ICGtesting.com
Printed in the USA
LVOW13s1539290617

539816LV00010B/665/P